Soul St

Stephen Riley

Copyright © 2022 Stephen Riley

ISBN: 9798849570006

All rights reserved, including the right to reproduce this book, or portions thereof in any form. No part of this text may be reproduced, transmitted, downloaded, decompiled, reverse engineered, or stored, in any form or introduced into any information storage and retrieval system, in any form or by any means, whether electronic or mechanical without the express written permission of the author.

Without whom…

Fiona Riley, Tim Bates, Kenny Lowe, Karen Seymour, Lesley Britton, David Smith, Jorge Lewis.

To my brothers, the ones given by birth and the ones I found and who found me along the way...

Soul Stories

The Diaries

The First Cut

Soul Stories Part 1

Soul Stories Part 2

Soul Stories Part 3

Millennium Tale

Afterword

Discography

Bibliography

Glossary

The Diaries

I guess the first thing I should say is that 'diaries' is perhaps a bit of an exaggeration. What I received that day 2 years ago was a bundle of old notebooks, full of spidery writing, and lots of scraps of paper, beermats and inside-out fag packets with notes scribbled on them, all wrapped in a brown paper parcel, comprehensively held together with an overabundance of packing tape. The material was, however, mostly dated, and where it wasn't I could interpolate, so there was chronology to be found and it all does amount to diaries of a sort.

There was no message and no return address, but I'm pretty sure why it was sent to me. I am a local historian, moderately well known in the area, with an interest in popular culture in the North of England from the middle of the 20th century onwards and, specifically within that, the various youth cults that have come and gone over that period: teddy boys, mods, skinheads, soul boys, punks and the rest.

The collection is the work of one Dan Brody – his name crops up time and again in and on the notebooks – though I am unable to say whether it was the man himself who sent me the parcel, or some relative/descendant, and my efforts to track him down have been fruitless. There are lots of Dan Brodys in the world, and none that I have reached is him, or admits to being him. It is clear, however, that whoever sent me this material expected me to do something with it – otherwise, why send it? So that is what I have done, and what you see here is my interpretation of it, set out as accurately as possible.

The first thing I did was try to grasp what exactly I was looking at, and then work out how best to interpret and re-present it. From an historian's perspective, it was an absolutely fascinating set of documents; a real time-capsule, filled with invaluable first-hand accounts of an era now passed; insights not only into lives and how they were lived at that time, but also into the inner workings of an individual who watched, experienced and recorded; not history as it is normally written, of great leaders and world-changing events, but folk history. These documents recount the ordinary and sometimes extraordinary experiences in the life of somebody who was a nobody and as such they no doubt reflect the lives of countless others whose stories remain untold.

Overall, the texts are an account of incidents in the life of Dan and his friends from 1969, when he was 14, on into early adulthood. Significant in this is Dan's involvement with the northern soul scene. The scene was not just some form of entertainment – it shaped his life and the lives of his friends in radical ways that could not have been dreamt of at the start. However, northern soul is not the only thing. What we see here is an account of a teenager's/young man's life in that period, in all its richness, in all of its highs and lows, involving love and loss, friendships, betrayals, work, football riots, smoky pubs, dodgy 70s cars and the rest of it. The choice of 'Soul Stories' as the title reflects not just the part that northern soul plays in the book, but that these are very much stories 'from the soul' and about the souls who populate the book.

I have endeavoured to be as faithful to the source as possible. All of the observations and details are Dan's. I have added nothing, just moulded the material into something more orderly and reader-friendly. And because this book is based on Dan's diary entries, it necessarily takes the form of numerous short stories, which appear in the first instance to follow no narrative. The tales are sometimes poignant, sometimes funny, and sometimes just matter of fact; some are several pages long, others are just a few sentences; and all seem at first to exist as separate entities. Where things are going only becomes apparent later. The charming innocence of the early stories gradually slips into something else as Dan grows older. I will go no further here, other than to say that it is that shift from innocence to experience that shapes the trajectory and forms the overall narrative.

To give readers a path into characters, time and place, there is an introductory/framework chapter called The First Cut, which outlines Dan's circumstances from 1969, when he was 14, through to age to 17; then come the actual Soul Stories, which also begin in 1969, but go on past the point where the framework chapter leaves off and take us into the early adult life of Dan and his friends.

This has been a labour of love. I hope you enjoy it.
Adrian Baxter – Historian, Manchester.

The First Cut...

It's 1969, and in the depth of a northern summer the big digital flip-clock of life clops over once more, and Dan Brody is 14 years old. Life revolves mostly around school, paper round and his mates. His family is in there as well, somewhere. They live in Dashley Dyke, in that strange liminal place where Manchester ends and the bleak wuthering heights of the Pennines begin.

School is in Hightown, four miles away – too far to walk, but not far enough to get your bus fares paid by the council. The town of Bradfield separates Dashley Dyke and Hightown.

The world beyond Dashley Dyke arrives mediated in black and white every evening via the TV news, and it is mostly concerned with extreme violence. The Americans are busy trying to kill everyone in Vietnam, as well as each other. British violence is visited upon its victims more by incompetence than anything deliberate – Brits can no longer afford carpet bombing. A badly maintained slag heap wipes out a school and nearly everyone in it; the side of a poorly designed, system-built tower block explodes and drops like dominoes onto its residents; a busted rail sends a packed express train into the sidings at 70 miles an hour; aircraft drop out of the sky with alarming regularity. There's the odd bit of positive, exciting news too, mostly about space: men doing spacewalks or going to the Moon. Dan absorbs it all, flopped on the *Family at War* armchair, munching cheese on toast.

Hormones have arrived and barged their way into Dan's consciousness like a demented rhino crashing through a brick wall. Dan falls deeply, passionately, devotedly in love at 20-minute intervals.

Social life comprises hanging around under the yellow street light outside Trev's off licence and trying to muster the money and courage to go in and buy a bottle of pale ale, then wondering how you're going to get the top off it without a bottle opener, and trying to bash it open on a low wall, pretending that you've done this a thousand times before.

There's a girl in the group – Susan Ford. Her favourite record is "Sugar Sugar" by the Archies, but this aside she is fashionably negative about everything and, by this means, holds everyone in thrall. Dan has never seen this before. He goes around in wide-eyed awe, thrilled by every new discovery. He didn't even know negativity was a thing, let alone a cool thing. He knows better now. Strangely, Dan doesn't fall in love with her. He tries to, he expects to, but somehow the frizzy yellow hair and baggy orange nylons keep him at bay.

And then Dan starts going to the youth club, which is better than hanging around outside Trev's off licence because it has a roof, which is handy when it's raining, and because there's more than one girl and because there's a record player and lads bring in soul and reggae records.

Dan's never heard of soul or reggae until now and he's blown away by it. His mate, Si, gets *British Motown Chartbusters Volume 3*, *Prince Buster's Fabulous Hits* and the *Four Tops' Greatest Hits*, and they sit listening to the Bush record player in Si's musty, never-used front room, and Dan can't believe the emotional impact of Levi Stubbs's voice and the lyrics and that powerful music and that driving beat. "Ask the Lonely", "Without the One You Love", "Baby I Need Your Loving" – they tear him apart. And then there's Prince Buster's irresistible rhythms and who-gives-a-fuck lyrics. The power of the music is overwhelming, ecstatic. He can feel it inside. It's almost a physical sensation. He understands why they call it 'soul'.

And they have a crack at Si's dad's gin in the never-used drinks cabinet, and it's horrible and they can't work out what all the fuss is about.

And Dan goes to his first nightclub – Mars, in Bradfield – and it's a mind-blowing experience. The place is mysteriously dark, except for the odd dim purple lamp that gives off a funny light and makes it look like his vest is outside of his shirt. The floor looks like the set from *Star Trek* when Kirk, Spock and Scotty beam down to an alien planet, with all craters and rocky lumps for seats. There's a riveted sheet metal bit in the middle for dancing on, and the DJs play more of this fabulous soul music, but a hundred times louder than in Si's front room. Dan doesn't know quite what it is you're meant to do in a night club, so he just stands around soaking-up the music.

And now it's December, and all Dan's paper-round customers give him tips, apart from that miserable old hag at 137 Albemarle Street, who fucks him off when he knocks. And he suddenly finds he has more money than he's ever seen – one advantage of having a paper round comprising hundreds of tiny terraced houses, with another front door every five paces – and he buys *British Motown Chartbusters Volume 2* and "Jimmy Mack" and "Return of Django" and a pair of Levi's and some red clip-on braces and a yellow-and-brown check Jaytex shirt. And his dad gives him a pair of work-issue bright orange steel-toecap work boots, which he paints black and hammers hobnails into, so they're like Si's army boots, more or less.

And it turns out that Dan isn't bad looking. This hasn't occurred to him before – either the fact of his own looks, or the idea that a male could be good looking at all. He's average height, average build and has a mop of black hair. That's it. He knows a beautiful girl when he sees one, but lads are much of a muchness. Sure, there's the odd freaky one, like Austin Iddon at school, who looks like the prototype for Plug from *The Bash Street Kids*, and there's the odd fatty, but all the other lads look like, well, just lads.

But the girls like him. Well, some of them do. Enough of them do. And soon he has a girlfriend, sort of, for all of two and a half weeks: Carol, from Hightown. But he doesn't know what it is you're meant to do with a girlfriend, and they sit twice a week in one of the craters in Mars holding hands and kissing occasionally. There's no conversation because he has nothing to say, and he has nothing to say because he doesn't know anything. The cat is more worldly than Dan.

Dan is a div.

And now it's the 1970s – a great open space with nothing yet in it.

Like every other little skinhead in East Manchester, Si Mitchell, Dan Brody and Adey Martin are now regulars at Mars. Adey and Si are also reasonably good looking, apparently. They are also of average height and average build, and they have brown hair, though Adey's hair is dark brown, and Si's is light brown, and Adey is marginally taller than Dan, and Si is marginally shorter. As well as weighing up girls they don't have the nerve to talk to and gazing at a dancefloor on which they wouldn't know what to do even if they had the nerve to step onto it, they spend their time standing around trying to look cool and struggling to work out what the records are. The DJs don't announce them and you never hear them on the radio. Dan calls them Mars records, because it's the only place he hears them. They pester the more knowledgeable, they try to read the labels on the decks before the DJs set them spinning, they try to guess titles from choruses. But the songwriters don't always make it easy – sometimes the chorus and the title are not the same thing. And sometimes the treasured track is a B-side, adding another layer of obscurity.

Once he's worked out what a record is, or what it might be, Dan goes to the various local record shops to try and buy it. Most are hopeless – they've never heard of these records – but then he gives The Record Box on Dashley Dyke High Street a try. And to his delight and relief, Dan finds that the lady who runs the shop, Anne, regards tracking down his record-wants an interesting challenge. Maybe it's a bit more stimulating than handing over yet another inane Top Ten pop record to yet another credulous pre-programmed Dashley Dyke kid. And each time he comes in with a list, she gives it her best shot. Most of the records are deleted, but there's no way of knowing which if you don't try: "At the Discotheque", "I'll Do Anything", "Get Out of My Heart", "What's Wrong With Me Baby" – no chance; but "Earthquake", "Billy's Bag", "Love Makes a Woman", "Philly Freeze", "The Who Who Song" – yes! And more. Sometimes it's iterative: his guess at the song or artist is wrong, but as Anne scans her catalogue, it's close enough and they work out what the real record is.

Dan picks up from older lads at school that there's this amazing club called The Twisted Wheel and that *it* is the origin of the music they play at Mars. It turns out that the DJs he's in awe of at his local club are themselves only little worshippers at this much more sacred altar.

Also, some of these lads write strange little code words on their school books, like 'SK&F' and 'Riker'.

Dan desperately wants to go to The Twisted Wheel. The thought of it is thrilling, frightening, exotic… But it's in central Manchester and Dan doesn't know how to get there and expects it'd cost too much to get in if he did and he might need a membership card and he wouldn't know how to get back from central Manchester in the middle of the night and they probably wouldn't let him in anyway because he's only 14. He's only been to Manchester once: his dad took him in 1967, when he was 12, along with his little brother Nicky, because the steam trains were about to be made extinct. They tiddly-popped in the smoky carriage from Dashley Dyke to Victoria and never left the station – just crossed the platform and tiddly-popped straight back. Dan was stunned to find that it was only a 20-minute journey. He'd always imagined Manchester was hundreds of miles away, like London.

Dan is 15 and gets laid for the first time. He studies his face in the mirror the next day and tries to work out if he looks any different – older, maybe. He fancies his voice has got a bit deeper. And is that a bit of stubble on his chin?

Now it's the final year at school. Dan is a big-time fifth-former and has a regular girlfriend for the first time.

He starts wearing his Doctor Martens boots to school, but gets into trouble when, on charging down a corridor, he skids on the worn-smooth vinyl soles and crashes into Kenny Ball, the physics teacher, and gets bollocked and told he can't wear them and has to wear proper black shoes, like school uniform regulations say. He retaliates by leaving a sucked-out Jubbly in the assembly hall piano, which melts and half wrecks the thing.

Some of the bad boys go to the school pub two streets away at dinner time: The Beehive. You have to tear your school badge off and shove your tie in your pocket or they won't serve you. Dan joins them now and then. He likes the smoky, beery smell of the pub, though the booze makes him drowsy all afternoon.

Dan hates school. It's not that he doesn't want to learn, it's just that the depressed indifferent teaching regime and casual sadism of Hightown High School for Boys makes survival a more pressing priority than learning, and being good at anything can be lethal. He discovers how easy it is to bunk off. You shout 'sir' as usual when the register's called, then at break time you slip out via one of several fencing poles that's been bent out of shape by previous escapees for this purpose. And then you're in the park, and then you stroll out of the main gate at the other side and no-one bothers you.

It's 1971, and the end of school, which till now had always seemed excruciatingly distant, is hurtling towards Dan's cohort at an alarming speed. Everyone is talking about what they want to do afterwards. The smart ones are staying on for A Levels, others are aiming for apprenticeships. With cotton now largely gone from the East Manchester towns, the options for lads are mostly in light engineering or Parkett's cigarette factory, where they make Park Drive and Senior Service. The psychopaths join the police. Anyone left over joins the army. Dan wants to go to art college. When he looks at the possibilities, it's the only thing that doesn't fill him with dread.

It's careers advice day. Dan queues in the green-tiled Edwardian corridor outside room 13B. He reaches the front. A voice yells from the room.

'NEXT!'

Dan shuffles in. The room smells of armpits and old blazers. He sits across the desk from the bald, permanently tetchy Mr Greenwood, who scans his file.

'So, Brody, isn't it. What do you want to do when you leave, Brody?' asks Mr Greenwood, briskly, efficiently.

'Go to art college, sir, become an artist,' replies Dan, hopefully.

'No, no, no. That won't do at all. Says here you're good at metalwork. Light engineering is the thing for you – a miller or a turner. NEXT!'

The Brody family living room is best described as flowery. It has red flowery wallpaper, a brown flowery carpet and a green flowery three-piece suite. Dan's mum and dad sit him down for a serious talk. His big brother Clive is also there. This must be serious. Clive is twenty-four and married with a kid. He's long since moved out and got his own place. He's been roped in especially for this.

Dan's mum and dad, Lily and Walter, always look worn out. They're both in their early fifties and have grey hair, though Lily dyes hers with various degrees of success. Walter is a lorry driver for a firm that makes plastic granules that get moulded into shoe heels, and he spends much of his time away, on the road, and often sleeps (badly) in his cab. Lily works on the school dinners at Foundry Street Methodists and does everything else.

It's the latest of several conversations about what Dan is going to do when he leaves school, and again he holds out for art college. But the time is drawing near and the pressure gets cranked up. It's ridiculous, the three elders tell him. No-one goes to art college. Art is a hobby, not a job. He says some people do: someone, somewhere is going to university to do an art course of some sort; someone designed this godawful wallpaper. They laugh, but seeing the hurt on his face, quickly convert laughs into indulgent smiles. Heads tilt to one side. The tone shifts to a sympathetic one. That's another world. They don't want to see him disappointed. People like them don't go to university. How could he imagine that anyone from their station in life could ever be smart enough to go to university? He's seen them on the telly, hasn't he? It's all Eton and Harrow and *University Challenge* and that. He doesn't know any of that stuff. He doesn't even talk right, let alone have the brains. He'd just make a fool of himself. He'd be laughed out of the place as soon as he opened his mouth. They're trying to protect him from that. And besides, they've already let him stay on at school – to do O Levels. He'll be 16 by the time those are finished. He's already been in education longer than anyone in the history of the family. Clive left school at 15, they left at 14, and granddad started at the dye works when he was just 11.

They can't afford for him to carry on studying. He needs to earn a living. He wants those trendy clothes doesn't he – the Ben Shermans, the tonic suits and all that – where's that gonna come from?

What he needs is a trade. With a trade you've always got something to fall back on. Dan's mind slips into abstraction: *falling back* – it's not something he's ever even thought about before, let alone contemplated as a thing he should insure against in life. He pictures himself in the future in a strange sci-fi wilderness, falling physically backwards onto some kind of soft Moon-dust surface. He imagines the quiet whump, the sensation of the soft, compliant surface on his back, and a cloud of pale grey powder rising up around him. He snaps back into reality at the sound of rustling paper, as Lily proffers the copy of the *Manchester Evening News* that had been behind her on the settee, already carefully folded back to reveal a chosen half-page in the adverts section. Rings of blue biro assertively highlight one particular small ad. This is what the intervention is about. *North Western Gas Board – Gas Engineering Technician Apprentices Wanted.*

Clive leans forward. This is his moment. Clive is a gas fitter. He explains what a brilliant opportunity this is. 'It's five years, block-release: work and college. You get trained *and* you get paid. You'll love it.'

Lily chips back in: he should at least give it a go. He can go on and study art later, if it doesn't work out.

Walter smiles encouragingly, but says nothing.

No-one in Dan's known universe thinks he should go to art college, except Dan, and he doesn't know where there is an art college, or how you apply to one, or what it takes to get accepted, or how you support yourself when you're there.

He shows up for the interview at the North Western Gas Board's offices in Verrington: red-to-blue tonic suit, black Brutus shirt with button-down collar, black Royals, red socks.

He gets the gig and a week later returns to sign giant archaic deeds of apprenticeship on imitation parchment with an embossed red seal at the bottom, and on 6th September 1971 he arrives at the Gas Board offices on Whitworth Street in

Manchester, opposite Gaythorn Gas Works, for his first day at work. He doesn't know it, but this is the same street The Twisted Wheel is on, albeit half a mile away on the other side of town.

Dan quickly gets familiar with the big city and how to get around it, and he's got a few quid in his pocket for the first time. True, it's only measly apprentice rates, but living at home means he's still got a bit to spend on having a good time and buying records. The only thing is, The Twisted Wheel has now closed down. He never made it. But still, Mars is still going and there's The Blue Parrot in Dashton and Dashley Dyke United Football Club – they play some soul at those too, though nowhere near as good a selection as Mars. They mix up the good stuff with crap from the charts and it can be frustrating waiting for their handful of good soul dance tunes. And there's only so many times a person needs to hear "Funky Street" and "Backfield in Motion" and "Move on Up" before they start to wear a little thin. And why do they always have to play "Montego"-fucking-"Bay"?

Dan quite likes the apprenticeship. It's a few weeks college, then a few weeks workplace training, and each time he goes back for the work period, they've moved him on to a new task or department, so he never gets the chance to get fed up of anything. And best of all, the college part of the training is at Stretford Tech, just across the road from United's ground. So when there's a midweek match, he can meet up with his mates in The Trafford and head straight on to the footy.

But the art thing is niggling away at him like a guilty conscience. And there's this bloke who also gets on the 153 in the morning from Dashley Dyke into Manchester, who carries one of those big black portfolios that artists and designers use. He's either working in art and design or studying it. Dan feels sick and angry every time he sees him. That should be him.

1971 turns into 1972, and Mars closes, but there's The Pendulum in Manchester, which is a fearsome, dingy place but which plays superb records. Tommy Coggins and Dan become regulars.

Then Dan makes it to his first big-time away club, Blackpool Mecca, and then to his first all-nighter, The Torch in Stoke.

And then he takes his first gear: amphetamine. To say he likes it is rather like saying George Best was fond of the odd beer. And gear becomes part of life.

And a new soul night opens in Bradfield, at the rugby club: Buffy's. And that's a really good place. The DJs are proper soul guys who get it and don't play the played-out stuff.

And it's 1973 and Dan is on top of his game. He goes to the right places, wears the right clothes, knows the right people.

Dan is cool…

Soul Stories Part 1: 1969-72

If you lived at the Bradfield end of Dashley Dyke or the Dashley Dyke end of Bradfield in 1969 and were too young for the pub, St Luke's youth club was the place to be, and Eleanor Fossett was the club's self-appointed queen bee. Dan wasn't sure if he was in awe of Eleanor or thought her absurd. She set herself apart from all those who spun their Motown and reggae records on the club's communal Dansette and jigged about on the dusty wooden floor. She liked sensible, grown-up music, like Joni Mitchell and Melanie and Lindisfarne, and you never saw her laugh. People said she was serious – a serious, sensible person. And she didn't dress like the other girls, either. No miniskirts and white tights for Eleanor; she wore maxi-skirts, long sleeveless cardigans and a medallion with a diagram on it, which meant something profound. She was 16 to his 14, so he saw her as the mysterious older woman, replete with exotic knowledge that he couldn't even guess existed, let alone grasp. And now she had his rapt attention, because she was holding forth on drugs.

Dan was interested in drugs. He wasn't sure why, but there was some kind of fascination there, about some kind of altered state of mind, about something taboo. And he'd never taken drugs. Well, not proper ones. He'd once found himself in a peculiar state whilst using some dodgy solvent his dad had nicked from work to take the dye off his boots. And then there'd been the incident with the cigarettes. He'd had the odd drag behind the chemi lab with some of the lads from his class, but apart from a bit of dizziness hadn't really felt much of an effect. There had to be more to it. So he'd gone to Trev's off licence and bought 10 Sovereign and smoked them all, one after another, to see what would happen. He'd then gone dizzy, turned sweaty white and thrown up comprehensively, and still couldn't work out what the big deal was.

But Eleanor was on about someone who'd taken acid. This was a different league. He listened reverentially.

Dan had heard of acid. He'd seen hippies on the telly off their heads on the stuff at Woodstock and in San Francisco. And pop singers snuck in surreptitious references to it in their songs. "Lucy in the Sky with Diamonds" – oh yes, he knew what that was about. This had to be worth hearing.

Eleanor, in apocalyptic tone, told the tale of some lad she knew at college: he'd taken acid and was dripping in front of the teacher.

'Dripping?' asked Dan, intrigued. 'You mean he was dribbling or something, like foaming at the mouth and that? Or he *wet* himself?!'

'No: *dripping*,' explained Eleanor, with the patience one reserves for those who aren't all that bright. 'It's what you call it when someone is high on acid.'

***

Dan was rummaging through Pete Storey's record box in the main hall of the youth club – "Private Number", "Harlem Shuffle", "Who's Making Love", "Respect" – *pretty good* – when there was a sudden kerfuffle. Bodies flew past him and a hand clapped him on the shoulder and an excited voice said 'come on.' He jumped up and joined the throng, completely oblivious to why he was doing so.

As Dan stepped out of the youth club door, he could see he was in a line of lads slowly moving up towards the cemetery gates. A few seconds later he saw Miriam Marsden lying on her back on a blackened old gravestone, stripped to the waist. The lads in the queue were taking turns to fondle her tits. He was in the queue. Soon he'd be at the front taking his turn with Miriam's mammaries. He was mortified, but there was no way out now. They'd call him a puff. He'd be ridiculed, banished.

The queue moved quickly forward.

He'd longed for an encounter with tits ever since he realised they existed and were not, after all, deformed ribs, as he'd once assumed. But not like this.

Al Fielding was in front of him. In cringing desperation, Dan tapped on Al's shoulder:

'Doesn't she mind?'

'Of course not,' grinned Al, 'it was her idea. Look at her – she's smiling.'

Wrong answer. He'd hoped Miriam had been coerced, so he could step out of the line in self-righteous indignation and be all decent and pious and castigate them all. But, no. There was no excuse. No escape.

And then he was there, at the front, and Miriam could see straight through him. In his grey school shirt and his home-knitted grey school jumper, he was a picture of embarrassment. 'Come on, it's OK.' He leaned forward and grabbed the floppy white orbs in his hands and rotated them a couple of times in concentric circles. He'd seen the lads in front of him do the same, so figured this was about right. Miriam grinned at him.

He ran off and joined a small circle of lads just outside of the cemetery gate.

'Phew,' he said, mustering what he hoped was a convincing grin, 'great, that,' then wandered off, still cringing.

***

Flirtatious youth club banter with a couple of the girls sent them scurrying off, giggling into the ladies' toilets. Dan and Si followed, but stopped at the door like uninvited vampires.

They sensed another presence, and there behind them was Hilda, the sanctimonious old battleaxe who opened the place at teatime and turfed them out at ten.

'It's disgustin',' spat Hilda, 'puritanical.'

Dan wasn't sure what puritanical meant, but was pretty sure this wasn't it.

***

The Alhambra picture hall had been closed and boarded up for as long as Dan could remember. But now something was happening. Vans and pick-up trucks appeared outside, dusty blokes in bib-and-brace overalls vanished into the now reopened main entrance, and scaffolding made its spidery way up the frontage. Dan watched it daily in time-lapse from the upper deck of the school bus.

Then, one day, the scaffolding had gone and the front of the building was completely covered in a bright shiny layer of metallic silver paint. Above and to the right of the main entrance was the word 'MARS' in massive fluorescent pink capitals.

***

Dan was at Colin Dugdale's house on a Wednesday evening. They were in the front room painting imaginary landscapes with poster paints, competing with each other for maximum realism.

Colin's dad, Frank, poked his head round the door: 'Wanna come to the club, lads? Yer can carry the muffins.'

'Er, yeah,' replied Colin.

'Club? What club?' asked Dan.

'Yer know, that new Mars club, where the Alhambra used to be. Yer must have seen it. Mi dad and our Gary are bouncers there.'

'Bouncers? What's that?'

'Doormen, like. They bounce people out who cause trouble.'

'Oh!' He laughed. *What a funny name.*

Dan and Colin travelled the mile or so to Mars in the back of Frank Dugdale's pale green Reliant van, trying to keep control of trays of muffins and frozen burgers as the three-wheeler slewed round bends and corners. In the passenger seat next to Frank was Colin's big brother, Gary. Both men looked like proper upper-class toffs, in black dress suits with patent leather shoes, white shirts and dickie bows. This sense was enhanced by Frank's large, magnificently-coiffured handlebar moustache, which made him look like a colonel from the Boer War. Both were enormous men, seemingly wedged into the front of the van, shoulders bulging over the tops of the seats. They were the ideal material for bouncers. The whole family was big. Colin's mum and sister were big as well. Colin was big, even though he was only 14. He confided in Dan that he'd hit 17 stone when he was just 11 years old. Anyone in the family could have been a bouncer, male or female.

Frank yanked open the club's freshly painted, metallic silver front door. It had only just gone 7pm, but the DJs were already at it. You could hear music pounding through from inside. Gary carried in the burgers. Colin and Dan each had a tray of muffins. They crossed the foyer, pulled open the heavy inner door and trooped in. Just as Dan made it through, the Isley Brothers' classic "Behind a Painted Smile" kicked off.

It was electrifying. He'd heard the song before, on Si's record player, but never like this, never at this volume. That delicate, almost classical flute intro exploded into crashing drums and insistent guitars, and the whole gorgeous cacophony bashed its way into Dan's body and mind, and powered on into his soul. He would never be the same again.

Then there was the extraordinary experience of the place itself: the unfamiliar musty smells and the deep, scarcely fathomable darkness, and then, as his eyes adjusted, the peculiar interior of the place, like TV pics of the surface of some alien planet: all dips and climbs and craters and strange rock formations. The great high ceiling of the cavernous former picture house was invisible – looking up, all that could be seen was endless blackness, just like real outer space – and the DJs were housed in a cylindrical spacecraft, made from sheet aluminium with Perspex for windows, all curved round to get that proper rocket-ship look.

Colin and Dan handed over their goodies to the lass working behind snack bar, then sat down in one of the silvery craters and watched the revellers start to arrive and tried to come to terms with what they were experiencing.

***

Si and Dan wanted to get pissed. Getting pissed was the thing. Real men got pissed. They wanted to be real men. But it wasn't at all straightforward. It took money to buy enough booze to get you pissed, and money was something that, as paper boys, they didn't have much of. And it was one thing to try your luck buying the odd pint at the school pub, or getting a bottle or two from Trev's, but getting visibly worse for wear while still wanting more might stretch tolerance a bit.

But then there was this poster outside the cricket club:

Charity Fundraiser.
Sherry Night
Saturday, 7.30 till late.

25p to get in and all the sherry you can drink – a chance too good to miss.

They showed up keen, spot on 7.30, faces washed, hair combed, shirts ironed. Both wore blue-to-gold tonic kecks and barathea blazers with a badge on the breast pocket: Si's, a Lancashire rose; Dan's, a crown, an anchor and some leaves – something to do with the navy. The outside of the low wooden structure was painted black with white window frames. They handed over their 25pees to the lady at the trestle table by the door and ambled in. The wobbly hardboard panels that lined the unfussy interior were uniformly covered in neat cream emulsion, punctuated with pictures of old cricket teams – rows and rows of grinning, arms-folded men in white uniforms – and the odd tattered, aged cricket bat, regarded as special because it had tonked the ball further and more times than other cricket bats. Plain chairs and tables lined the edges of the scrubbed wooden floor; in the middle a space had been cleared to create an area for dancing. The room was empty but for two middle-aged couples who sat at opposite ends and muttered inaudibly.

Across the way from where Dan and Si took seats were the bar, then, to its left, separate and set up on one of the tables, a big upright barrel of sherry and a tray of glasses. A man of about fifty, who looked like he ought to be called Ken, with white hair, white shirt and fawn slacks, served.

Dan strolled over first. 'Can I have a glass of sherry, please?' He asked, with the kind of studied, grown-up politeness he hoped would circumvent any discussion of his age.

The glasses were the smallest Dan had ever seen – narrow, concave things, somewhere between the size of a thimble and a school chemi-lab test tube. The guy picked one up, filled it to within half an inch of the top and gave it to Dan. Si got the same. They returned to their seats.

They drank the sherry. It was disgusting, but it went almost immediately. They weighed up their options. It was 'as much sherry as you could drink,' and they wanted to drink a lot, but it would be a bit embarrassing to keep going back again and again, especially while everyone else was sitting around, sipping sensibly and slowly, and making one of those farting little glasses last ages.

A plan took shape in Dan's mind. He turned to Si: 'What if we go the bar, get a pint, drink it, then go and ask the bloke to fill the pint pot with sherry? He can't say no, can he? It's all the sherry you can drink, innit?'

They bought pints of Tetley's bitter in big, dimpled glass jugs and returned to their seats. Dan drained his glass and sauntered casually over to the sherry guy with his pint pot behind his back.

'It's all the sherry you can drink, right?'

'Yeah, yeah,' said the bloke, looking at him quizzically.

Dan whizzed the pint pot from behind his back and said 'here you go, then. Fill that.'

The sherry guy looked a bit unsettled, but said nothing. He took the pint pot, shoved it under the tap and filled it three-quarters full. 'To the top, if you don't mind,' said Dan. And the guy huffed and filled the other quarter. With the plan a success, Si took his pint pot over and also came back with it brimming with sherry.

Now they had to drink the bloody awful stuff.

Another white-haired, slacks-wearing guy, also probably called Ken, or maybe Don, chatted conspiratorially with the sherry server. They both looked over at Si and Dan as they spoke, but did nothing.

The place was filling up. As daylight faded outside, the lights inside turned the room a subtle peach colour. Wanky pop music drifted from the feeble PA: "Julie, Julie, Julie do Ya Love Me", "Goodbye Sam, Hello Samantha", "Blue Spanish Eyes..." There was a genteel atmosphere, except at Si and Dan's table, where drunkenness, nausea and a desire for anarchy had taken hold.

They stumbled outside, dodged round the back of the club, grabbed a few of the empties from the crates behind the toilet block, smashed them on the wall and cheered like they'd scored a goal, then staggered up the slope to the cricket pitch and ran round it, screeching, bellowing and singing football songs, before stopping, doubling up and vomiting profusely.

The following morning they experienced their first ever hangovers, as well as the first day of a lifelong hatred of sherry.

***

Reena Davies and Ruby Hobbs invited Si and Dan to Ruby's house near the top of the hill on Lime View Estate on a Tuesday night. Ruby's mum was out at the bingo. Si and Dan had discovered that if you slid a penknife into the return coins slot in a pay phone, quite often a stuck sixpence would be persuaded out. They scored in two of the three phone boxes they passed on the way up to Ruby's.

Si and Dan both wore their skinhead gear: denim jeans and jackets, boots, braces and check shirts with button-down collars. Both girls were small and pretty, and both wore miniskirts. They looked like they'd stepped off the set of *Ready Steady Go*. Reena wore knee-length white plastic boots and had black hair shaped into a bob, with a white Alice band at the front. Ruby had blonde hair and one of those long half-wigs, where the wearer's own hair is visible at the front, and the wig, which is meant to be a spot-on match for the natural hair, forms a high-up false bit at the back, *à la* Mandy Rice-Davies. Dan found this very seductive.

The girls played some of their favourite records: "Terry" by Twinkle, "Single Girl" by Sandy Posey, "Chapel of Love" by the Dixie Cups and "Leader of the Pack" by the Shangri-Las. Incompetent motorcyclists and longing seemed to be the key themes. And Dan and Ruby, on the settee, and Si and Reena, on the armchair, snogged and engaged in what they called heavy petting.

***

Adey Martin had been bought a tent, complete with all necessary accessories, for his birthday. Adey's parents had a few bob. His dad was an ice cream man and didn't have to pay tax because he was self-employed. They lived in a bungalow on the new estate on the hill.

It was a good tent – mostly green with an orange fly sheet and sewn-in groundsheet. So far it had only been pitched in the garden, but now Adey wanted to do something more adventurous, so he and Dan decided to spend the night on Leaches Moor. It was only half a mile from town. The Pennines have jagged edges, and Leaches Moor is an outcrop that pushes out into Dashley Dyke and shapes and overshadows the town.

They trudged up the winding lane, boots scrunching on old crushed sandstone. Adey had a bulging rucksack with aluminium pans tied to it, which bounced and clattered as he walked. Dan had a duffle bag slung over his shoulder. Stuffed into it was a sleeping bag made from an old eiderdown, which his mum had folded then sewn across the bottom and up one side, to make do. In one hand he carried a Diana .22 air rifle, in the other his mum's blue Ever Ready transistor radio. The plan was to warm up some tinned soup on the Gaz stove then smoke some cigarettes and flop out and listen to Radio Luxembourg on the tranny. It wasn't entirely clear what the air rifle was for, but when you go off into the wilderness you have to take precautions. They might be raided by bandits or attacked by wild beasts.

Now, the thing about Leaches Moor, which distinguished it from most other moors, was that it was haunted. In the nineteenth century, a cotton magnate called Frederick Stubbs had built a fine sandstone house right on the top of the moor, overlooking the town: Leaches Moor Manor. And just at the end of that century, a villain had got into the house and shot Mr Stubbs dead. No-one knew whether the assailant was a burglar, who Mr Stubbs had caught and fought with; or an enraged, defrauded business associate; or someone from his resentful, ill-treated workforce. But, whatever the case, the murderer was never found, and the ghost of Mr Stubbs's dog – a giant, fierce Alsatian – was said to roam the moor in the dead of night in search of his beloved master's killer.

No-one wanted the house after Mr Stubbs's horrific murder, so it gradually fell into disrepair and was eventually demolished by the council in the 1950s. All that was left were a few footings and, incongruously for the Pennines, an abundance of now unwieldy rhododendrons, which had once graced the carefully cultivated gardens.

There was still a bit of light when Dan and Adey reached the top. They found a clearing, a nice flat bit among the rhododendrons, and pitched the tent. Adey set up the Gaz stove and they scoffed Jacob's Cream Crackers with a tin of cream of vegetable soup in aluminium bowls. Kit-Kats for afters. They then laid back in the tent with the radio and fiddled around with the dial, looking for Radio Luxembourg, hoping to hear some soul. But the tuning drifted in and out. There was the odd hint of music, then a whining noise, then white noise. Multiple efforts produced only the same: a few seconds of unidentifiable crackly music, then nothing.

They gave up and instead started to wind each other up with ghost stories. Then it was time to sleep, but Adey needed a piss first. He pushed the flap back and eased himself out of the tent. Seconds later he came crashing back through it like a man possessed.

'It's the dog! It's the fucking dog!'

'Yeah, right,' said Dan, cynically.

'No, seriously, I've just fuckin' seen it. I'm not joking. It's the fucking dog!'

The look on Adey's face confirmed his seriousness.

Dan was sceptical about anything supernatural, but the terror in Adey's eyes was real and that wound him up too. He tried to keep his cool. He cracked open the air rifle, slotted a slug into the breach and snapped it shut. He slipped a handful more slugs into his pocket. 'Come on then, let's have a look.'

They stepped out into the darkness. Their only light source was a feeble Woolworth's torch, which illuminated nothing more than three feet away.

'There,' said Adey. And some thirty feet in the distance was a shape that looked roughly like a large dog on its haunches, scarcely discernible in the near total blackness. Dan went cold. He wasn't sure if it was moving. It seemed to hover and shimmer in the chill black air. He took aim with the air rifle and fired. The shape didn't move. He loaded and shot it again, and again – twenty times. The shape remained impassive.

'Well, whatever it is, it's fucked now, isn't it. I mean, an air rifle won't kill anything, but it'll certainly give it a bad day. If it was gonna do anything it would've done it by now.'

They slipped back into the tent, closed the flap and secured it conscientiously. Some hours of fitful sleep followed, and then it was light.

They extracted themselves from the tent with only one thought: the dog. And there it was: the end of a low ruined wall, part of the footings of Frederick Stubbs's old house, roughly the shape of a large dog on its haunches, the pale yellow of the sandstone making it stand out from the dark green rhododendrons that surrounded it.

***

Paper round done, tea done, homework done – it was time for the youth club. Dan bowled briskly up dusty Chatters Hill Road and crossed over towards the gap between the terraced houses.

The kerbs turned in as though someone had once intended to build another street there but changed their mind. Instead of tarmac, a short stretch of dirt track, just the depth of the houses and their backyards, mended here and there with crushed clinker, led to the space behind: a loosely rectangular patch of wasteland, about 150 yards across, bound where Dan stood by the backs of the terraced houses on Chatters Hill Road, to his left by the bungalows on Northumbria Avenue, to his right by the tangle of bracken and fly-tipping that led steeply down to the lock-up garages, and on the far side by the grey asbestos panelling and tar-paper roof of the youth club.

The rectangle dipped in the middle and was covered in thick scrubby grass, generously manured by local dogs. A path created by decades of footfall cut diagonally across from the dirt-and-clinker track to the entrance of the youth club.

Dan had walked that path a thousand times. Today it was different, though. Halfway across the otherwise featureless space and just to the left of the path was a tent. A green and orange tent. Adey Martin's tent. There were clearly people inside it. Dan could hear whispering voices and the sides bulged and receded as bodies shifted. He approached it, wondering how you knock on a door made out of calico, but Adey must have heard his footsteps. He poked his head out just as Dan reached the tent. His face seemed to combine self-congratulatory pleasure with a hint of embarrassment. He was grinning like a chimp, but scarlet. Smells drifted out from the tent flaps: sweat, bodies, jizz. On the groundsheet was a torn-off piece of brown corrugated cardboard, and on it were little grey-white globs of the offending substance. Beyond that was Irene Bottomley, lying on her side, her massive hips like the rolling hills of the Pennines, still in her green Bradfield Girls' Grammar School uniform. She said nothing; just gazed back at Dan with a smirk – a mixture of triumph and defiance. She always looked at him like that, even when they passed on the street, but today it seemed to have a bit more meaning. Dan's eyes switched back to Adey.

'Erm, right,' said Dan. 'I'm just off to the youth club. Probably catch yer there later, yeah?'

'Yeah, sure, yeah,' said Adey, abruptly, keen to have the encounter over as soon as possible.

And Dan wandered off up the well-trodden path with his mind churning: *why, when Adey reckoned he'd had nearly every girl in the youth club, was he exchanging hand-jobs with Bradfield's answer to Olive from* On the Buses?

***

Dan thought he was a skinhead. Well, he *was* a skinhead – he had all the right clothes: the Levis, the braces, the hobnailed boots and all that, and he liked soul, ska and reggae – he just didn't have the right hairstyle. In fact, he didn't really have a hairstyle at all. He just had hair, which, when it got to being about an inch longer than it ought to be, would be cropped by Ukrainian Joe the barber, so that it looked like it did the previous time he cropped it, and the time before that...

But now Dan was becoming more style conscious, so this time he took himself off to Joe's place on Inkerman Square with a new, uncharacteristic sense of purpose.

On the walls of the tiny salon hung cascading steel racks that displayed all the things a man could need: combs and razorblades, mints and chewing gum, cigarettes and matches, Durex johnnies – Gossamer and Fetherlite – and hogs-hair shaving brushes. Around and above were aspirational photos of footballers and film stars, and monochrome models with unfeasibly neat haircuts that no-one in real life ever had and would have been beyond Joe's skills anyway, if anyone ever actually had the nerve to ask for one – fancy haircuts were not the thing in Dashley Dyke. The air was thick with the whiff of hair stuff of various sorts: Vitalis, Brylcreem and pomade, whatever that was. On the shelf at the side were black and brown Bakelite trimmers, along with the bottle of light machine oil that Joe applied to them assiduously to keep them moving efficiently. Next to these was a large glass jar containing combs, scissors and a cut-throat razor, all drowning in deep blue sterilising fluid. Facing the mirror was the big, important-looking, black-and-chrome adjustable chair – the sort of chair James Bond would be strapped into by the evil genius to face a horrifying death, but would escape from because the baddy would be foolish enough to leave the room and give our hero the chance to exercise his unbeatable 007 secret-agent escapology skills.

Neat, polite Joe hovered around the impressive chair, snipping away at the head of a grey-haired, middle-aged man. Two more blokes were waiting. Dan sat on the red plastic bench, which was busted at the corners and had old horsehair stuffing coming out, and flicked absent-mindedly through year-old copies of *Titbits* and last week's newspapers (which he'd delivered), and waited his turn.

Dan had only heard of two hairstyles: 'square neck' and 'short back and sides'. He knew it was the former he was meant to ask for, but he'd always found barbers unsettling. Something about having someone messing about with your head and wielding sharp objects around behind you where you can't see them was disconcerting – only one up from the dentists'. And as he settled into the special chair and Joe loomed up behind him, he lost his nerve and blurted out 'short back and sides' instead of 'square neck'. And whereas he'd expected to leave the shop looking like a cool thing on a cool day in a brisk northerly breeze, he looked more like a tragic 1957 National Service conscript.

***

Si was 16 months older than Dan and so reached the magical age of 17 while Dan was still only 15. He'd been saving up his paper-round and birthday money for driving lessons and a car, while also getting unofficial lessons from his dad in the family Ford Anglia. But at 17, he could finish the job. He passed his test first time and bought a 1960 Austin A40, finished, like most of them, in an institutional-looking milky turquoise with a black roof.

Si picked Dan up for a quick whizz round town, to show off the car and his newly acquired skills. He pulled off from outside Dan's house, taking care to apply all of those freshly learned safe driving measures, except putting on seat belts – it was an old car and didn't have them, and they wouldn't have known what to do with them even if it had.

They cruised carefully around Dashley Dyke's side streets, but Si itched to get out onto the open road and put his foot down a bit.

They reached the start of Leppings Road, the dead-straight, derestricted, one-and-a-half-mile stretch of smooth tarmac that ran due north, linking Dashton to Glodhill.

Si put his foot to the boards and the Austin picked up speed at the rate it felt reasonable. And then they were doing sixty. And as they passed the peak by Hartford Farm and started to descend towards Glodhill, the dial moved up still further – to seventy. Si wanted to see just how fast it would go, and with the help of the downward slope, it got up to 75, just as the sharp left-hander at the Glodhill end of the road came into view.

They weren't going to make it.

Si slammed on the brakes, but the boxy old cross-ply tyres couldn't cope. The bonnet dipped and the Austin careened left and right. Si wrestled with the wheel but had no control. They did a complete spin, Dan's head slammed against the side window, and they were now on the wrong side of the road, still moving, still out of control. Si turned the wheel this way and that and fought to bring the beast back to the left. It rose up onto its two right wheels and threatened to roll over, but didn't – it crunched back down onto all four wheels and shot back leftward. At which point, with a few more side-to-side lurches, it finally stopped, at right-angles to the oncoming traffic.

***

The key uses for a nightclub, Dan learned, were listening to music, dancing, getting off with girls, drinking and fighting. You could also, in Mars, if you'd successfully done the third of these, slip easily through the door into the boiler room for a bit of privacy and a knee-trembler.

All of these activities were popular at Mars, but none more so than fighting. The place was filled with skinhead gangs representing each of the East Manchester towns, and sometimes specific estates within or next to a town. Each group fought for prestige and dominance, to right the wrongs of previous lost battles, and to meet the expectations of skinheads created by outraged but vicariously-thrilled print and TV media.

Periods of calm would be interrupted by sudden bursts of violent action. A group of people, who at one moment seemed to be chatting peacefully, would suddenly erupt. Fists, feet and glasses would fly. Folk chatting in other groups would break off and throw themselves into the melee. Previously invisible bouncers would appear from dark corners and wade into the fracas, pulling, shouting and separating. Faces streaming with blood would be dragged out and despatched from the front door.

But not all skinheads were part of a gang. Some were hard enough to get by on their own.

Adey told Dan about this guy called Frankie, who carried a cut-throat razor and would stick it in your mouth and slice up to your ear if you crossed him. And crossing him wasn't hard to do: if you happened to brush past him and touch his tonic suit, he would demand money for dry cleaning, and if you argued the razor would appear.

And then there was Steve Mahoney. Some foolish little skinhead took a pop at him outside Mars one night. The lad ended up in hospital fighting for his life after being kicked repeatedly in the head with hobnailed boots. Guys like Steve Mahoney were more dangerous than a whole skinhead gang put together.

And some lads weren't even skinheads, like Bob Hindley. He was mates with most of the Bradfield lot, but wore just regular clothes: flared kecks, tank top and side-gusseted slip-on boots. He was his own man. He even thought "I Never Promised You a Rose Garden" by Lynn Anderson was a good record and didn't mind who knew. But he could handle himself better than most skinheads and was completely devoid of fear. One night, he left his girlfriend on the dancefloor and went off to buy a couple of drinks. When he got back, some guy was trying to chat her up, and when Bob intervened it turned nasty. The bloke, who was quite a bit taller than Bob, poked a finger into Bob's face. And Bob, with a full pint pot in one hand and a wine glass in the other, demolished the interloper with a succession of well-aimed kicks to the bollocks with those slick, side-gusseted boots. Only a tiny amount of Wilson's Best and Cherry B was spilled.

And then there was a touching and strangely incongruous moment. The Hatterston crew and the Hightown crew had been fighting battles small and large in Mars and The Blue Parrot for months. But then came the accident. Billy Hobday, on his way one evening from Hatterston to Mars in his blue Crombie and check Ben Sherman, leant out of the open platform at the back of the Number 30 bus, as it made its way down Furnace Street. And just a hundred and fifty yards from the club and with all the momentum of a ten-ton double-decker hurtling down a hill at thirty miles an hour, Billy's face smashed into a concrete lamppost and his neck snapped and his skull disintegrated and he never knew anything else. The Hightown crew sent a wreath.

***

At least once a week, if he had the money, Dan would nip out of school at dinner time, trot down the hill past Bieberstein's throat-rasping dye works, and check out Terry's record stall in Hightown Super-Market.

The Super-Market wasn't a supermarket in any conventional sense. What it really was was an old picture house that had fallen out of use and been converted into a market hall. Apart from its rather grand frontage, which still retained a few hints of its more elegant former life, it was no different from any other northern indoor market hall. But since supermarkets were now all the rage and Hightown didn't have one, the council decided to re-label Hightown's indoor market 'Super-Market', hoping that no-one would spot the difference. The words were emblazoned in great swirling red letters on the art deco facade to eliminate any doubt.

Dan had called in several times, breezing past the whiffy cheese stall, the haberdashers and the place that sold those tedious Tru-Form shoes, to try and buy some record he'd heard in Mars. Terry never had it, but would always say that it would be in next week. And a week on, Dan would get all excited and go back expecting to buy a nice crisp new copy of "Baby Do the Philly Dog" or suchlike, but when he asked if it had arrived, Terry would look at him vacantly and say that it would be in *next* next week.

After several rounds of this, Dan concluded Terry was a bullshitter. And finally, to put it to the test, he called in and asked Terry if he'd got "Tell the Truth" by The Liars. Terry said he didn't, but he'd have it in next week.

***

Adey went on a school trip to Lucerne and came back with a flick knife. Everyone in 5T was envious. It was so supremely sharp that you could almost cut yourself by looking at it. A small group of knife enthusiasts stood round Adey in the tech drawing room and watched as he repeatedly flicked it open and dramatically stabbed the door frame, like a juvenile delinquent in a 1950s Hollywood gang fight. And there was discussion about the difference between a flick knife and a stiletto: with a flick knife the blade came out of the side; with a stiletto it came out of the end. Adey's was one of the side-egress type.

Wanting to try it out properly, Adey got Dale Fletcher to stick out his hand, whereupon he sliced a cool, effortless, clean cut right across the back of it. It was a surreal moment. The way Dale put his hand there and kept it there seemed inexplicable – almost as though he didn't think this was really happening. And Adey himself seemed shocked, as though he expected Dale to jerk his hand out of the way before he got going, but he didn't. There was disbelief all round.

For an instant there was just a neat red line across the back of Dale's hand, which looked like it had been drawn with a felt-tip pen. Then the cut opened up and the blood spread outwards and started to drip onto the parquet flooring. And then the pain hit, and Dale flung open the door and ran howling into the corridor and up to the school office for first aid.

Adey was in the headmaster's office for a long time, but didn't get expelled.

Dan coveted the knife, but there was no chance of getting one here in the UK. So he bought a wooden-handled penknife from Dashton Market and broke the spring at the back so the blade could be made to fly out with a flick of the wrist and then held in place by squeezing the handle. He took it everywhere with him in his back pocket in case of trouble. When *A Clockwork Orange* came out, a year or so later, he felt vindicated.

***

Dan and Si stood on the platform half way up the stairs in Mars, the bit where it turned before heading up to the balcony. The platform was a vantage point, with views over both the dancefloor and the DJs' mock-space-landing-craft booth. Some of the girls on the dancefloor caught their attention but, more urgently, they watched what the DJs were putting on the turntables, trying to work out, if not what a record was, at least what label it was on. This could form part of the investigative process. If you knew the label and had an idea of the title via the chorus, you might be able to work out what it was and who it was by, and from there maybe get a copy.

Suddenly, there was a bang in the back of Dan's leg. He didn't look round. He just assumed it was some drunken sod reeling into him on his way up or down the stairs. But then it happened again – much harder this time. Once could be an accident; twice not. He spun round, and there set out before him, blocking the way both up and down the stairs, were ten or so lads wearing black Harringtons, check Jaytex's and Doctor Martens boots: the Hatterston crew, with the trouble-maker-in-chief, Pete Halfpenny, at the front. Dan didn't know them, he just knew who they were, and this looked like trouble.

Halfpenny got in his face and snarled something, but it was inaudible, drowned out by the pounding music. Dan didn't know quite what to do. What was the protocol when someone kicks you in the back of the leg in a night club and says something aggressive in your face, but you can't tell what? 'Sorry, I didn't quite get that,' which might have been appropriate in another time and place, didn't quite work for these circumstances. However, Dan figured the guy wanted a fight, so he obliged and punched him in the face. Halfpenny flew backwards and was caught by his friends. He seemed surprised. Dan was surprised that he was surprised. Wasn't this what he wanted? What did he expect when he'd kicked someone and then snarled in his face? It seemed Dan had got the protocol wrong.

But, whatever the case, the odds – ten onto two – didn't look good, and before Dan could further contemplate his social faux pas, Si had hold of him by his shoulders and was pushing him through Halfpenny's mates down the stairs. They followed him, fast. Then they were on him. He tripped on the bottom stair and went down under their weight. He hit the ground face down and covered his head, waiting for the inevitable kicking. There were a few kicks, but nothing much, and then there seemed to be air around him and he was being dragged upward by his collar by the mighty right fist of Gary Dugdale. Another bouncer, big lanky Terry Wardle, was dispersing the mob.

***

The Blue Parrot was alright, but not a patch on Mars. They had some decent soul – "Sock It to 'Em JB", "Free for All", "Chills and Fever" and a few more – but you had to wait an age, during which you were compelled to listen to garbage like "Chirpy Chirpy Cheep Cheep", "Cracklin' Rosie", "Yellow River", "In the"-bloody-"Summertime" and T-Rex's latest warbling. And then there was the pop-chart soul, like "I Want You Back" and "Up the Ladder to the Roof" and "Stoned Love", which was nearly as bad. And even when you did get to the soul bit, it was only about half an hour's worth and always selected from the same dozen or so records. It had been OK at first, but had started to wear thin. Folk hung on, nevertheless, in the hope that it would get better, because there was nowhere else to go on a Monday night.

The building itself was a long, narrow affair with a curved roof, a bit like a dark aircraft hangar, with a small, low stage at one end, steps up to the balcony and bar at the other, and a human-scale, Victorian-style, pale pink birdcage in the middle, where the djs did their thing. Between the cage and the stage was the dancefloor; at the other side of the cage was a carpeted area for sitting and standing around with drinks. Along the edges were alcoves, a bit like compartments in an old-style train, like the one where Richard Hannay snogged the startled blonde girl in *The 39 Steps*: mauve-veloured glory holes, where couples could hide away in darkness and something a bit, but not entirely, like privacy. Here, lips met lips, fumbling fingertips flicked bra hooks asunder, and hands made expeditionary sorties between flesh and fabric. Limits were tested. Luck was pushed.

Above the alcoves a balcony ran around the whole perimeter of the building. When Dan was there with his mates, they'd wander round it, doing slow, leisurely laps, chatting and periodically stopping to gaze at the dancefloor and djs below, and to see if anyone had come in who they knew, or fancied. But on this particular night Dan was with Lucy. They snogged in one of the alcoves.

Fights broke out sporadically, as was the norm. There seemed to be some kind of feud being played out between the Dashton lot and the Clayton crew. Dan knew most of them by sight, but no-one personally.

Suddenly, the whole place erupted into a vortex of violent energy. Bodies, bar stools and beer bottles flashed past the entrance to the alcove. The air was filled with shouting, screaming and the crash of smashing glass. Dan got up to take a look. Lucy grabbed his sleeve and yanked him back into his seat.

The music stopped and the lights came on and it was strangely quiet. Dan and Lucy poked their heads tentatively out of the alcove. The place was nearly empty. A few couples and small groups stood around the edges, talking among themselves in whispered tones. Bouncers and uniformed police picked their way through the mess and surveyed the damage. The floor between the cage and the steps up to the bar was covered with a continuous glittering shroud of shattered glass. Dan and Lucy picked up their coats, stepped out into the cool night air and found an unlit corner in the multi-storey to consummate what they'd started in the alcove.

A girl on the bus said that someone had been thrown off the balcony and was in Dashton General in a bad way.

***

It was late on Wednesday night. Dan was upstairs, towards the back of the last Number 90, on his way home from Lucy's, wearing his rolled-up Levis, the long pale-blue cardy he'd nicked from his dad, and his beloved cherry-red Doctor Martens boots. The bus pulled up at a stop in the nondescript suburban bit where Hightown merged into Bradfield. A cool looking guy emerged from the top of the stairs, sporting a neat suedehead haircut, a pure white button-down Ben Sherman shirt and a pair of silver-grey tonic kecks, which looked like the bottom half of a suit. He pivoted and dropped into a seat a couple of rows in front of Dan on the other side of the aisle. As he turned, the entire back of his shirt – from shoulder to shoulder, neck to waistband – was saturated with blood, which continued to be topped up by a seeping dark red wound on the back of his head.

***

It was half-nine in The Blue Parrot, and still there'd been no soul. "Love Grows Where My Rosemary Goes", "Knock Three Times", "The"-fucking-"Banner Man"... And it was a weeknight – most everyone had to be gone by 10.30 for the last buses. This just wasn't on. Rob Brierley had had enough. Rob was a wiry little fucker, with a look of Lee van Cleef from *The Good, The Bad and The Ugly* about him. He strode up to the giant pink birdcage, agitation visible in his jerky skinny body, and yelled and poked an angry finger at the DJ. 'Put some soul on, you tosser. Haven't you got any decent bloody records?'

Seconds later Rob was carried out horizontally, wriggling, by the bouncers.

Dan was incensed. It was time to show solidarity. He tapped one of the bouncers on the shoulder and said 'come on, he's got a point, this music is fuckin' awful. We didn't come here to listen to this shite. It needs sortin' out.' And seconds later he was carried out horizontally by the bouncers. He didn't bother to wriggle, though.

***

There was a knock at the front door. Dan's mum pulled back the net curtain and nosed out of the window. 'Looks like one of your mates.'

Dan prised himself out of the creaky armchair, turned the worn brass Yale lock and swung open the door. There was Bernard Wainwright. Bernard knocked about with the youth club lot and went to Mars now and then, but fashion didn't register with him, and with his floppy fair hair and brown check shirts and baggy cords, he always had the look of a farmer's lad about him, though he was in fact the eldest son of Joe Wainwright, the window cleaner. The Wainwright's house was where Dan had spent the previous evening.

'OK, give it back and we'll say nowt,' said Bernard.

'What? Give what back? What are yer talkin' about?'

'The record you nicked from my party last night?'

'What? What record? I never touched your bloody records.'

'Yes yer did: "Skinhead Moonstomp". Someone saw yer. And then yer left early.'

'"SKINHEAD FUCKIN' MOONSTOMP"?! I wouldn't have it given me, let alone nick it... And I left early 'cos it was a shit party.'

'You didn't nick it then?'

'No, I bloody didn't. Who says I did?'

'Oh. No. It doesn't matter.'

Bernard turned and walked away.

***

Every Tuesday Dan and Lucy went to The Regal in Hightown to see the latest movie. Dan caught the Number 90 one way and Lucy caught it the other way and they met on the corner of Market Street and Warrington Street, a few yards from the cinema entrance. They'd seen *Love Story*, *Soldier Blue* and *Straw Dogs*, and this week it was *A Clockwork Orange*. There was always a nervous moment when the film was X rated. Sometimes they were challenged at the till. 'Are you eighteen?' Naturally, they always said they were, like in the pub. It seemed a futile exercise. They would hardly say 'no, we're not – you'd best chuck us out.' And no-one ever argued. No-one said 'no you're not, you're only sixteen.'

They bought Paynes Poppets in the foyer and filed into the dark musty space. It was busier than usual. They flipped forward a couple of the aged maroon velour seats and made themselves comfortable, ready for this week's celluloid thrill.

As the narrative played out before him, Dan could scarcely believe what he was seeing. He was both aghast and exhilarated, and he left the building on a cloud, euphoric. He could hardly put into words what he was feeling. To a sixteen-year-old skinhead, violence was thrilling – as long as you were on the winning side – but it wasn't just that.

It had always felt like the skinhead world he inhabited was invisible to anyone who was not part of it, like he was part of some cultural force that meant something, but something that the world at large would not acknowledge. And now here it was, big, bold and unignorable. OK, it was slightly shifted, there was something futuristic about it and there were stylistic differences: it had had the movie-land treatment. The hair and clothes were different, and Dan didn't know anyone who'd murdered someone with a four-foot fibreglass penis, but these minor details aside, it was palpably a skinhead parable.

Previously, all there had been were various bits of scandalised media coverage, reporting skinhead antics in the usual censorious tone, to thrill the curtain-twitching, oughta-be-a-law brigade. But here, now, in glorious Technicolor, there was something that spoke not from the culturally illiterate viewpoint of Mr Outraged of Orpington, but from the birthplace of it all: from the perspective of the teenage protagonists. As perverse as they seemed from the outside, there were values and reasoning. There were hierarchies, power struggles and codes of behaviour, though these were mutable and under constant renegotiation, because this was all part of growing up. And there were music and style, places and pleasures, and camaraderie, loyalty and betrayal. And there was love. There was something culturally rich in the land of the teenage skinhead. Adults, if they looked at all, seemed to see it as a brutish, stupid, *Lord of the Flies* sort of place, but were skinhead battles and power struggles really any worse than adult ones? Wasn't what happened between skinheads considerably less wicked than the brutal, Machiavellian manoeuvrings amongst the historic warlords and Mafioso who schemed, tortured and murdered their way to the top before proclaiming themselves divinely-appointed royalty and aristocracy? Was it skinheads who were dropping bombs, napalm and Agent Orange daily onto Vietnamese civilians? Brawl on a beach and you're sub-human; burn a few thousand brown people alive and you get a medal.

It became a minor obsession. Dan watched the film several more times, bought the book and read it twice, and bought the soundtrack LP and listened to it over and over again.

***

The tonic jacket was *de rigueur*, and you had to have one with a centre vent; side vents would just not do. And there was a kind of arms race going on in the clubs to get your tailor to make you the tonic jacket with the biggest vent. Vents went from scarcely discernible, to 6 inch, to 9 inch, to 12 inch, and even to 15 inch. And then one night in Mars, a guy breezed past Si and Dan with a vent so long that there was only about 5 inches of unvented cloth between it and the collar. As he walked by the back of the jacket flapped about like a pair of curtains in a draught.

'Bloody hell,' said Si, 'a two-part jacket.'

***

Four of the six East Manchester towns stacked on top of each other, north to south: Crossley, Dashley Dyke, Bradfield and Hightown. To the east were the Pennines, to the west, the other two towns: Dashton and Hatterston. Beyond those was the mighty city of Manchester itself. To the north was the great sprawling mass of Glodhill, which drifted off into South Lancashire. To the south was the even bigger sprawling mass of

Verrington. It spread most of the way around the south of Manchester and linked the city to the airport and separated it from rural Cheshire. Together, the six towns formed a jagged, grey-brown Siegfried Line of houses and mills that separated the city from the wilderness. Folk from the city seldom ventured out to the moors, and the wild men of the Pennines didn't have much use for the city. Those who lived in the six towns were inbetweenies – not of the inner city, but not country folk either.

The pre-cast concrete shelters on Hightown bus station looked like they had once almost been elegant. The curves at each end suggested a bit of art deco influence, as well as echoing the shapes of the trams they served a couple of generations ago. And there had once been glass in the windows and lights in the ceiling – you could still see remnants of the fittings – but the council had long since abandoned any hope of keeping ahead of the vandals. They were now dark, draughty places that always reeked of piss. Dan normally waited outside the shelter, but tonight the rain was lashing down so there wasn't much choice. He avoided touching the sides, didn't lean on anything.

It was quiet. The teatime rush was long over and the chucking-out-time melee had yet to start. A couple of people in front of him stood silently, silhouetted against the glow of the sodium street lights.

The Number 4 lurched in around the corner and straightened up as it slowed for the shelter, like a staggering drunk struggling to maintain some semblance of dignity. A handful of people stepped off: a tired-looking bloke in a donkey jacket who looked like he'd just finished a shift; a dolled-up hairspray girl going out on a date; two laughing, chatting lads on their way to the pub.

Dan hopped onto the open rear platform and jogged upstairs. He didn't smoke, but sitting *downstairs with the virgins* wasn't for him, so, as always, he sat on the top deck in a cloud of other people's tar-and-tobacco pollution. This was a matter of no concern – smoking still wasn't bad for you in those days and the concept of passive smoking did not yet exist. And anyway, the bus was three-quarters empty at this time of night. He slunk back in his seat and put his knees up on the one in front. His black parallels rode up and exposed his red socks and black Royals. The windows were coated in a smelly grey film of condensed breath and nicotine. He wiped a small spy-hole with the back of his hand, gazed out absentmindedly over the bus shelter to the service road at the back of the shops, watched the rain flash past a street light and tried to understand what had just happened.

The evening had started well enough. Dan and Lucy had gone to The Joker coffee bar on Market Street. They'd had hot blackcurrant juice in funky, low cups and saucers, made out of Pyrex glass. And someone had commandeered the turntable and played "Love, Love, Love" and "What's Wrong with Me Baby", and those two new ones they'd just started playing at Mars: "The Next in Line" and "You're Ready Now".

They had set off up the hill towards Lucy's house: he would walk her home, then begin his journey back to Dashley Dyke from the bus stop outside her place. But then the rain started, and he tucked in under her umbrella. And with the rhythm of their walking, the brolly hit him on the head and he got a bit pissy. She held it higher up and they carried on walking. But it gradually slipped down and hit him again, and he got pissier. Then it happened a third time and he blew up into a ludicrously disproportionate rage. They yelled at each other in the street, and he stormed off down the hill in the driving rain, back past The Joker, towards the bus station. He looked back, but she didn't, and they both kept on going in opposite directions.

The diesel engine grumbled into life. The bus shuddered and rolled out of the bus station.

What had he just done? This was the latest in several such absurd incidents. And she hadn't looked back. He knew he'd blown it this time.

He'd never heard the word 'angst' or of the concepts that attached themselves to it. He just knew that two vicious, angry ferrets had been fighting to the death in his chest for the last few weeks, and he was struggling to articulate why, even to himself.

They were both 15 when they met in Mars. He was crazy about her. She was lovely: soft, warm, voluptuous, gorgeous – looked like she was made out of peaches. She wore one of those Wonderbras, which made what was already irresistible overwhelming. They made love in the park among the fragrant blooms at dusk after everyone had gone home, or on the hearth rug at her house whenever they were left to babysit her little brother. It was wonderful, idyllic.

Dan lived right on the border of Dashley Dyke and Bradfield. In fact, the border probably ran through the last few feet of their house – you could see the change in the colour of the tarmac where one council finished and the other started, and you could see where that line would go – but the front door was in Dashley Dyke, so Dashley Dyke was where he lived. And Lucy lived in Hightown, but right on the far side, almost in Verrington. There were effectively two towns between them – Bradfield and Hightown – but the Number 90 bus ran both past his house and hers. What luck! What a joy that discovery was when they first got together. It was perfect! But then Dan's parents moved the family to the other side – the Crossley side – of Dashley Dyke, so now there were three towns between them: Bradfield, Hightown and Dashley Dyke. And the Number 90 went nowhere near where he now lived. That shouldn't have stopped two besotted lovers. Climb the highest mountain, swim the deepest sea and all that… But the practicalities soon became frustrating. Dan now had to catch two buses to get to Lucy's house, and hope that the first didn't come late and make him miss the second. And a journey which had previously taken three quarters of an hour could now take an hour and a half. If he went to hers in the evening, he had to leave at 9.30 to make sure he got the last second bus. And they were both nearly 17 now, and he'd started work at the Gas Board and she was doing her A Levels. In another year she'd be off to university, probably at the other end of the country, and he'd never see her, and the aching would be unbearable. And she'd probably – *inevitably* – take up with some other guy on her course, who was smarter and cooler and posher than him, and she'd offload Dan because she'd realise she could do better, and that would be humiliating as well as devastating. And they'd been together since they were 15 – how on earth could that be expected to last? He couldn't see a time when he would want to be without her, but who ends up getting old with their first love? It had to end in disaster. He couldn't bear to lose her, but he couldn't bear to live with all this impending horror. So he'd blown up over an umbrella. *A fucking umbrella.* And why didn't he just grab it and hold it himself? Maybe he wanted this to happen...

The bus lumbered up Gartside Street, past Felix Brothers' towel factory, towards the plateau on which sits most of Bradfield. The land levelled out and the bus chugged sedately along Beeches Lane in the direction of the rugby field. And then he saw it, a little black block-house of a building, with a small, scarcely noticeable sign over the door: Buffy's. He'd heard about that place; he'd seen its squat, nondescript form from the bus a thousand times, but never thought anything of it. But just lately Jez Reeves had been banging on about it. They played soul, and really good soul too, not like that thin crappy gruel served up at The Blue Parrot. But he'd missed the stop. He jumped up quickly, hopped off at the next one and walked back.

He didn't know what to expect, and it was odd to be going to a place for the first time on your own, and given what had already transpired that evening he was hardly in the mood. But he paid at the desk and stepped into the darkness. The music was pounding: "I'm Standing" by Rufus Lumley. This had to be good. And then his eyes adjusted to the dark, and there was Reevesie, and there was Rob Brierley, and then he saw Graeme Stafford, dancing.

Later, as Dan rode home on the last Number 4, he had a feeling that wouldn't quite translate itself into words; a strange, elusive feeling that somehow his life was about to change.

Soul Stories Part 2: 1972-75

Dan was apprenticed to Tony Green till his next stint at college. Tony was unlike any of the other gas fitters who operated out of Dashley Dyke depot. Although he was only 26, he was completely indifferent to the stuff the other lads obsessed about. Football, fashion, music, girls and the rest held no interest for him. He was of slightly stocky build, with a pale white face, unremarkable but for the fact that it seemed to belong in another time. This sense was no doubt added to by the sensible, old-fashioned short-back-and-sides haircut he always wore, which made him look like the old guys who'd served in the army way back and never quite shed its habits. The only time he drank was at Christmas, when the whole depot piled into The Cricketers and got arseholed before heading home for the festivities. Tony only had one thing, and it was an all-consuming thing: he did up old cars. His house had a large, brick-built garage fastened to it, and he'd supplemented that with a big wooden workshop out the back. He was currently rebuilding a 1937 Austin Seven. Every now and then he would drive one of his completed or nearly-completed projects to work, and everyone would drop what they were doing and congregate in the car park to marvel at another pre-War relic turned into something that looked like it had just been driven off a movie set. So, although he was a bit of an oddball, Tony wasn't bullied and suffered no more leg-pulling than anyone else, because everyone respected him for the miracles he worked on old cars.

Tony sat in the driving seat of the orange Gas Board Mini-van, which was parked outside 49 Filbert Street in Dashton West End, and flicked through the various job and parts sheets on his blue plastic clipboard. Dan, seated next to him in the passenger seat, waited to hear the plan. It was 10.30am and they'd just finished installing a gas fire.

'Right,' said Tony, 'this should take us up to dinner. 25 Buckingham Drive: faulty gas cooker, only six months old.'

The little Mini engine chugged into life, Tony checked the rear-view mirror, and they pulled off for the brief, two-mile trek to Buckingham Drive. They both knew what Buckingham Drive was, though neither said anything. Of Dashton's sink estates, it was the one that had sunk the most, and no gas fitter ever relished going there.

As they pulled up outside number 25 – a cream-stuccoed, 1930s, homes-for-heroes semi, placed high on a grassy embankment – they both realised they'd been there before: six months before; they'd installed the cooker which was now faulty.

The lady of the house let them in and led them to the kitchen. She scarcely spoke and avoided eye contact. Her face was mostly covered by large, bottle-bottom glasses, which magnified her dark, bovine eyes. She wore beige nylon flared trousers and matching blouse, both of which were visibly losing the battle to contain her bulbous body.

'There,' she said, pointing, then took a seat alongside the kitchen table, crouched with her elbows on her knees and her mouth open, and stared across the room at some featureless patch of grubby woodchip wallpaper.

Tony and Dan looked at the faulty appliance. What had been a pristine white stove just six months earlier was now a mountain of grease with something cooker-shaped inside it. The front and sides were streaked in layer upon layer of congealed brown fat. The eye-level grill was caked in it. Worst of all was the hotplate, the white ceramic floor of which was invisible beneath half a year's worth of fat, gravy and other, unrecognisable coagulated matter. Here and there an unidentifiable fragment of food, perhaps a rotting chip or desiccated marrowfat pea, punctured the surface, like the aft of a tiny half-sunk ship in a slimy brown sea – itself, a primal swamp in which some life forms died and decomposed, while other new ones shimmered into being, fed on the remains of their forebears, and flourished. And it smelt *bad*.

Tony leaned towards the cooker and looked closely at the hotplate, arms firmly by his side. 'It's your burners, love. They're blocked with grease and gravy and whatever the rest of this brown gunge is. That's why it won't work.' The woman looked at him vacantly and said nothing. Tony continued: 'The holes round the burners are blocked. See.' He pointed, but didn't touch. 'The gas can't get out properly and it'll not stay lit. But, anyway, I'm not working on it like this. It's unhygienic. I'm not touching it. You need to clean it. Get it cleaned up, and that'll probably do it. There's almost nothing to go wrong on these. It's just the muck in the burners. If you get it cleaned up and it's still not working, ring it in, and we'll come out again and sort it for you. OK, love?'

The woman glanced in their direction and nodded, then returned her gaze to the piece of wall opposite, which she'd been looking at throughout.

***

Dan Brody, Jez Reeves and Pete Jones caught the coach from Mosley Street Bus Station in Manchester city centre and arrived in Blackpool late afternoon: destination, the legendary Blackpool Mecca club – the Saturday night soul session.

Dan and Pete were 17, Jez was 18, but they'd been friends since school days, even though – or perhaps because – they all went to different schools. Jez and Pete lived a couple of doors apart on Fir Tree Estate, and Dan used to go up the steep hill to theirs on his bike to play football in the street, exchange gossip and trade records. Jez was tall, blond, good looking and a dyed-in-the-wool soul boy. He was also unfeasibly thin – Pete called him a narrer-back. He'd been going to the clubs for as long as they'd let him in, he owned some cracking records and he wore the right clothes. Jez was cool while Dan was still trying to work it all out. Pete, on the other hand, was no more than 5' 6', with mid-brown hair in a centre parting, which curtained his face and seemed to draw unnecessary additional attention to his slightly oversized nose. If Pete's looks were not his most engaging aspect, he made up for that with a wicked, incisive sense of humour. Little escaped his sharp observation and acerbic wit. He routinely wore the green Harrington he'd bought second-hand off a mate of his older brother, and nearly-matching green army pants, though he had something smarter in his holdall for tonight.

There were loads of B&Bs on Central Drive, but the one they'd heard of, because it had been recommended to them by Lenny Hughes, was just a couple of hundred yards from The Mecca; one of a line of big old bay-fronted terraceds on the other side of road. Its real name was The Ambleside Guest House, though everyone called it The Purple Haze Hotel on account of the violet and white paint job. It was probably no better than thousands of other Blackpool B&Bs, but it was good when you were new to a place to go somewhere that had been used and endorsed by someone you knew, and it could hardly have been handier for the club. They knocked and exchanged polite words with the landlord and handed over money, then dumped their bags in the room. It had one single bed and a bunk. Pete bags-I'd the bed, Dan chose the bottom bunk, Reevesie the top one.

The great grey edifice of the Mecca entertainment complex, with its giant 'Mecca Dancing' sign emblazoned across the frontage, was easily visible from The Purple Haze Hotel's front door.

On their way to the club they bumped into four lads from Dashton. Dan knew them vaguely from The Blue Parrot. The guy at the front was Degsy, in his usual wire-rimmed, John Lennon glasses. He couldn't put a name to the others. Reevesie knew them, though.

Degsy asked them – well, Reevesie, mainly – if they'd got any gear. *Odd question*, thought Dan. Of course they'd got gear, they were wearing it – Dan had on his red-to-blue tonic jacket, his freshly-pressed black parallels and his bright-red penny-round shirt. Though he suspected maybe they meant something else, so he kept schtum so as not to look a div. Reevesie said they hadn't got any gear, and Degsy and his mates continued their prowl along Central Drive in the hope of finding someone who had.

Dan, Jez and Pete dismissed the incident and headed on to the club, trying to be cool while bursting with excitement inside. And then they were there: Blackpool Mecca! Then on up the escalator to the famous Highland Room. They'd made it!

The venue was unlike any they'd been to before. It was large, clean and box shaped, with a low ceiling and subtle lighting. It felt modern and upmarket, like the lobby of a funky hotel. In keeping with the Highland theme, the walls were adorned with embossed steel shields and crossed Celtic swords. Beyond the edges of the slick wooden dancefloor a fitted tartan carpet spread out under rows of neatly arranged tables and chairs.

In their keenness, they'd arrived early and the place was sparsely populated, but it soon filled up, and in no time the room was heaving and the dancefloor packed.

The music was superb – and loud. The DJs spun all the latest sounds. Archie Bell, Johnny Copeland, The Inspirations, The Four Larks, Dobie Gray and the rest kept the rapturous, throbbing crowd on the jam-packed dancefloor energised all night.

Dan, Jez and Pete were in their element, ecstatic. What a place they'd found! And they swigged ale and told jokes and danced the night away under the ornamental shields and mock claymores.

Mid-evening, Dan got hunger pangs and bought a hot dog with onions and tomato sauce from the snack bar. It would be the last time he'd ever feel hungry at a soul do.

***

In the early-70s the idea of creating mass unemployment in order to make working-class people apprehensive and docile, so they'd work for less and turn their backs on unions and stay out of politics, was still inconceivable, whichever party held sway, and anyone who wanted a job could have one. And most people did want one, or, if they didn't want one they generally accepted that they ought to have one because that's what people did, so they got one and did it, and even if they moaned a bit and changed to another job with some regularity, they still remained almost permanently in some form of employment. But there was the odd individual who would studiously avoid work, and one such was Rob Brierley. And such was the uniqueness of his position that he acquired a nickname: aping that well known Edwin Starr record "Agent Double-O Soul", Rob became known as "Agent Double-O Dole".

***

The Highland Room aside, few soul venues were what you'd call salubrious, and Buffy's was no exception. From outside, it was a black-painted, flat-roofed, single-storey box. It looked like something left over from the War, though in fact it was the last remaining vestige of the coal pit that had stood behind it and been closed down after being worked out in the 1940s. What was now Buffy's had once been the miners' social club. Inside, it was no more prepossessing. About thirty feet square and also painted uniformly black like the outside, it had an entrance and cloakroom in one corner, the dj's set-up in another, and the bar and toilets in the other two. Chairs and functional rectangular tables lined the sides, leaving the middle open for dancing. The only nod to indulgence was the parquet flooring, but even this could not be relied upon. Odd bits were missing, some wobbled, some stood proud – all particularly hazardous for soul folk with their side-to-side shuffling dancing style. Regulars knew where to dance and where not.

Seated around a sticky, beery table, Dan Brody, Jez Reeves, Rob Brierley and Graeme Stafford chatted urgently about Saturday night – a trip to The Torch in Stoke-on-Trent. This would be their first all-nighter.

They met as planned at Hightown bus station and caught the Number 30 to Verrington. From there they caught the train to Longport, near Stoke. Although The Torch was supposed to be in Stoke, it was really in a suburb called Tunstall, and Tunstall didn't have a station, so you had to go to Longport and walk the rest of the way. It was as well to know these things before setting off – landing in the middle Stoke on a Saturday night and looking for The Torch would be a disappointing experience. And such follies were not without precedent: Jane Clarke and Julie Ramsbottom, who were also regulars at Buffy's, went to Blackpool Mecca one night and were really disappointed with the selection of music: all chart crap. They didn't realise until they got back and told others their tale of woe that they'd been in the divvy disco downstairs – they didn't know that the soul place was The Highland Room, upstairs. It was important to do your research – *no-one wants to travel hundreds of miles to listen to Gary Glitter and The Osmonds.*

The journey was an experience. Dan was stunned that the train ride was only three quarters of an hour. He knew they were going to the midlands and expected that to be hours away. If the train journey was shorter than he'd anticipated, the walk from the station to the club was considerably longer. They traipsed through dreary terraced streets, which looked no different from those in their scraggy old bit of East Manchester, and over some ancient, hump-backed canal bridge where the tarmac was so worn away that an old cast iron gas main was visible.

And then they were there. The setting was at once strange and unremarkable. It seemed odd that such a legendary place was parked in so anonymous a backstreet: Hose Street, Tunstall. And the facade itself was less than inspiring – it hardly boasted the swagger and self-confidence of the giant neon-concrete pillbox that was Blackpool Mecca. But then they got inside, and that was something altogether different.

The music was pounding, fast and sublime – "You Don't Want Me No More", "Baby Boy", "Love You Baby" – and the place was heaving. The atmosphere was happy and upbeat. Excited, laughing people relaxed and chatted and danced, though some had strange staring eyes and slightly agitated mannerisms. Lads wore wide, dark parallels and Simon pin-tuck T-shirts in numerous colours – it was too hot for jackets. Girls wore loose-fitting skirts and dresses, and had their hair up in pig-tails to combat the intense heat. Hard-looking guys with tattoos, sinewy arms and midlands accents glanced around warily, while chatting urgently with other hard-looking guys with midlands accents.

The interior was long, narrow, dimly-lit, painted almost entirely black, and nowhere near as big as Dan had expected such a famous venue to be. Over the stage, where the DJs' set-up was, hung a huge day-glow orange banner that proclaimed 'Another Boooooooming Success at the Torch' – the proprietors were clearly proud of how loud the place was. Dan ditched his coat at the cloakroom and went off for a blast on the packed, writhing dancefloor.

By 1.30am Dan was feeling really tired. By 2am he was dropping. He went to find the others, hoping they'd still be energised and up for it, and that their enthusiasm would infect him and energise him for the rest of the night, but they were in the same state, and after a brief conversation there was the unanimous view that they should go home.

Quite how this was to be accomplished was never resolved. They just set off walking with some vague hope of finding a train station and that there might be still some late trains running.

With heads down, collars up, hands in pockets and little conversation, they marched purposefully along the dark, deserted streets. A bitter wind blasted between the shops and houses and chilled their bellies and rattled their skinny teenage ribcages. Dan was freezing. All he had on under his flimsy fly-front mac was his green pin-tuck T-shirt with the fly-away collar – fine for a night club; not so good for the middle of a cold, black autumnal night in the Potteries, especially with the sweat drying after all that dancing.

Suddenly there was the roar of an engine. A police panda car swept up onto the kerb and stopped right next to them. Two big brawny coppers jumped out, lined them up against the wall and leered at them menacingly.

'Where are you off to, then, lads?' said one of the coppers, face leaning into each of them in turn.

'Home – Manchester,' said Graeme.

'Oh, aye,' said the cop, in his best sarcastic tone. 'And where've you been?'

'The Torch,' added Dan.

'*Really*, and who was selling all the drugs in there tonight?'

'Dunno, I was looking for him all night,' said Rob.

The cop grabbed Rob by his lapels, crushed him up against the wall and shoved his face into Rob's face. The thick-necked, sneering officer opened his mouth to speak, but in that instant a crackly voice chirped from inside the blue and white Ford

Anglia, and he put Rob down and turned to listen. His colleague had already jumped into the driver's seat and picked up the mic. Without another word, the blue bully hopped urgently into the passenger seat, and the car sped away into the night as quickly as it had arrived.

The trek continued, on and on... And then there was a train station: Kidsgrove. The gate to the gloomy, desolate platform was open. They studied the timetable in the dim light: nothing until 9.15am. They searched again, looking for a loophole. Surely there had to be something. Weren't there night trains or mail trains or something? But no, the timetable was implacable: 9.15am it was.

They tried the waiting room door. It was locked. They shoulder-charged it collectively. Inside were hard wooden benches, and it was just as cold as outside. They took one each and tried and failed to sleep.

At around 7am the sky completed its transition from black to dark blue to light grey, and the first station staff arrived. A fifty-something guy in cap and uniform wanted to know how they'd got into the waiting room. They told him they'd found it open. He scoffed and went off to open the ticket desk.

The Manchester train trundled in at 9.15am, as advertised, packed with hundreds of other soul devotees, who'd also been at the Torch but had left at 8 and boarded at Longport, as non-divs tended to. The four fugitives boarded sheepishly, glanced at quizzical faces and took seats away from the others, in the hope of not having to explain. None of them would ever go to an all-nighter drugless again.

***

Reevesie had a job as delivery driver for a fish firm, carting his slippery cargo around the shops, markets and chippies of East Manchester and the west Pennine towns in a smart, cream-coloured Escort van. At the end of the day he had to hose out the big fishy aluminium tray in the back, and then the van was his for the evening.

Having this unusual access to a vehicle, Reevesie, Dan and Pete Jones would make the most of it and head out of town for a pint or two up in the hills in Halterworth, where the old blackened sandstone pubs were a bit more picturesque and select than those in Bradfield and Dashley Dyke. But the van, of course, only had two seats, so Pete and Dan had to take turns at being the guy who sat in the fish tray in the back, hoping that Reevesie had done a good job of washing it out.

Along the route was a hump-back bridge, which rose and fell abruptly on an otherwise straight stretch of road. On the way there they drove over it quite sensibly and at a reasonable speed. On the way back, after a few bevvies, the project would be to hit it as fast as possible so that the van would fly as far as possible, and whoever was in the back would get a brief, chaotic theme-park ride involving hitting the sides, roof and floor in quick succession, though not necessarily in that order, to the roaring amusement of the safely seat-belted pair in the front.

***

The Number 30 wound its way out of Hightown bus station and started to climb up the gradually steepening slope of Market Street, on the first leg of its sluggish, rumbling journey to Verrington. On the upper deck, Jez Reeves pulled a small paper bag out of his jacket pocket.

'Blueys, ten a quid,' he said in hushed tones. 'Five apiece.'

'Great stuff,' said Dan, and slipped the five precious pale-blue pills stealthily into his pocket and handed over a fifty pence coin to Jez.

'If we take 'em just before we reach Longport, they should just be kicking in when we get inside,' added Jez.

Dan was itching to take the pills, both because he was desperate for this new, thrilling experience, and because he wondered whether there'd be police at Verrington station who might search him and find them. Certainly it was already clear that the police knew what was going on at The Torch. But he held his nerve and kept his enthusiasm at bay, and he and Jez necked their gear just before the train pulled in at Longport station. Dan expected swallowing pills without a drink to be a bit of a trial, but it was easier than he thought and it was something he would soon become expert at.

The trudge from the station to Tunstall was filled with excitement and anticipation, in spite of the dreary surroundings: The Torch! And what would this drug be like?!

Dan could already feel his heartbeat picking up as he handed over his tonic jacket at the cloakroom. And then this wonderful ecstatic feeling ran through his body. He took deep breaths that quivered in his chest.

The place was hot and heaving, alive with energy. Five hundred amphetamised bodies jiggled and jerked in the half-light on the jam-packed dancefloor. Jez and Dan shoved and wriggled their way to the middle and danced side by side. After a time, Jez vanished, but Dan kept on going. The music was sublime and incredibly loud: "Exus Trek", "Lonesome Road", "Thumb a Ride"... Dan was in ecstasy. And the records kept coming: "Blowing Up My Mind", "Cheyenne", "Crackin' Up Over You"... He was weightless, flying: "Soul Self Satisfaction", "I Got My Heart Set On You", "Thock It To Me Honi"... His body and the music were one – he was made for this. This was what he had been put on planet Earth for! And still the records kept coming: "Crying Over You", "I Love You Baby", "I Need Help"...

In the middle of "Bok to Bach", where it hits that crescendo, it felt like the top of his head might fly off and he would explode with joy. He'd never felt anything like it. This was better than love, better than orgasms. It was like one long continuous climax for his whole being. The music and the drug and the dancing and the atmosphere – it all became one wonderful whole in his joyous mind and body.

And on it went: "Compared To What", "Purple Haze", "This Beautiful Day"... He dripped with sweat. His arms glistened in the stifling heat. His pin-tuck T-shirt stuck to his chest. It occurred to him that maybe he should take a break, but every time he thought that, another record came on that seemed even better than the one before, and he couldn't leave: "Quick Change Artist", "Here She Comes", "Change Your Ways"...

Now and then a drop of cold water landed on his head. Sweat from the steaming revellers was condensing on the invisible black ceiling and dropping back down onto them.

Then Reevesie reappeared and leant into his ear: 'you better get off the dancefloor. You've been at it for two hours. The Squad are watching you.' And without looking up and without a word, Dan turned to leave, and the pair squeezed through the writhing crowd, took a seat in the bar and ordered a couple of cokes.

And then, after what he felt was a sufficiently Squad-pleasing period, Dan slipped back onto the dancefloor and it all started again: "Walk Like a Man", "K-Jee", "The Penguin Breakdown"... "Gonna Get Along Without You Now", "Too Late", "Last Minute Miracle"... And Reevesie was back dancing alongside him again.

And then Dan suddenly had a mild feeling that the drug wasn't quite as intense at it had been. This wouldn't do. He cupped his hand into Jez's ear: 'Reevesie, it's wearing off. Do something!' Jez vanished for ten minutes or so and reappeared on the dancefloor. 'I've got something. It's not proper gear. Just a substitute: ben-somethings. But they'll do. They'll prop us up on top of the other stuff.' They snuck off to the toilets, divided the ten ben-somethings, necked their share, then slipped back onto the dancefloor and kept on going till 8am, when they played "Long After Tonight Is All Over" and the doors opened and the dreaded white daylight bled into the place.

***

Unable to get gear for the all-nighter, Rick Cooper ate a Benzedrex inhaler instead. He reckoned it was half-decent high, but everything he ate the week afterwards tasted of inhaler.

***

It was Sunday teatime and Dan was at home trying to come to terms with his delicate physical and mental state after the Torch all-nighter the previous night. The phone rang – it was Adey Martin wanting to know if he was coming out for a few pints.

Dan didn't feel up to it.

He had to, pressed Adey: Phil Burns was home from the Navy; he'd only be around for a couple of days, then he'd be gone for months.

At 8pm on Sunday night Dan walked into The Clarence in Hightown, having not seen a bed since 8am Saturday morning. Adey and Phil had just arrived with an old friend of Phil's called David Watts, who was good at karate. Phil was a tall, lanky fellow with a narrow, slightly beaky face and fair hair. He was always cheerful and sanguine – nothing seemed to bother him. David Watts was a small, muscular bloke with short cropped hair and a furtive expression, which suggested he was always on the alert for trouble. He didn't say much, though after a few pints he loosened-up and joined in and laughed at the others' jokes.

The Clarence had this new beer on, called Gauntlet. It didn't taste great, but it was better than Whitbread's regular bitter and it was very strong. They drank till near closing time and were regaled with Phil's Navy stories and Dave's karate stories. And then they were faced with the question – where next? They staggered down to the bus station, caught the 211 into Manchester and headed for Dotty's – a regulation city centre disco, with red walls, black beams and bad music; open 7 nights, 8 till late. They paid in and drank Watney's Red Barrel.

For Dan, the place became a dream. He wasn't sure if he was awake or not. The walls seemed pliable, nothing would stay upright, and "Stuck in the Middle with You" seemed to be playing continuously. He went to the toilets and saw himself in the large mirror near the door, and, strangely, that version of him seemed to be much more real and present than he was. Its face was mostly white, with flushed red cheeks, and the eyes seemed more alert and focused than his, as though they were in contact with a brain that wasn't experiencing all the weird stuff his was, and that was reassuring, for a moment. If he and that other, more assured-looking him could have stayed together and come to some sort of mutually supportive arrangement, he might have been OK. But that wasn't possible, and as he turned for the door, the other him slipped off the edge of the mirror and Dan was on his own again. And back out in the club the madness resumed with a vengeance. The sounds were strange, echoey and unreal, the people were synthetic, frozen and almost certainly from another world, and the floor sloped this way and that, like the bridge of the Starship Enterprise under Klingon attack.

Dan came back into consciousness, having evidently been somewhere else, and found himself leaning on the bar. In front of him was a dimpled pint glass with an inch or so of stale, varnish-coloured liquid in the bottom. He looked up and around. Adey was stood next to him, also propping up the bar. Dan looked down – there was vomit on his shoes. 'Fuck! Someone's been sick on me shoes,' he yelled; his mind wrestling with the question of how someone could have got close enough to throw up on his shoes without him noticing. 'Who's done that? Bastards!'

'You,' replied Adey.

***

Dan and Reevesie grabbed the only available couple of seats close to the dancefloor at The Torch. Side on to them was a guy in his mid-twenties who looked like he'd been caught in a time-warp. His hair was puffed up in a kind of male bouffant, he had a big Zapata moustache that fell over his top lip and wrapped round the edges of his mouth, and he wore a multi-coloured suede jacket with patch pockets. He looked for all the world like Roy Wood in his The Move days, circa 1967.

They'd only been there for a few moments when the guy spun round and snarled at them and accused them of dipping into his pockets. They vacated the seats and wondered if this was why they'd been free in the first place.

***

Tommy Coggins and Dan Brody had been mates since they lived across the road from each other, when they were little more than toddlers. The Brodys' gritstone two-up-and-two-down on Widnes Street faced the bit of bombsite wasteland at the back of the Coggins's redbrick terraced, which in turn fronted onto Sheffield Road. Their families had a lot in common and were close. Dan was a few months older than Tommy, while Tommy's sister, Wendy, was a year older than Dan, and so was the responsible senior when the three trotted off to school at Foundry Street Methodists.

The youngest Coggins was Shaun, who was four years younger than Tommy and the same age as Dan's younger brother, Nicky.

But when Dan was ten, their friendships drifted. The Brodys moved to the other side of town, and calling round after tea to play footy on the street was no longer possible. And a short time later, Dan, Tommy and Wendy all found themselves at different secondary schools with their lives taking different paths.

But Tommy was 17 now. He'd been at work for a year, had money in his pocket, and had begun to assert control over his life. And he'd started to come to Buffy's, where Dan was already a regular, and to ditch Chicago, Velvet Underground and Cream in favour of soul. Dan and Tommy's friendship resumed.

Tommy was perhaps not the best looking of Dan's mates. He was always slightly portly – he had been even when he was little. His brown hair was cut in the collar-length, centre-parted style that was now obligatory for all fashionable young men, and whereas this looked cool on the other lads, it somehow failed on Tommy and bore more than a passing resemblance to spaniel ears flopping down either side of his forehead. And the stubble on his chin never quite made up its mind whether it had arrived or not, leaving him with a few fuse-wire bristles that hardly seemed worth the effort of shaving, but left him looking kind of unfinished if he didn't. To top all this off, Tommy never had much in the way of dress sense. He hadn't been around for the mod/skinhead/suedehead thing and had never understood 'cool'; a thing made palpable when he showed up at Buffy's wearing red and white loon pants. These monstrosities were white and tight-fitting from the top to the knee, where began a wide flare in deep crimson that spread out over his shoes. His belly swelled out over the fiercely tight waistband. But Tommy was evidently very proud of these kecks, as he visibly kicked forward the flared bit for maximum visual impact as he moseyed across the dancefloor.

'What have you got on, Tommy?' asked Dan, trying not to sound exasperated, but failing.

'Loon pants.'

'Yeah, I can see that, but why are yer wearing them here? You look like strawberries and cream.'

'They're cool. Y'know: two-tone.'

***

Dan answered the door. It was Reevesie.

'Oh. Hi, Jez,' said Dan. 'Don't normally expect to see you on a Monday tea time.'

'Yeah. Well. I know. It's a bit awkward.'

'What is?'

'It's me hook.'

'Your hook?'

'Y'know – that bit where your bell-end and your foreskin connect round the back of your dick. That little narrow bit.'

'Oh, err, yeah, right.'

'I was getting it on with this girl at weekend and, well, it was a bit dry and I pushed a bit too hard and it kinda split.' Jez started to undo his jeans.

'Fuck's sake. Not here. What are yer doin'?' They were still on the doorstep. 'Yer better come in. We'll go up to the bedroom.' They trotted upstairs. Dan closed the door. 'Right you were saying.'

'Yeah, it's me hook,' and he reached for his pants again.

'No, no, stop. I don't need to see it. I know what you mean – where you mean. But what do you expect me to do about it? Why not go to the doctor's? I'm a gas engineer.'

'I can't. I just *can't,*' pleaded Jez. 'It's the same doctor who sees me mum and dad. How can I look him in the eye? And I thought, you bein' a man o' the world and that, you'd know what to do. It must have happened to you.'

'I can't say as it has. I've come close, though. You can feel it when it's getting too much, but I've always stopped before it snapped.'

'But what would you do... yer know... if it did?'

'I dunno. I s'pose there's three choices: go to the doc's, go to A&E, or just leave it be – let it heal itself.'

'So you reckon it'll get better by itself?'

'Yeah. Don't see why not. I mean, it's in an embarrassing place and all that, but really it's only same as cutting yer finger, innit.'

'Oh, that's a relief.'

'Is it? I mean, I don't know anything more than you do. I'm just... it's just speculation. I'm guessing,' said Dan, palms upwards.

'I know, but it's common sense. I'll do that. I suppose I could put some ointment on it as well.'

'Yeah, that and keep your hands off it for a few days.'

***

It was Adey's birthday and he wanted to try out Manchester Beer Keller on Wood Street in town. He'd heard about it. Someone said it was a good, wild place. The music wouldn't be any good, but it was ideal for a whacky night out with the lads.

As Adey, Tommy and Dan all hailed from Bradfield/Dashley Dyke area, and Phil Burns, David Watts and some guy with a beard were coming in from Shipman's Fields Estate on the far side of Hightown, Hightown town centre was the place to meet – specifically, The Clarence.

Pulling six pints of Whitbread Gauntlet, which dribbled from its preposterous iron-fist pump like it had prostate issues, took an age. The landlord said, half-jokingly/half seriously, that they should ring in advance so he could start pouring the stuff half an hour before they got there.

They each got a round in, then it was time to head off into town. The 211 dropped them in Piccadilly and they slipped into the dark, narrow backstreets towards Wood Street and The Beer Keller.

The low, crowded space was modelled on some Mancunian businessman's idea of what a real Bavarian bierkeller ought to look like: all the fitments were made from unpainted wood and there were rough-hewn tables and communal benches instead of stools. The multiple small rooms and dense smoke gave the place a claustrophobic air, and no-one was even remotely sober. The venue served three kinds of lager: ordinary, super-strength and imbecilic. Naturally, the lads had to have imbecilic, and they found a table and set about having a further six pints of that.

The music, as predicted, was bloody awful: "Son of My Father", "Telegram Sam", "A Horse with no"-fucking-"Name", Noddy Holder shouting about something... Then, as they were halfway down their tenth pint, a miracle! Millie Jackson: "My Man a Sweet Man"!

Dan jumped up, found a space on the dancefloor and started to move.

Then... nothing...

Consciousness came back to Dan upstairs on the 211. A glance out of a steamy window suggested they were in Ardwick, probably somewhere near the 5-a-side pitches, speeding along Hightown Road in the deep black and dim yellow of a Manchester Saturday night. Tommy, Adey, Phil, David Watts and the bloke with the beard were having a singsong: "Shine On Harvest Moon", followed by "Long After Tonight is All Over", followed by "We All Hate Leeds and Leeds", and other all-night-bus singalong favourites. Dan had some vague recollection of being carried pall-bearer style along some Manchester back streets. He'd seen parking meters flash by.

***

Dan, Rick and Sally were perched on tall stools at the bar in The Torch, sipping coke. Tommy had gone for a pee and a stroll.

Rick and Sally had been together for as long as Dan had known them, and they'd got married a year ago. Rick was good fun, but also a rogue and highly volatile with an explosive temper. He had fair hair which was already receding even though he was only 19. He operated a lathe at Bradley and Bagnall's engineering works and spent his days surrounded by brass, bronze and steel, yanking, pulling and lifting. His muscular arms and burly upper body bore testament to that. Sally was blonde and dainty and, to Dan, always seemed too delicate and sensitive to be with a guy like Rick, but it was clear she was absolutely devoted to him, and that was the way it had always been.

Tommy, in his brown parallels and matching brown penny-round shirt, came back from his ramble. ''Kin 'ell! You see some things in 'ere. There was a syringe with the needle bent up on the toilet seat in the gents – don't know if you were meant to sit on it or something – and some bloke was battering seven shades out of a guy on the stairs. Making a right mess of him, he was.'

***

Dan was standing in his usual dark, smelly bus shelter on Hightown bus station, waiting for the last Number 4 back to Dashley Dyke. Across the way, in the shelter that served the buses that went the other way, out to Shipman's Fields Estate, stood an old man in a dark grey gabardine raincoat and flat cap. A group of four lads – teenagers, perhaps a year or two younger than Dan – appeared behind the old bloke and started taking the mickey out of him and jostling him. Then another guy arrived, fast, suddenly and seemingly from nowhere – a wiry-looking fellow in his early/mid-twenties, with close-cropped black hair and a tash. Dan thought he recognised him from Mars. If it was who Dan thought it was, it was Joey Wilcox – a real local hard nut, not someone you mess with.

The probably-Joey-Wilcox guy got in the face of one of the mickey-taking teenagers – the mouthiest one, the one at the front. 'You don't pick on old folks. You don't pick on old people, got it?' he said, poking his finger into the lad's face. Then poking wasn't enough, and he started punching the lad in the face. And then he worked himself up into a frenzy, and he punched and he kicked, and he punched and he kicked, and his voice got louder and louder as he went on: 'you don't pick on old people, you don't pick on old people...'

The lad hit the ground, and probably-Joey-Wilcox booted him in the face again and again. 'YOU DON'T PICK ON OLD PEOPLE...' With each ferocious kick, the back of the lad's head crashed against the foot of the concrete bus shelter. He flopped about like a rag doll, his bloodied blond head jerked back and forth, each sickening thud of boot against face answered instantly by a sickening crack of skull against concrete. The lad's three mates backed away and cowered at the other end of the shelter.

It crossed Dan's mind to intervene. He could try reason: *come on mate, he's had enough*. Or maybe he could try self-interest: *come on mate, that's enough – you don't wanna get yourself sent down*. But then, that could all go wrong, and Dan didn't fancy seeing out his days in a hospital bed, gazing vacantly up at institutional ceiling tiles with a plastic feeding tube up his nostril.

And the Number 4 swept in and obliterated the view, like a curtain closing on a dreadful scene in a theatre.

***

Jez Reeves had two nicknames; well three, really: Reevesie, Boot Boy, and then just Boot, as a shortened version of the latter. It wasn't that he was some sort of vicious, football-rioting, 'Paki-bashing' skinhead. He had been a skinhead like everyone else at the time, but that was just a fashion thing, and he was a gentle, happy soul. The most violent thing he ever did was take the piss out of you now and then. He had a cheeky grin – he *was* cheeky – and the girls loved him for it. The reason he was called Boot/Boot Boy was that he had a habit of showing up at Buffy's straight from work, still wearing his rolled-up Wranglers and clapped-out Doctor Martens. These skinhead styles had long since gone out of fashion in favour of wide Trevira parallels and Skinners jeans, with brogues or tasselled loafers, so were relegated to second-division use as work-wear. Most of the other lads would have worn similar garb to Reevesie's during the day, but got scrubbed-up and changed into something more fashionable for the all-important Thursday night out at Buffy's. So Reevesie stood out in his work clothes and acquired the nickname.

Reevesie was also a good source of gear. He was, however, some way down the distribution food chain. Essentially, he bought what he needed and a bit of excess, then divvied up and sold the surplus to pay for his own, which meant that what you got was of reasonably reliable quality, but the quantity wasn't great. Some years later, when wraps of amphetamine sulphate were the thing, rather than pills, a joke circulated which tipped a nod to that old adage 'more haste, less speed': 'you get a lot of haste in one of Reevesie's wraps'.

But Reevesie didn't mind being called Boot or Boot Boy; in fact, he rather revelled in it. And one night he showed up at Buffy's and stood in front of the DJs' decks, grinning like a simpleton, holding up his for-sale gear for all to see in a paper bag emblazoned with a big blue logo that read 'Boots the Chemists'.

***

Scooter was one of those acrobatic soul-boy dancers, who did back-drops and front-drops and spins and all that. A space would clear around him at The Torch; everyone would get out of the way of his flailing limbs while he did his demonstrative thing. And on Thursday nights he would come to Buffy's and practice new moves.

Dan, Tommy and Reevesie chatted in front of the turntables, made plans for the next all-nighter and negotiated gear deals. Pete Griffin and Ritchie Baker spun the tunes.

The Du-Ettes' mid-tempo masterpiece "Every Beat of My Heart" faded out, the storming fanfare that marked the start of The Triumphs' floor-shaking "I'm Coming to Your Rescue" kicked in, and Scooter hit the floor. And then he hit it literally. He took off with great energy, like a startled cat, and for an instant was horizontal at about head height, evidently having in mind some kind of extravagant front-drop. But he seemed to lose concentration while in mid-air and crashed down, still in a kind of sky-diver position, onto the rock-hard parquet flooring. His mates helped him up as he spat out bits of busted tooth from his bloodied mouth.

***

Dan, Rick and Sally joined the bustling queue for tickets at Verrington station. There was a throng of others who, by the style of their clothing, were also headed for The Torch. The buzz going round was that you only needed to get a ticket to Smithy Gate – the first stop out of Verrington – because no-one checked the tickets on the train and the ticket collector at Longport was usually overwhelmed by the huge numbers disembarking for the all-nighter and didn't bother to collect the tickets, or didn't look at them when he did. So Dan just got a Smithy Gate ticket, like everyone else.

But the ticket didn't look like the Longport ticket – he'd bought one many times before. The Longport ticket was paper, pink and large; the Smithy Gate one was card, blue and small. And it emerged as they approached Longport that all those who'd bought a Smithy Gate ticket also had an old Longport ticket, retained from a previous trip, to give to the ticket collector in the event that he was actually paying attention this time.

If he was, Dan was sunk.

Dan stepped off the train and glanced around quickly for a solution, but there was no escape route, and the ticket collector, in proper official navy-blue railway uniform complete with peaked cap, was barring the exit and making sure that he got a ticket from every traveller, even if he didn't look carefully enough to see the date stamp. Dan tried to brass it off and stuck the blue, wrong ticket into the ticket collector's hand, and when collared tried to make out that it wasn't his ticket – scores were being pressed into the bloke's hand at the same time.

Dan knew it wasn't much of a ploy, but it was all he'd got, and he wasn't at all surprised that the guy wouldn't have it.

Dan was marched off to the office and given a form to fill in with his name and address. As Dan wrote, the ticket collector scanned him up and down and jotted a description of him on a pad. Naturally, Dan wrote down an invented name and address, but he knew the police would be there waiting for him with the ticket collector in the morning when The Torch turned out.

He went off to the club and made the most of the night, regardless. The ticket incident was one of the topics of conversation as he sat at the bar with Rick and Sally, but they moved on to other things. And Dan was telling Sally the titles of the songs as they came on – she didn't know many of them.

"'I'm in a World of Trouble",' said Dan.

'Oh, no, it'll be alright,' replied Sally, 'you'll be OK, they won't do anything.'

'No, I don't mean me. It's "I'm in a World of Trouble" by the Sweet Things – that's the song, that's what's playing.'

'Oh.'

'Div.'

As they walked back to Longport station in the chill of the morning and the beginnings of an amphetamine come-down, Dan discussed his predicament with Lenny Hughes and Ross Oldham, and they came up with a plan. Dan was 5' 8", had collar-length jet black hair, a tash and long bushy sideburns, was wearing a sheepskin jacket and did not wear glasses. Lenny had a curly blond mop, no facial hair, was at least 5' 10" and wore a dark blue Crombie. Curly-haired Ross wore glasses. They did a swap-around. And at Longport station, wearing wired-rimmed glasses and a long blue Crombie with the collar up, Dan bought a ticket for Verrington and strolled, unhindered, past a cordon comprising the ticket collector and two uniformed police officers.

The ticket collector might have spotted a sheepskin coat that looked vaguely familiar pass through the line a little further back, but the wearer was a tall blond bloke, so it couldn't have been the ne'er-do-well he'd apprehended the night before.

***

Dan and Tommy stood in The Oak Tree, chatting and drinking Robinsons' Best on a Tuesday night. They never knew quite what town the pub was in because it was right on the border of Dashton and Dashley Dyke on the main Manchester Road and they'd never bothered to resolve this pedantic detail.

It was 10.20 – last orders – and it was Tommy's round. He reached into the pocket of his salmon-coloured parallels and pulled out a fifty pence piece, which slipped from his fingers. They both saw it happen and tried to chase the coin with their eyes, but it bounced instantly into invisibility in the low light and the legs and feet of the numerous bar-proppers. Though, just as it fell, they both saw amongst the throng a guy reach down and pick something up from the floor.

Tommy strode purposefully over to him: 'have you just picked up a fifty pence piece, mate?'

'No,' came the resolute response.

Both were doubtful over the bloke's reply. Was that expression on his face one of defiance or puzzlement: 'fuck you,' or genuinely 'I have no idea what you're talking about'? And at a time when an apprentice got a tenner a week, and fifty pence would buy four pints of bitter, this was no trivial matter.

They seethed quietly. This was the end of their evening. Dan had already spent up, and Tommy had just lost his last coin.

Outside the pub's front door, they debated the matter and concluded that the guy had obviously picked up the fifty pee and lied when Tommy confronted him, even though they weren't entirely sure of what they'd seen. And the more they talked, the more angry they became, and they decided to wait for the evil thief and work him over when he came out.

After ten minutes, the criminal hadn't appeared. After fifteen minutes, he still hadn't shown up.

Tired of pacing up and down, Tommy sat on the dwarf wall that separated the pub frontage from that of the house next door. Making himself comfortable, he swung round and lifted his feet up onto the wall, and a fifty pence coin dropped out of his turn-up.

***

Tommy showed up at Dan's house with the news that Jed 'Molly' Moberly had died of a barbiturate overdose. Tommy had heard the news from Degsy, who'd called round with his mates to Molly's house the day after it happened. The worst thing, Degsy reckoned, had been Molly's mum, in bits, crying and shrieking 'couldn't someone stop him taking drugs?'

***

Dan and Tommy loved The Pendulum, but getting there could be just as much fun as the club itself. They'd meet on Friday night at 7.15 at the junction of Holmfirth Road and Sheffield Road. They'd then walk together down to Dashley Dyke bus station and hop on the 7.30 218 into Manchester city centre and catch up with each other's stories and gossip. The buses terminated at Piccadilly Gardens, while The Pendulum was down near Victoria, on Long Millgate. So there'd be a fifteen-minute or so walk between the two, but it was a walk that went past several pubs, most of which seemed too inviting to miss. And sometimes they'd get off one stop before the terminus to sample the delights of the rickety old Coach and Horses, opposite Piccadilly train station, with a pint and whisky chaser. And they couldn't really walk past The New Mancunian, just a bit further up the road, without popping in. That was the one next door to The Dolls' Hospital, with the Hornby train that to-d and fro-d over the bar all evening. It had started to be a thing that pubs were themed or had to have a gimmick of some sort. Then there was the bar under The Piccadilly Hotel, smack in the centre of town. That was a very cool, trendy place, with Simon Dee and Peter Wyngarde lookalikes and elegant ladies in pastel frocks perched on spindly bar stools, sipping cocktails. As well as their pint and chaser, Dan and Tommy would sometimes have one of those little Hamlet cigars in there.

By now the conversation had moved on from the superficial stuff to profound philosophical discussions about the meaning of life and Monty Python and such; discussions of a kind that only those who'd drunk a substantial amount of beer with whisky chaser could appreciate. They'd have another drink or two in the dark underground hovel that was The Auld Reekie on Market Street. And then they'd pop into The Wellington, which, because the pub proper was inaccessible because it was in a place that was being redeveloped, was now unconvincingly recreated in a big Portakabin, which had sepia pictures of old Manchester on the walls in an effort to make up for its painfully banal grey-panelled blandness. But it was worth having a pint in just for its utter strangeness – like a Soviet works canteen, thick with blue-brown smoke and wall-to-wall bellowing drunks. They would sometimes also call into The Swan with Two Necks on Shudehill – you could hardly *not* go into a pub with a name like that – and they'd also sometimes have one in Rowntrees Sounds. Then they'd have one final one in The Mitre Hotel, which was just round the corner from The Pendulum. By now the profound philosophical discussions had got so distended and blurred that each would start off a sentence, then get pulled aside by related issues, each of which had in turn its own related issues and so on, until they were so far adrift from the initial point they were trying to make that they were unable to find their way back to it, which was pretty disappointing, because that initial point, had it been possible to say it, would have been one of the most profound things said that evening – possibly, even, ever.

On one occasion, they were so thoroughly spannered by the time they got to that part of town that they never made it to The Pendulum. They sat in the best room at The Mitre Hotel and watched as the doorway to the bar started to rotate. Dan jumped up abruptly, ran outside and threw up next to the cathedral. Tommy followed him out and, on seeing the mess Dan had just made, threw up himself. Dan could never face whisky again after that night.

***

There was a knock at the door at the Coggins's house. Tommy's big sister, Wendy, answered it.

'Is Shaun in?' asked the diminutive figure on the doorstep.

'Wait there,' replied Wendy.

Back in the living room, she told Tommy and Shaun: 'You've got to see this!'

The three of them trooped to the front door. And there was Duncan Fraser. Duncan was one of Shaun's classmates – fourteen years old and of slight build. His dad had a good job at the wallpaper factory, and Duncan always got all the new fashions and gadgets.

Tommy, Shaun and Wendy gazed at the spectacle framed by their front door: Duncan was wearing a giant floppy denim cap – a Donny Osmond/Michael Jackson/Huggy Bear pimp cap – jauntily tipped to one side, and an enormous pair of black sunglasses, which almost entirely obscured his face. Beneath, he wore a long denim shirt with embroidery and chrome studs on the shoulders and a pair of wide, patchwork denim flares. Both the hat and the sunglasses appeared to have been made for someone with a face at least twice the size of Duncan's and gave him the appearance of a large fly in a blue bonnet.

Tommy, Shaun and Wendy fell about laughing. Duncan didn't get it.

***

It was one of Phil Burns' trips home from the Navy, and a pub crawl round Hightown was called for. Dan, Tommy and Adey arrived in Hightown on the Number 4, but Phil now had a car – a pale yellow Triumph Herald. He parked it near the bus station and met the others in The Clarence.

They had a few rounds in The Clarence, then strolled up Market Street to The Farmer's Arms and had a few more rounds in there. Then they went to The Chapel – a Boddingtons' house. They definitely enjoyed the beer in there and questioned why they routinely went in The Clarence and drank that dodgy Gauntlet stuff when there was Boddies a few hundred yards away, and then they remembered that they drank Gauntlet because it was exceedingly strong and they liked the effect, and even if Boddies tasted better, it was nowhere near as potent. And then they finished off at The Drover's, by which time they were so addled that Adey went into the ladies' by mistake and had a row with a woman who he accused of being in the wrong bogs and some kind of pervert, though he did find it a bit odd that there were no urinals.

They staggered back down Market Street to collect Phil's car. This was OK because drinking and driving was only a bit illegal in those days and no-one really cared, except those whose loved ones had been killed by drunk drivers. And those whose husbands and brothers and dads had gone off the edge of the Snake Pass or Woodhead pissed in the middle of the night and ended their days in a burning Vauxhall Cresta or Ford Zephyr at the bottom of a ravine – they probably cared as well. And the police cared a bit. But no-one else.

The Triumph was a two-door vehicle. Dan and Tommy tipped the front seats forward and climbed into the back, Tommy on the driver's side, Dan on the passenger side. Adey took the front passenger seat and Phil took the wheel.

They all agreed that curry was the next thing they needed, and no-one did curry sauce quite like Wangs. This was because Wangs' curry sauce wasn't quite like any conventional curry sauce. It had an indescribable colour, somewhere between army green and dayglow orange, and its flavour, while having overtones of curry, also had hints of other things – perhaps custard, possibly fish. And on a Saturday night, after a few pints, there was nothing better than a tray of chips with curry sauce from Wangs.

They clambered back into the yellow Herald and got stuck into their trays of chips and dayglow sauce. Everyone finished, except Dan, who'd only got about a third of the way through his before he started to feel queasy. Phil offered to drive everyone home, while Dan was still struggling to make progress with his food.

They'd only gone about half a mile when Dan gave up and announced: 'Look, I'm not gonna finish this. Can we chuck it out?'

They agreed that rather than just chuck it out like some feckless litter lout, he should do something worthwhile with it and chuck it at some passer-by. But the thing with Triumph Heralds is that, as well as having no back doors, they didn't have opening back windows either, so Dan would have to launch his curry over Adey's left shoulder and out of the front passenger-side window. Adey wound the window down in readiness, while Phil scanned the mostly-deserted streets for a potential victim. Then they saw this guy walking alone along the footpath, coming towards them on the passenger side. Phil slowed the car, Adey leant out of the way and Dan took aim. As they got alongside the poor unsuspecting sod, Dan launched the curry with all his might. But the impulse to get as much pace behind the throw as possible came at the expense of accuracy, and the food bomb never left the car – it hit the door frame, and a two-thirds-full tray of chips and Wangs' thick, inscrutable bitter-sweet fluid flew back into the car. As well as the rebound from Dan's throw, the wind whistling in through the window caught hold of the stuff and sprayed it – over the seats, the carpet and the dashboard, but mostly over Adey's treasured blue-green tonic suit. Most of the chips came to rest in his lap, though a few were stuck to his face and a couple lodged in his hair. A few fragments got as far as Phil on the driver's side. Dan had some of the sauce on the sleeve of his throwing arm and a bit on his legs. Tommy, in the driver's side rear seat, escaped mostly unscathed. The guy at whom the package was aimed saw none of this and went on his way without ever knowing he'd been the target of such an outrage or that he'd played such a pivotal role in this perfect moment of karma.

When Phil sold the Triumph a year later he still hadn't managed to rid it of the smell of Wangs' curry.

***

Adey had stayed on at Hightown High School to do A Levels. University wasn't his thing, but he discovered that he could do a two-year Education Diploma, after A Levels, and from there he could become a woodwork teacher, which was what he wanted to do. And he got a place at Shoreditch Teacher Training College in Egham in Surrey.

Dan, Phil Burns and Dave Podmore drove down for a weekend in Phil's curry-flavoured Triumph. A student in the same dorm as Adey had gone away for the weekend and loaned Adey his room for his mates to use.

They drank dodgy southern beer in Adey's posh southern local on the Friday night, then went back to the dorm and tried to sleep, two to a single bed. Dave shared with Adey in his room; Dan shared with Phil in the other student's room. On one wall it had a poster depicting a new band called Queen and advertising their new record: 'Seven Seas of Rhye'. Funny looking bunch of blokes -- the goofy one in the middle looked like he was wearing a white frock. Opposite was a poster of a big fat man in a dinner suit with a napkin shoved into his collar and a silver knife and fork in his chubby hands, tucking into huge mounds of excrement, with the caption 'eat shit – fifty billion flies can't be wrong'.

Dan figured top-to-toe would be the best bet in the narrow bed and spent an almost entirely sleepless night within inches of Phil's whiffy feet. Maybe this was payback for the curry incident.

On Saturday Adey showed his guests the delights of Egham town centre. And then, there it was – the record shop. Dan and Dave shifted instantly from absent-minded indifference, suffering from hangovers and sleep deprivation, to being men on a mission. Adey and Phil gave it a miss. Adey didn't buy records nowadays – he was focused on his studies and didn't have the space or money for records. Phil wasn't that bothered about music – he liked Elton John. The shop was wonderful, an absolute time capsule, chock full of deletions: loads of old soul, Motown, Stax, Atlantic, HMV, Liberty, Stateside... going back to the mid-60s. It was amazing. They rummaged and rummaged. And then the bloke behind the counter said that if they were so interested in old records, he'd got thousands more in a store room at the back. They could have left the place each with hundreds of records, but they had hardly any money. They'd brought what they had, and that was only just enough to get through the weekend. Food and drink weren't cheap here, what with this being the pricey South. And neither had a bank account, so what they had in their pockets was all they had, and it wasn't much, and they could hardly go out on Saturday night unable to buy food or beer, and there was still petrol to get for the trip home.

Dan bought just one record: "Too Much of a Good Thing" by Karen Young on Major Minor – something he regretted almost instantly. Why buy a jerky, singalong, pop ersatz-soul thing when there was all that other stuff? But he'd been so bewildered by the sheer amount of records that he'd lost focus.

Over more beers on Saturday night, Dan and Dave resolved to come back in a few weeks with quids in pockets and have a real do at that record shop. They'd save up and make sure they were ready next time.

Three weeks later Adey wrote to say that the shop had burnt down and everything in it was destroyed.

***

Dan went to Rita's on Vincent Street in Salford straight from college. They ate tea, which comprised, as always, boiled potatoes, something green and some form of meat, none of which tasted of anything. Rita's nan had the ability to remove the flavour from any set of ingredients.

Dan had met Rita at Bob Hindley and Anne Betts's engagement do in the function room upstairs in The Diamond in Dashton. He had not long since broken up with Lucy and was really not in the mood, but Rita had been persistent and chatty and had almost cheered him up, and they'd exchanged phone numbers. She was a couple of months younger than Dan and could not have been more different in appearance from Lucy. Whereas Lucy was all curves and voluptuousness, Rita had a slim, athletic build with pert little breasts. There was a knowing, astute look to her pretty face, which was framed by long, streaked blonde-brown hair and illuminated by sharp, intelligent green eyes.

After tea, Rita put on a bit of slap and they headed out for the pub. It had been The Broughton last week, so this week The Sun, right on Rialto Corner. The Sun was the better bet anyway, as not only was it a Boddies' house, it was less than a mile from the brewery in Strangeways – the beer could hardly have been any fresher.

In a lot of pubs they would ring the bell and hang up the beer towels spot on 10.30, and it didn't matter how much you begged, you would not get another drink. *Y'wanna get me my licence took away?!* But it was 10.45 and there was still a buzz around the bar and they appeared still to be serving. And Dan felt he could fancy another. But maybe they were only serving well-known locals... He thought he'd try his luck anyway, and at 10.50 he joined the throng at the bar, and after a brief wait placed his order: another pint of bitter for him and another snowball for Rita.

He took his change and picked up the drinks, then suddenly became aware of an uncomfortable presence behind him – something dark and too close, breathing down his neck. He swung round, and there was a copper in full uniform, complete with pointy hat. And there was Dan with the evidence in his hands. I'm nicked, he thought. It was a good half hour since closing time. But the copper just reached past him to the bar and shouted 'pint of bitter please, Betty, when you're ready.'

***

Phil Bowden – 'Philbo' to his friends and most everyone else he knew – was a small fellow, probably no more than five foot three, and very young looking. Although he was 16 and had started work as a general labourer at Newall's Builders'

Merchants, on a good day he could easily pass for just 12 or 13 years old. This might have made it difficult for him to get into clubs, but because of his boyish looks the older ones couldn't help but look after him like a younger brother, and more often than not they were able to smooth his way past difficult doormen, and if that didn't work they'd knock open the crash bars on the fire doors and let him in that way.

It was Monday evening. Philbo had had his tea and now stood in his peach-coloured bedroom and gazed at his chest of drawers, which had once been brown but had now been painted by his mum in a bright royal blue, to help cheer the place up. On top were a packet of Player's Number 6, half done, a few coins and crumpled notes, and a deep green bottle of Brut 33 aftershave, not that he had much use for shaving. Fastened to the wall above with drawing pins was a team shot of United, from the Law, Best, Charlton glory days. He squatted down and pulled open the sock drawer at the bottom. He rummaged past the contents to the back and pulled out an old sweetie bag that had been scrunched-up into a ball. He carefully unpicked it, and there was his gear – six beautiful, shiny green-and-clears. He'd done this several times over since he scored them off Plonka the Pole in the pub, Sunday dinner time, and once again he held the precious capsules in his hand. He studied them up close, mesmerised by the semi-transparent green bit and the wholly-transparent clear bit encasing those magical little white balls, and he anticipated the joy they contained. He loved the capsules and they loved him back. They seemed to glow in his hand. These simple little gelatine tubes could transform the utter tedium of his life and lift it into some beautiful other dimension. All he had to do was swallow them and that wonderful otherness would be his.

But it was only Monday night – the all-nighter was nearly a week away.

But there was Buffy's – the Monday night session. Could he? Should he? He had to. He knew he wouldn't sleep and would feel like death all day Tuesday at work, but resistance was futile.

He had the best night at Buffy's he'd ever had, but, in bed by 11.45 and with nothing to do, and bored and agitated and about as wide awake as it was possible to be, he started to scratch out the myriad tiny bumps from the woodchip wallpaper on his bedroom wall with his fingernails.

In the morning, after he'd gone to work, Philbo's mum went to his room to make his bed and was bewildered to see a whole arc of what had previously been pristine Sunset Peach satin-finish emulsion defaced by countless tiny scratches and little white dots, and a thousand minute fragments of chipped wood and wallpaper on his bedspread.

***

The Pendulum was another of the soul scene's unpromising looking clubs. In fact, from the outside, it didn't look like anything at all, because it was underground and invisible. All that was discernible to a passer-by was a doorway and a discreet sign that said:

Manchester Sports and Social Guild
Sports and Social Centre

– no mention of The Pendulum. You had to know it was there. At the bottom of the stairs was a smoky, low-ceilinged room; the bar to your left, dj's stand to your right, dancefloor in between. It looked like what it was: a cellar – dark, damp, and dingy, with a rough, stone-flagged dancefloor – the natural successor to the also-subterranean Twisted Wheel, in spirit and style. And like The Wheel, the music was magnificent and the place always packed.

After an abbreviated and circumspect pub crawl, which did not include whisky chasers or cigars, Dan and Tommy arrived safely at the club. They hung their coats in the cloakroom: Dan's tan sheepskin and Tommy's dark blue overcoat – some sort of double-breasted, ex-military thing he'd bought from the Army & Navy store, with anchors on the buttons.

They chatted, had a few more beers and danced to favourite tunes. And there were some good ones: "Cat Walk", "Standing in the Darkness", "Walk Like a Man", "I Need Your Love So Desperately"...

Dan was chugging away happily on the dancefloor, minding his own business, when a guy walked up to him and got in his face, nose on nose. He looked a serious guy – sunken cheeks, wiry, fearsome. If Dan wasn't mistaken, this was the probably-Joey-Wilcox guy he'd seen kick that lad half to death – or maybe all the way to death – on Hightown bus station a few months earlier. He stopped dancing.

'Yer wanna buy any gear?' growled probably-Joey-Wilcox, glaring into Dan's eyes and twisting his head sardonically to one side as he spoke, for added menace.

Dan would have very much liked to have bought some gear, but figured that wasn't what this was about and this situation could turn out one of two ways: he'd say yes, hand over his cash, and the guy would waltz back over to his mates by the bar and have a laugh at how easily he'd extracted money from that idiot on the dancefloor. There'd certainly be no gear, and Dan would get his head kicked in if he complained and asked for his money back. Or he'd say no, and the guy would use this as an excuse to kick his head in for being a poncey, straight, drug-free phoney soul boy. Neither outcome looked promising. So he said he *would* like to buy some gear but couldn't because he had no money because he was on the dole. This wasn't true, but the guy seemed stumped by an answer that wasn't one of the expected two, and that ended the encounter, for now at least, and he turned on his heels and walked away.

As did Dan – straight over to Tommy who was stood by the bar.

Tommy looked at him: 'What's up? Who was that guy?'

'Get the coats – we're off. I'll explain later.'

***

With the day's apprenticing in Dashton West End finished, Dan strolled back into the town centre in his grey-green North Western Gas Board overalls and dark blue donkey jacket to catch the bus home. The standard-issue donkey jacket had NWGB in white lettering on the collar: the company's initials, though some of the gas fitters who Dan was apprenticed to reckoned it stood for 'Not Working Gone Boozing', or 'No Wonder Girls Blush'.

As he reached the newsagents on Stanniforth Street, opposite Peter Rosen's gentleman's outfitters where he'd bought that crappy imitation Crombie that fell to bits after six months, he had an overwhelming urge for a Mars bar.

As well as mags, newspapers and every conceivable kind of chocolate bar, there were two of those tall, rotating circular display racks, one containing birthday cards, the other, old deleted singles in tatty, much-thumbed sleeves. Dan munched his Mars bar and rummaged through the records. Among the Roger Whittakers, Engelbert Humperdinks and Shirley Basseys, two caught his eye: "Mellow Moonlight" by Roy Docker on the Domain record label and "What Kind of Lady" by Dee Dee Sharp on Action – twenty pence each. The price seemed reasonable and he bought them both.

A couple of weeks later, there was a guy selling old deleted records from a stall on Dashley Dyke outdoor market. Dan bought "Train Keep on Movin'" by The Fifth Dimension for fifteen pence.

***

Closing time had long passed at The Cricketers' and numbers were thinning. Dan and Tommy drained their dimpled pint pots and stepped out into the cool night-time air. They made outline plans for Buffy's later in the week and set off home. For Tommy, the journey was a straightforward one: straight down Sheffield Road to their house near the bottom. For Dan, there was a choice: back towards the town centre and up Holmfirth Road, which took twenty or twenty-five minutes, or the short-cut, which took about half that. Given that it was well past eleven and it was a week night and there was an early start for work tomorrow, the choice was an obvious one. But the thing about the short cut was that it was through St Mark's graveyard. And the thing about St Mark's graveyard was that it was both very large and completely devoid of light, making it a dubious affair at night.

It was roughly the size of three football pitches, though no particular configuration of three football pitches as you normally see them would match its irregular shape. Nor do you normally see a couple of thousand buckled and toppled gravestones on a football pitch. It had been first created in the early 1800s, when St Mark's was built. In daylight, you could still see the old drystone wall that surrounded the small cemetery that was originally set out alongside the church. But you could then see vestiges of other dry stone walls, which had once divided up the fields that were overtaken as the graveyard grew rapidly in size with the dizzying advancement of the Industrial Revolution. In that era of mining, cotton and cholera, dying young was the height of fashion – everyone was at it – and the graveyard was extended over and again to cope with the relentless demand.

A narrow, informal path, which was dust in summer and mud in winter, cut right across and made a loosely diagonal link from Steggs Lane, off Sheffield Road, over to Crowley Street, which led to Holmfirth Road, but zig-zagged occasionally, where some inconsiderate sod had chosen to be buried on what would otherwise be a reasonably straight line. It was a handy link and people had been using it ever since there had been people in Dashley Dyke. But at night, it was a tricky prospect: if there was no moon, darkness was total. You could hold your hand up a couple of inches from your face and be unable to see it. The plot was a long way from any streetlights and was screened from what there were on all sides, about half of it by the backs of the houses on Steggs Lane and Crowley Estate, on another part by the massive bulk of Longbottom's Mill and finally by St Mark's itself and the rows of tall old trees that surrounded it and marked the edge of the original cemetery. In short, on moonless nights all you had to go on was your memory of where the path was.

This was reasonably OK for Dan, as he'd used it so many times. Even so, in such complete darkness, as there was on this particular night, it was possible to veer off the path and trip over urns and gravestones. And it was creepy as hell. And totally silent.

Dan's mind was telling him, there's no such thing as ghosts, and his mum's expression, 'you have nothing to fear from the dead – it's the living you need to worry about,' kept flashing through his mind. But still, it was *creepy as hell*.

About halfway through, there was a bit where you had to be especially careful, where the path went through a gap in one of the old drystone walls. It was only about 18 inches wide and in the dark you had to take care to meet it right, so as not to bash your legs on the wall. He felt OK, he was still on the path, he could feel its curved, worn shape under his feet, and the gap must be coming up shortly. And then he reached it.

They reckon a human being walks at about 4 miles per hour. So, when Dan's face slapped into that of a silent invisible stranger coming the other way at the bit where the gap was, it must have been at a combined speed of about 8 miles per hour. Not that the force of the impact was the prime concern of either. Much greater was the shock and horror of their clammy faces meeting full-on, without warning in a graveyard in total darkness in the middle of the night. They both let out an involuntary 'waah!' then 'whoa!' as their confused and horror-struck minds fought to make sense of the encounter, and they shuffled awkwardly and invisibly round each other in the inky blackness.

And then the other guy carried on, on his silent way towards Sheffield Road, and Dan, heart pounding out of his chest, pressed on to Holmfirth Road.

***

Dan and Phil Burns took a trip down to see Adey at teacher training college in Surrey again. This time Dan had the delightful Linda with him, which would make the bed-sharing experience a much more pleasurable one. The gulf between the joy of waking up to Linda's lovely face and facing Phil's fetid feet first thing in the morning was perhaps one of the largest known to man. Linda was sexy. She was tall, slim and shapely, with big brown eyes and long auburn hair, like something out of an old painting. She was also fly, and Dan knew she wouldn't be around for long, but intended to have as much fun with her as possible while he could and do his best not to fall in love. They were allotted the same room as before, the one with Queen and the fifty billion flies guy on the wall. Phil would bunk up with Adey.

After the long drive, they freshened-up, got changed, and skipped down the institutional-looking 1960s staircase to the Students' Union bar for beers. A friend of Adey's, a hippy-looking guy called Robin, with long scraggy hair, murky green loon pants and a grey granddad shirt, joined them. After not very long the conversation turned to drugs, and Robin reckoned he had some – well, one. Well, a half, really: half a tab of acid. Dan could have it for fifty pee. Dan was interested. He'd only ever had speed. Acid, the famous LSD, was something he longed to try. Robin went and got it from his room, and there it was in his palm, a mauve semi-circle of microdot acid: 'purple haze', about an eighth of an inch in diameter. Dan was both intrigued and sceptical. How could something so tiny do anything? He was used to a handful of pills and/or capsules. Even so, it was too much to resist, and he handed Robin a fifty pence coin and pocketed the half pill. He couldn't take it there and then as they'd all be in bed in a couple of hours, so he reluctantly exercised a bit of self-discipline and agreed with himself that he'd take it the next day.

The four sat round the blue-topped table in the student refectory and breakfasted on eggs on toast. Dan swilled down his half-tab of acid with his mug of tea. Adey and Phil went off for a drive into the country in Phil's smelly Triumph. Linda and Dan decided to catch the train into London, after a potter around Egham.

They walked past the burnt-out, boarded-up record shop. In spite of the tragedy of that, Dan started to have feelings of giddy pleasure. They found themselves looking into the window of a clothes shop. A lantern-jawed manikin with shiny nylon hair sported some nice, bright blue cord baggies – so bright, in fact, that they seemed to glow. Dan *had* to try them on. And there were any number of things that Linda wanted to check out. They picked possible choices from rails and shelves and disrobed together in the same changing cubicle, much to the tut-tutting horror of the bouffant ladies who ran the place, which had them both in giggles.

They bought nothing and headed on to the train station. It was one of those early spring days, when it was bright and sunny without being all that warm. They sat on the platform on an old cast iron and timber bench, which had its back to the waiting room wall. The flue of a gas heater blew warm air out at their backs. Dan found this hilarious, but wasn't sure why.

Dan had never been to London before, but he'd seen pictures and always imagined it as a place where the buildings stood still. Not today they didn't. Everything swooped in and out of his presence: shops, buses, cars, people... Nothing would stay put. And every time a bit of sky appeared, the GPO Tower leapt into it and peered at them from its great height, like a giant robotic mother, concerned at what her kiddies were getting up to. Noises were similarly uncooperative, swishing in and swooshing out of his consciousness, unbidden. And the people... there were far too many of them. But then, this was the capital and lots of people wanted to be there, so *fair enough,* but he'd be grateful if they wouldn't get so close, and maybe standing still for a bit would be nice too. And where were they all going? OK, it was a big city, but how come everyone who lived there wanted to be somewhere else?

Dan's exploding synapses fought to make sense of it all. *What kind of city is it where everyone is permanently in the wrong fucking place? Gobshites! Fucking southern cockney jessie gobshites. Why didn't they just get where they were going and stay there, then there wouldn't be all this commotion? And what about a bit of planning? If someone was in place A and was headed to place B, and someone was in place B and was headed to place A, why didn't the person in place A do what the person in place B was going to do when s/he got to place A, and vice versa? That way no-one would have to go anywhere and all this rushing madness would stop. And this was just on the surface – there were loads more of these fuckers squirting from place to place in that tube thing they kept hidden underground. This was a place that could do with some proper Northern organisation. No wonder London was down fucking South.*

The drug brought alternate moments of joy and discomfort. A siren call from somewhere deep inside invited him to panic, but he could see that for what it was and refused to have it. He resolved to make the most of the drug, to enjoy the good bits. There was certainly no doubt now that half a tab of acid worked. He ought to apologise to Robin for thinking he was a charlatan. And he was with the lovely Linda. Really, he could do with being in a quieter place, a park or something, but this was the West End of London on a Saturday afternoon – probably not the best place to try out your first hallucinogen. *Oh well, fuck it.* He concentrated on the GPO Tower – a thing that was relatively familiar and comforting, if only from pictures and the telly. It seemed to be following them everywhere, keeping an eye on them, *so why not roll with it.*

***

After two years of manual work – gas fitting and digging trenches and laying gas mains in them – Dan's apprenticeship moved on, and he was allowed into the office to work with the intelligent, sophisticated people. Here, he was given more complicated and mind-stretching tasks to advance his skills and understanding, like putting things in filing cabinets in alphabetical order or with other things of the same ilk, or transferring information from cards that the blokes on the road used onto similar but cleaner cards that lived in the office, and putting them away in a filing cabinet, where they could be ignored until they next needed to be updated.

Jud Greenway was the office cad. He was thin, hunched and grey-haired, and he sloped around the place in a caddish way in kipper tie and washable grey flares. He chain-smoked and flirted incessantly with the ladies in the office.

The tracer, Doris Jackson, who like Jud was in her mid-fifties, wore Crimplene suits. She had three in pastel colours – pink, blue and lemon yellow – so she never wore the same one on two consecutive days. Each comprised a neat short jacket and a neat short skirt. Beneath the jacket she wore a sensible, business-like blouse, usually white, and an imitation pearl necklace, and beneath the skirt, tan-coloured tights and big white knickers. The reason everyone knew she wore big white knickers was that they got to see them several times a day. Doris was a hefty woman, and it didn't take much leaning over the Dyeline printer to reveal her not insubstantial backside. When this happened, most in the office looked elsewhere in mildly amused embarrassment and pretended they couldn't see. But not Jud. He would yell out 'way, hey, hey!' or 'keep bending over like that, love, and I'll buy yer a new hat,' or 'blimey, Doris, you look like a pig that's just had its throat cut,' or 'I see the moon's rising early today.' And sometimes he wouldn't be able to resist some kind of physical engagement and would leap out from behind his desk and pretend to mount Doris from behind, to which she would cry, in a seen-it-all-before tone, 'Oh, give over will yer, Juddy.'

Not everyone in the office was as tolerant of Jud's antics as Doris, however; Muriel Date being a case in point. Muriel was in her mid-forties, with a hard, unsmiling face, bony fingers and the sense that she was bitter about something that she didn't care to disclose. She seldom said anything more than was necessary to do her job, and when she did, it was usually to have a dig at someone. Jud would periodically tease her in the hope of drawing her out of herself or making her laugh. He never succeeded. One day he followed her into the ladies' and, after giving her time to sit down and settle to her task, threw a paper cup full of water over the toilet door, which landed entirely in Muriel's upturned gusset. A livid Muriel stomped back into the office with a gait like a cowboy who's been on his horse too long, screaming, shouting and threatening, before waddling home to get a change of underwear.

She made an official complaint against Jud, and he was given a written warning.

***

Dan and Reevesie waited impatiently on the southbound platform of Verrington station for the Longport train. Fifty yards further along the platform were two guys, obviously soul boys, from their parallels and tonic jackets and bushy sideburns. Suddenly, there was music pumping out from somewhere near them – James Bounty's thundering masterpiece "Prove Yourself a Lady" – and they started dancing, right there on Verrington station's concrete platform.

Dan and Reevesie couldn't resist going for a look.

'What are yer playing this on then, lads?'

'It's a Discassette.'

They took a look. It was a silver box with a flap on the top that opened so you could put a cassette in, and a slot where you could slide in a 45. One of the lads, the one with the gold-to-blue tonic jacket and bushier sideburns, ejected the James Bounty single, waggled it in front of them for an instant, then slotted it back in to show them how it worked. There was a clicking noise and then the music started again.

'Wow.'

Dan and Reevesie were impressed and came to the view that it was a handy thing, but also felt that entrusting a precious, rare single to some clunky mechanism you couldn't even see and a stylus you could never change was a bit much to take.

***

Everything was beyond. She wasn't just pretty, she wasn't even just beautiful, she was perfect. And maybe not just in his eyes – men stopped talking when she walked into a room. Even women stopped to look, sometimes with admiration, sometimes envy. She had big dark eyes that glinted in the light when she laughed, a neat perfectly symmetrical little nose, and perfect cupid's-bow lips, which she kept permanently painted in a deep passionate red. Her dark brown hair was cut in an irresistible bob that matched the colour of her eyes and framed her perfect face. If this part of her was brunette, her figure was pure Jayne Mansfield. She was all curves – as one swelled provocatively outward, another swept seductively inward. And this being the early 70s, she routinely wore halter-neck dresses, exposing acres of gorgeous, creamy-white female flesh. The perfume she used was Estee Lauder Youth Dew, which sent Dan crazy. Even her voice was sexy. She was a delight to all the senses.

And he wasn't just in love; he was out of this world, off the scale, into orbit, crazy in love. He'd been crazy in love with Lucy too and been devastated when that ended. The same with Rita. But this was something else. He was rapturously, dementedly, besottedly in love. And to his joy and amazement, she felt the same. She even wrote 'Dan Brody is my Magic

Man' on the wall of the ladies' toilets in The Blue Parrot, quoting that Wilson Pickett record.

He'd never have had the nerve to talk to her, but friends could see what was going on and conspired to manoeuvre them into each other's path.

At first they tried to be cool and meet just a couple of nights a week, but the longing was too much and soon they saw each other every night, except Wednesdays. It was important to have at least one night off, to get things done and because it was the last day before pay day and Dan had always run out of money by then.

They couldn't keep their hands off each other. They made love whenever and wherever they could, but given that neither had their own place and both were a long way from owning a car, this always involved improvisation, and after a few drinks there were no inhibitions. They did it in parks, in alleys, behind bushes, on car bonnets... The best time was at weekends, when it was OK to go back to hers. They'd creep in after a pub or club. Her parents and sister would be in bed and hopefully asleep. Eve would go upstairs and take off her underwear but leave on the rest of her clothes. They'd make love on the settee or on the rug in front of the gas fire, and if they heard anyone stirring upstairs, she could stand up and in an instant her dress would fall back into place and no-one would be any the wiser. Dan's embarrassment might be a bit harder to hide. He had to yank his kecks up sharpish, taking care not to catch anything vital in the zip, then position himself strategically on the couch, leant forward, elbow on knee, hand placed thoughtfully under chin. They also met at dinner time from work, if they could, if things matched up right. Eve worked as a shorthand typist at the asbestos factory, and if it was one of the periods when Dan was at the Dashley Dyke depot, they were only two hundred yards apart. Her parents both worked, so for a few precious minutes they had proper privacy and the use of her bed. There'd just be time afterwards to wolf down a pie from Stubbs's Bakery, and then Dan would show up back at work, looking a touch flushed and sweaty, to the restrained amusement of the office ladies and highly vocal amusement of Juddy the Cad.

Dan was on a cloud, he had a smile for everyone, and if they weren't happy, he'd be happy for them. The world glittered with love and wonder. The sun shone every day, and when it didn't the rain was soft, vibrant and life-giving, and the snow was gentle, pure and beautiful. Breezes were fresh and uplifting, strong winds were vigorous and romantic. And all the love songs seemed made for them. The juke box in The King's Head had Gladys Knight's glorious "The Look of Love" and the Detroit Spinners' celestial "Could it be I'm Falling in Love". They pumped it with coins and listened to them over and over. The rapture of the songs met perfectly the rapture of their hearts. These were *their* songs. Even old Dashley Dyke had gone from godforsaken, falling-down shithole to proud and ruggedly beautiful vestige of the Industrial Revolution. The sickly, throat-clogging vapours that drifted up from the plastics factories in the Dash Valley now seemed playful, sweet and charming. The miserable old bastards who drank in the tap room of The King's Head were now loveable old rogues with hearts of gold behind those gruff exteriors.

At seventeen, he'd met the girl he wanted to spend the rest of his life with. By the time of his eighteenth birthday, it was over.

He struggled to grasp it going wrong, even while it was doing so. It was like a dream in which a beautiful ornate building, filled with love and life and happiness, is cursed, and a grey shadow falls across it, and suddenly it is old, abandoned and derelict. And it begins to collapse before his eyes... and there is nothing he can do to stop it.

At first there were scarcely perceptible little things: a moment's indifference – a solitary slate sliding unnoticed down a buckled roof. A thoughtless comment – a puff of brick dust escaping silently from a twisted chimney stack gradually giving way under its own weight. Then things accelerated: a few bricks fell, then floors began to twist and slide as beams gave way, then window frames buckled and shards of shattered glass shot out across the street, and then, with a sickening subterranean rumble, the whole festering edifice crashed down in an ugly brown cloud of poisoned dust. He just seemed to say and do the wrong things – over and over again. He couldn't stop himself. His clumsy words thudded down like great clumps of sodden old masonry onto sullen unyielding earth. Each time it happened, she didn't argue, she just went quiet. His favourite shirt, the grey one with the sketchy pattern, was washed out and looked a bit ragged. So she bought him a new one from Grattan's catalogue. When she asked if he liked it, he said it was OK, but not a patch on the old one. Silence. His taste for soul took him on into blues and he fancied learning to play the harmonica, like those old delta blues guys. So she bought him one. But he reckoned it was the wrong sort and he couldn't get the right noises out of it, not those howling delta blues noises, and they couldn't return it for another because he'd used it, had his mouth on it. Silence. It had cost her most of a week's wages. They bumped into Lucy in Dotty's in town and, at the sight of her, all those feelings he thought were in the past rushed back and overwhelmed him, and he was beside himself with grief for their lost love, and naturally he couldn't help but share his distress with Eve. More silence.

If someone had asked him what he thought he was doing, he'd have said he was just being honest. Not that anyone did. And that didn't really explain what was going on anyway. It was more the case that he could only see the issue at hand. The human needs, the emotions that pertained to a situation were not visible to him. No-one had explained to him that sometimes you had to prioritise how someone might feel ahead of the bald facts. And it dawned on him that he'd been doing this all his life and either not noticing that he was doing it or, if he noticed, not knowing either that it mattered or why he did it. There was that time he needled the bouncers outside the Piccadilly Club and when they reacted he did it some more and their eyes widened and their fists clenched and Tommy had to shove him away before he got his head kicked in. And then there was that time he'd insulted Greg Fowler's girlfriend. He hadn't meant to – it just came out all wrong – and as anyone who knew Greg Fowler would tell you, no-one who valued having teeth in his head would insult Greg Fowler's girlfriend. And there was that incident with Arthur Pratt in the canteen at work, when Arthur wanted to talk about music because he'd heard Dan was into soul. Arthur was into jazz, and Dan didn't think much of jazz and he asked Arthur if he hadn't noticed that when someone uttered the word 'jazz', the word 'wanker' was never far away, and Arthur had walked away all crestfallen and hurt. And there was that time with Rita, when she'd bought some red French knickers because she thought he'd like them, but he didn't, he was horrified – they reminded him of football shorts – and he told her to burn the bloody things because they made her look like Kevin Keegan, and she was all deflated and upset. And his mind flashed back to that time at school when the English teacher, Mr Dunn, had completed a long diatribe on *Catcher in the Rye* and, proud of his spiel, had asked the class if anyone had any questions, and Dan had asked if there was something wrong with the clock because it was behaving in a funny way with the minute hand swinging backwards and forwards and that, and not really going anywhere, and the class had fallen apart laughing and Mr Dunn looked as much hurt as he did angry.

'Aspergic' was another pertinent word that Dan would not encounter for many years.

Dan had always thought of himself as quite a nice guy, but now he thought about it, the evidence did not seem to back that up. It turned out he was a bit of a git, even though most of the time he didn't know it.

But it was over. And now it was the pain that was beyond, out of this world, unbearable, off the scale. And the world was no longer generous, bright and pretty, but meagre, dark and ugly. Every day was grey and miserable and all the people he passed on the street were wretched bloodless creatures living out meaningless, shitty lives, like his. Now it was the sad songs that got to him, tormented him, wrenched his heart out. "Looking for You", "I'll Always Love You", "I Hurt on the Other Side" and a million more got him in the corner and smashed him sickeningly around the head till he was dizzy and pummelled him with dark thudding blows to the gut until he heaved. He thought he'd die. He couldn't understand how it was possible to feel this bad and still be alive. Maybe he was dead, but the news hadn't reached his body yet. All the people on the street, the older ones, they must have been through something like this when they were young. How could they still be alive? How could they still smile and carry on as normal?

And now Dan saw the world through the prism of his own wretchedness and loathing. His soul had turned as black as the soot-covered walls of Dashley Dyke town hall. And the town was back to being its old shithole self: a grim, derelict dump of a place; a zombie-land, dead since the mills closed and cotton vanished; a living necropolis, not where dreams were shattered, but where they were never had in the first place; a vapid village of vomiting drunks and fifteen-year-old mothers. A place where no-one was going anywhere, where every night on some grubby backstreet there was always some pissed-up old tart screeching 'leave 'im Terry 'e's not worth it.' A place where only bookies and money-lenders got fat and where ignorance was a thing to be celebrated – *Dashley Dyke, born and bred, strong of arm, thick of head* – and where uttering a word of three or more syllables could get you your head kicked in in the post-chucking-out-time chippy. The sickening plasticky pall that crawled up the banks of the river was now an evil cancerous miasma, cloying in its synthetic sweetness. And the miserable old fuckers in the tap room of The King's Head were just hateful, cirrhotic old bastards with no redeeming features, save that one day soon they would be dead and their putrid corpses could feed the weeds in St Mark's cemetery, though maybe they'd poison even them.

He wondered if it would be possible to rekindle things. But how could someone who was so dead inside, whose soul was so black, charm anyone, especially someone whose love he'd managed so thoroughly to obliterate? It just wasn't in him anymore. In any case, she wouldn't come to the phone and her dad always answered the door and wouldn't let him in. He tried to find ways of accidentally bumping into her, not that he knew what to say to her if he did. He looked for her in the soul clubs where they'd both been regulars, where they'd met. But she wasn't there. She was never there. And when he finally found her, months later in the early hours on one of the all-night buses coming back from Manchester, she was cold and indifferent. It was like their history together – all that love, passion and intensity – had never happened and he was just someone she knew vaguely and what little of him she did know she despised. He tried to be chatty, tried to lift the stilted conversation, said he hadn't seen her at Buffy's or The Blue Parrot or The Pendulum or anywhere. And she said she didn't go to dumps like that anymore. She wasn't into soul anymore. She liked David Bowie and Roxy Music now. All that soul stuff was *so* last year's model, and the fashions were a joke. And then she turned her back on him and carried on talking to her friend.

The bus stopped and a bunch of half-drunk blokes filed down the aisle past Dan. He swung a fist into the gut of one of them, in the hope of starting a fight, but the guy, anaesthetised by ale or just not interested, ignored the slight and went and sat with his mates at the back of the bus.

***

Dan sat with Reevesie, Rob Brierley and Tommy Coggins at one of the beery tables in the dark at Buffy's, and fought to make themselves heard over the loud, pounding music. All-nighters, or the dearth of them, was the subject of the conversation. The Torch had closed. The Drug Squad had stuck their oar in, just as they had at The Twisted Wheel. Va-Va in Bolton had gone the same way. But there was this new place in Wigan: Wigan Casino, it was called. There was derision, snorting down noses. How could there be anything worthwhile in Wigan? It was the back of beyond. Sheep country. The only time Wigan came up in conversations was in the punchline of a joke. A comedian dying on stage could always revive his fortunes by throwing in a gratuitous quip about Wigan. The audience was bound to laugh.

Nobody fancied it; it was bound to be crap.

A week later and the four were back in Buffy's again, and this time there was news. Rob had bumped into a few guys from Dashton who'd been to this Wigan place the first weekend it was open and they reckoned it was pretty good – really big venue with some good DJs and great sounds. The 'Casino' thing was misleading – it wasn't a casino; it was just a club, and it had a good big dancefloor as well. It was OK. They should try it. 'Only thing was, it didn't open till 2 in the morning. There was a divvy disco on in the same place, and they had to chuck that lot out and sweep up a bit before the soul night started.

There was muttering, scepticism.

Back at home, Dan found himself fancying this Wigan place ever more. He'd scored some dex midweek and was itching to take them, and with the break-up with Eve still getting him down he wanted to go out and have a good time, forget about it all for a few hours. He made plans with Tommy. They'd get the train from Dashley Dyke station into Victoria and get the Wigan train from there.

Saturday came and Tommy rang and said he was off colour and didn't want to go. Dan looked around the living room: his mum knitting, dad snoring, Nicky and Janet sat on the floor arguing over something, shite on the telly. And he thought, *fuck it, I'm going anyway*.

He had a bath and a shave and splashed on some Avon Blue Blazer and set off on foot down Holmfirth Road. Dashley Dyke station was deserted, but at the next station, Dashton, a bunch of lads and girls he half-knew from The Blue Parrot and Buffy's got on, and he sat with them and chatted for a bit. Then, at Victoria, there were a quite a few souly-looking folk waiting. And when the Wigan train filled up, it had so many of them that it started to look a bit like a Wigan Casino special, though the atmosphere was quite muted. This was only the second week and, like Dan, most seemed a bit nervous about what they were letting themselves in for. *What if it was crap? What if it was some sort of poxy church hall kind of place? Would they know any of the music?*

The train disgorged and Dan followed the crowd through the dark Wigan streets, assuming they knew where to go, because he didn't. And then they were there. The building was pretty impressive – a substantial red-brick affair with a great veranda that reached out over the footpath with the words 'Casino Club' plastered across it in big, confident red letters. But then they had to wait ages in the Beachcomber Café because the main club wasn't open yet. The Beachcomber was part of the same building, but it was also next door, in that it had its entrance on the opposite corner from the main one into the club, and there was no access between the two – you had to go back outside and queue to get into Wigan Casino proper. Dan didn't much care for the Beachcomber. It was too bright and noisy, with the wrong kind of noise – the racket of chatter, the opening of coke cans and the movement of people and furniture and stuff. He wanted music. He wanted to be in the dark, dancing. And he wanted his gear.

After what seemed an age, there was a sudden upturn of noise. Chairs slid back, lads stood up, girls picked up handbags. It was time to go in. Dan joined the queue. It was busy. Clearly a lot of people had picked up on this place. The long queue filled the full width of the footpath and bustled and swayed under the deep veranda. It reminded Dan of the mischievous, impatient throng shoving towards the Stretford End on a Saturday afternoon.

Dan glanced around cautiously in the half-light, rummaged in his pocket, picked out the dex, fed them furtively into his mouth and swallowed. No drink. He was expert at doing it dry now.

Dan reached the desk and handed over his money. He then turned up the steps to go through the inner door, and just as he reached for it someone else pushed it open from the other side. It was Reevesie! And the music blasted out from behind him: "Soul Self Satisfaction" by Earl Jackson. One of Dan's favourite records! They grinned and hugged and backslapped, and Dan thought, *I'm gonna like it here.*

***

Dan didn't much like it that folk called Charlie Broadhead 'rat face'. It was true that there was a certain rodentiness about his appearance. He had a slightly pointed face and pale hair and complexion. His whiskery little tash bristled over his top lip, and years of excessive speed consumption had left him thin, fidgety and jittery, with overtones of a prey animal. But Dan preferred to think of him more as a ferret. They had similar physical characteristics, but ferrets were generally regarded as more wholesome animals – mankind had never quite forgiven rats for that bubonic plague thing – and the word 'ferret' didn't sound anywhere near as nasty as 'rat'. Even so, Charlie himself wouldn't have much cared for either epithet, and Dan didn't bother sharing this proposed revision with him.

Charlie had passed his test, taken out a loan and bought a car – a shiny red Datsun Cherry – and he wanted to go to Tiffany's in Newcastle-under-Lyme on Sunday night. It was an odd night to be travelling, with work the following day, but it wasn't that far, really, and there were good DJs on: Colin Curtis, Dave Evison and others. It was a cracking night – Charlie had seen reviews in *Blues and Soul*. They'd hear all the latest tunes. And Charlie wouldn't be drinking – he wasn't about to wreck his lovely new car. And he'd given up speed, on account of all that jitteriness. He was only going for the music.

Early Sunday evening, Charlie picked up Dan in Dashley Dyke and Chris and Mel Halliwell in Withington, and they all chipped in for petrol and set off for Newcastle.

Chris and Mel were decent, clean-living, non-identical twins and both were trainee electricians at NORWEB. Their mum was a jolly, rotund woman who always seemed to be laughing about something and always overfed Dan whenever he called round to their house. Their dad was a maintenance technician at Kellogg's cornflake factory in Trafford Park. Both lads were always immaculately turned out in the latest soul boy fashions and neither had ever fallen prey to the temptation of drugs. The only negative with them was that their capacity for drinking beer was not matched by their enthusiasm for buying it. Both, but especially Chris, would always find a way to be last to the bar. As you walked up to the pub door, he would suddenly discover that his shoelace needed tying, or he'd politely open the door for you, so you would be the first in and the first to catch the barman's eye. By these stratagems, he might, if there was an odd number of rounds, manage to buy only one to everyone else's two, and if the crowd was big enough – if, say, there were seven in the group and everyone sank six pints – he might stagger home at end of the evening, agreeably addled, without having once put his hand in his pocket.

Tiffany's was another great modernist beast of a place, part of the same chain as Blackpool Mecca and not too different in appearance. The interior, too, was smart and slick, like that of its more famous Lancastrian counterpart, though this being a Sunday night, not a Saturday, the crowds were thinner and the atmosphere less frenetic and more laid-back. It was easier to do your thing on the dancefloor without repeatedly colliding with your neighbour. And the music was fabulous, all new stuff: "Come on Train", "You Better Keep Her", "Love Don't You Go Through No Changes on Me", "You've Got to Try Harder", "Ella Weez"...

And all too soon it was over. They had to get away and get on the road at a reasonable hour, what with having work the next day.

As they clambered into the Datsun, rain began to fall. Charlie put on the windscreen wipers, but all they did was smear. There was some vague semblance of road and streetlighting before them, but the whole vista was streaky and blurred. Each stroke of wiper blade produced only a fresh, curved kaleidoscope of red, white and yellow shapes set in unfathomable blackness.

'I can't see a blind thing,' complained Charlie, anxiously.

They struggled on out of Newcastle with this limited view of the road and speculated that maybe this was as good as it gets. Maybe Datsun windscreen wipers weren't all that good. Rain was wet stuff – you had to expect some smearing. Did he put some detergent in the washer pot or was it just plain water? Were they old wiper blades?

The rain never stopped, and all the way home the Datsun's windscreen wipers did little more than wipe a smeary mess across the windscreen. Charlie fidgeted and complained and turned the blower up to full tilt and squirted the washers. Occasionally they stopped in a lay-by and got out and Charlie wiped the windscreen with a rag he kept in the glove box, while the others inspected the wiper blades and ran fingers over their edges and looked hopelessly for a solution. And all the way back Charlie repeated over and over again 'I can't see a blind thing. I can't see a blind thing...'

Dan rang Charlie after work on Monday night. Had he got home OK? Charlie said he had, though it had been very stressful. And he'd discovered what the problem was: before setting off on Sunday night, he'd topped-up the oil, but he'd forgotten to put the filler cap back on, so the engine had been spraying a fine mist of oil up and onto the windscreen all the way to and from Newcastle.

***

It was a grim thing when United got relegated to the Second Division, but it did have a couple of upsides: firstly, the team was improving just as they were relegated, so when they kicked off in the second tier they played some great football, which was thrilling to watch, and they beat nearly everyone and were soon reinstated in the top flight; secondly, it meant that, as a fan, you went to loads of different places you'd never been to before: Bristol Rovers, Leyton Orient, York City and elsewhere.

This particular weekend it was Blackpool away. *Great stuff!* This meant Dan and his mates could go to the footy then on to Blackpool Mecca. Dan had invited his new girlfriend too, busty Brenda, so he'd get laid as well. *Fabulous! A three-parter: footy, soul and sex.* That was pretty much everything there was.

Dan had met Brenda on the crammed teatime bus, coming back from Stretford Tech. He kept dozing off, lulled by the rumble of the wheels, the stuffy heat and the exhaled breath of seventy other dispirited sardines, and she was amused by this and started chatting and woke him up. Brenda was undeniably hot – black hair, blue eyes and a statuesque figure that was impossible to ignore. In truth, however, he hadn't felt what he ought to because he hadn't got over Eve. But they had good times, and showing up at the pub with Brenda on his arm made all his friends jealous.

Coming into Manchester from a few different directions, they met at a dusty, breezy Mosley Street bus station to catch the Blackpool coach; seven of them: Dan, Brenda, Tommy Coggins, Jez Reeves, Chris Halliwell, Lenny Hughes and Dave Podmore. Dave Podmore didn't have a clue about football, but he wanted to go to Blackpool Mecca, so he came along for the whole event.

Dan liked Dave. He seemed somehow to combine a persistent, resilient cheerfulness and a good, generous heart with the demeanour of a Victorian undertaker. No-one could accuse him of getting by on his looks, however. He had a narrow, craggy face, pock-marked and flushed with acne. His dark brown hair, when it got to more than a quarter of an inch in length, turned to frizz, and his body seemed devoid of even the merest hint of muscle. The only protuberance was his belly, which the rest of him seemed to sag into. And whereas the shape and hang of everyone else's baggies were defined by their hips or buttocks, Dave's were defined by the swell of his gut. His baggy corduroy kecks hung down from it like a saggy old theatre curtain.

By the time everyone had arrived at the bus station and found each other, time was getting tight. And then, when they went to get on a coach, there were no seats – everyone from within twenty miles of central Manchester had had the same idea and everything was booked out. They considered the trains, but no-one knew what time they ran or even if you had to go to Victoria or Piccadilly for a Blackpool train. And what if they were all booked-out too? They'd waste time getting over there and still be stuck. Even though it was a 70-odd-mile journey, a taxi was the only solution.

Dan approached a black cab, lined-up in the rank next to the bus station:

'How much for Blackpool, mate?'
'Twenty-two quid.'
'There's seven of us.'
'Forget it.'
He tried another:
'How much for Blackpool?'

'Twenty quid.'
'There's seven of us.'
'Twenty-five quid.'
'Fair enough.'
'Up-front, mind.'
'Sure.'

They handed over the money and bustled into the back of the cab. There were only five seats, so two of them had to sit on the floor. They agreed to take turns on the floor because it was uncomfortable and it was a long way – except Brenda, because it wasn't right that a girl should have to sit on the floor – and once every fifteen minutes or so they rotated, and two of the seated ones gave up their places and took a stint on the deck.

One such switchover happened in Chorley. Tommy swung his well-upholstered backside out of his seat in the same instant that the cab rounded a tight left-hand bend, lost his balance and sat on the handle of the right-hand door. It flew open and the centrifugal force threw him halfway out, arse first, like a motorbike sidecar racer, white knuckles wrapped around the door frames. They dragged him back in and pulled the door closed and resolved to take more care over the seat-changing procedure for the rest of the journey. The driver gasped, swore and shook his head.

There was just time to book into a B&B. The Purple Haze Hotel didn't have enough space for seven of them. They knocked on other B&B doors and soon found a suitable one about a quarter of a mile further away from The Mecca. It was dingy – not a patch on a fine establishment like The Purple Haze Hotel – and it didn't smell too good, but it could take seven. It would do. Dan and Brenda got a double room to themselves, for a bit of privacy. Three were in another room, two in a third.

They just scraped into Bloomfield Road in time for kick-off. And United won, three-nil – Forsyth, Macari, McCalliog – though Dave Podmore spent the whole ninety minutes plus half time and injury time looking thoroughly bored and bewildered, scarcely grasping what he was looking at. 'Which is our side, again?' he asked, half way through the first half.

They got cleaned-up and changed back at the B&B and went out for a burger and a few beers before heading off to The Mecca – The Highland Room – which was its usual wonderful self. The atmosphere was cheerful, the music hot and cool but always insistently up-tempo. Ian Levine and Colin Curtis did their thing on the decks – new sounds and old – and the soul faithful hammered it out on the stifling, super-smooth dancefloor. The seven friends danced and drank and chatted until the doors closed at 2am.

Dan and Brenda made love in their squeaky, dubiously fragrant double bed and fell fast asleep. They woke early, as the milky autumnal light bled in through the thin, shabby curtains, and did it again.

Dan felt there was something strange, some odd feeling, but the business was urgent so they carried on until things reached their natural conclusion. Then, when he extracted himself, he discovered the cause of the odd sensation. Scrawny flaps of flaccid beige rubber told the tale – the condom had broken.

Shit. Shit. This was how lads ended up married and shackled to misery and nonsense while still in their teens. And not to Brenda. *Please, God, no. Not Brenda bloody Burgess.* OK, she was a laugh, sort of, in small doses, and her bosom was legendary, but you would hardly call her conversation scintillating, and her way of expressing herself, through endless repetition of sayings, figures of speech and recently-invented proverbs had you wanting to bash your head on a wall after a short time in her company. 'Ooh Brody, be'ave, be'ave,' or 'Ooh Brody, yer give me the 'orn,' every time he started kissing her neck and coming on to her – it was almost enough to put him off. *Almost.*

And he was only just nineteen. The thought of spending the rest of his days with Brenda filled him with dread.

And then she missed her next period.

And Dan was in turmoil.

And the days and the weeks went by.

He'd not long since bought that Ruby Andrews record, "Casanova (Your Playing Days Are Over)", and now it haunted him – the lyrics ran round in his mind and he couldn't bear to hear it. And that Paul Anka song, "You're Having My Baby", was in the pop charts and was played everywhere he went. Who could have contrived that that record was the big hit while all this was happening? Dan could feel his bowels grip every time it came on. It was on the radio, on pub jukeboxes. He fled from a clothes shop in Verrington after it started to burble from the PA. Some twat at work was humming it one day; Dan wanted to strangle him. And then there were media discussions about it, because somehow it was controversial, as though, for some folk, news of the means by which every person who has ever lived on this fucking planet got here was a revelation they just weren't ready for.

And then, some four weeks late, Brenda's period started.

***

Dan's apprenticeship had taken him to the North Western Gas Board's facility in Verrington. The north west of England was half-converted to natural gas now, but some places, including Verrington gas works, continued to make gas from steam and coal in crumbling old Victorian gas manufacturing stations and pump it into as yet unconverted sections of the distribution system.

Dan leant over his drawing board in deep concentration, as he tried different configurations to make a governor system fit into a restricted space in Sorbay's sweets factory in Milltown. Suddenly, the near silence was interrupted by fuss, dismay and sobbing. One of the old engineers, Albert Clegg, had gone to inspect the filter beds in the old gas production plant, and the rusty old cast iron catwalk had given way. Albert had fallen through, down to the concrete apron twenty feet below, and had hit his head on the unforgiving jagged metal as he fell.

Everyone was very upset and said what can you expect when the plant was so old, and what a shame it was when Albert was only a few weeks away from retirement. And there was a whip-around to send flowers to his widow.

***

Wigan Casino was a traditional turn-of-the-century dancehall, built big enough to serve the Saturday-night needs of a whole town of mill workers – a great, high barn of a place, with a huge polished dancefloor, a high stage at one end and a balcony that ran round three sides, decorated with gilt-painted plaster swags. And the Saturday night all-nighter, which in reality ran from 2 till 8 on a Sunday morning, was what everyone said it was: six hours of unbounded amphetamised elation, dancing without inhibition to frenetic, up-tempo soul – the ultimate expression of the joy and pain of ghettoised black America, presented in ten thousand bits of precious black plastic to British working-class youth. The dancefloor was always packed and stifling, and as the temperature soared from hot to tropical to steam room, some discarded even their singlets and danced bare-chested. This was not like jigging about in a jacket and tie with a girl in some ordinary night club, this was pure Dionysian communion with your transcendent inner self. You danced alone, body, soul and mind infused with substances that felt so good they had to be made illegal, all in sync with pounding, unstoppable, ecstatic music. And while everyone did his own thing on the dancefloor, there was a sense of communal endeavour too, as loud, whip-crack claps went down sharp, in unison, on those well-known special beats, those crucial stops and crashes that everyone knew on the most loved records. The place lived in tension between joyful camaraderie, amphetamine elation, amphetamine anxiety, and the threat of being rolled in a dark corridor. And no-one much cared for using the toilets.

The dangers they presented were not only hygiene-related – there were numerous tales of people being mugged in there, including Dave Podmore. Mind you, there was something about Dave's daintiness that said 'mug me', and possibly even someone who had never mugged anyone before in their life and had not gone in there to mug anyone had seen Dave and suddenly felt compelled to do so. But Dan had never had any trouble. He wasn't sure if that was to do with his being a bit chunky nowadays, after all that road work, or if it was just good luck. Nevertheless, there was always a first time, and a trip to the gents was still a time for vigilance, to be ready for defensive action, if necessary.

Whatever the case, Dan's bladder was sending urgent messages to his brain. He had to go. He wriggled off the heaving dancefloor and shoved open the ominous black door. The place was empty. He stepped into the eye-watering stink and picked his way to the urinals over the giant Petri dish that was the floor. Deed done, he swung over to the mirror, pulled his comb from the back pocket of his green cord baggies and set about combing the sweat-sodden hair off his forehead and out of his eyes.

Suddenly, he was aware of another presence, another Simon-shirted body next to his in the mirror. Dan steeled himself, wondering if this was trouble. The lad looked at Dan's basic, brown plastic men's comb and, grinning, presented his own. It was a long-handled comb, a woman's comb, made from aluminium. But it was unlike the regular ones you saw in the shops: the handle had been filed so it had sharp, blade-like edges and a lethal-looking point.

'Here,' said the guy, 'you wanna get yourself one of these, mate – my little insurance policy.'

For an instant Dan wondered if there was any more to this, if the blade was coming his way. But it didn't. The bloke was just showing off. So Dan smiled and nodded and said 'nice,' and left it at that and resumed the important business of giving it some on the teeming dancefloor.

***

Dan waited to cross Chatters Hill Road, on his way to Buffy's. The Number 90 was opposite, at the stop in front of The George. It had just dropped off its passengers and was pulling away. He crossed the road and found himself following a girl who had evidently just got off the bus. Judging by her clothes – fitted black leather jacket, pale green midi-skirt, black stack heels – she was probably a soul girl, though he'd only be sure if she turned up Kenway Lane, then she'd almost certainly be going to Buffy's. Her hair was light brown and healthy looking and it bounced like something from a shampoo ad as she walked, and the way her hips swayed had him mesmerised.

Then she spun round, and there was this vision of classical beauty – big green eyes, high cheekbones and full pouty lips.

Though maybe the lips were just a bit *too* pouty – she looked a tad narked, probably because here was this wide-eyed, beguiled geezer following closely behind her. *Hmm.* Maybe he'd got a little too close. He slowed down to give her a bit of space and see what happened at Kenway Lane. Sure enough, she turned in. She had to be going to Buffy's.

She paid in and hung her cool leather jacket in the cloakroom. Then she walked across the room to Reevesie and they flung their arms around each other and kissed. And Dan went to the bar.

***

It hadn't been that much of a night, really. Not that there was much wrong with The Blue Room, that dark little tucked-away spare room, the bit dedicated to the faithful mid-week soul fraternity, round the back of the main Sale Mecca complex on Washway Road. There'd been some fantastic music as always there – "Bet You If You Ask Around", "Cool Off", "Branded", "Sending My Best Wishes" and many more gems – but Adey and Dan had to leave early because it was work tomorrow and they had to get all the way back to Piccadilly and from there back over to Dashley Dyke. And the beer had been bloody awful. It always tasted like someone had chucked a handful of gravy browning in it, and tonight it had been particularly nasty, so after forcing down a pint each of deeply unpleasant bitter they'd reluctantly moved on to shandy.

So, at 11pm, Adey and Dan were sat in an appalling state of cold, cheerless sobriety, upstairs on a sparsely populated 211, waiting for it to pull out of Piccadilly Gardens bus station. Adey sat by the window, Dan by the aisle, and they jointly felt that special kind of boredom known only to those who have waited on a bus after an unsatisfactory, sober night out, with only home and bed to look forward to.

Suddenly, something caught Adey's eye, down on the edge of the gardens.

'Look at that cunt,' said Adey.

Dan looked, and a uniformed police officer was dragging and pushing a ragged old tramp, gratuitously dead-legging the guy with every step. The helpless old fellow yelped and howled with every kick.

'Bastard,' said Dan.

Adey opened the window and yelled at the copper: 'Hey! Leave him alone you bastard. He's doing no harm.'

Within seconds, the upstairs of the bus filled with police officers, waving truncheons and rubber torches. The two at the front grabbed and pulled at Dan and Adey. Dan wouldn't move. 'What have I done? Am I under arrest? If so, what for?'

'You're coming with us,' yelled the copper.

'I'll come with you if I'm under arrest, but if I'm not, I'm staying here.'

'YOU'RE COMING WITH US,' and more dark blue arms closed around Dan and he was dragged off the bus. He lost sight of Adey.

The group of police officers rushed Dan across a wide stretch of footpath towards a parked police Mini with a blue-and-white panda paint job. The door was open and the front seat was ready tilted forward so he could be shoved into the back.

As they reached the car, Dan swung up his right leg and jammed his foot on the edge of the car roof, over the door space. He knew what happened at Bootle Street nick. If they weren't arresting him, this was just about giving him a kicking. His leg jammed, and the more the police shoved, the more solidly his leg locked at the knee. He wasn't moving. One of the cops swung round and threatened to hit him in the face with his heavy rubber torch.

'All right,' yelled Dan, 'if you stop shoving I might be able to get me leg down.' The pressure stopped, briefly, Dan's leg came down, and with forceful encouragement from behind, he squeezed into the back of the Mini.

Coppers jumped into the front two seats and the car sped off.

'Am I under arrest or what? If so, for what?' pressed Dan, again. The passenger-side copper swung round and again shoved the black rubber cosh into his face and told him to shut it.

At Bootle Street, Dan was frogmarched across the yard and thrown into a cell, which already had Adey in it.

After about half an hour they were taken out and fingerprinted.

After another half an hour a charge sheet was bought in. It said they were going to be charged with 'Behaviour Likely to Cause a Breach of the Peace' and told how PS Harris had been patrolling Piccadilly Gardens in a quiet and orderly manner, when suddenly and without provocation, Dan and Adey, who appeared to be in an advanced state of intoxication, had started to hurl torrents of foul-mouthed abuse from the top deck of the Number 211.

'But none of this is true,' said Dan. 'We weren't trying to cause a breach of the peace; we were trying to stop one. Your mate was kicking a tramp, and there weren't torrents of foul-mouthed abuse, we just told him to leave the poor guy alone. And we're not drunk.'

'Think yourself lucky we're not doing you for resisting arrest,' said the copper.

'But I asked if I was under arrest and I would have gone peacefully if I was, but no-one would answer – you just attacked me.'

'Let's put it this way: if you sign this now you can go home and go to court in the morning. If you don't, you're here for the night. Alright?'

Not wanting their parents to know they'd spent the night in the cells, Dan and Adey gave in to the blackmail and signed.

The following day, the coppers' work of fiction was read out in the Magistrates Court in Crown Square, and Dan and Adey were convicted of Behaviour Likely to Cause a Breach of the Peace and were each given a two-year Conditional Discharge.

***

Sunday morning, 8am, and Dan Brody, Tommy Coggins, Jez Reeves, Philbo, Rob Brierley, Graeme Stafford and Mick Henshaw piled out of Wigan Casino, struggling to deal with the vengeful daylight. They'd arrived 7 hours earlier in Mick's big, dark green Bedford van; one of those with the sliding front doors. He'd borrowed it from work. And now they climbed back into it for the trip home, a couple in the front, the rest scattered in the back, with various bits of discarded cardboard.

Mick shoved the key into the dashboard and turned. The starter motor whirred and whirred, but the engine wouldn't have it. He tried again, and again, and again. Whirr, silence. Whirr, silence. Whirr, swearing. They'd have to bump start it.

With Mick at the wheel, the rest climbed out and shoved the van up Station Road. The van picked up a bit of speed, Mick let out the clutch and the engine grunted begrudgingly into life. They all jumped back in and the van pulled away from the club.

After about half a mile the engine cut out and again refused to start. They got out and pushed again, and again it sparked into some form of life, and they jumped back in, hoping that would be *it* this time. Maybe it had warmed-up properly now. It sounded OK, reasonable – it would be fine, it would get them home. But after a few hundred yards it conked out again. And again. And this procedure went on mile after mile: a few hundred yards of the van running, followed by nearly as many with them shoving.

It broke down again in Hindley town centre. Mick rolled it into a car park and lifted the bonnet, and they all gazed in to see if there was any explanation for what was happening, or failing to happen, not that any of them had any grasp of how the black oily thing they were looking at did what it did, or how any fault it might have would make itself visible. A friendly policeman saw them. They saw him look. They hoped he wouldn't come over, but he did, and they all looked away or gazed at the floor, knowing what their amphetamine-addled pupils looked like. He asked if he could help. They told him they would manage and there was nothing he could do – thanks anyway – and he mercifully went away.

Once more they shoved. The stricken Bedford started again and it stopped again. All the way along the East Lancs Road it was the same: shove then ride, shove then ride. And then they were in Salford.

And after that thing with Eve and that other thing with Brenda and a few other things with a few other girls, Dan was back with Rita, who lived in Salford. The van limped up to

Rialto corner and they dropped Dan there, Mick still revving the engine in the hope of keeping it alive. And Dan wished them luck and gave the side of the ailing green beast a couple of slaps and snuck away round the corner towards Vincent Street, with a tinge of guilt, while the others alternately pushed and rode the rest of the way back to Dashley Dyke.

***

Seated in a corner of a bland Blackpool pub, fruit machine rolling and bleeping a few yards away, they drained their glasses. It was still early evening, still time for another pub or two before The Mecca opened.

'Wheatsheaf next, then?' suggested Tommy.

The rest – Chris and Mel Halliwell, Dave Podmore and Dan – agreed. 'Hmm. Yeah. Sure.'

'But I want to check out the seafront first. I fancy a bit of sea air,' added Dave.

'Fair enough.'

It had been a pleasant day when they'd gone into the pub. Now, as they stepped out, the sky was dark and threatening. At just gone seven on a May evening, there still ought to be some hours of daylight left, but this was climatic darkness, not night-time darkness. And as they set off down Talbot Road towards the prom, it got so dark so quickly that someone from a more superstitious age might have thought they'd riled the gods. Then, suddenly, the fearsome black clouds burst open, and they found themselves in a raging gale-force wind, complete with face-flaying downpour. The prom at the end of the road vanished into the grey void, and a biblical storm blasted in almost horizontally from the Irish Sea. None of them were dressed for this – no coats or even jackets. They were getting drenched.

They darted down the street, into the storm, looking for shelter. The shops were closed, but one had a doorway deep enough to provide a bit of cover. They dived in – all except Chris, who'd dawdled, looking in a shop window just before the storm broke, and was now forty yards behind. He sprinted to join the others in their makeshift shelter. But as he braked to turn in, his treacherous wedge-soled shoes went from under him and he flew past the entrance horizontally, legs splayed like a pair of open scissors, and splattered down on his rump on the filthy, saturated footpath and skidded to a halt. As he stood up, his beige baggies were black and sodden. A great dense stain covered the whole backside and the backs of the legs.

The storm subsided, and they made their way to The Wheatsheaf. Chris tried to wipe off the mess with green paper towels in the gents, but made little impression. Blackpool grime was evidently a permanent dye when applied to beige Trevira, and for one night only in 1975 the two-tone trouser was back in fashion at Blackpool Mecca.

***

A governor, in the gas industry, is a device that reduces and controls the pressure of gas at various stages on the distribution system. There's a little dinky one on top of your gas meter, there are giant, high-pressure ones on the national grid, and there are lots of district governors of various sizes dotted around towns and cities, which deliver gas into the mains that run up and down urban streets and roads. You have probably walked past one a million times without noticing, as they are usually housed in non-descript little buildings, like small lock-up garages. The maintenance of these devices, however, is an important and sensitive task, and the fitters who do the job are generally seen as a cut above ordinary gas fitters.

Dan was to spend a month apprenticed to governor fitter Lee Braithwaite, who covered the south Verrington area, which extended into rural Cheshire. On this particular morning, they travelled to Prestbridge in East Cheshire to carry out a scheduled inspection of the village's district governor.

Prestbridge was the sort of place where the big Mercedes was the little family runabout, next to the Bentley and/or the Ferrari, and where any mention of left-wing politics might result in the police being called and possibly a stint in a ducking stool, followed by stoning or burning at the stake.

Lee was twenty-five, had been a qualified governor fitter for seven years and was generally regarded as one of the most skilful and reliable in the depot. He was a smart, funny guy, who was full of stories and never seemed down about anything.

He was also the only male Dan knew who had had the nerve to have a perm – his dark brown hair had been turned into a Kevin Keegan poodle mop. Dan didn't necessarily like or envy the perm, but he admired Lee's ballsiness, as he walked every morning at 8am into the macho atmosphere of Verrington depot without giving a stuff about the stick and ironic wolf-whistles the others gave him.

It was a beautiful sunny spring day, already warming up even though it was still only 9am when they arrived on site. Lee parked the big orange North Western Gas Board Transit a short way from the governor building at the end of leafy Astley Drive, so as not to block the hammerhead turning area, and they walked the rest of the way.

Suddenly, the serenity was shattered by a small yapping terrier, which hurtled down a long sloping lawn towards them. Lee squatted down to greet the dog, which leapt into his arms like a long lost friend. The animal was closely followed by a shrieking, howling woman, who galloped down the garden in peach twinset and pearls as fast as her legs would carry her. Everything wobbled but her hair – an oversized blonde crash helmet, sculpted into waves evidently held rigid by huge quantities of hairspray. Lee stood up, smiling, still cradling the tiny dog. The woman squinted at Lee, with disgust and hatred in her eyes and, in the haughtiest tone she could muster spat 'you mast be jeauking,' and snatched the bewildered bowser from his grasp. She then turned and waddled urgently back up the perfectly-manicured lawn, shouting something about 'oiks' and hissing vague threats to report Lee and Dan for the act of profound evil they had just committed.

***

Saturday dinner time, and Dan and Tommy hopped onto the Victoria train at Dashley Dyke station. They'd got the number of a hippy in Salford who sold good, reliable acid: lettuce, a pound a tab. They mustered twenty quid from their own pockets and from friends who wanted in, made a deal on the blower, and were on their way to meet the guy in The Crown near Strangeways.

They'd have no trouble finding it, the hippy said. It was on Ducie Street, almost under the railway arches that led from the station. Ask for Vince.

And he was right. There it was, smack in the city centre, right on the Salford-Manchester border. And what a find it was. Unlike all the other blokes/beer/fags/fights pubs that typified Manchester city centre, this place was full of hippies and bikers, with a loud, rocking juke box and walls plastered with posters for rock acts and events. From the outside, it was just another bland, turn-of-the-century pub. On the inside, it was a proud piece of counter-culture – a bit of San Francisco dragged 5,000 miles and plonked on England's Route (A)56. It had been right under their noses, a couple of hundred yards from Victoria Station and only a few more from The Pendulum, but they'd never known about it till now.

They sat down with Vince and a couple of pints of bitter. Vince wore a tired-looking black suit jacket over an orange tie-dye T-shirt. He had long brown hair and his mouth was hidden somewhere beneath an abundant yellow-brown tash and beard. There wasn't that much of his face left to see.

'Twenty, then?' said Vince.

'Yep, twenty,' said Tommy. And Dan put two tenners on the table and tucked their corners under his pint pot to make sure they didn't blow away.

Vince reached into his pocket and pulled out a misshapen coil of something. He then pinched one end and unfurled what looked at first like a strip of lumpy sellotape. But as their eyes settled to it, it was two back-to-back strips of sellotape with, trapped neatly between them, a series of eighth-of-an-inch diameter green dots at one-inch intervals. More than anything, it looked like those strips of caps they'd had for their toy guns when they were kids.

'Twenty,' confirmed Vince, cheerfully, as he held the strip up to the light. He produced a pair of scissors from another pocket, counted the dots and snipped the tape just under the twentieth tab.

'There you go.' Vince handed over the strip and picked up the tenners. Dan and Tommy gazed lovingly at the green and translucent wonder, each little jade dot a moment of joy, beauty and ecstasy yet to be had. Dan carefully re-coiled it and prodded it into his jacket pocket.

Vince got up, shook hands and went off to do more business elsewhere. Dan and Tommy sank several more pints of bitter and enjoyed the atmosphere of the pub. Sure, the jukebox wasn't the greatest from a soul boy's perspective, but it was loud and it was more rock than pop: Eric Clapton and Cozy Powell and Golden Earring and such, which was considerably better than you'd normally get in town on a Saturday afternoon – no Osmonds or Rubettes or "Y Viva"-fucking-"Espana". And later in the afternoon they made their way back to Victoria for the train ride home, very satisfied with the pub and the drugs and the day's business overall. And they planned their first dip into the acid that night and talked about how funny it was that you could buy Class A drugs right there, almost within touching distance of Strangeways nick.

***

Tommy's little brother, Shaun, had watched Dan and Tommy's lives with envy. He'd seen them set off for The Torch and Blackpool Mecca and Wigan Casino and the rest and having all that delectable gear, while being told he was too young to join in. Now, at fifteen going on sixteen, he felt he had a case. Dan and many others on the scene had started younger than that, so in spite of wanting to look out for the little guy, it was hard to resist his arguments.

Shaun was like a young pup – all energy, curiosity and mischief, and with great enthusiasm for just about everything, but especially soul and United. Dan and Tommy, both in their late teens and having been at work for four years, felt like jaded old men by comparison. And Shaun wasn't that little any more – a thing made palpable by his ferocious sliding tackles when they played football in the park on Sundays.

Shaun loved the music, and as he and Tommy shared a bedroom and the same record player, it made no sense for there to be two record collections, so Tommy and Shaun both contributed to what was now their joint and ever more impressive haul.

And he wasn't as backward in coming forward as his older brother when it came to girls. Tommy's awkwardness around girls was well known, but Shaun knew what he wanted and he went for it.

If such things made him different from Tommy, other things made him visibly a younger adaptation of his older brother. They looked similar and both always carried a bit of excess weight – not because there was an overabundance of food in the Coggins house, but because their diet relied substantially on those heavy, calorific staples of the northern working-class diet: things like chips, white bread, fried eggs, fish fingers and pies. And if a meal wasn't big enough, they'd top-up afterwards with jam butties. Shaun also shared his brother's lack of dress sense, or maybe indifference to fashion. Both gave it a bash – they had to wear something after all, so it might as well be moderately fashionable – but the colours wouldn't work, or the fit would be wrong, or they'd get the naff 'Empire Made' version from Dashley Dyke market. But really, neither of them much cared about clothes and both gave Dan stick for his pernickety attention to his appearance.

And so it was that there was now a new addition to the group for the pub, the footy, the all-nighters and the gear. And soon friends from Shaun's class at the secondary modern, Eddie Froggatt and Marty Baldock, latched on and started going to these events with them.

Eddie and Marty seemed to go everywhere together, but they were very different in both appearance and character. Eddie was small, stocky and dark haired. Marty was tall, skinny and fair-haired – almost blond.

Eddie didn't say much, but when he did it was always marked by as much bluster and swearing as he could muster. His stories always seemed to concern some outrage that had been visited upon him, or which he'd seen or heard of, and he would eff and blind and go red with rage as he relived the affront. Eddie quickly absorbed himself into the northern soul scene. He got himself a black leather bomber jacket and baggies, and grew the obligatory, half-convincing tash, which, if you ignored the collar-length hair, made him look like some long-vanished soldier from a faded old First World War photo.

Marty was totally scatty and eccentric. He'd been adopted, but didn't know anything about his birth parents – or preferred to pretend he didn't – and liked to fantasise that his dad was an American GI who'd tubbed his mother while stationed in the UK. The fact that he was born in 1959, fourteen years after the War had ended and long after most American soldiers had gone home, did not impinge upon this belief. He self-identified as an American, even though he had seldom set foot outside of Dashley Dyke. Marty never really absorbed himself into the northern soul scene, though he came along to quite a few events. And he never adopted the fashions. His dress code was as eccentric and unpredictable as he was and generally involved bright, mismatched colours, and fashions from another time and place. He once showed up at Wigan Casino looking like something from the Flower Power era, in turquoise flares and a bright yellow roll-neck sweater. The fact that all the people around him were dancing in T-shirts and singlets because of the sweltering heat failed to register. Marty lived in a state of cognitive dissonance. He liked American movies but couldn't separate actors from the roles they played. The fact that Al Pacino and Robert De Niro were artists – performers, expert at simulating events they had no personal experience of, and were not really the sort of people who gunned down their enemies or tortured them to death – would not take hold in Marty's mind. He talked about them as though they really were gangsters, whose lifestyles he wanted to emulate. Clint Eastwood really was a psychopathic 1880s cowboy, except when he was a psychopathic 1970s cop. And when the group Barnaby Bye, who had a northern soul hit with "Can't Live This Way" turned out to be the Alessi Brothers, who at the same time had a pop-chart hit with "Oh Lori", he speculated that another northern soul hit, "Right On" by Al De Lory, must also be by the same people: a performer with Lory in his name had to be the same person/people who made a song with the word Lori in it. And there was that time when they were playing footy, when he'd intercepted an attack and got the ball off his opponent on the edge of the penalty area, but, finding himself in such a perfect location for a pop at goal, couldn't resist firing a low, hard shot past his own flailing, bewildered goalkeeper.

It was fair to say that the addition of Shaun, Eddie and Marty enriched Tommy and Dan's social group, but also brought new challenges.

***

With the football season over, there was nothing for it on a Saturday afternoon but to go out and quaff some ale, and Tommy, Shaun, Dan, Mick Henshaw, Dave Podmore and the Halliwell brothers were in the venerable, half-timbered Shakespeare pub on Fountain Street in Manchester, knocking back pints of bitter.

The conversation turned to what you have to do to deal with Sundays after an all-nighter, and Tommy related a tale: Tommy, Shaun, Dan, Mick Henshaw and Eddie Froggatt had gone to Stanniforth Park in Dashton on a Sunday after Wigan Casino. It was a sunny day and it was OK for a while lying on the grass, but then they got a bit unsettled – too many kids, too much racket, people chucking things about – and they strolled out of the top of the park, past the boating lake, up to Paddock Dam. Paddock Dam was a small, unmaintained, loosely circular body of water, too big to call a pond, too small to call a lake. It was fed by a small stream that wound down from the Pennines, and it in turn fed the boating lake, a couple of hundred yards away. Blokes fished in it, more for its relative tranquillity than for the hope of catching anything particularly interesting. On this particular day the water had been very low, what with it being the height of summer. The depth increased only very gradually from the muddy bank and it was no more than eighteen inches deep even at the deepest part in the middle. But it was hot, and Mick was determined to dive in and cool off.

There was something stolid about Mick. He was kind of average height, like the rest of them, with centre-parted dark brown hair and the near-obligatory tash, but he was quite heavily built, muscular, and there was something odd about his teeth, a certain unevenness when he grinned. He was also a very determined character, which probably explained why he'd managed to pass his test and get a set of wheels long before most of the others, who saw that as something they would not be able to afford for years.

Y'can't dive in, Tommy told Mick, it's far too shallow. But Mick was having none of it. He'd been school champion diver, nearly, and he knew how to dive in at a shallow angle to deal with shallow water. You'll hit the bottom, maintained Tommy. No I won't, insisted Mick, and he stripped down to his striped purple underpants and carefully shaped his posture for a suitably shallow dive. I'll bet you a quid you hit the bottom, said Tommy. Right, you're on, replied Mick.

Mick made further fine adjustments to his posture, gazed thoughtfully ahead, envisaging the perfect low dive, and then threw himself headlong into the dark brown Pennine water. Great clouds of mud billowed up around him and there was just enough water to close around his pasty white back. And then he stood up. And there were mud and grazes on his face, down his nose and all over his reddening torso. Tommy and the rest were doubled-up with laughter, and Mick, trying to maintain some sense of dignity said, I didn't hit the bottom – I know I should have, but I didn't. And the laughter grew even louder, and Tommy didn't get his quid.

And they laughed about it again in the Shakespeare and had a couple more pints. Then someone said they should pop into Rowntrees Spring Gardens. It was only round the corner and they played some soul in there now and then.

They piled out of the door onto Fountain Street. After several pints in a dark, dingy tap room, the daylight came as quite a shock, and Mick, somewhat distracted, turned and walked full-tilt into a lamppost and shuddered back, reeling from the impact.

'It didn't hurt. I know it should have, but it didn't,' said Mick, in all seriousness, while the others fell about laughing in the street.

***

A red Datsun Cherry, with Charlie Broadhead at the wheel and the Halliwell twins and Dan Brody in the passenger seats, approached Blackpool Prom from a side street in the shadow of the famous tower. The four were going to Blackpool Mecca, but it was early so a bit of a tour around town was in order.

What you met when you approached Blackpool Prom from a side street was at first identical to what you would encounter on meeting any other main road from a side street: first there was a footpath, then a main two-way carriageway, then the far footpath. But this being Blackpool, things went further, and beyond the far footpath were, first, the tramlines, then beyond them, the big main promenade footpath, which was then finally separated from the beach by the sea wall and Victorian wrought-iron railings.

And for most people, a right turn was a pretty straightforward thing. You waited in the side street for a gap both ways, then drove out to the centre of the carriageway and made your right turn. But Charlie Broadhead was no ordinary driver, and as he approached the prom he saw the layout differently and acted accordingly.

Things started well enough. He positioned the car near the middle of the side street and waited for a gap. Then there was one, and he pulled out. But instead of turning right onto the far side of the carriageway, he kept on going. Having evidently seen the far footpath as the centre of a dual carriageway and the tramlines as the other half of the road, he drove over the footpath and turned right onto the tramlines.

The Datsun bumped along the tracks in a Fleetwood direction. About two hundred yards away, a St. Annes-bound tram was heading straight towards them. There was panic and yelling from Charlie's passengers: 'Aaaagh! Woah! Charlie! What the fuck?! What are you doing? Charlie, Charlie, for fuck's sake! Look out!' But Charlie was bewildered and couldn't work out what it was he'd done wrong.

'Charlie, we're on the tramlines, the fucking tramlines!' yelled Chris.

'What? What'jer mean? Oh.'

'Look, there's a fucking tram coming!'

At this Charlie wrenched the steering wheel sharply to the left and pulled the Datsun onto the prom. People, prams and walking frames scattered in all directions. Yelling and driving advice came loudly and in great abundance from both inside and outside the car.

'We're on the prom, now, the fucking prom! Look out! Kids! Watch that dog!'

But Charlie was even more confused. He'd got off the tramlines. What more did they want?

He pulled even further to the left, so the sea wall and its painted iron railings skimmed the left side of the car. More terrified pedestrians leapt for cover.

'Waah! Fuckin' 'ell, Charlie! What are yer doing?!'

'I can't get any further over,' pleaded Charlie.

'You need to be back over there!' yelled Chris, pointing a diagonal finger in front of Charlie's nose. 'Over there.'

'You didn't want me to be over there. Tramlines, you said.'

'No, not the tramlines! Past the tramlines! The road! The fucking road! What have you got against driving on the road?!'

Finally, they made Charlie see where he was in relation to where he ought to be and he swung right, rumbled over the tramlines and made it safely back onto the road, and red-faced, fist-shaking, V-sign-wielding holidaymakers vanished in the rear-view mirror.

***

Dan, Tommy and Shaun were sat with Black in Dashley Dyke Labour Club (East Ward), having a dinnertime pint.

Dan never knew why Black was called Black. He wasn't black, though his hair was and he was fond of a bit of black in a spliff. Maybe that was it. And he could bullshit for England.

The jukebox vomited up Daniel Boone's "Beautiful Sunday" and the busy, booze-mellowed room swayed side-to-side and sang along with the monosyllabic bits:

'Hey, Hey, Hey,'

'Haah, Haah, Haah,'

'Maah, Maah, Maah.'

Tommy winced. Dan pictured himself wringing out his brain and beating it to death on the table. And Black told the amazing tale of what had happened the night before.

He was still shocked and reeling even now, he reckoned. He'd been walking home, late on, after a few too many sherbets in The White Hart, and he staggered out onto the zebra crossing at Johnson's Cross at the wrong moment, and an Austin 1100 screeched to a halt. And in his shock and confusion, Black fell down in front of the car. And the driver got out to see if he was OK. And they'd never guess who it was...

Elton John!

***

Tommy, Dan, Shaun and Eddie were tripping on Leaches Moor, enjoying the soft grass, the views over the town, the warm sunshine and the assorted flowery smells that drifted around them and into their nostrils. The conversation turned to music, and Dan told the others how wonderful the soundtrack to *A Clockwork Orange* was. No-one else had got a copy or even heard it, so they all decided they needed to go and listen to it at Dan's.

They traipsed down the winding path from the moor and up High Street to Dan's place on Bessemer Street. Tripping was not a state in which you would want a conversation with your parents, so Dan just shouted quickly through the living room door 'we're just gonna play some records,' and they climbed the stairs to the room Dan shared with Nicky.

Dan switched on the Rotel amp, extracted the LP from the shelf and placed it carefully on the turntable. They listened attentively to side one. He flipped the disc and they listened equally attentively to side two. At the end he asked what they all thought of it. There were positive, approving noises all round. Dan, however, felt there was something wrong. While acknowledging to himself that acid changed perceptions of everything, including time, the music did seem a bit more strident than it normally did, and it all seemed to be over more quickly than usual. And then he looked at the turntable again and saw that it was switched to 45 rpm, not 33. No-one had noticed.

The ramifications of explaining this now seemed too daunting. He'd reveal it at some later date. And they all set off back for the moor to continue their trip.

***

United were away at Stoke City. Tommy, Shaun, Eddie, Dan and Mick Henshaw had travelled down the M6 in Mick's dark maroon Austin 1800 to watch the match. There had been a hiccup on the way. Not knowing the area, apart from single-purpose late-night train trips to The Torch, they'd pulled up near an impressive looking stadium, found it curiously deserted for a Saturday afternoon, then driven away realising they'd almost gone to see Port Vale reserves.

They finally found the right place and were stood on the terrace at Stoke City, reading their programmes, waiting for kick-off. The place was filling up. The latest chart hits chirped from the tinny PA system. A few lukewarm chants broke out here and there and quickly dissipated.

Many football grounds had a 'popular end', and it was in Stoke City's popular end that the five friends now stood. The popularity of popular ends was a dubious thing. No doubt they got that name because they were the cheapest standing space in the ground, being open, unroofed terraces, but they could be very unpopular when it rained, and given that football is an autumn/winter/spring sport, this was not an uncommon thing. No doubt, for this reason, the popular end was normally allocated to the away fans, because their discomfort was of no concern to the home club. Indeed, if they got cold and wet and fed up, they were more likely to be subdued, and the home fans could more easily out-shout them. Plus, a roof amplified the noise and directed it forcefully at the players; the absence of a roof meant that the sound would drift off more readily into the ether and would make fans' enthusiasm seem feeble and half-hearted, and this might make the away team feel not so well supported and maybe they would lose a little vigour and passion as a result. Stoke's popular end was even more crude than most, in that the slope behind the terrace was made of nothing more than a huge pile of old clinker, no doubt from the furnaces that were once a major part of industry in the area.

Suddenly and seemingly from nowhere, a copper barged through the crowd, got hold of Eddie by the collar of his bomber jacket and yelled in his face:

'I've warned you – shut it.'

Eddie was bewildered. He'd done no more than stand on the terrace in silence reading this week's team news and manager's message.

'Whaddaya talkin' about? I'm just stood here. I haven't done anything.'

'I'm telling yer. That's yer last warning.'

'But… I don't get it. I'm just stood here.'

'Right. That's it. I've had enough. I warned you,' barked the pissy policeman, wagging the forefinger of his free hand in Eddie's face. And he dragged Eddie though the crowd up to the top of the terrace. Dan and Tommy followed and tried to argue with the copper that Eddie hadn't done anything, to which he replied if they didn't shut it he'd nick them too.

As they emerged from the throng onto the narrow path at the top of the terrace, the officer lost his footing and his grip on Eddie's collar and surfed down twenty feet of rusty old clinker in a murky cloud of brown dust. Eddie stood and watched him vanish down the slope and seemed for one strange moment to be waiting for the guy to come back up and arrest him again.

'What are yer waitin' for, yer fuckin' idiot. Run!' yelled Tommy. And the three slalomed quickly back though the crowd and vanished into the numbers.

Talking about the incident on the way home, they concluded that probably the police had quotas and that successful policing of such an event was demonstrated by achieving a certain number of arrests. It didn't matter whether you'd done anything. The police could fill that in later.

***

Dan arrived home Sunday mid-morning. Hungover and hungry, he headed straight for the kitchen, where he found Lily standing over the grumbling twin-tub, prodding steamy flollopping clothes with a giant pair of wooden tweezers.

She regarded him contemptuously. 'Where've you been till now?'

'Erm, we had a few in The Bay Horse, then went off to Coffers.'

'Coffers closes at two. It's quarter to eleven. Where've you been since then?'

'Well, I got invited to a party at Gill Bradley's, if you must know, not that I have to explain meself to you.'

'No? Look at the state of yer. You're bog-eyed, your hair's all over the place and there's lipstick on your face and make-up on your jacket. You're a tart. You're a bloody disgrace. You're just like your father. And you've got Rita coming round later, poor lass. I don't know how she puts up with yer.' Lily glanced at the wall as if looking for inspiration, took a deep breath, and continued: 'Anyway... I've got news... I'm leaving. I'm moving out.'

'Oh aye. You've been leaving for as long as I've been alive.'

'Yeah, well, I'm really going this time. The house goes up for sale next week and when it goes through I'm off to Brighton and taking Nicky and Janet with me. We'll be staying with Auntie Pam and Uncle George till I get a place.'

'So, I'm not invited then?'

'You've got your own life. You're a grown man.'

'I'm 19.'

'Yeah, well, at 19, I was in the Land Army, hundreds of miles from home.'

'Aye, and that was all found, wasn't it: housemates, accommodation, meals, bills paid...'

'We got paid hardly anything. They worked yer like a slave, then took half of it back for food and board.'

'But still, you got somewhere to live, didn't yer? It was covered. What am I supposed to do? I'm on apprentice pay and I've got another 18 months to go. It's less than half a real wage. I can't live on me own on that.'

'Well, you'll just have to sort something out, that's all. You'll just have to stop all yer drinking and gallivanting.'

'What the hell's that supposed to mean? Even if I stopped doing *anything*, there still wouldn't be enough – a flat, bills, buses...'

'You could get a place with yer dad.'

'Jeezus! With 'im?! Bleedin' 'ell. The only reason we haven't killed each other is that we hardly ever see each other.' Dan paused, looked at the floor, then back at Lily. 'What if I wanna come?'

'You can't. It's all decided. And there's no room anyway. *And* you've got your apprenticeship to finish.'

'I'm sure the South Eastern Gas Board has apprentices too. But, that's not the point, is it? I've always been the outsider in this family. I was never gonna be invited.'

'If you're an outsider, it's your own doing. You're never here; you treat this place like a hotel.'

'I didn't when I was ten though, did I? It's always been the same. Janet and Nicky are your cosy little family. I don't know who I'm supposed to be.'

Lily returned her gaze to the twin-tub and shoved back under the scummy water some squirmy grey thing that had come up for air. 'Well, like I said, you'll just have to sort something out, that's all.'

***

At work, as part of his continuing apprenticeship, Dan had been placed with Ken Gilson, a distribution supervisor. Ken oversaw the work of pipe-laying gangs, each comprising two or three blokes, whose job it was to dig trenches and install gas mains in central and west Verrington. Ken's task was to give the teams plans, showing what needed to go where, and to order materials, monitor progress, and work out how to overcome problems, like, for example, there being a gigantic water main in the path of the proposed gas main. Dan's brief was to learn as much as possible from Ken, as this might be the kind of job assigned to him once he completed his apprenticeship.

Ken had six such gangs to supervise, and his managers worked out that he and his fellow distribution supervisors should each be able to get round three gangs in the morning and three in the afternoon. In reality, Ken was usually able to get round all six in a morning, leaving the afternoon free for things he'd rather do. And there were two of these things: going to the pub and buying caravans.

Ken was quite a presence: a forty-odd year-old of heavy build, with a bulbous nose, a ruddy complexion that still carried vestiges of adolescent acne, and naturally frizzy hair, which when it got beyond a certain length looked like a brown afro. He might have borne a passing resemblance to Angela Davis, were it not for the fact that his hair was brown and he was white, male, rotund, and bearded, and had a face that only a mother could love. Some in the Gas Board's Verrington offices found Ken a bit intimidating, and it was true that he could get pretty pushy when he wanted his own way, but he and Dan got on very well and revelled in each other's funny stories.

By twelve noon, Ken was usually to be found in The Three Crowns in Verrington, eating pies and drinking Boddies' Bitter, while thumbing through the day's freshly-minted Manchester Evening News, looking for second-hand caravans at bargain prices. If he found something promising, he'd ring from the pub call box, negotiate a deal, then head over to whatever part of Greater Manchester the caravan was in and tow it back with his gas van – which conveniently had a towing hitch, as most of them did – before tarting it up and selling it on for a profit. Dan went along on a couple of these jaunts: one to a place on the outskirts of Warrington, the other in Bolton, then back to Ken's modern detached house on one of the new, hill-side estates between Dashley Dyke and Crossley, to drop off the caravan.

If there was nothing worth buying, or if someone else had got there first – buying and selling caravans was a competitive business – Ken would carrying on drinking for another couple of hours then wobble back into the office late afternoon to deal with his paperwork.

Dan, assigned to Ken for a four-week period, would join in with the practice. Not that he minded: Dan wasn't much interested in caravans, but he liked pubs and he liked beer, and both were far more interesting than looking into a muddy hole with a cast iron pipe in it. And the pies in The Three Crowns were stupendous.

If it was a long stint in the pub, Dan, being on apprentice pay, soon ran out of money, but Ken, glad of the witty, uncritical company, happily plied Dan with further pints long after his pockets were empty. And Dan, after six pints of Boddies' Bitter and two pies (one steak and kidney, one meat and potato – he believed in a balanced diet), also wobbled back into the office, where he quietly cursed the piercing fluorescent light, battled to keep his eyes open and tried not to breathe on anyone.

***

It was twenty past eight on a Sunday morning at Wigan Casino. The music had stopped, numbers had thinned, daylight and cold air crept in from the open doors. A few stragglers stood around and chatted on the dancefloor. Dan stood waiting for Tommy, who'd gone for a final neurotic pee before the trip home. Chris Halliwell appeared. Dan hadn't come with him and in the great throng of the all-nighter hadn't seen him till now.

'Any chance of getting a lift back with you, Dan? I came on the train and it's a pain in the ass,' asked Chris.

'I dunno. I'm with Mick Henshaw. Wait here. I'll ask him.'

Five minutes later, Dan was back.

'Sorry. No. Mick's already overloaded. There's six of us going back in his car. Hang on though. I've just seen Al Waterhouse. I'll ask him.'

Al cut an unusual figure in a northern soul club. He wasn't speed-freak thin like most of the others. Not that he was an abstainer: he loved his gear as much as the next guy, but somehow this failed to impact on his portly frame. Nor did he comply with the routine all-nighter fashion of baggy kecks and tight T-shirt. With his curly hair, tweed jacket and fawn slacks, he looked more like a country gent out on a grouse shoot than a soul boy.

'Al, I've got a mate who needs a lift back. Any chance?'

'I dunno. I've got a few on board. Who is it?'

'Chris Halliwell. Comes from Withington.'

'I don't know the guy.'

'He's alright. Decent bloke.'

Al scrunched his face and shrugged. It wasn't looking promising. Dan cranked up the persuasion.

'Come on. He's no trouble. Doesn't even touch gear – he's straight.'

'Straight?! Then he can definitely fuck off. I'm not having anyone straight in my car.'

And that was Al's last word on the subject, and he turned and strolled off towards the exit.

And that was the last time Dan saw Al alive. Two weeks later the news reached Buffy's that he was dead. Accidental barbiturate overdose, they reckoned – *easily done with that Tuinal.*

***

Dan arrived at The Bull in Bradfield. He glanced into the busy best room, looking for Jez and Philbo. It had dark wood furniture, red wallpaper and a thick, squishy carpet, all bathed in subtle low lighting, signifying 'luxury' – a place where a chap could take his missus on a Saturday night. They weren't there. The tap room, in contrast, was starkly bright under harsh fluorescent tubes, with a scrubbed wooden floor, a hotchpotch of no-nonsense kitchen-style tables and chairs, and plain emulsioned walls, which would have been white were it not for the decades of nicotine that coloured them a browny yellow. Each table had a low aluminium ash tray, with 'Senior Service' or 'Park Drive' in raised letters on the side, which was rapidly filled by the punters and emptied at regular intervals by the glass collectors. The room was packed with heavy-drinking men and a couple of loud, sozzled women, who veered between the bar and the tables and periodically flopped onto the lap of one of the men. Layers of grey smoke hung in the air, and the noise was deafening. Three lads with *Top of the Pops* hairdos, best jackets and flares, and wide, half-fastened ties mucked about and played darts at the other end of the room, no doubt getting tanked-up ready for Coffers disco after closing time. The bit of music that bled through from the jukebox in the best room was emphatically drowned out by voices, which increased in volume exponentially as each person fought to be heard over his neighbour and because, as the drink took hold, it was necessary to relate all anecdotes with ever greater passion, vehemence and outrage. The beer was 2p a pint cheaper in the tap room. Or rather, it was 2p a pint dearer in the best room, to pay for all that luxury.

Dan struggled at first to find Jez and Philbo, what with the crowd and the noise and the smoke. But then, there they were, hemmed tightly into a corner of the tap room, with their pints on a small round table.

The rushed-off-her feet barmaid, with beads of sweat on her forehead, served Dan a foaming pint of Boddies' Bitter, and he squeezed in next to Jez and Philbo.

'Got the gear?' asked Dan, all wide-eyed and enthusiastic and looking forward to a big night out at Wigan Casino.

'Yeah. Got the money?' replied Jez, coolly.

Dan rummaged.

'Don't give it me 'ere. Wait till we're in the car.'

'OK.' Dan shoved the notes back into his pocket.

'Terry should be here in about twenty minutes,' explained Jez.

'Great stuff! A three-litre Capri then, eh? Our Clive had the two-litre. I didn't know they made them bigger than that.'

'They do,' proffered Philbo. 'They're pretty rare, though. Goes like shit off a chrome shovel.'

'Woo-hoo! Can't wait!'

Terry arrived. Grins and handshakes all round.

'Having a pint then, Terry?' Asked Jez.

'No. Let's get moving. I'm keen to get off. It's nearly closing anyway.'

Parked outside was the metallic bronze Ford Capri, still glinting and gorgeous, even under street light, and with that tell-tale extra bump on the long bonnet that marked it out as a three-litre. Dan and Philbo climbed into the back, Jez and Terry into the front, and they roared off down Corporation Road, first to Dashton, then onto the wide main drag into Manchester, then up through Salford via Regent Road.

Dan reflected on the strangeness of going to Wigan Casino with Terry Wardle. Terry had been a bouncer at Mars when Dan was only fifteen. Big, lanky Terry – he'd seemed like a man, an adult, someone older and more sensible. And here he was necking speed and all-nightering like a teenager. Mind you, he'd probably only been in his late teens back in the Mars days

– his size had got him the job – and was probably only 22 or 23 now. Age difference seemed to matter less as you got older.

They stopped at traffic lights on the East Lancs Road. A red Hillman Avenger pulled up alongside.

'Looks like he wants a race,' said Philbo.

11.30 on a Saturday night – the road ahead was dark, empty and derestricted.

The lights changed, Terry's foot hit the floor, and the Ford took off like a tracer bullet. Exhilarating force sucked the four soul fiends back into their seats. The dial moved up – forty, fifty, sixty... It breezed past eighty and continued to climb. Whoops and yelps of delight met the roar of the engine and filled the car. Ninety, a hundred... The Hillman was nowhere to be seen.

***

It was Wednesday evening, and United were away at Derby County. Mick Henshaw picked up Tommy Coggins, Dan Brody and Graeme Stafford in his big, comfy Austin, took a whip-around for petrol and loaded up with fuel at Charles Street service station. The light was already fading as they made their way down the winding, rocky Derbyshire stretch of the A6.

As they pulled up on a side street half a mile from the ground, Mick looked at the dashboard with a puzzled expression on his face.

'Bloody hell. We've used a lot of fuel. I don't get it. I put in easily enough to get us here and back. Anyway, we'll worry about it later. Let's get to the match.' And with that they set off on foot to the stadium.

With only a few minutes left to play, the game seemed to be fizzling out to a one-all draw. But then United's goalie, Alex Stepney, bowled the ball out inexplicably to the feet of Charlie George, who gleeful smashed it back past his head into the net. And that was how it ended: from a creditable away draw, United had slipped to a 2-1 defeat. The Derby fans were ecstatic; the United fans were livid.

With the match over, fans tumbled out of the gates into the red-brick terraced streets. The houses were of the kind that had a low wall and tiny, tokenistic five-foot strip of garden to separate the frontage from the footpath. The police syphoned the away tribe out into a chosen side street to keep them from the Derby fans, who were ushered down a second, parallel street. But the police plan was flawed, because a few hundred yards away there was another street that ran across at ninety degrees and linked the two. The United fans ran down their allotted street, turned right and right again, and there was the wall of Derby fans, marching towards them. The outraged Mancunians screamed like banshees and sprinted towards the unconcerned midlanders, who, in the dark, seemed not to have grasped what was happening. Dan and Tommy were in the front line, with the joy of battle coursing through their veins. But then Dan looked to his right and there was no-one there, and to his left, where there was only Tommy. And he looked round, and his fellow warriors had all fallen away and were heading back towards the rest of the United fans at the far end of the street. Hemmed in on a seamless terraced street, with no escape route, it was just Dan and Tommy against twenty thousand Derby County fans.

Dan yelled 'TOMMY!' and dived for cover over a low brick wall into a little front garden, much to the bewilderment of the man and lady of the house, who were stood on their doorstep, keeping an eye on their property until the mob moved on – they looked at him momentarily and said nothing. But Dan's warning was too late – Tommy was at full tilt and only a split second from the leading edge of the Derby crowd as Dan shouted, and couldn't have heard him anyway over the joyful chanting, and he launched himself at some random body at the front of the Derby line and vanished into the implacable, unstoppable mass. Dan waited to be spotted by the Derby fans or to be grassed-up by his impromptu hosts, and steeled himself for the inevitable kicking, but it didn't come. The horde just trudged slowly forward and no-one even noticed him. He got up, stuffed his red-and-white scarf down his jumper, slipped into the crowd and tried to remember where they'd left the car.

Mick and Graeme were already there. Tommy arrived a couple of minutes later.

'Are you OK?' said Dan.

'Yeah, I'm fine. Feel like shit, though.'

'Why, wassup?'

'I kicked a girl. I kicked a fucking *girl*. Not on purpose. There were hundreds of people – just a mass of bodies, and I just leapt in and kicked some random person. And when I looked, it was girl – about thirteen at a guess. I've got me fuckin' steel toe-capped boots on an' all. I gave her a right crack in the shin. I'm a cunt. I feel terrible.'

'Oh, shit. So what happened?'

'Nothing. I was just swallowed up in the crowd and that was it. I got swept along and followed them back here.'

Mick started the engine and again looked with great seriousness at the fuel gauge. 'Sorry about this, lads, but there should have easily been enough to get us home, but there's not. It's nearly empty. I don't get it. I'm gonna need more money.'

They emptied their pockets and handed the proceeds to Mick, who turned in at the first service station and topped up the tank.

After a few more miles, he sounded desperate: 'it's going down again. We're not gonna get home. Has anybody got any more money?'

'No, I'm out,' said Dan, and so did Graeme and Tommy.

'Then we're fucked. I don't know what we're gonna do.'

'We'll have to mug somebody,' said Dan. 'I mean, it's not something I'd normally suggest, but what choice have we got?'

Tommy concurred, Mick reluctantly agreed. Graeme said nothing.

They cruised along a dark empty stretch of road, looking for a victim. A bloke of about their age appeared, walking down the footpath towards them on the passenger side.

'Right, Mick – he'll do,' said Tommy.

The car slowed, Dan and Tommy grabbed the door handles. 'Wait,' said Graeme, 'I've got another quid.' There were sighs of relief, as well as irritation that Graeme had not owned up sooner. Mick put his foot down, the Austin picked up speed, and the innocent passer-by was left unmugged.

'This should be enough,' said Mick, as he got out at another petrol station and fed the whole quid's worth into the tank.

But as they zoomed back up through the blackened limestone villages of central and northern Derbyshire, the dial plummeted again, and they only just made it back to Dashley Dyke, with the needle firmly at zero and the engine running on vapours.

The following night, Mick rang Dan. 'You know what it was? I had the choke out all the way, all the fucking way. Didn't notice. Didn't occur to me.'

***

A sunny Sunday afternoon – perfect weather for a trip in the park. Dan called round for Tommy and Shaun. In their bedroom, Tommy picked up the Airball air freshener from the mantelpiece, dismantled it and extracted a coil of Selloptape containing the acid: a tab each of lettuce. They sat on the beds and peeled apart the tape and swallowed the tiny green pills, then put on a few soul sounds and waited for something to happen.

The Coggins's house was a flat-fronted, red-brick Victorian terraced on Sheffield Road, and Tommy and Shaun's bedroom was at the front. It had two tall, narrow windows, which lined up loosely with their two beds, and an old cast iron fireplace, which was never used for its intended purpose – the grate stood in as a makeshift litter bin. Mrs Coggins and Grandma shared the second bedroom, and Wendy had the box room at the back. All that separated the front wall of the house from the road was six feet of footpath. Tommy and Shaun's room had net curtains, otherwise folk sitting on the upper deck of the bus as it queued for the traffic lights, fifty yards further down the hill, would have been able to gaze straight in. And the whole house shuddered when the great, heavy quarry trucks bringing limestone and sandstone down from the Pennines thundered by, or battled, brakes squealing, to come to a halt at the lights.

Tommy had a music centre – cassette player, radio, turntable and amplifier, all in one impressive-looking imitation-teak-veneered box, with knobs and dials and a smoky grey Perspex lid – made by Sharp. You could record straight from records onto cassettes without putting a microphone in front of the speakers and having to shout 'shurrup I'm recording' whenever someone barged into the room. He'd got it on HP from Currys. He dropped the needle on "I've Got Something Good" by Sam and Kitty, then "Time's a Wasting" by the Fuller Bothers, then "Just Ask Me" by Lenis Guess...

Dan noticed that the edge of the wardrobe had started to twitch, and overall it seemed to have developed slightly bendy characteristics, which it didn't have earlier. 'I'm starting to feel it,' he said, 'are you getting owt?'

Tommy and Shaun were still contemplating their replies when there was a rumble of feet on the stairs.

'Oh shit! That's our Wendy. Dinner'll be ready. Dan, think up some excuse, some story,' said Tommy, flapping his arms like an overweight penguin.

Tommy flung open the bedroom door just as Wendy arrived at the other side, and without a word, he and Shaun shoved urgently past her and out of the doorway. Wendy's irritated, curious gaze followed them down the stairs, then turned to Dan, whose attention was split between her and that capricious wardrobe, which he could see behaving irresponsibly in the corner of his eye.

'We're tripping,' said Dan, and before Wendy had time to assimilate what she'd just heard and respond, he also shoved past her and followed the other two down the stairs.

He caught up with Tommy and Shaun directly outside the front door on Sheffield Road.

'What story did you tell her, then?' asked Tommy.

'I said "we're tripping".'

'Bloody hell! Is that the best you could do?'

'I thought it was rather good.'

They set off up the hill towards the park in the lovely afternoon sunshine, past the sweet shop, where they sold Vimto lollies and nut brittle, past Murphy's TV repair shop, where they repaired your telly but it broke down again a week later, and past the takeaway where the world's most tolerant Chinese people put up with Dashley Dyke's drunks six nights a week.

They took the short cut through the mill yard, snuck into the park through the gap in the fence and lay down in the grass.

It was the greenest, most beautiful grass ever. Dan lay looking at it with his head on one side. The grass was higher than his eyes. He could see sunlight filtering through it and, above, the perfect blue sky. Time passed, then Dan lifted his head and, a dozen or so feet away, Tommy and Shaun did the same. They smirked at each other, then giggled. This peeping thing was a bit like in the cartoons. They stood up and decided to explore some other parts of the park.

As they rounded the steep hillock just above the kids' playing area, they came abruptly face-to-face with a young couple with a baby in a pram and a toddler. It was a shock. They stopped in their tracks. So did the couple. There was a moment of confusion and silence as the two groups faced each other.

Dan suddenly had the idea that he was Spock from *Star Trek* and that it was his job to take charge. He stepped forward and raised his right palm in what he felt was a proper, dignified, Spock-esque salute. He looked at the family, then turned slightly to address his friends and said: 'humans – ignore them.'

The three then diverted round the bemused couple and strolled on up the path, doubled-up, laughing.

Soul Stories Part 3: 1975-79

The removals truck vanished round the corner of Bessemer Street, closely followed by Uncle George's beige Marina. In the passenger seats were Dan's mum and little brother and sister, all heading off for a new life in Brighton.

Dan's dad, Walter, opened the boot of his dark green Vauxhall Victor. Dan chucked his suitcase in on top of Walter's, and the two set off on the short journey to The Silverdale Old People's Home in Bradfield, dropping off the house keys at the agents' en route. A bloke Walter worked with at the plastics factory had told his sister, Mrs Thwaites, who ran The Silverdale, about Dan and Walter's impending homelessness, and she had offered to give them a room for some indefinite period.

The Silverdale was a big old redbrick Victorian villa house, set in its own leafy grounds. When it was built a hundred years earlier as a private home for a wealthy mill owner, it was surrounded by verdant countryside. It was now pinned down on all sides by Bradfield's biggest council estate.

Mrs Thwaites was very kind and gave them both ham and mustard sandwiches, made with soft white bread, and showed them to a nice flowery room with two beds and an odd smell – sort of disinfectanty but with a slightly sour undertone. It was a nicer room than Dan had shared with Nicky back at Bessemer Street, but nevertheless Dan had a slight feeling of unease about the situation because when he asked Mrs Thwaites how much she wanted for board and keep, all she would say was not to worry about that for now, and Dan *was* worried because he didn't want to run up a big debt. Apprentice pay wouldn't keep a person in a flat, let alone B&B accommodation.

Dan's bed was comfy enough and that night he might have slept well, were it not for Walter snoring like the Queen Mary leaving Liverpool in a fog.

Dan went to work and college as usual, but there wasn't much to do back at The Silverdale in the evenings for a fidgety

19-year-old, unless it was your thing to sit around in the lounge with all the nans and granddads and watch the most mind-numbing pap imaginable on the telly, all at ear-splitting volume because everyone was deaf. So Dan would arrive back very late after the pubs had chucked out and everyone else had long since gone to bed. And the problem with that was that once everyone was tucked-up in their room for the night, Mrs Thwaites turned off every light in the building and left Keith, her Doberman, roaming free to guard the place, not that Dan ever understood why anyone would want to break into an old people's home. What would they nick – Zimmer frames, hearing aids, Velcro-fastening slippers? So each time Dan returned late at night, he would unlock the back door, step into total darkness and, with his back to the wall, feel his way to his and Walter's room with Keith, invisible in the blackness, growling and shadowing his every step. Then he'd get to the room and shut the door quickly around himself so the dog couldn't follow him in, though he privately nursed the wish that one day he might trap the fucker's head in it and give it a good kicking. And then he'd undress and realise he needed to expel a bit of beer before settling down, so again he would creep out and slide along the corridor to the bathroom with his back to the wall, menaced by the snarling beast all the way there and all the way back. And if he got taken short during the night, which after all that beer wasn't unusual, the process would be repeated again.

Dan was grateful to Mrs Thwaites for giving him and Walter somewhere to stay – it beat homelessness – but the place soon became unbearable. It wasn't just the terrifying night-time encounters with the demonic Doberman that were getting him down: an eye-watering stench of piss and disinfectant permeated the whole building, and someone died nearly every night. Some old geezer who'd been dribbling down his beige acrylic cardigan in front of *Coronation Street* on the communal telly in the evening was a heavy, ill-defined shape wrapped in a blanket being bumped down the stairs by a couple of dead-eyed porters at breakfast time. Dan watched each morning over his boiled egg and soldiers as the corpses were carried through the kitchen and out the back door.

Dan had accumulated a huge pile of washing. He had never done his own washing before and wasn't sure what to do, but Mrs Thwaites said he could use the giant commercial washing machine in the basement. It was pretty straightforward, she reckoned. So, one Saturday morning Dan opened up a shirt to use as a carrying sack, put everything in it, slung it over his shoulder and skulked off down to the musty cellar. A feeble yellowy lightbulb dangled from the ceiling and gave just enough light to see what he was doing, but not enough to see the walls, which vanished into gloom. He gazed at the big stainless steel cube. He'd never seen one like it. It was a front-loader; his mum's had been a twin-tub, with a fairly obvious A-to-B trajectory for the laundry. He opened the door and shoved all his stuff into it: white shirts, blue jeans, black socks, playfully colourful underpants and the rest, and weighed up the settings. He figured that 95 degrees C would be the one, because of the whiffy socks and skanky underpants. He then scrutinised the carton of Omo he'd bought. How much should he use? Well, it was a big batch, so it would probably need most of the box. He emptied the blue and white powder in on top of the clothes, pressed the 'on' button and took a seat across the room on an old, upturned milk crate. He felt that as this was his first effort it would be wise to stick around for a while and keep an eye on things.

The machine started up OK. It churned the clothes, then stopped for a rest, then did it some more. And then it stopped and did it again, and again. It wasn't making any funny noises, so Dan concluded this was normal for a front-loading washing machine. This must be what they do. It was probably heating the water up.

Then, after about fifteen minutes, foam started to appear from a little drawer at the top-left corner of the machine. It wasn't much, and Dan hoped that would be the end of the matter. Then the machine got into its stride. It was getting on with some serious washing now: no longer the stop-start stuff, things were really moving. But now the foam seemed to be coming from all corners of the thing – from the little drawer, from around the circular loading door and from underneath –

and spreading out along the floor in all directions. This couldn't be normal. He went up close and took a look. He couldn't see his clothes. Dense white foam completely lined the glass door. Maybe three-quarters of a large box of Omo was too much. But how were you supposed to take it out? How did you stop the thing when it was so vehemently into its stride and washing with such vigour?

The wash had been on for more than half an hour now, and the foam was coming out at an even more alarming rate. He had to do something. It was clear that what he needed to do was open the door to release the pressure. But it wouldn't open. He returned to his milk crate and thought. Maybe the foam would die down of its own accord. But it didn't; it continued to build and pour out. He pressed the off button on the fascia and tried the door again. Still it would not budge. He followed the lead and switched the machine off at the mains. That was probably a good thing to do anyway – *water and electrics and all that...* But the door remained steadfastly shut. He paced around in the foam on the sodden flagstone floor. Then he heard a click. He reached once more for the catch. The door flew open, and with great pent-up force, huge quantities of foam and steaming grey water swept out around his legs and across the room. As things settled he could pick out items of foam-covered clothing, like dead bodies washed up on a beach after a shipwreck, all of them grey – dark grey socks, light grey shirts, blue-grey jeans and murky grey underpants.

Dan didn't last much longer at The Silverdale. The night-time encounters with Keith and the morning ones with the daily crop of fresh corpses became too much. He kipped on a roll-up mattress in Adey's bedroom for a while and then on the Coggins's settee. And then Tommy and Shaun got a sun lounger and set it up in their bedroom for Dan.

Some months later, Walter told Dan that someone had died in his bed at The Silverdale the night before they moved in. He didn't dare tell him at the time. He also told him there was a rumour that the place was under investigation because people sent there seemed to die much more quickly than at other old people's homes in the area. And there'd been another circulating at the time they were there, that any old curmudgeon who crossed Mrs Thwaites would very quickly join the list of deceased.

***

It was Wednesday: getting-clean day, and Tommy, Shaun and Dan set off for Dashley Dyke baths for a good soapy shower and a swim.

A wall of warm, humid air and the familiar smell of chlorine greeted them as they arrived. They each collected a galvanised steel rack from old Ted at the hatch in the wall, put their clothes and towels in, memorised the number on the top and handed it back.

The shower was a twelve-foot square tray with a scratchy floor. A couple of rusty pipes passed overhead with a shower head here and there. The water temperature could be anything from freezing to super-heated steam – there was no knowing till you got in there, and it could change from one to the other suddenly and without warning. If it was at a reasonable temperature, it was wise to get the job done quickly, before it changed into something intolerable, though, for lads who never otherwise got to bathe or shower, it was also tempting to bask in it while you could.

They washed using odd-shaped slivers of brick-coloured soap picked up from the floor after previous users. Ted would monitor the soap situation, and when the fragments got too small, he'd saw off a fresh bit from the bar behind the hatch and chuck it into the tray, like feeding animals at the zoo.

After they'd thoroughly washed and rinsed, the three stepped into the pool area. As it was early evening, the place was almost empty: the daytime lot had gone; the serious evening swimmers had yet to arrive.

They swam a couple of lengths, then stood and chatted in the shallow end, caught up on gossip and made plans for scores and the weekend. It may have been a swimming baths, but swimming was incidental; it wasn't what they were really there for.

They got out, quoted their memorised numbers to Ted and collected their racks.

There were forty cubicles in the men's changing room: two rows of twenty, facing each other across a narrow tiled aisle, which had a gulley in the middle and occasional grids, so you could wring-out your trunks. The cubicles had no doors, so if there was someone in the one opposite, you had to tolerate each other's nudity – or perhaps enjoy it, if you were so inclined.

A cheeky kid of about ten or eleven took the cubicle opposite Shaun and started giving him lip about his pasty white body and flabby belly. Shaun took his sodden, heavy towel and flicked a perfect whip-shot across the aisle. There was a resounding crack, the kid yelped in pain and started to whimper, and Shaun, in his best *Dad's Army* Captain Mainwaring voice, said 'stupid boy.'

***

It was Saturday night at 64 Sheffield Road, and with Wendy, Mrs Coggins and Grandma having now gone to bed, Tommy, Shaun, Dan and Rick had the front room to themselves. They necked their tabs of acid and waited.

After half an hour things started to change. The room went from ordinary to magical – and potentially complicit, if they wanted it to be. The world at large was a different place.

They held deep, thoughtful, philosophical conversations that never quite came to a conclusion. They gazed at the grubby old 1950s Dashton-market curtains, which had a picture on them, repeated over and over again, of a stream, a little rustic bridge and a thatched cottage with a water wheel, and found them extraordinarily beautiful. They suspected that Marvin, the Coggin's ageing grey tabby, was in fact a spirit in possession of profound wisdom which he brought to bear whenever he looked at them but never shared, possibly because he didn't think they'd understand, though more probably because he couldn't talk. And in between they tried to make sense of the telly.

Rick was suddenly overwhelmed with feelings of hunger. The Chinese chippy was only a few doors away, and as it was only just after 11pm they'd still be open, serving folk who'd just spilled out of the pub. But in full dissociative mode, the last thing he wanted was a conversation with people from the real world. He came up with a solution: *fish*. He could just say that one word, that one syllable, and they would serve him a nice piece of freshly-fried, battered fish, and that would be great. No problems.

He stepped out of the Coggins's front door and turned towards the chippy. The smell of frying filled his nostrils. He *really* wanted that fish now. He longed for it. He anticipated it: his teeth breaking through that crispy batter, the rush of warm chip fat onto his tongue, the soft light texture of fish...

He joined the queue, which made a narrow U shape around the brightly lit chip shop. When he reached the bottom of the U and turned up the other side, he would be in front of the counter and it would be his turn, and all he had to do was say 'fish'. Not even 'please'. Just 'fish'. Manners were thin on the ground this late, post-pub, in Dashley Dyke. It wouldn't be out of place not to say 'please'. 'Fish' would do.

Fish, he kept saying to himself. *Fish*. It's all he had to say. One word: *fish*. Just *fish*.

And then it was his turn and there was the Chinese lady.

'Next please.'

'Fish.'

'Cod or haddock?'

'What?'

'Cod or haddock? You wan' cod or haddock?'

Rick felt a surge of panic. This wasn't going to plan. It had the makings of a conversation.

'I dunno. Just a fish. I just want a fish. Cod or 'addock? I dunno. I dunno. What's the diff'rence? Cod. No, 'addock. No, cod.'

'You wan' chi'?'

'What?'

'You wan' chi' with your fish?' She pointed at the chips in the range.

'No, just a fish.'

'Sore finger?'

'What?'

'Sore finger?'

'WHAT?!'

The sensible-looking middle-aged man behind Rick in the queue chipped in: 'salt and vinegar, she means. It's the accent.'

Rick turned back to the Chinese lady and tried to regain his composure, but as he looked at her, her face melted and reassembled itself several times over, which did nothing for his concentration. And the stainless steel range behind her was glowing in an unfeasible way, as if trying to communicate something to him. But what the hell was it doing, doing that when he'd got all this to cope with? There's a time and a place for everything.

'You wan' sore finger or noh?' snapped the Chinese lady, with growing exasperation.

'Salt and vinegar? Mmmm. Yes. No. I mean yes. No, just salt.'

'Wrapped up or to eat now?'

'Waaaaah! I just want a fish. Fish! FISH! I just want a fucking fish. I've been queuing here for ages. I JUST WANT A FUCKING FISH. I've got your money, look: your money.' He slammed coins on the counter. 'Just give me a fucking fish.'

***

Walter put his half of the house money together with a loan and got a tiny mid-terraced on Steggs Lane in Dashley Dyke. He thanked Mrs Thwaites and left The Silverdale Old People's Home. Dan moved out of Tommy and Shaun's place, and for the first time in six months had his own room and bed. Walter had a phone installed so he could keep in touch with the rest of the family in Brighton. The house didn't have a bathroom, but then neither did Tommy and Shaun's, so getting clean continued to comprise washing as far up and as far down as possible at the kitchen sink, plus the weekly trip to the baths.

Dan never could work out why people got sniffy about council houses. In Dashley Dyke it was the private stuff that was a nightmare. The house he grew up in on Widnes Street was supposed to have been knocked down as part of the council's slum clearance programme, but they changed their minds when the bulldozers were only two streets away – they'd run out of money or changed policy or something. Lily, who'd been looking forward to a nice pristine council semi, cried and almost had a nervous breakdown. When Dan was eight he'd gone for tea at a school friend's council flat and was amazed. It had a bathroom and an indoor toilet. In the kitchen it had a long row of smart, matching cabinets with everything you needed in them. It couldn't have been more different from their kitchen, which had a damp flagstone floor, a big chipped old sink that looked like it was meant for horses to drink from, a small mesh-fronted cupboard that was supposed to keep butter and milk fresh, but didn't, and rats. And best of all, the friend's flat had little vents that warm air came out of and kept the place all balmy and comfortable, even when it was really cold. In Dan's house you froze to death all winter and ice ferns coated the insides of the windows as well as the outsides. And then there'd been Auntie Pam and Uncle George's council house in Brighton, where they'd gone a couple of times for summer holidays when he was a kid. That was like paradise. It was a semi. He'd never been in a semi before. And it had two toilets – one upstairs, one down, so you were OK wherever you got took short – and a big grassy garden, with a vegetable patch and two cherry trees with a hammock slung between them. Cherries just dangled in the air above you, loads of them, and you could pick them and eat them on the spot, and no-one minded.

The phone rang. It was Tommy and Shaun in the call box on Sheffield Road. They'd got some gear. Was it OK to come round? It was. Walter was in the pub.

Tommy and Shaun walked in, looking very pleased with themselves.

'What have you got, then?' asked Dan.
'Amphet sulphate.'
'Right. Any good, is it?'
'Well, they reckon so. Haven't had any yet. Have yer got a spoon?'
'A spoon? You eat it with a spoon?'
'No, you div. You dissolve it in a spoon and inject it.'
'Inject it? Bloody hell. Really? Have you got a syringe?'
'Yep. We'll need some water.'

Dan went into the kitchen and came back with a dessert spoon and a mug of water, giddy with excitement.

'Is it clean,' asked Tommy.

'Course it's bloody clean. What do you take me for?'

Tommy peeled open a small silver package, revealing a flattened wodge of white powder, some of which he shook into the spoon. From a polythene bag, he produced a plastic syringe and a little tubular plastic cap that contained a needle. He fixed the needle onto the end of the syringe and drew water up into it from the mug. He squirted the water into the spoon. The powder dissolved almost immediately, but Tommy gave it a stir with the end of the needle for good measure.

Tommy looked at Dan: 'first hit then?'

'Bloody hell, yeah... if you guys don't mind?'

'Right, we need a tourniquet.'

Dan trotted upstairs and came down with his old school tie. He rolled up his right sleeve, wrapped the tie around his bicep tightened it. The vein in the crook of his arm swelled.

Tommy pulled up the mixture from the spoon into the syringe, then held it up to the light and squeezed the plunger to expel the air. He then flicked it like a nurse on the telly and gave it another little squeeze to get any final air bubbles out.

'You know what you're doing, then?' asked Dan, betraying a tinge of doubt and nervousness.

'Yeah. Rick showed me. You've got to get rid of the air bubbles. They'll kill yer... Anyway, prepare yerself for the rush of a lifetime. Rick calls it a "wap", cos that's what it feels like when it hits the top of your head.'

'Woo-hoo!'

Satisfied that everything was ready and in order, Tommy levelled the hypodermic at Dan's arm. The needle went in softly. Tommy pulled back the plunger, a bolt of dark red blood shot into the plastic tube.

'We're in. Are you ready?'

Dan slackened the tourniquet. 'Oh yeah.'

Tommy emptied the syringe steadily into Dan's arm.

In an instant Dan was rolling around on his back on the settee, gasping with delight. 'Fuck! Fuck! Fuck! Oh my God!

Oh my God!' This was like his first ever speed at The Torch but a thousand times more intense. 'Jesus! Fuckin' 'ell! Waaaah!'

'Oh goody,' said Tommy, in playful understatement, rinsing out the syringe and preparing Shaun's hit. 'Good stuff then?'

'Good?! It's out of this fuckin' world, man. Fuckin' 'ell! My God! I can't tell yer. It's just... It's just... Oh! Wow! You've gotta have some!'

Dan reached for the phone. Words rattled out of him like machine-gun fire: 'I've gotta phone somebody. I've gotta tell somebody. Who can I phone? I've gotta phone somebody. Everybody's got to know about this. Who should I phone?'

***

"Help Me" by Al Wilson had been rereleased on Pye International. Tommy had loved that record since he first heard it at Wigan Casino, and as soon as it was reissued, he rushed down to Spin Inn in Manchester and got himself a copy. Back at home, he slapped it onto the turntable in his bedroom, lowered the needle and cranked up the volume, and out came the song in all its brilliant dynamic power. Tommy danced joyfully around the room. Then, at the first instrumental break, the needle skipped. Tommy took the record off the platter and studied it closely. No scratches – it was a brand new record, after all. He gave it a careful wipe with his Emitex and put it back on. The song started up with its renowned vigour and gorgeousness, but as it reached that same point the stylus again jerked itself out of the groove. And again Tommy scanned the record, but it wasn't faulty. It just seemed that the record player couldn't cope with the violent rhythms in the instrumental breaks. He tried it again, and again, always with the same result. His exasperation grew. He increased the weight on the tonearm, and still the needle jumped. Heat built under his collar. He turned the tonearm weight up to maximum, and still the stylus skipped. He gave it another chance, then another, then another, and still the player mangled the music. And then he'd had enough, and in a state of blind rage he grabbed the record from the turntable and threw it out of the window. And folk walking home from work on Sheffield Road were treated to the sight of an unusual-looking pink and black Frisbee, which spun down from a first-floor window towards the tarmac and was crushed under the wheels of the Number 11 bus.

***

Babel Brook in Thursbury was the only remaining few acres of wilderness in inner-city Manchester. It comprised a couple of winding lanes, a stream and some densely wooded areas. It also had a pub, The Babel View, and Rita and her friends had planned to come over from Salford to spend an evening there with Dan and his mates.

Of course, it was important to prepare properly for a night out. So, early in the evening, Eddie Froggatt and Dan Brody called round to the Coggins's place and went up to Tommy and Shaun's room, where they all had a wap of speed. Dan was a little disappointed. It just wasn't the high he was expecting. So they all fixed up again. But while the others were now seemingly content with their drug intake, Dan still wasn't high enough, and Tommy fixed him up once more with a third hit. He then scrutinised Dan's frantic speedy eyeballs and said, 'that's it, Dan. That really is enough.'

'You reckon? I could really... I dunno... I'm just not there yet.'

'Yeah. Give it a rest, man. You're gonna be getting yourself in a state. You look off yer head. Yer eyes are like saucers. Look in the mirror.'

With that, Tommy trotted off downstairs to the kitchen for a wash and shave, ready for the big night out.

Unconvinced, Dan still wanted more speed. But he didn't yet have the skill to fix himself up, so he persuaded Shaun to give him another hit and not to tell Tommy. And it still wasn't enough, so Shaun fixed him up again and they had just enough time to put the wrap and syringe away before Tommy returned.

Dan still wasn't feeling the sort of speedy high that he wanted. It wasn't like that first time at his dad's on Steggs Lane. That was the feeling he always longed to get back to. He was high, sort of, and it was a speedy feeling, but now there was a bit of unwelcome dizziness and sweatiness attached. Maybe he had had too much. Five hits in thirty minutes... He tried to hold it together.

Tommy reached out a fresh shirt from the wardrobe, a white one with lots of little pictures of bowler hats on it, and he pulled on his brown baggies with the high waistband and the turn-ups, and so they were all cleaned-up and ready for the evening.

The four drove down to Babel Brook in Tommy's crumbling 1958 Morris Oxford and met Rita and her friends just after eight as planned. Dan still felt a bit odd. He downed a few pints to calm himself down. After an hour or so, he stood up to go to the toilet. As he did, his insides suddenly seemed to compress or expand or twist, or maybe all three of those at once or in quick succession. Bits of him felt numb, but he wasn't sure which. Sensations moved and mutated. He could feel himself reeling. But he couldn't let Rita know he was in this state. They lived with a kind of double-think about his gear-taking: she knew he took it, but he didn't discuss it, so she was able to believe and tell her friends that he didn't take it, and he was able to think she didn't know. And he couldn't let Tommy know because then he'd have to reveal that he'd snuck in those extra two waps. And he couldn't let Shaun and Eddie know because they'd helped him have those extra two waps and they might feel bad about it. And what would anyone do if he did tell them this was going on, anyway? The stuff was inside him now and there was nothing to be done. And then, as he tried to ease himself from behind the table with his insides still engaged in some powerful destructive project way beyond his control, he thought he might wet himself, but he didn't, which was just as well, given the off-white flares he was wearing.

***

Dan, Tommy and Shaun were drinking, chatting and listening to the jukebox in the best room at The King's Head. Dan loved that "Haitian Divorce" by Steely Dan. He couldn't work out why; it wasn't his usual kind of music, but somehow its world-weary ironic chirpiness seemed to capture his mood.

It was getting late when a blonde woman in her late twenties, wearing a pale blue sleeveless dress, kicked off. She was all over the place, screaming drunk, reeling, and yelling at the man and woman she'd been stood with at the bar – and anyone else who looked at her. Dan and his mates tried to work out what she was yelling about, but it was something that only she and the two at the bar were party to, and there was no sense to be made of it. Fred, the landlord, and a few others tried to calm her down, but to no avail. They offered to call her a taxi, but she wasn't having it, and she carried on screeching and flailing. Having exhausted all other possibilities, Fred and a few tap-room regulars ushered her outside onto the street.

Seconds later there was an ear-splitting crash and the big frosted-glass window on the far side from where Dan and the Coggins brothers were seated exploded into a thousand pieces and fell into the room, most of it over the wizened old chap with the flat cap who always sat on the bench seat in front of that window. Cold evening air rushed in, along with the woman's even louder shrieking and wailing. Fred and the regulars ran outside and brought the woman back in. Blood poured profusely from her right wrist. Fred ran upstairs and returned in moments with his wife and a bandage. The woman sat sobbing on a barstool while Mrs Fred wrapped the wound and Fred rang for an ambulance.

Dan looked across to the great, empty, seven-foot by five-foot opening, which now framed an unfettered view of night-time Kirkby Street. The old fellow hadn't moved. He sat there, splinters of glass on his flat cap, on his shoulders, in his beer and all around him. He looked back at Dan:

'Third time it's 'appened to me, that.'

Dan gave a wry smile in return.

As they walked home, Tommy asked Dan, 'do you know who that old codger is?'

'No. I've seen him in there a million times, but I don't know him, don't know his name or owt.'

'D'you remember, must have been all of ten years ago now, when that quarry truck went out of control down Sheffield Road and demolished The Alma Tavern and killed that woman and her kids?'

'Yeah, course I do. Terrible thing. She was just walking past the pub with a pram and toddler, and the lorry went straight through them.'

'Aye, well, it was his wife and kids. John, he's called. That's all he does now. Sits quietly and drinks his beer in The King's Head. How old do you think he is?'

'I dunno – seventy or something?'

'He's about fifty. Martin Shorrocks's dad worked with him. That's what it'll do to yer.'

***

It was a Monday night, and Dan, Tommy and Shaun met up, as planned, with Rick Cooper in The King's Head. Rick had scored a big bag of sulphate and needed to sell some on to recoup his money. They drank till about half ten, then went over to Rick and Sally's place, above the cake shop, for a fix. Sally was still up, but didn't seem to mind the invasion of their flat. She sat up with them for a while, then at about midnight went to bed.

The flat seemed mostly orange. The carpet was orange, as were the curtains, and whatever wasn't orange was bathed in orange by street light filtering through the curtains and by a table lamp with an orange shade, which stood on top of the telly.

They chatted, smoked, played records – quietly, so as not to wake Sally – had further fixes of Rick's very good sulphate and laboured over a newspaper crossword underneath the orange lamp.

Rick got paranoid. Every slam of a car door out in the street was the Drug Squad, and he'd turn off the lamp and they all had to sit in silence and darkness for a few minutes, so if the Squad came to the door they'd think everyone was in bed, asleep. But it never was the Squad, and the orange light went back on and they were left in peace, until the next time a car door slammed.

And the hours passed and they injected more speed, and then that dreaded daylight started to creep in round the curtains, and it was morning and they had to go to work.

Dan contemplated the day ahead. To step out of the cosy, druggy warmth of the flat onto the street was to walk into another world. Outside was the brutal, indifferent ordinariness of a new Dashley Dyke day – cold morning air, dusty streets, unwelcome baking whiffs coming from the cake shop under

Rick and Sally's flat, buzzing milk floats, steamed-up buses, stone trucks thundering down from Pennine quarries on their way to some building site or road construction project in Manchester or beyond – all of this was met with the realisation that somehow, without sleep and filled to the gunnels with amphetamine sulphate, work and people and the rest of it had to be dealt with. The buses would be awful – always the upper deck, crammed full of people puffing away on Park Drives, Woodbines and Number 6s, turning the air a sickly browny grey, then the smell of diesel and the nauseating throb of the engine which pulsated right through the filthy, seventy-seat aluminium sarcophagus as it idled in the bus station. Then there was just the fact of being at work – the tedium, the sweat and discomfort, having to talk seriously about things he didn't give a flying fuck about to people he'd rather not know, some of them looking him in the eye when he didn't want them to see his dilated pupils, others making sly comments, hinting that they knew he was on something. It all had to be faced.

Dan dragged himself home. He could hear Walter stirring in the back bedroom and didn't fancy a conversation. He ran upstairs, got changed, ran back down, washed his face and cleaned his teeth in the kitchen sink, all before Walter came downstairs. Then, trying to be as normal as possible, Dan blended in with the other bodies that shambled down Steggs Lane towards their various workplaces, and turned down to where Sheffield Road met Holmfirth Road to catch the Number 4 on the first leg of the journey to Verrington.

By Tuesday evening, Dan's speed-suppressed appetite had still not returned, but he thought he ought to eat something, so he forced down a yoghurt – *healthy food, yoghurt* – and an orange. And then he called for Tommy and Shaun and they went round to Rick and Sally's and did it all again.

And they did it all again on Wednesday night.

On Thursday night, Dan had had enough and was exhausted and so didn't have any drugs and just had a few pints in The Cricketers and went to bed for the first time in days.

But on Friday evening, paid and partially reinvigorated, he called round for Tommy and Shaun and went again to Rick and Sally's and again stayed up fixing speed all night.

And on Saturday night.

On Sunday night, Dan went to bed to get himself in some sort of shape for work the following day, and looking back at the week he realised he'd only gone to bed once since the previous Sunday.

***

Late in the dark of a Lincolnshire Saturday night, Mick Henshaw's burgundy Austin whizzed eastward along the A18 towards the coast, with Tommy Coggins in the passenger seat and Dan Brody, Rob Brierley and Ian Caldwell in the back. This would be their first trip to the Cleethorpes all-nighter. For entertainment, they'd got Tommy's Phillips cassette player on the back seat. A smart one, it was – futuristic styling, black and silver, with slider controls for tone and volume. They'd bought fresh batteries – six U2s – for it before setting off, and Dan and Rob had brought a selection of home-recorded cassettes for the trip – all all-nighter soul (or 'northern' soul as it was now pretty universally known).

Dan had necked his gear; a mixture of things – some dex, some Pirellis and a couple of bombers – and he was starting to feel the effects.

The cassette deck was playing all unknown stuff: Rob's new discoveries, records he hoped might one day make it big at the all-nighters. Suddenly this wasn't good enough for Dan. 'Quick, me gear's kicking in. Put something on I know.'

Rob picked out a cassette and held it up to catch light from the street lamps as they flashed by. Soul Volume 5, it had written on the spine in biro. 'See if this is any good,' he said, and clicked it into the machine. A few seconds later, the devastating power and passion of Linda Jones's "My Heart Needs a Break" filled the car. Dan leant back in the seat, closed his eyes and took deep breaths. The surging updraft of the drug and the infinite gorgeousness of the music met in his body and produced an overwhelming ecstatic rush.

'Oh my God,' said Dan, slowly, dreamily. 'I love this record... I fuckin' love this record... and I love Linda Jones. And I love speed.' His eyes opened at this realisation. 'I *love* speed. I mean, I really love it. I want to marry it. Yes. That's it. I'm gonna marry speed.'

He grabbed the seat in front and pulled himself forward. 'Did'jer get that Tommy? I am now officially betrothed to speed.'

'I'm sure you'll make each other very happy,' replied Tommy, slightly miffed that his gear hadn't kicked in yet and that he wasn't quite getting what Dan was.

Ian chipped in: 'You know, I have a theory about all-nighters. Every time we go to a 'niter and stay up all night, we have eight hours more life than all those folk who went to bed and slept all night.'

'Hmm,' said Dan, thoughtfully. 'I think they get theirs added on at the end.'

Being on the town's pier, the 'niter wasn't at all hard to find. They parked the Austin in a side street and joined the numerous small clusters of people who converged quietly onto the pier. A long, slow-moving queue led out over the wooden walkway, above the rushing, lapping water, to the whitewashed wooden building that contained the dance hall. And it was cold. Very cold. Dan wore only a pair of dark blue A-line flares and a white cheesecloth shirt. No jumper. No jacket. No nothing. And as a vicious North Sea wind shaped to skin him alive, he reflected on the fact that as he looked northwards at the limitless black sky and the icy black water, there was nothing but a few microns of cotton between him and the Arctic Circle.

But inside was another world. The hot, dark ballroom buzzed with positive energy. The space was large and roughly square, the music incredibly loud. In the middle, bodies jerked and writhed on the big, slick wooden dancefloor. To the left was a high stage with the djs' kit set back under the lights. Around the edges, hundreds of young soul fiends packed the gold-painted tables and chairs, swigging coke and taking a breather between stints on the floor. The atmosphere was friendly, the dancefloor frenetic. The place lacked that slight air of menace that Wigan Casino often seemed to have, and the music was fabulous: "Heartbreaker", "Your Autumn of Tomorrow", "Baby Without You", "She'll Come Running Back", "Rona's Theme" and hundreds more. The dancefloor went wilder and crazier with each stupendous track, and that familiar feeling of elation that only happened at all-nighters swept through Dan's body.

After a couple of hours on the floor, Dan took a break, climbed up onto the stage, sat on the edge, legs dangling down the front, and soaked up the vibe of the place. And as he looked out over the sweating, swirling bodies, World Column's "So is the Sun" kicked off at immense volume, and the energy in the room, which was already colossal, went off the scale. The dancefloor was alive – a throbbing mass of primal human dynamism and joy. Their energy could have lit up the whole town. A thousand people, each individual pounding the dancefloor in his own moment of ecstasy, joined the one euphoric whole in common purpose – that of experiencing limitless rapture. He knew what they were feeling and he felt it with them: that unalloyed joy that could only happen in a northern soul club; the boundless bliss that came from the convergence of up-tempo soul music, wild uninhibited dancing, the gorgeous uplift of amphetamine, and the fellowship of friends and strangers who got it, who felt exactly the same things as you and were with you as one. They were him; he was them: a brotherhood and sisterhood of ecstatic hedonists. He wondered for a moment if they'd go at it so hard they might pound their way through and plunge into the sea. *Maybe they should. Maybe everything should stop right now and this moment should be frozen forever and preserved, because it could never be beaten.* Generations in the future could look at it recreated as a hologram in a museum from their own insipid *Logan's Run* lives and see how things once were, how the reckless youth of the 1970s found that one perfect formula. This was *the* Golden Moment. Nothing was better than northern soul.

***

Rick Cooper had a score lined up at Rowntrees Sounds in town. Dan, Tommy, Shaun and Rick trundled off to the city centre in Tommy's Morris Oxford.

They stopped in Fennel Street, by Rowntrees Sounds' not-much-used side doorway.

'Right. Keep the engine running,' said Rick. There was audible edginess in his voice. He climbed out of the car and slipped into the pub entrance.

Ten minutes later, Rick leapt back out of the door and into the car like a demon was on his tail. 'Drive! Drive! Fuckin' drive!' he yelled, frantically. 'Let's go! Come on! Come on! Move it!'

Tommy jabbed the accelerator and the car and its now slightly unnerved passengers slowly picked up speed and lumbered down Fennel Street, while Rick looked over his shoulder to see who if anyone was following. His eyes were wild, agitated: 'Come on! Come on! Move! Won't it go any faster?'

It was rumoured that the old Morris did nought to sixty, but no-one had ever had the patience to find out in how long. With Tommy's foot hard to the floor, it had approached a stately twenty miles an hour by the time it reached the cathedral frontage and the turning for Victoria Street and the safety of the crowd.

And then they were on the main roads and safely away from Rowntrees Sounds. Rick opened the wrap and held it up for the others to see. 'Hey, hey! Check it out,' said Rick, to grins all round. It was a big, healthy looking wrap. It would have been good value for money, if it had actually been paid for. But it hadn't, and there was a certain unspoken discomfort about what had just happened. Dan, Tommy and Shaun had chipped in up front, and Rick had taken their money but not paid the guy in Rowntrees Sounds. He'd said he was just going to the toilet to look at the wrap and check it was OK before parting with his quids. He'd then done a runner. So Rick got his gear for free, as well as Dan, Tommy and Shaun's money. But they let it go. It was all dodgy business, and a big bag of gear when you really wanted it tended to render all ethical questions moot. They would still get what they'd paid for, and it was up to Rick if he wanted to shoulder the gigantic risk he'd now taken. There'd now be places he couldn't go and people he dared not bump into. Rick had turned himself into a marked man.

***

When Dan and Tommy were little, they played with Tommy's next-door neighbour, Martin Shorrocks. Dressed in woollen balaclavas and hand-me-down grey V-necks, they played football and cricket in the almost entirely car-free streets, or they stalked and ambushed each other in the back alleys with chrome cap guns in white holsters until it was time for tea. And they were well known to everyone, both because they were always around and visible, and because they were in trouble not infrequently, when the odd sliced clearance or wayward cover drive made contact with glass. The neighbours preferred it when they were Jesse James, Geromino and Billy the Kid to when they were Bobby Charlton, Stanley Matthews and Jimmy Greaves, or Ted Dexter, Raymond Illingworth and Fred Titmus. But as they got older and became teenagers, and Tommy and Dan started going to the pubs and clubs and the footy, Martin drifted away. He just wasn't that kind of guy. When he left school he started as a trainee at the local branch of the Yorkshire Bank, and going to work became the only time he was ever seen leaving the house. And as Tommy and Dan grew up into outgoing, hedonistic good-timers, Martin matured into a boring stay-at-home with a personality as interesting as chipboard, and their years-old friendship fizzled out to nothing. But if Martin turned out to be what Tommy termed a 'micey fucker', that was nothing compared to his younger brother, Andy.

Andy didn't even do the playing-out thing when he was young. There'd been the usual fuss amongst the women up and down the street when he was born – lots of popping by with gifts of home-knitted cardigans and bootees, and to coo and admire his podgy pink complexion and comment on how firm the grip of his tiny fingers was and how much he looked like his dad. But once this was done, he was seen even less than Martin. He went to school, he came back from school – that was it.

People who moved into the area after his infancy scarcely knew who he was. Some didn't know he existed. He was the same age as Shaun, and Shaun tried to encourage him to come and play out, as Tommy and Dan had with Martin, but Andy would have none of it.

And as time passed, the Shorrockses became forgotten nonentities. They were only the other side of the party wall from the Coggins's house, but they were never seen and there was nothing to say about them.

And then there was the incident.

Wendy opened the Dashley Dyke Gazette, which arrived every Friday tea time with its usual mixture of news, gossip, obituaries, and how Dashley Dyke United had gone on in the Northern Premier League the previous weekend. And there was Andy Shorrocks's picture on the court reports page – all kind of grown up and whiskery now, but still unmistakably him. And if there was any doubt, there was his name. And there were the sordid details: how he'd been had up before the magistrate for jerking off in his bedroom window at the women in the bus shelter on the other side of Sheffield Road.

***

Shaun, Tommy and Dan, along with Marty Baldock and Eddie Froggatt, were at Blackpool Mecca to see The Miracles. The band, in their post-Smokey Robinson line-up, had a big hit on their hands – "Love Machine" – which had been a monster at the northern soul clubs and had now also broken through to the charts and the regular discos. This made a tour of the UK worthwhile for the legendary Motown act.

For once, the event wasn't in the Highland Room – it was downstairs in the main ballroom where the divvy disco was usually held, with its fake deciduous trees stretching their fake fabric leaves out over the dancefloor. Dan and his mates had never been in there before. It was a much bigger space and it had a large stage for the group and their backing musicians.

The five passionate soul fans had made the seventy-five mile journey from Dashley Dyke in Tommy's ancient but well-appointed Morris Oxford. Preparation for the trip had included a mighty successful score, and they each had twenty-odd assorted amphetamine pills in their pockets, to make the night go with a swing.

The place was completely rammed, and the band was sharp, loud and on it – all thumping, powerful driving energy, pounding bass and soaring horns, with superbly soulful vocals over. The sweltering crowd went as wild to the group's current top-forty hit as they did to their much-loved 1960s classics; though, as this was a flat-floored disco rather than a sloping auditorium, viewing was sometimes difficult, unless you were tall or close to the front.

Some guy climbed up one of the trees to get a better view. As he got to the top, it collapsed under his weight, and as bogus branches crumbled, faux rustic gave way to the trite predictability of chicken wire, plaster and structural timber. For an instant there was alarm, as the lad and bits of phony foliage fell into the crowd, then quickly, amusement, as revellers realised what had happened. Dan laughed at first, as well, at this moment of unscripted slapstick, but then felt something else, something he couldn't quite put his finger on.

That token of bucolic idyll was nothing more than a crude gewgaw thrown together by some Lancastrian handyman from stuff bought at the local builders' yard. The ballroom's seductive ambiance had been exposed for what it was: a facility, a hard-headed business venture; an illusion, complete with all chimeras necessary to create a fantasy world for willing, weekend fantasists. Not that anyone thought it was anything else; it was just that, for Dan, the prop's all-too-easy collapse and frank exposure of its crude entrails burst the bubble. The enchantment of the magical night, conjured up by booze and drugs, coloured lights and glitterballs, and Top Shop's best dresses and Burton's finest Saturday-night flares all fell away into the cold banality of a building site.

The band completed their set and djs took over the task of providing the musical entertainment. The group of friends sat down at a table in a corner, speeding off their heads and downing pints of bitter. A bloke at the next table with a Yorkshire accent, big pupils and jerky mannerisms confided in Dan that he was going to beat someone up because he'd looked at his girlfriend. Dan started to argue that people can't help looking at people – it's part of life. How would you know you were in the presence of someone you knew if you couldn't look and see who it was? But this seemed too deep a concept for the paranoid, speedy Yorkshireman, and Dan let it be.

Tommy vanished for a while and then returned. 'I've found a bloke selling chalkies, four a quid. There's eight apiece if you want 'em.'

Shaun, Eddie, Marty and Dan each handed over two quid, which Tommy shoved into the pocket of his toffee-coloured baggies. Dan wondered what the chalkies would do, how he could possibly be any more off his chops than he was now.

Tommy returned and they each necked their chalkies – thick, long Tenuate Dospan tablets, nicknamed 'tombstones' by some. Dan surprised himself by successfully swallowing them all at once, without using his drink. He'd got pretty good at swallowing pills dry, but eight chalkies, and with his throat dried by the gear he'd already had? It was an achievement, of sorts.

Shona Stringfield's glorious, fragile voice poured out of the speakers, singing "I Need a Rest". Then came the stunning Three Degrees instrumental, "Reflections of Yesterday".

It was 2am. The club closed and the friends stepped out into the cool night air with the other goodtimers, who quickly dispersed. What were they going to do now, in the middle of the night and off their faces?

None of them had more than a few pennies left. It had all gone on petrol, getting in, gear and beer. A jaunt over to Wigan Casino was out of the question. Even if they'd had the money, the state they were in would have been bloody obvious in the harsh light of the foyer and they'd have probably been busted. Home was the only answer.

They climbed into Tommy's Morris Oxford and within ten minutes it was clear they were hopelessly lost. Tommy knew a short cut, then he didn't. Then he was pretty sure where they were, then he wasn't. The suburbs of Blackpool all looked the same – endless rows of bow-fronted redbrick semis. They cruised up one street then down another, then turned a corner, then another, and then found themselves in what looked very much like the place they'd been in three streets ago. What they needed was a main road – that, sooner or later, would have to have direction signs, and even if they were going the wrong way, they'd be able to work it out.

But they couldn't find one.

They were arguing amongst themselves on yet another unremarkable suburban street when there was a sudden ear-splitting crash. The front of the car became airborne, the bonnet reared up and filled their vision, then the whole body whumped down on its suspension with a loud dull thud. Tommy jammed on the brakes and they all jumped out to find the cause of the outrage. A hubcap rolled down the street with a vaguely metallic noise and vanished out of sight. The street was dark – just a few miserly streetlamps provided little pools of yellow light here and there. The Morris had come to rest next to a small roundabout – a grass mound about fifteen feet in diameter, surrounded by upturned flagstones about two feet high. Tommy had completely failed to see it and the car had hit the left hand side of it at about twenty-five miles an hour.

They inspected the front end. The bumper bar had been bent upwards, and the bottom of the right front wing had been bashed back under itself, so that it pressed into the tyre. They pulled and yanked and shoved, and finally managed to drag it back far enough for the wheel to be able both to spin and turn directionally, so they could get home. There was a brief conversation about searching for the hubcap, but they quickly concluded that, considering they were drugged to the eyeballs and this was the middle of the night and they were on some Blackpool back street they had no particular business being on, they'd loitered long enough. The last thing they needed was some concerned resident, shaken from their sleep by the racket, calling emergency services, or 'help' from a random patrolling police car.

They eventually found a main road. And then there were direction signs and they were able to find their way back – first to Kirkham, then to Preston, then towards home. But by now Tommy was experiencing severe hallucinations, especially on the unlit A-roads. Trees kept appearing and he couldn't see past them, he reckoned. That was why he'd hit the roundabout. He hadn't seen any roundabout – only trees. And no-one else knew how to drive. So the journey back was a joint effort: Tommy operated the controls, while the others watched the road intently and advised how close to the edge and middle they were and what in the wide variety of plant life Tommy was seeing was real and what wasn't.

***

It was Sunday morning, and the five friends rattled back to Dashley Dyke from Wigan Casino in Tommy's Ford Cortina – Dan next to Tommy in the front; Shaun, Eddie and Marty in the back.

The venerable old Morris Oxford, with its dignified, understated dashboard and crackly red-leather seats, had died. Tommy had never had the bonnet up and didn't know what went on under there. He'd put fuel in at the back, but no-one had told him about oil and how you had to check it and keep it topped up. The engine had dried out and the big ends had gone, and the faithful old motor had taken its last sad journey to the scrapyard on Kirkby Street amidst loud bangs and clouds of blue smoke.

The Cortina was a Mark II, F-reg, finished in silver, though odd bits of missing paint near the headlights and trim told the tale that it had once been dark blue. The top part was painted matt black, so it looked like it had a vinyl roof, like one of the more upmarket ones – a 1600E, maybe – but it was in fact a 1300L. Dan had gone with Tommy to buy it off a bloke in Hightown. They looked it over. The bodywork seemed OK and the engine sounded OK, which, given their knowledge of what an engine ought to sound like, was essentially meaningless. It did have one leaf of the rear suspension cart-springs broken, but Tommy decided he could live with that because the other leaves were OK and because he liked the way it looked, especially with that imitation black vinyl roof, and he handed over a hundred and fifty quid in fivers.

Marty had bought a copy of "That's Alright" by Ed Crook from a guy flogging bootlegs in the club. It had the word 'time' and '2.24' on the label, which intrigued Marty. He'd noticed that most of the northern soul records he'd bought had the word 'time' on them, followed by a number, usually between about 2.10 and 2.45, and he pondered aloud why it was that all these records seemed to be recorded at roughly the same time of day and always in the early afternoon. There was silence and head-shaking in the car – no-one was in the mood for trying to explain that that was the duration of the tune in minutes and seconds, not the time of day it was recorded. And Marty went on to speculate that maybe the artistes did their rehearsals in the morning, and it was always early afternoon, after they'd had their dinner, that everyone was re-vitalised and ready for the final cut. Again, no-one took the bait, and Marty was left to his ruminations.

They were most of the way home, on the ring road in Collyhurst, when a sudden rush of steam shot vigorously skyward from around the bonnet. 'Fuck,' said Tommy and steered the Ford to the roadside in front of a row of terraced houses. All you needed, feeling the way you felt after an all-nighter, was car trouble, but there it was and it had to be dealt with. They all got out and took a look, though Marty after one quick glance got straight back in. Tommy clicked open the bonnet. They gazed in. There was nothing obvious that might have caused the leak – hoses were intact, Jubilee clips were fixed firmly in place. They looked underneath. A pool of water under the radiator was slowly spreading out under the engine. In the middle was a small brass object: a cylindrical thing about 3/8ths of an inch in both length and diameter, with a recess in the middle, where a sealing ring might have been expected to fit. Tommy and Dan lay on the road on their backs and slithered under the car, and there, in the casing that housed the shaft that drove the fan was a small hole, also about 3/8ths of an inch across. That had to be it. The car must have overheated, and the pressure in the cooling system blown out this little brass plug. The only thing was, the plug was round, as plugs usually are, while the hole was more the shape of a television screen:

square-ish with curved corners. But this had to be it, because there was a hole and there was a plug, and water and steam had come out.

They set about putting the plug back into the hole. Dan had a go, then Tommy had a go, then Dan had another go, then Shaun had a go, and on it went, as the sporadic Sunday morning traffic swished past them. Eddie paced up and down on the pavement and swore at intervals. Marty, superior to all this greasy-hands stuff, stretched out on the back seat and lit a fag. But the plug just would not go back in. And they had no tools. So, in a further attempt, Dan held the plug approximately in position, while Tommy used the dipstick and a piece of random house-brick to try and bash the bloody thing back into place.

After about an hour of trying, they realised it was never going to work. They looked up and down the road for answers. A couple of hundred yards away was another Mark II Cortina – a dark blue one. They slithered under that and had a look. It too had a small television-shaped hole in the casing that housed the shaft that drove the fan – but it didn't have a small brass plug, just the hole. And then it dawned: the car must have overheated and squirted out steam from somewhere, but the plug was a red herring. It just happened to be on the road at precisely the place where they stopped.

They climbed sullenly back into Tommy's Cortina. It started first time, showed no signs of overheating, and they drove the rest of the way home without incident, if feeling a bit silly. Marty smirked in silence. He knew they were all fools. His decision not to help was clearly the right one.

***

Dan hopped off the Number 4 at the junction of Holmfirth Road and Sheffield Road and strode off up the hill for the last quarter mile of the journey home from work.

When he was half way along Steggs Lane, a bright blue, shiny new Ford Escort slowed down and stopped alongside him. He glanced inside. Brenda Burgess was at the wheel, wearing a yellow skinny rib jumper, yellow suede mini skirt and yellow knee-length leather boots. She wound down the window.

'Get in. I'll give you a lift,' she said.

'I'm nearly home. I'm only there,' said Dan, pointing diagonally across the road.

'Oh. You're not at Bessemer Street anymore? No wonder I haven't seen yer.'

'Bloody hell, no. So much has happened since then. You wouldn't believe it.'

'Well, get in anyway.'

Dan swung in onto the passenger seat, and Brenda drove the remaining 75 yards and pulled round the corner onto Grover Street, next to the triangle of grass and trees and privet hedges that locals called the 'cat park', because it was where all the local cats went to relieve themselves. And the dogs.

'Interesting outfit, Brenda,' said Dan.

'Yeah, I'm a go-go dancer at The Phoenix in Manchester, now. Just got off the afternoon sesh.'

'So, you what – wriggle about on the stage in that stuff while blokes drink their dinnertime pints and have chicken in a basket and watch your tits jiggle?'

'Yep. That's about the size of it. But the money's OK and I get lots of tips.'

'I bet you do. And where'd this car come from. It's brand new, isn't it?'

'Yeah. Mi dad bought it me for mi birthday. Alright, isn't it?'

'Alright? Bloody hell, yeah! Mine gave me a fiver.'

'Mind you, it's only an eleven-hundred. With a full load it doesn't want to know about hills.'

'Still, it's a car though, innit,' said Dan, scanning the dazzling new interior and inhaling the seductive smell of new car.

'Anyway,' said Brenda, 'I'm off to Maxie's tonight. Do you want to come?'

'What, go-go dancing?'

'No, just as a paying punter.'

'It's a bit posh, Maxie's. It's where all the ten-bob millionaires go. D'yer think they'll let us in?'

'Of course. I'm a regular there. They know me.'

'Yeah. OK. Why not. What time?'

'I'll come for you at half seven.'

'It's a deal,' said Dan, smiling. And he jumped out of the car, and Brenda sped off up Steggs Lane.

Dan had the house to himself, which was pretty normal. His dad's driving job for the plastics firm meant he frequently spent nights out, and then when he was back in town there were his marathon pub sessions, so Dan never knew when he'd be there. Similarly, Dan's pubbing, clubbing, all-nighters, stays at girlfriends' houses and all-night speed sessions at friends' places meant his visits to the house were also unpredictable and often brief. They were like two almost-strangers who shared a doss house and occasionally bumped into each other and nodded.

Dan had bacon and eggs for tea, then cleaned his teeth and had as thorough a wash as he could in the kitchen sink – face, neck, armpits, bollocks – and then vanished into his bedroom with a mug of clean water and a dessert spoon. He reached into his record box, where the records were filed by alphabetical order of record label, and separated the discs at the flap that said D, which stood for Deram, Dynovoice, Duke and the rest, but also for 'drugs'. He reached down to the bottom and pulled out a self-sealing polythene bag containing a dozen or so small salmon-coloured pills – Ritalin. He crushed five of them in the spoon, added 2 millilitres of water from a syringe and stirred. He then pulled up the mixture into the syringe, using a cigarette filter to keep out the chalk. He tourniqued his left arm with a tie, held it in his teeth, and with his right hand emptied the syringe into the big blue tube on the back of his triceps.

He felt good. He weighed himself up in the full-length mirror on the wardrobe door: collar-length hair, still jet black, with the odd scarcely perceptible grey strand, centre parting, and a nifty little black tash. The big bushy sideburns had got a bit passé and he'd shaved them off a couple of years ago. But, hell, he'd got really thin with all that speed. He took the smallest adult sizes: 30 inch waist, 36 chest, 14½ inch collar. Sizes smaller than that were on the kids' racks. His face had started to sink in – his cheekbones had become noticeable for the first time. His collarbone protruded like a coat-hanger. The boyish looks had gone – he looked like what he was. But this was OK – he was still getting away with it and it was better than being fat. He got out his best cream-coloured A-line flares and the shirt with the pictures of people from the Caribbean or somewhere, dancing and playing bongos. He always seemed to score when he wore than one. Over this he slipped his black double-breasted blazer. He'd bought it as one of those dreadful brass-button affairs that all the old blokes wore, from Henderson's Gentlemen's Outfitters on Dashley Dyke High Street, but he'd cut off the buttons and sewn on big grey-and-off-white imitation horn ones, and now it looked cool as fuck and everyone admired it and no-one could work out where he'd got it from. He pulled up the shirt collar and straightened it over the jacket collar – that's how they were wearing them now – and splashed on some Yardley Black Label.

Brenda showed up just after half seven, dressed slightly more demurely than before, in a short black velvet dress and a little black jacket with a red brooch on the collar.

They went for one in The Diamond first and talked about old times and caught up on the latest gossip. Dan told Brenda about his mum buggering off down south and the old people's home and his stint at the Coggins's. Brenda told Dan about her mum and dad's latest crisis. Dan remembered Bill and Marjorie well from the few months Brenda and he had been an item: Bill the pompous know-all who knew hardly anything, and who, after you'd explained something to him, would make out he knew that all along and was just testing you; and Marjorie, a woman who always seemed to be quietly seething with rage about something, but you never knew quite what – living with Bill, probably. It seemed now they were on the brink of divorce. Bill had written Marjorie a letter saying that he was at the end of his tether with her. He'd tried, God knows he'd tried, it said. Dan asked why he wrote a letter and didn't just say it. Brenda said that was because he never got to finish a sentence without Marjorie bawling him out.

And on they went to Maxie's. Brenda was right about them knowing her. The bouncers were more like concierges. They exchanged a few jokey comments and smiled and opened the door for her. They weren't so smiley with him, though.

The club was all glitter, mirrors and plush black seating – posh for a place dedicated to getting pissed and laid – though, predictably, the music was no better than was to be expected from a divvy disco. The big tune of the moment was "Oh What a Night" by the Four Seasons. They played it at least hourly. And Dan reflected on the fact that the all-nighters were playing "The Night" and "I'm Gonna Change" by the same outfit, but they wouldn't have touched "Oh What a Night" with a drain rod, and the people in Maxie's were completely unaware of these other, infinitely better songs.

Brenda drove Dan home and again pulled round the corner onto Grover Street, and in the dark and with the cover of the cat park trees and bushes she straddled him and they fucked on the passenger seat.

Brenda climbed back into the driver's seat. Dan did up his fly.

'D'you want to do this again some time?' asked Brenda, smiling seductively.

'Oh, give over, Bren. You know I'm back with Rita.'

'Yeah, so I heard. The Queen of Higher Broughton... What's she got that I haven't got?'

'Come on,' cajoled Dan. 'Don't ruin a lovely evening. It's been nice, annit?'

'Oh, it's OK. *Really.*' said Brenda with a smile. 'But you still fancy me, don't yer? You stood to attention quickly enough.'

'Course I still fancy you, Bren. I always did, but what can I say? It's just time and place or chemistry or something. I dunno. Things just happen.'

'So Rita's *The One* then, is she?'

'The One?!' exclaimed Dan. 'No-one's *The One*. I was only twenty the other week. I'm just not thinking about anything like that. I'm just, you know, getting on with life. The One! Jeez.'

'Anyway, you remember what I told yer?' said Brenda, demurely.

'What's that?'

'That if you marry anyone but me, I'll show up at your wedding and sing that song: "It Should Have Been Me".'

Dan let out one of those sad little down-the-nose laughs, then so did Brenda.

***

Early evening, and Dan was in high spirits on his way to Buffy's. He crossed Sheffield Road at the junction with Steggs Lane and called for Tommy and Shaun. To his surprise, instead of it being a member of the Coggins family that answered the door, it was a bald bloke in his fifties wearing a dark blue rain mac. 'Ah, the insurance guy,' thought Dan. The Coggins's always seemed to be taking out little, a-few-pennies-a-week insurance policies. 'This'll be the guy from United Friendly.'

'Tommy and Shaun in?' asked Dan.

'Yeah, sure,' said the man, swinging open the door. Dan stepped in.

As soon as the door was closed, the man said 'CID,' grabbed Dan by the arm and shoved him brusquely down the narrow corridor and into the Coggins's living room. Tommy and Shaun were sitting ashen-faced on the settee. Another man in a mac was standing over them. On the opposite side of the room, Wendy was consoling a tearful Mrs Coggins and Grandma.

This other cop told Dan to empty his pockets. Dan complied. Keys, money, comb, half-done packet of Wrigleys Spearmint, grubby white hanky – nothing incriminating. The cop had a rummage himself, to make sure. Then he told Dan to roll up his sleeves. Dan did so and the detective scrutinised his forearms carefully, from the crook of his arm to his wrist. There were no marks. The forearm veins had got a bit worn out and Dan been cranking in the veins on the backs of his arms for weeks. The officer didn't look there.

Satisfied with, but disappointed at Dan's apparent virtuousness, the coppers sent him on his way, slammed the door behind him and continued with their interrogation of Tommy and Shaun.

***

It was Thursday night at Buffy's. Tommy explained that his boss had a job for him to do in Preston on Saturday, and since he was going to be up that way anyway, it made sense to make the most of it and go on to Blackpool Mecca. Was anyone interested? Dan was and so was Dave Podmore. Eddie Froggatt couldn't afford it, Reevesie wasn't around and Shaun was at home, sick with flu.

They made a plan. Tommy would finish his job in Preston then drive over in his van to Blackpool, and Dave and Dan would travel up Saturday teatime in Dave's funky new Citroen GS Pallas. And they would meet in The Bloomfield. Everyone knew where The Bloomfield was. Tommy had a score set up for Friday, so that was the gear taken care of.

On Saturday morning, Tommy called round to Dan's and gave him a small silver paper package. 'Sort yourself and Dave out and bring mine to The Bloomfield. See yer about half six,' said Tommy.

'Will do. See yer later.'

Dave Podmore showed up at Dan's place at just after 5pm. He and Dan went up to Dan's room. Dan emptied the sulphate into a dessert spoon, filled the 2 mil works with water and emptied it onto the crystalline powder – three times. He stirred briefly and the nearly-white substance dissolved completely. *Must be good stuff.*

He drew 2 mil of the mixture up into the works. Dave wrapped a tie around his scrawny white arm and Dan searched for a vein. It took time. Dave's arms were flimsy and white, more like those of a ten year-old girl than a twenty year-old bloke. He'd never done a stroke of manual work in his life, sport was an alien concept, he didn't even walk anywhere, so there was no muscle to speak of, and his veins didn't have much to do. Eventually Dan spotted the hint of a pale blue line in the crook of Dave's arm. He sunk the needle, pulled back the plunger and watched with satisfaction as the blood ball confirmed he was on target. Dave relaxed the tourniquet; Dan slowly emptied the syringe, then carefully extracted the needle.

Dave gasped and flumped onto the bed, with his hands on the side of his head, like blinkers. 'Whoa! Whaaat?! Fuckin' 'ell! Fuckin' 'ell!'

'Good stuff then, Dave?' laughed Dan.

'Bloody hell yeah! My God! Oh, wow, what the...? Fuckin' 'ell! Jeez!'

Dan rinsed out the works, pulled up 2 mil for himself and got Dave to fix him up. The rush hit the top of his head, his fingertips, his toes, his eyes, his brain. He caught his breath, gasped, gulped. *Good stuff?!* 'Bloody 'ell. Ha! Phew! 'Kin 'ell! Waah!' It was absolutely bozzonks. Instant madness. This was nearly as good as that first time, when he'd rolled around on his back and phoned Mandy Walker and bent her ear for half an hour about how magical it was. Dan and Dave grinned at each other, giddy and breathless – a shared moment of ecstasy.

Now quivering with the power of the drug, Dan rinsed out the works and pulled up the remaining fluid. He looked carefully at the lines on the side – the meniscus was right on the 2 mil line. He felt good about that. He'd split it into three precisely. Tommy would get his share exactly. He put the plastic cap on the needle and stowed it safely in his pocket for Tommy.

Outside, the white Citroen looked like it had sunk into a gulley. They climbed in, Dave turned the ignition and the car's strange pneumatic suspension system slowly raised it to the height of a normal car. But inside, it was like no car Dan had ever seen: soft, luxurious grey nylon seats, all-singing, all-dancing dashboard, and soundproofing so effective that it made you feel completely isolated from the real world. Compared to Tommy's Cortina or even Mick's Austin 1800, it was like a spaceship. Dave slipped it into first, and they swept off up Steggs Lane and heard only the sound of the wind as it whooshed over the car.

The Bloomfield was busy, noisy and smoky. Thin Lizzy blasted from the jukebox, singing "Whiskey in the Jar-o". But Tommy wasn't there yet. Dan and Dave fought their way through the bustle at the bar and got a couple of pints: bitter in a dimpled pint pot for Dan, lager in a sleever for Dave. There was one remaining empty table – by the wall next to the gents. They sat. Dave dropped a packet of Sovereign on the table and lit one up.

Tommy arrived ten minutes later, bought a pint and sat down. 'Got the gear then?'

Dan slapped his right jacket pocket. 'In here, all ready to go.'

'Right, I'll go in first,' said Tommy. 'We don't want to look like a pair of turtles.' He stood up from the table and turned through the door to the gents.

Dan gave it a couple of minutes, then followed Tommy. There was no-one else in the room. They went into the first trap and locked the door. Tommy took off his jacket, hung it on the hook and rolled up his shirt sleeve. Dan took the plastic cap off the needle and held the syringe up to the light: still 2 mil and no bubbles. Perfect. Tommy took off his trouser belt and pulled it tight on his right arm. Dan scanned for the most suitable, least damaged vein. And then he was in, and then he pulled back, and then he squeezed. Tommy gasped and, heart pounding, and conscious of his surroundings, kept his reactions to a minimum: 'phwa, phwa, errrr, errr,' and then some deep breaths. Gasps.

'Good stuff, eh?' grinned Dan.

'I'll say,' said Tommy, shaking his head and blinking as though trying to regain some clarity. 'Fuckin' 'ell!'

Dan rinsed the syringe in the sink, put the cap back on the needle and slipped the assemblage safely back into his pocket.

'Give me a minute,' said Tommy.

'Sure,' said Dan and returned to the lounge and Dave and his beer.

It was more than a minute – more like five. Tommy emerged from the toilets, and with his eyes fixed firmly forward, marched straight past Dan and Dave as though they weren't there and right out of the front door and onto the street. Dan and Dave looked at each other. *Strange.* Dan jumped up and followed Tommy out of the door. Tommy stood on the footpath with his back to the pub and scanned the street left and right as though he was looking for something, or somebody.

'Tommy, what are yer doing?'

Tommy spun round and seemed for a moment surprised to see Dan there.

'What? Oh yeah. I was looking for yer.'

'We're in the pub. You walked straight past us.'

'Yeah. What? Oh yeah. Didn't see you there.'

'You were sat with us ten minutes ago.'

'Was I? Yeah. Sure. That's right. Hmm.'

And they turned back into The Bloomfield and sat at the table, and Dave lit another Sovereign.

'So, where's the rest of the gear?' asked Tommy.

'The rest? There isn't any rest. We've had it all.'

'You mean we've cranked the whole lot?'

'Yeah, you said divide it up into three for me, you and Dave. And that's what I did. A third each.'

''Kin 'ell! I didn't mean the whole lot. I meant sort us out a fix each. It was supposed to last the rest of the week. Bloody hell! No wonder we're off our tits.'

'Ah. Right. That explains it then. I thought it was a pretty monstrous hit. Old Dave here didn't know what had hit him.'

Dave smirked.

'Well, anyway,' continued Dan, 'we'll have a good time, won't we. We'll be the most off-our-tits fuckers in Blackpool Mecca – and we'll probably not sleep till Tuesday.'

***

They'd cranked speed in Tommy and Shaun's bedroom for months, and now they'd run out. They'd used up what they'd got, their source had been busted and they'd yet to find a new one.

They looked at the sideboard where they prepared their fixes – an old, brown varnished thing. But the top was no longer brown. Countless tiny splashes from spoons had combined to create a thin white veneer that spread across much of the surface. That was sulphate, or maybe some of it was – some of it would have been the chalk padding left behind when the good stuff was pulled up through the filter. Still, it was there, looking at them, and they had nothing else. They looked at each other, knowing each was asking himself the same question: should they? Could they? Was this a level of abjection too far? Of course they could – they were junkies. Tommy got a razor blade, carefully scraped the surface and accumulated an amount of grey powder, which they hoped contained more amphetamine than varnish. He sorted out 3 fixes, filtered rather more carefully than usual, and they each had a hit and tried to persuade themselves they could feel just a hint of something, but they weren't sure.

***

It was a rip-roaring night in The King's Head. A big crowd of them, mostly lads, some girlfriends, crammed in around the oversized oval table in the best room and laughed and told stories and swilled back the Boddies' Bitter. The flowery red-flock and gold wallpaper gave a comforting glow under the subdued orange lights and the jukebox banged out the hits of the moment: "The Hustle", "Disco Stomp", "I'm Not in Love"...

Tommy bragged about how the Drug Squad had raided their house again a couple of nights ago. Searched the place from top to bottom, they did, but found nothing. And they all howled with laughter when Tommy explained that this was because he kept his gear inside the Airball air-freshener on the mantelpiece, and the dumb-arses never thought to look in there.

Two nights later, Tommy answered a knock at the door and three Drug Squad officers barged past him into the house. Their commanding officer, Detective Inspector Coleman, in his blue fly-front mac, calmly followed them in. He paused in front of Tommy and looked him in the eye and said 'we won't miss the Airball this time.'

***

It was Saturday night, and Dan, Tommy, Shaun and Mick Henshaw were on their way to the St Ives all-nighter in Cambridgeshire. Injecting wasn't an easy thing to do in the car or a club, and there was always the risk of having the paraphernalia hanging around for the Squad to find, so they scored pills instead. Lots of them, too: ten Dex and twelve Filon apiece – enough to blow the socks off anything.

Mick swung the Austin into the St Ivo Centre car park and the four friends piled into the blocky, beige modernist building, ready for a night of druggy dancefloor euphoria.

It was a pretty unremarkable place – a multi-purpose provincial community centre, with plain décor and simple furnishings. The dancefloor was smooth and easy to glide on, though, and the music was top-drawer, with Soul Sam behind the decks. And as always at all-nighters, it was hot and crowded.

Dan had a bit of a dance, then a sit down, then another dance, then another sit down. Then, after a couple of hours, he had to admit to himself that he wasn't really feeling it. He didn't seem to be getting much out of the drugs and the place seemed to lack atmosphere: neither the joyful, uplifting vibe of Cleethorpes, nor the dark intensity of Wigan Casino. It felt more like a youth club... Though maybe it was just him – the way he was feeling. He went and found Tommy on the balcony.

'How're yer doin', Tom?' asked Dan.

'OK, yeah, I guess,' replied Tommy, with little apparent enthusiasm.

'Are you getting much off this gear?'

'Well, a bit, yeah.'

'But we've had twenty-two pills. We oughta be flying. It can't be bum gear. It looked right and you can't fake Filon.'

'No, it was good stuff, straight from the chemist's. I saw the bottles and everything.'

And reality gradually dawned – they'd had so much amphet sulphate for so long that twenty-two normally potent pills scarcely touched the sides. And the whole night continued in this dreary half-life – enough gear to keep awake but not enough to feel good.

And then it was morning, and for the first time Dan didn't much mind that an all-nighter had come to an end. They sat on the low wall outside, next to the car park, chatted, caught up with gossip, had conversations not possible in the ear-splitting din of the 'niter.

Suddenly, the Sunday morning come-down quiet was disturbed by loud, ugly noise. There was the roar of an engine and the screech of tyres. The glint of a fast-moving car roof was just visible beyond the first few rows of parked cars. A metallic green Triumph 2000 flew out from behind the line and turned sharply left. Its tyres squealed, it dipped on its suspension and blue smoke billowed. It screeched and roared and turned left again and accelerated back down to the bottom of the line, rounded the last few cars, then tore back up and did the whole thing again, and again...

'Who's that div?' scowled Mick. 'You come out of an all-nighter full of gear and give the police a reason to come and look at yer. What a knob-head.'

Dan weighed-up the car. 'It's one of our lot, that: Pete Clayton. He's from Bradfield. Goes in Buffy's.'

'Ah, yeah. I know him – by sight. Fuckin' pillock.'

'He's young – only seventeen, I think,' mulled Dan, 'new to the scene.'

And the following week the news filtered through to Buffy's that Pete Clayton was dead. He'd been screwing chemists' and the police had got him, and he'd hanged himself in the cells because he couldn't face what was coming next.

***

Tommy and Dan showed up at The Cricketers with the big bag of back-street blueys they'd just scored in Chorlton, and joined Shaun, Eddie and Marty, who were already into their third pint in the best room, under the portrait of Ena Sharples. Everyone knew that back-street blueys weren't much good, but there wasn't much else around and they were relatively cheap. You had to neck a lot of them to feel anything, so the plan was to crush them up and inject them. You might get more out of them that way, and you'd certainly get it quicker. Even this was iffy, though, because what you seemed to get in the mixture was mostly blue ink. Still, it was better than nothing, if only just.

But tonight there was a problem. They couldn't go to Tommy and Shaun's place. Wendy and Mrs Coggins were on the warpath after the recent run-ins with the Drug Squad. Walter was home, so they couldn't use Dan's place. Eddie's house was similarly compromised. There was one remaining option, but it was tricky. Marty's parents were away, but they locked him out and took his key and sent him to his sister's when they went on holiday, because he couldn't be trusted with the place. He'd set fire to his bedroom the previous year, when they were in Prestatyn. So he couldn't get in... but they might try breaking in.

They finished their pints and headed for the Baldock residence: an end-terraced on Cuthbert Street. The front was implacable and impenetrable – door and windows tightly locked. They filed round the back into the narrow cobblestone alley and climbed over the gate into the yard. The light wasn't good, away from the streetlights, but when eyes adjusted they could see enough, and Marty knew it intimately. The narrow, top kitchen window was slightly open.

Tommy cupped his hands. Dan placed his right foot on the makeshift step and his left on the windowsill, then pushed himself up. He lifted the window open and dragged himself into the gap. Pivoting on his stomach, he brought his knee up and got one leg through the window, then the other, then lowered himself towards whatever was underneath him in the darkness. He poked with his toes for something hard. His right foot came to rest on something that felt reasonably reliable. He cautiously let his weight down onto it. Suddenly, there was a loud cracking noise, and whatever it was that was supporting him gave way. For an instant he thought he was doomed, but he only dropped six inches. He jumped down to the floor, felt for the light switch, clicked it on and looked back. There was the electric cooker, with three good rings and a hole where the fourth should be. He looked into the hole, and there, lying in the grill space below, was the ring.

Dan unlocked the door and let the others in. 'Some good news and some bad news, Marty,' said Dan as they filed past him, 'we're in, but I've busted the cooker.'

Tommy looked at the sad sunken hole. 'Never mind that. We'll sort it in a minute. Let's get this fix sorted first.'

They had their fixes, of blue liquid with a tiny amount of amphetamine in it, then set about dealing with the cooker.

They all looked at it studiously. Dan reached into the grill and pressed the ring back up into place, but it wouldn't stay put – the welds that held the brackets had broken.

'I've got some Araldite in me room,' said Marty.

'Well, yeah. Let's give it try,' said Dan, hopefully.

They mixed the Araldite and Dan applied it carefully to the broken welds with a matchstick and pressed the ring back up into position. And when the glue set the ring stayed put and felt solid, and you'd never know it had ever been damaged. They turned the lights off, locked-up and went back to The Cricketers.

Two weeks later, when Mrs Baldock was cooking up a big pan of Lancashire hotpot on her stove, the ring suddenly and inexplicably gave way and it and the pan fell through the hotplate into the grill space below.

***

It was half nine. They'd been at Buffy's for about an hour, and Dan had just taken a break from dancing. He sat at one of the tables by the wall next to the DJ's stand, swigged from his pint of bitter and looked absentmindedly around the dimly lit room. The dancefloor was half full. Tommy stood with Jez, Philbo and Rick Cooper on the far side, leaning into each other's ears, setting up a gear deal.

A fair-haired man in his early twenties, wearing a denim jacket and tapered denim jeans, appeared at the entrance, spoke to no-one, ignored the dancers and strode purposefully across the room to the bar, where he struck up an inaudible conversation with the barman.

Squad, thought Dan. *No-one wears tapered kecks; no-one wears a denim jacket and matching jeans. Plain clothes my arse!* In a room full of baggy pants and tight cotton T-shirts, this guy could not have been more out of place and more visible.

Tommy concluded his conversation with Jez and the others, plonked himself down on the chair next to Dan, took a pull on his beer and lit a Number 6.

'Seen that guy at the bar?' said Dan. 'He's Squad. Has to be. Look at him.'

'Give over. You're just being paranoid,' said Tommy.

'Really?! Look at him. Just look at what he's wearing. Two lots of denim and tapered kecks – he has to be Squad. Who else could be that uncool?'

Before Tommy had a chance to reply, the lights came on and dozens of police officers – male and female, plain-clothes and uniformed – rushed into the place. The denim guy at the bar turned to meet them. The music stopped.

'Everyone against the wall,' shouted the main, plain-clothes cop. 'Don't move and don't touch anything.' The denim guy approached him, leant into his ear and pointed variously around the room.

Cops grabbed some of the recalcitrant and bewildered ones by the arm, dragged them off the dancefloor and pressed them against the wall. Some of the girls shrieked as they were grabbed; a couple of them dissolved into tears.

Everyone was inspected in turn. A plain-clothes cop walked up to Dan and told him to empty his pockets. Dan complied. The cop forced his hands into Dan's pockets to make sure: the side pockets of his waxed-cotton bomber jacket, the breast pockets of his white cheesecloth shirt, the front/groin pockets of his Falmers baggy jeans. Mercifully the Falmers didn't have back pockets, so he was spared the bloke fondling his buttocks. The cop found nothing. He then rummaged in Dan's blow-dried hair to see if there was anything lurking beneath his black locks, but still found nothing. Finally, he made Dan roll up his sleeves and scanned for track marks on his forearms, but Dan was still giving his front veins a bit of recovery time and cranking into the backs of his arms, and as with the raid at Tommy's house, the cop didn't look there.

Next to Dan another cop subjected Tommy to the same procedure. Both he and Dan were deemed clean and sent out of the building.

They waited outside, free men. The less lucky ones were rushed, arms twisted up behind their backs, into dark blue vans. Rick was amongst them. The cops had seen him throw a wrap onto the floor as he waited to be frisked. Greg Platt, who was already well known to the Drug Squad, was taken out back to the store room and strip searched. He had nothing on him and was allowed to leave.

Rick wasn't released till the next day. Normally loud and ebullient, Rick came out of the police station changed. He was quiet, cowed, visibly shaken, and refused to talk about what had happened to him in there.

***

Dan Brody, Chris and Mel Halliwell and Charlie Broadhead stumbled out of Blackpool Mecca at 2am on a piercingly cold Saturday night in the depth of winter and made for the back street on the far side of Central Drive, where Charlie's red Datsun Cherry was parked.

Chris and Mel pulled Dan's leg about the attractive girl he'd been chatting to in the half hour before the club closed. Dan took it in good heart, told them she was called Carmen and said he'd got her phone number.

'Whoop-whoop!'

When they reached the Datsun, it was, like everything else, hidden under a couple of inches of snow. Dan poked a finger though the layer on the car roof and wrote. The word 'DAN' appeared in crimson letters against the pristine white. Mel then took a turn, and after DAN he wrote, in brackets, '(ROMEO)'. Charlie had been sauntering some way behind. He arrived seconds later and looked at the writing on his car.

'What? DAN CROMEOD?! Who's DAN CROMEOD?'

The others laughed at first, then realised that Charlie really had misread it, and they explained that the shapes on the ends were brackets, not a C and a D, and the word in the middle was ROMEO, and they were giving Dan stick about his insatiable appetite for women.

They got back to their various bits of Greater Manchester at about four in the morning. Dan slept till two in the afternoon.

He remembered Carmen and searched his last-night's clothes urgently for the scrap of paper with her phone number on it. He turned jacket and trouser pockets inside out, but it had gone. He'd lost it. And she lived in some village outside Blackpool, the name of which he couldn't remember – if he'd heard it correctly in the first place over the club's thundering sound system – and the odds of bumping into her again were close to zero. But anyway, he had to get cleaned up and get his act together because Rita was coming round at four.

***

After necking a tab of acid each, Tommy, Dan and Shaun were enjoying the endlessly transformative décor of the living room at 64 Sheffield Road. The hands of the brown clock in the middle of the mantelpiece semaphored that it was just short of 2am.

'I'm getting a bit micey in 'ere,' said Shaun. 'Let's go for a walk or something.'

'OK.'

'Make sure you've got a key. Have we got a key?'

'I've got a key.'

'OK.'

Sheffield Road was deserted, magical and strangely wide, like something from a post-apocalyptic movie. The sound of screeching and grinding drifted up from the night-shift engineering works' in the valley, along with random clanking noises from the goods yard. The sky was dark and moonless, but the road, being a main trunk road, was well lit with lots of tall, powerful streetlamps – gangly *War of the Worlds* aliens that dyed everything yellow and black. The less well-lit Steggs Lane, across the way, beckoned.

They trooped past Walter's house and the room that contained the bed Dan ought to be asleep in. After about half a mile, Steggs Lane steepened, turned gently right and ceased to be Steggs Lane. From here, it became Old Sheffield Road.

Old Sheffield Road was ancient. It climbed and wound and occasionally dipped, then climbed and wound some more, as it wended its way up and over the Pennines. It had been there for millennia, since before Dashley Dyke existed; when what became a bustling industrial boomtown was still just scraggy grassland, fit only for sheep grazing, stretched out across the River Dash between the market town of Dashton and the crossroads village of Butterworth. The feet of Brigantian tribesmen had first defined the route; legions of Roman soldiers had metalled and marched on it; ragged, hungry people escaping an unsatisfactory life on one side of the Pennines and believing there was a better one on the other had staggered up or down it with their few pathetic possessions on their backs.

Steep, narrow and inconveniently bendy, Old Sheffield Road lost most of its purpose when, in the early 19th century, a new, straight, wide and slow-gradient Sheffield Road was built, as a job-creation scheme for soldiers left over from the Napoleonic Wars. And having lost most of its traffic and having the only bit of olde worlde charm to be found in Dashley Dyke, Old Sheffield Road became a desirable place to live. It had some of Dashley Dyke's oldest houses, as well as newer ones, which got described as 'architect designed' when they came up for sale in estate agents' windows. Most of Dashley Dyke's houses were not architect designed. It was just a stroke of luck that bricks got piled on top of each other in the right order and suitable gaps were left for doors and windows. This might also explain why most of the houses didn't have bathrooms – an oversight an architect would have spotted immediately.

They stopped outside an age-old gritstone house. It had a low front wall and a narrow garden filled with jumbled green stuff of various sorts. More green stuff, with the odd pale flower here and there, climbed up the front of the house and wrapped itself around the door and the mullioned windows, which had diamond shapes on them, made out of thin strips of lead.

'Bloody hell,' said Tommy, 'Snow White's cottage.'

They cackled and continued their exploratory stroll.

Shaun fiddled with his watch. It was new, and he was still fascinated by it and coming to terms with how to use it. It was one of those cutting-edge LED digital ones – a Casio. It was blank and inert most of the time, to save the batteries. You had to press a button to wake it up. Shaun stopped walking and gazed at it aghast.

"Kin 'ell! Wow! Look at this.'

Tommy and Dan looked, and there, in the dark of Old Sheffield Road in the middle of the night, on the watch's silent, implacable black face, the word 'THIS' glowed at them in bold pink letters.

THIS! *THIS!* Fucking THIS! Everyone knew that 'is-ness' was a key aspect of the trip experience, but a watch?! How could it know? And here it was trying to communicate with them, announcing its presence. It knew! It knew they were tripping. It was letting them know it understood and was with them. THIS!

They shook their heads in disbelief. Astonished. Gobsmacked. Flabbergasted. *Wow! Wow! THIS! THIS!*

Things were much less exciting 24 hours later, when the watch, in spite of all the great expectations now placed upon it, could only muster FR16.

***

Rita had persuaded Dan to bring one of his friends along for a blind date with one of hers. Dan had taken Adey Martin, and the night had been an unmitigated disaster. They'd met in a little street-corner pub in Blackfriars. Rita's friend, Deborah, lived in one of the tower blocks nearby. Deborah had curly yellow hair – a bit like a blonde afro – and what Dan thought was a reasonably attractive face. This wasn't a view shared by Adey, and the night was characterised by stilted, forced conversation, as Adey tried to be polite to a girl he found as alluring as lard.

On the bus on the way home, Adey gave Dan all sorts of stick. What was Dan doing inviting him out to meet a dog like that? Dan tried to excuse himself on the basis that Rita had said she was very attractive and he himself didn't think she was that bad. In the end Adey blew himself down, and they agreed to differ.

So it was that some weeks later, when Rita wanted another trial run with another of her mates and another of Dan's, he baulked. But Rita kept up the pressure. This really, genuinely, was a great looking girl, said Rita; so hot in fact that she was almost frightened to show her to Dan in case he ran off with her. This girl, Monica, was something else – had to be seen to be believed. She'd swear it on a stack of bibles. There was no way any of Dan's mates could find Monica unattractive – it was impossible – and Rita would take responsibility if it was another embarrassing, crap night, but there was no way it could be.

Rita had covered all the angles, exhausted all of the arguments. Dan acquiesced and persuaded Chris Halliwell to come along, using all the arguments Rita had put to him.

They met in the newly-opened House That Jack Built on Bury New Road in Higher Broughton. Dan and Chris arrived first, got a couple of beers in, and chose a secluded alcove with space for the girls when they arrived. Ten minutes later, Rita and Monica arrived. Rita was foremost, looking as hot as ever – her startling green eyes brought out by expertly-applied make-up, hair freshly streaked and wearing her stylish, knee-length black leather coat. As she stood aside and proudly introduced her friend, the contrast could not have been more stark. There was this plain, brown-haired, mousy girl, with shifty little eyes and a tight lipless mouth, which made her look like the only emotions she'd ever felt were anger and disappointment. Dan's heart sank. Rita either had eyesight problems or she was a liar. Dan and Chris took dark half-glances at each other. Dan felt both angry that he'd been misled by Rita and awkward and embarrassed that he'd been tricked into misleading Chris. He hoped his glance would convey that. Meanwhile, Chris was mad at Dan because he'd been had, while accepting that he was there now and he'd have to be polite and friendly with this girl, even if he felt she had all the appeal of a sack of hardcore. It was going to be a long evening.

Dan tried to persuade himself of what people had long tried to persuade him – that he shouldn't be such a shallow git and what mattered was personality, not looks. The trouble with Monica was that she failed to trouble the scorers on either count. Chris, Dan and Rita did their best to sound upbeat and involve her in the conversation, but it was like trying to breathe life into a dead weasel. The lads told their best stories and their funniest jokes. They told self-effacing anecdotes about times they'd made fools of themselves, in the hope of making her feel a bit bolder. They wondered if a few more drinks might loosen her up as the evening wore on. But nothing worked. Monica just sat there, tight-lipped, hands clasped firmly in her lap, inert.

Chris and Dan argued all the way back on the bus into town: Chris seethed at what he'd been set up for, while Dan argued that it wasn't his fault, that Rita had misled him. Thankfully for Dan, once in Piccadilly Chris stomped off to get the Withington bus, while Dan made for the Number 8 back to Dashley Dyke.

On Saturday night, Dan, Chris and Chris's brother Mel were out doing a few city centre pubs, along with Charlie Broadhead. Against a backdrop of the usual uproarious Saturday-night racket in The New Mancunian, the Monica incident was the chief topic of conversation. By now Chris had calmed down and the whole thing was a joke, albeit one from the gallows end of the genre. Chris gave Dan playful abuse about setting him up with a dog, and whereas Dan had stood up for himself against Adey because he felt Deborah was alright, he offered no defence in the case of Chris v Monica. And the four of them laughed at what a nightmare both the evening and Monica had been. But Charlie's laughter ended abruptly, and to the astonishment of the others, he said he wanted to meet her; he wanted a blind date with Monica.

At first there was disbelief: he couldn't possibly be serious… but he was. Then they tried to talk him out of it. He wouldn't like her – she was about as interesting as an old filing cabinet, but not as good looking and without the classy dress sense. But Charlie was both serious and adamant – he wanted to meet Monica. Eventually Dan was persuaded, both of Charlie's seriousness and to risk expanding further his own burgeoning reputation as someone who sets up dodgy blind dates, and he agreed to set the thing up on the absolute understanding that this was at Charlie's insistence and that he, Dan, would take no responsibility if it was another fucking nightmare – this would be the third time he'd been had like this. Charlie agreed to the terms, and on Sunday Dan phoned Rita and another blind date was set up for Wednesday.

Charlie picked up Dan from Dashley Dyke in his Datsun and the pair sped over to Rita's place in Higher Broughton. They transferred to Rita's Cortina, picked up Monica in Pendleton, and drove out to a new disco pub Rita had heard about in Eccles – Dan next to Rita in the front; Charlie with Monica in the back. Dan was naturally anxious about Charlie meeting Monica, and there was little conversation in the car.

They found an almost secluded spot in the loud, bustling disco pub. Van McCoy, K C and the Sunshine Band and B T Express pounded from the speakers. Conversation wasn't easy across the wide wooden table and over the thumping disco beat – which was piped into every corner of the place so no-one would miss out – but after a short time Charlie and Monica were in their own little world. Dan and Rita couldn't hear what they were saying, but were content that they seemed to be getting along, against what had seemed insurmountable odds.

And then they were more than getting along; they were all over each other: hands, lips and the odd raised knee. But suddenly Charlie had swept off to the gents and Monica was in tears. Rita swung round the table and slipped into Charlie's seat, next to Monica, and asked what he'd done, what she was so upset about – they'd seemed to be getting on so well. But Monica wasn't upset. These were tears of joy. Charlie had declared undying love before going off for a pee. In a couple of hours in an Eccles disco pub, with the Bee Gees, Barry White and Gloria Gaynor enhancing the romantic vibe, Charlie and Monica had fallen rapturously in love.

That was the plus side. On the minus side, Charlie had told Monica all about the conversation on Saturday night: how Dan and Chris had laughed at her and called her a dog and said she was about as sexy as office furniture and tried to put him off, but Charlie, steadfast, had refused to believe their word and had manfully come through and this was his reward. It seemed the mousy girl and the ferrety guy were made for each other.

So it was that on the way back to Pendleton, Monica, enraged at what she'd heard, started to hurl abuse at the back of Dan's head from the back seat of the Cortina. And as the journey went on she worked herself into ever more of a tizz and got ever louder. Dan tried to protest that it hadn't been him that called her names; he'd just not disputed Chris's account. Well, he'd kind of backed it up, really. But Monica got bolder and angrier and more aggressive. She screeched and she effed and she hurled insults at Dan. Dan tried to keep his cool. But as the car sped down Broad Street, Monica started to hit him on the back of the head. And, as anyone who knew Dan would tell you, if there was one thing that would make this normally placid guy explode, it was messing with his head. Way back in the fourth form, there'd been that kid sat behind Dan who kept flicking the back of his head with a ruler. Dan warned the fucker once, but he persisted, and in the next instant found himself lying on the floor, wearing his desk. And then there'd been that incident with Lucy and the umbrella. And there was his perennial disquiet at the barber's.

Dan lost it. He spun round as best he could, restricted by the seat belt and a clip-on head restraint, and poked his finger into Monica's face and told her to shut it. But on she went, and Dan swung round still further, now half out of his seat, and told her he'd never hit a woman before, but she was going the right way to be the first. Monica slunk back into her seat, still hissing and seething, while Rita and Charlie tried to shut her up and defuse Dan.

Charlie got out of the Cortina in Pendleton with Monica, in spite of the fact that his car was a couple of miles away in Higher Broughton. Monica slammed the door and spat on the windscreen.

Dan went back to Rita's and spent the night there. Neither of them ever saw Monica or Charlie again.

***

Dan Brody, Mick Henshaw and Tommy and Shaun Coggins set off from Dashley Dyke for the Cleethorpes all-nighter at dusk – just after 7pm – in Mick's Austin 1800. This was early, given that it was a two-and-a half/three-hour journey and the 'niter didn't start till gone midnight, but they fancied the idea of breaking up the trip by checking out a few pubs en route.

As they passed through Gosden, the last town before they climbed up into the wilderness of the Pennines, it started to rain. Mick flicked on the wipers, which scudded into action but did no more than create two streaky wet semi-circles. A four-inch strip of loose rubber flapped about like an old shoelace on the driver's side.

'Shit. I meant to replace the wipers. They're buggered.'

'There's a dealership just up the road,' said Tommy.

Mick brought the motor to a halt next to the showroom. The new cars were inside, the used ones on the concrete apron outside. The place was shut and deserted.

In a move that looked so slick that you got the sense he'd done it many times before, Tommy jumped out, looked up and down the street and took the wipers off Mick's car, then stepped over the low wall that surrounded the forecourt, sought out an identical, but beige, Austin 1800, removed its wipers and put Mick's on in their place, before returning and slipping the new ones onto Mick's car.

Mick gave the new wipers a try. They worked a treat, and Mick declared himself happy with the job, and the trip resumed.

They sampled the beer and hospitality in a selection of Yorkshire and Lincolnshire pubs and, at about twenty to midnight, were closing in on Cleethorpes. Suddenly, ahead, on the otherwise deserted road, there seemed to be something going on. Torches pierced the gloom, silhouettes shifted, cars lined up at the roadside.

'Shit! It's a fuckin' road block. Hide yer gear,' said Mick.

'Where? Where won't they look?' yelled Shaun, urgently.

'Down your underpants,' said Dan.

'What? For fuck's sake. You serious? You've got to eat them afterwards.'

'Would you rather be busted?'

They each extracted pills and capsules from trouser and jacket pockets and shoved them down under belts and waistbands into their underpants.

Mick slowed the Austin. A policeman waved them down with a torch and directed them into a layby. Mick wound down the window.

'Got any drugs in there, lads?' enquired the officer.

'What? No. Of course not,' said Mick, in what he felt was a pretty grown-up, business-like tone.

'Out of the car, all of you.'

They stepped out into the dark, sweet country air. The cop went through their pockets. A second cop plundered the car – glove box, under seats, boot...

Relieved and begrudgingly exonerated, they re-joined the road.

Still nervous they might be followed and caught out, they left their gear where it was for a mile or two. Then, with nothing in the rear-view mirror, Mick pulled into another layby and they extracted their pills and caps from their dubious hiding places and necked them, with cola and a hint of distaste.

The gear kicked in and the Cleethorpes 'niter was its usual stifling, frenetic, fabulous self. The top sounds of the moment were "Supership" and "Time Passes By" and "Control Tower" and "What a Difference a Day Makes". They also played an earlier Esther Phillips track – "Catch Me I'm Falling" – which Dan loved.

But then it was morning, and in the savage, uncompromising daylight, the sweaty, come-down drive home had to be faced.

They needed petrol. The Austin, with its 1800 engine and especially with four up, was a guzzler, and Cleethorpes was quite a way from Dashley Dyke. Mick pulled into a petrol station and hopped out.

On the far side of the pump was a mustard-coloured Allegro. Dan recognised the car – it belonged to Dave Podmore's big brother, Benny. He also recognised some of the passengers – soul boys he knew by sight from around Dashley Dyke and Manchester. The bonnet was up and Benny was looking at the engine, perplexed. His hands moved around in the engine compartment. He was doing something, but it wasn't clear what.

Mick left the pay booth, saw Benny and went over. They had a brief conversation, which wasn't audible in the 1800. Mick seemed to be explaining something, pointing.

Mick jumped back into the car, slammed the door and started the engine.

'What a fucking pillock,' said Mick, pulling out onto the road.

'Why? What was he doing?' asked Tommy.

'He'd checked the dipstick, and the oil was low. So he'd got some to top it up with, and he was trying to pour it in down the dipstick hole!'

The car erupted with laughter. 'What a knob-head!'

'I had to show him the oil filler cap and what you have to do. Pillock.'

***

Dan lifted up his head from his drawing board, gazed down the vast, first-floor, open-plan office and allowed his eyes to escape from the myriad fine black lines he had been labouring over and readjust for a moment. Down at the far end, past desks, filing cabinets and scores of other busy heads, was the exquisite Penny.

A short distance from Penny was an empty seat which, until a fortnight earlier, had been occupied by old Joe. Their workplaces were the same distance from Dan's in Distribution Planning, but ten feet apart across the aisle: Joe in Parts, Penny in Domestic Billing. They, it had always seemed to Dan, were the most opposite people in the whole of the Gas Board's Verrington facility.

Joe was in his early sixties, but could easily have been taken for someone a couple of decades older. He had always been a small man, but with age had become ever more wizened, and by now bore more than a passing resemblance to a turtle. His small, wrinkled, hairless head protruded from his sensible cream coloured shirt and tweedy green tie. Joe, the office gossip said, had never been with a woman. He'd come close, once – Elsie, she was called. They met at a dance at the Astoria during the War, but she rapidly tired of him and dropped him in favour of a succession of American airmen. Joe was left bereft and never mustered the courage to try again. Elsie hadn't seen it the way Joe did; she was just having fun, and when Joe ceased to be fun, which was pretty quickly, she was off. What Elsie didn't know, or if she did, didn't care about, was that for Joe, this was his moment; while he was just some boring Verrington bloke she'd met, she was the love of his life. And now, all these decades on, he was still a virgin and still lived with his aged, domineering mother.

Penny, on the other hand, was just twenty and so breathtakingly beautiful that she hardly seemed real. She had the most delicate features and flawless, almost translucent, skin, which made her look like a Dresden figurine. Her hair, of the palest blonde, was always perfectly brushed and reached most of the way down her gracefully arched back. She wore light coloured clothes, to complement her exquisite complexion. In a white angora top and pale muslin skirt she was an angel that floated weightlessly through the office and bewitched all but the most self-disciplined of men. But in spite of her captivating beauty, she was modest and quiet. She just came in, did her work and went home. Few in the office knew much about her, though she was rumoured to have a boyfriend.

Dan was mercifully inured to her allure. For all his promiscuity outside of work, the need to keep his druggy other life from his employers ensured that he never dated girls from the office. Plus, he always seemed drawn to the dark-haired, red-lipped vampish types, his nascent sexuality having been defined by Fenella Fielding writhing and smouldering on a *chaise longue* in a skin-tight red velvet dress in *Carry On Screaming*, and nearly everyone he had ever slept with he'd met in the shadowy netherworld of a nightclub. For Dan, the dark mystery of the intoxicated night and the combined whiff of hairspray, booze and cheap perfume were the ultimate aphrodisiac. Penny was just too pure, too virginal. Still, it didn't stop him looking and wondering, now and then.

Joe, on the other hand, looked at her and looked at her and looked at her, day after day after day. He lusted and fantasised. But he was so much older – she would never go with him. But maybe she would. He'd seen all those things on the telly – Benny Hill and such – where gorgeous girls somehow found ugly old men irresistible. And in the movies, it was always the craggy old geezer who got the slender, wraithlike goddess who was only just out of her teens. It had to be possible – he wanted her so badly – it just *had* to be. And then there were the lascivious fuckers who worked next to him on the other side: the comb-over brigade, the sweaty, moustachioed, fag-stained reps from Commercial Sales, who came back daily half-pissed after a three hour dinner break – or rather *lunch* break, as they preferred to call it in Verrington – and thought they were great because they sold gas to clients who couldn't buy it anywhere else. They were always full of it, cracking dirty jokes and making out they'd groped this or that lass in the stationery cupboard and had it away with all and sundry. If they could do it, so could he.

He'd never even spoken to her.

The unfortunate occurrence happened at 1pm on a rainy grey Thursday. Penny, having taken an early lunch, ascended the stairwell from the ground-floor canteen, just as Joe set off down the stairs for his. There was no-one else around. Their eyes met. Penny smiled sweetly and innocently at the harmless old man who worked near her. Joe saw the object of his lust and obsession smiling at him. His chance had come at last. The blood rushed to his head. Her exquisite form filled his consciousness. She was there, now, *for him*. But he didn't know what to do. Action was needed, but what should it be? He was overcome, overwhelmed with passion and desire, struck dumb.

As they crossed on the landing, he reached out and touched her angora-covered breast, with a short jab of the hand, like a kid playing tick in a schoolyard. Penny shrieked and recoiled. Joe's legs buckled beneath him and he fainted where he stood.

There was a disciplinary, and Joe was never seen again.

***

The guy walked diagonally across the dancefloor at Buffy's, making a bee-line for Dan. And then he was directly in front of Dan, smiling and looking in Dan's eyes – a lightly built fellow of about twenty, with delicate features and wavy blond hair.

'Hi,' said blond man.

'Hi?' said Dan, slightly bemused at the stranger's familiarity.

'I'm Kelly,' came the reply, in a distinctly effeminate tone.

'Oh, hi Kelly.'

'D'you remember me? Kelly from Barnsley.'

'Errrrr...'

'You remember me, don't you – Saturday night at Cleethorpes?'

'I'm struggling if I'm honest, mate.'

'We chatted at the Cleethorpes all-nighter. You said I must come and check out this place – Buffy's in Bradfield. Don't you remember? You must remember. We chatted for ages.'

Dan racked his brain, tried to piece together Saturday night. He'd only got fragments. He'd sunk five pints of bitter in pubs en route to Cleethorpes, as they all had, and arrived at the place with a belly containing more pills than a hypochondriac's night stand. He remembered queuing on the pier and getting into the club, and he remembered dancing to fabulous tracks like "I Travel Alone" and "I'm Com'un Home in the Morn'un" and "Uptown Saturday Night". He remembered Tommy having one of his hallucinations again – a Triumph Herald had materialised briefly on the stage but had vanished before anyone got hurt. Graeme Stafford had hitched a lift with them and Dan remembered him coming up and wanting to talk about something at some point during the night, but he was incomprehensible, partly because the music was so loud, but also because he was slurring his words and foaming at the mouth because he always took a handful of Valium with his speed, to ward off the edginess. Dan remembered wandering off on his own to the Winter Gardens half of the all-nighter, a couple of hundred yards away along the seafront, and the others doing their nuts when he got back to the pier because they couldn't find him and were beginning to wonder if he'd fallen into the sea. And he remembered the toilets being brightly lit and less threatening than the ones at Wigan Casino, and he remembered a good humoured vibe in there in the morning, as lads got changed and sprayed themselves with Arrid Extra Dry and splashed on Brut 33. He did vaguely remember some random conversations with some random people – speed made him very talkative – but he wasn't sure if he remembered this guy. But then he started to concede to himself that the bloke couldn't have shown up at Buffy's out of the blue with this clear recollection of a conversation if it hadn't happened – he couldn't be making it up – and at this he started to picture himself chatting to the guy, as described. But then he wasn't sure if he was really remembering, or if he was inventing this image because he thought he should, and in the end he had to conclude that, no, he really didn't remember the bloke or the conversation they were supposed to have had, even if it all rang true.

'I'm sorry, no. I don't remember. I was off my tree on Saturday night. I always am at the all-nighters.'

'Oh, oh,' said Kelly, in a disappointed tone.

'Sorry, but I really don't remember,' emphasised Dan, but on seeing the disappointment on Kelly's face set about trying to rescue the situation. 'But, anyway, yeah. It's a good place, Buffy's. I'm glad you came. Barnsley, eh? A nice trip over the Pennines. I can understand why I recommended it, even if I don't remember the conversation. I always recommend it here. It's a great place. They play some fantastic stuff. You'll love it.'

Kelly turned halfway away from Dan and pointed to a guy on the busy dancefloor: a skinhead, in rolled-up bleached Levi's, Doc Martens and check shirt with braces. He stood out from the rest, all in their soul-boy baggies and flares. 'That's my friend, Kevin. That's who I came with.'

'The skinhead?'

'Yeah.'

'Oh, OK.'

'He wets the bed, you know.'

'Erm. Right. Odd for a man his age,' said Dan, quizzically.
'But what's that got to do with you?'
'We share the same bed.'
'Ah, erm. Right. You wouldn't be gay by any chance, would you, Kelly?'
'Yes. Is that a problem?'
'Well, no. Not as long as you understand that I'm not,' said Dan, trying to strike a balance between firmness and sensitivity.
'Hmmph.'
'Oh, look. I'm sorry if I've misled you, if you've had a wasted journey. But if I was raving about this place, it really was only about this place. I'm a chatty, friendly guy with a passion for this music. If you get me talking, I don't shut up – especially at an all-nighter. And I love this club. There's no more to it than that.'

There was a long pause. Kelly looked at Dan, then at the floor, then back at Dan. 'Well, thanks for being honest.'

'No sweat.'

Kelly smiled a disappointed smile and walked over to Kevin, and the pair vanished into the crowd. Dan took a swig from his beer.

***

It was half six on a Wednesday evening. Dan had finished his tea and wondered what to do with the evening: pub, later... maybe... probably... almost certainly.

The phone rang. It was Tommy.

'Johnny Caswell's just come round with some gear – opium tincture.'

'Ooh. Right. I'm on me way.'

Ten minutes later, Dan was in Tommy and Shaun's bedroom. Three fresh 45s – Tommy's latest soul purchases – waited their turn by the Sharp Music centre, after "Baby I'm Still the Same Man" by James Wells, which was booming from the speakers as Dan arrived. Johnny held up a brown bottle – a proper pharmaceutical bottle with liquid rolling around inside it – and looked very pleased with himself.

Johnny was younger than Tommy and Dan but older than Shaun, and he'd been a regular at Buffy's since he was fourteen and a frequenter of Wigan Casino since it opened. He was slim and good looking, with intense blue eyes, angular features, and dark brown hair that went curly if he allowed it to grow, which he generally did, giving him a look of the England fast bowler, Bob Willis.

'Opium tincture.' Johnny proudly announced, as he wriggled the bottle in his fingers for the others to feast their eyes upon.

'Gradely,' said Dan. 'What do you do with it?'

'Fix it. A mil apiece ought to be a decent start.'

Tommy jogged downstairs and came back with a mug of clean cold water. He extracted the syringe and needle from his bedside table, fitted them together and gave them a couple of rinses, squirting the used water into the old cast iron fireplace. He handed the works to Johnny.

Johnny inserted the needle into the bottle and pulled up the plunger. The mysterious russet-coloured fluid followed it into the plastic hypodermic. No need for diluting or filtering – this was proper hospital stuff. Johnny stopped as the liquid reached the middle line – 1 millilitre – then tipped up the syringe, held it up to the light and squeezed out the tiny bubble that had settled at the top. A minute bead of liquid at the very tip of the needle confirmed that all the air had been eliminated.

'Who's first then?'

'Well, it's your gear. You better have first dibs,' said Tommy. Dan and Shaun nodded in assent.

Johnny tourniqued his right arm with a trouser belt and Tommy gave him the fix. Johnny gasped with pleasure, closed his eyes, dropped the tourniquet from his arm and flopped onto Tommy's bed.

'You wanna go next, Dan?' asked Tommy, as he re-rinsed the works and again sprayed the fireplace.

'Well, yeah, don't mind if I do – if you and Shaun don't mind.' This was an understatement. Dan loved speed, and with opiates having that reputation of being the pinnacle of drugs, he anticipated the speed experience, but at much greater intensity. He prepared himself for the thrill of his life.

Tommy pulled a further 1 mil from the brown bottle, expertly found a vein in Dan's right forearm and pressed the plunger. Dan felt a sudden warmth and hot tingling in his face – and not much else. There was a brief silence as the others looked at him, seeking a reaction.

'Is that it?!' exclaimed Dan, in loud disappointment. 'That's opiates?! Fuckin' 'ell. I was expecting speed squared. It's hardly anything.'

'Is that it?! Is that it?!' yelled Johnny, outraged. 'That's fucking opium, man. The Cream of Drugs. Aren't yer getting anything from it?'

'Well, yeah, something... But it's a bit mild.'

'Jeez. A bit mild, he says. A bit fuckin' mild. Fuck me!'

Tommy studied their faces, trying to make sense of the contradiction: one of them in ecstasy, calling it the Cream of Drugs; the other wondering if it had even tipped the dial. Bemused, but intent on finding out the truth for himself, he rinsed the works and sorted out fixes for Shaun and himself. The four of them then set off down the hill to The Apple Tree for a game of darts and few pints of Robbies'.

Dan searched inside himself, trying to grasp the effects of the opium, psychologically and physically. By the end of the evening, he still wasn't entirely sure what he was feeling, but he was sure that he wanted some more.

***

It was half-one on Sunday afternoon; overcast but not raining – just the job for a kick-about in the park. Dan called round for Tommy and Shaun, to see if they fancied it. Wendy answered the door.

'Hiya, Wendy. Just wondered if Tommy 'n' Shaun fancied a bit of footy?'

'Oh, come in, Dan. You'll have to wait. We're about to have our Sunday dinner.'

The family was seated around the table – Tommy, Shaun, Mrs Coggins and Grandma – each with an empty plate in front of them, with a knife and fork parked alongside, on the tan and white flower-patterned plastic table cloth. At the far end of the table a fifth place-setting awaited Wendy, who was server.

They exchanged greetings and Dan took a seat on the yellow and brown check blanket on the settee on the other side of the room. Wendy came in with a large plate, stacked high with steaming cabbage, placed it in the middle of the table and took her seat.

'Tuck in,' said Wendy.

They each took from the charger, filled their plates with cabbage and started to eat.

Tommy had had the push from the GPO for too many drug-induced sick days, and had yet to find another job; Shaun had been made redundant from the carding room at Moorcroft's Woollen Mill in Crossley, which wasn't entirely a bad thing because now he didn't smell so bad; their dad had walked out in 1959, shortly after Shaun was born, and had not been seen since; Mrs Coggins had long since given up work at Henderson's anorak factory because the rheumatism had frozen her hands into useless claws; Granny was ancient, crippled and way past work of any kind; and Wendy was at college. So, Sunday dinner was cabbage.

***

Dan's come-downs and dissociative moods made work a trying experience, and today Muriel Date was getting on his wick. It was the way she spoke on the phone. Whenever she asked to speak to someone, she'd end the sentence with 'at all': 'Is Mr So-and-So there, *at all?*' The 'at all' bit was presumably so the sentence didn't sound quite so assertive and demanding. 'Is Mr So-and-So there, *at all?*' was softer than just 'Is Mr So-and-So there?' Even so, it put Dan's back up, partly because the excessive deference made him cringe, and partly because it defied logic.

The matter rolled around in Dan's irritable mind. There were circumstances in which 'at all' tagged onto a request would make sense:

'I'm kind of skint till Friday. Could you lend me a tenner?'

'I can't. I'm a bit skint myself.'

'How about a fiver, then?'

'Err, no, not really…'

'Well, if you could lend me anything *at all* it'd be a help.'

But Mr So-and-So could only be there or not be there. He couldn't be slightly there. There couldn't just be some vestige of Mr So-and-So hanging round the place – it was all or nothing.

Dan fantasised about being on the other end of the phone when Muriel made one of these calls:

'Hello. Is Mr So-and-So there, at all?'

'Yes, he's slightly here. We've got his left leg. The rest of him popped out on an errand half an hour ago. Will this do?'

***

Dan finished work in Verrington at five and rode home to Dashley Dyke, first on the Dirty 30, and then, from Hightown, on the Number 4. He disembarked and strolled up Sheffield Road, thinking about what he would have for tea. At the junction with Steggs Lane stood Crosby's grocers' shop, where Shaun now worked.

Shaun, in his long white grocer's coat, was busy with other customers. He clocked Dan and nodded discreetly. Dan nodded back and vanished into the aisles to choose his shopping. He picked up a Mother's Pride white loaf, a box of Cadbury's chocolate fingers, six medium-sized eggs and a Longley Farm black cherry yoghurt, then joined the queue at the counter.

Then it was his turn. He placed the four items on the high glass counter, which had butter, cheeses and various cooked and fresh meats in the brightly lit display beneath. 'Right. It's these, and can I have half a pound of pork sausages, please.'

Shaun cut off and weighed the sausages, rolled them up efficiently in greaseproof paper and slapped them on the counter in a flourish. 'Right. That's it?'

'Yeah.'

Shaun produced a white carrier bag from behind the counter and stuffed Dan's goodies into it. 'That's err... one pound fifty-seven, please.'

Dan handed over two pound notes.

Shaun rummaged in the till and dropped the change into Dan's waiting palm. 'See yer later.'

'Sure. Cheers,' said Dan, turning to leave. The change seemed heavy for forty-three pence, but he waited till he was outside the shop before checking – just under two pounds in silver and copper coins.

***

Jez Reeves walked into Buffy's looking worse than anyone had ever seen him look, and everyone had seen him in a variety of states. He was pale and pipe-cleaner thin at the best of times, but today, on top of all that, he looked grey and washed out as if in shock, in the starkest possible contrast to his long black leather coat.

Dan and Tommy went over.

'Wassup, Jez?' asked Tommy.

'Terry's dead.'

'If this is a wind-up, Jez, it's not funny,' said Dan, in stunned disbelief.

Jez's eyes filled up. 'It's not. It's not. I wish it was. I've just seen his wife. She's just... And he's got two young kids. It's fuckin' awful.'

''Kin 'ell. What happened? We only went to Wigan with him the other week. He was right as rain. He was on good form.'

'Palfium. He had Palfium.'

'Palfium? What's Terry doing with Palfium? I didn't know he even touched junk.'

'He doesn't. Well, he didn't. Well, he didn't *really*. There was a deal: a few of us were in but didn't have the money, so he stumped-up the dough up-front and was looking after the gear till everyone paid up. Had it in his locker at work. And I guess he couldn't resist having a bit. He started the night shift after few pints, got the Palf out of his locker, fired it up and... well... you know what Palfium's like. Someone found him a few hours later, but he was already dead.'

***

It was a sunny Sunday afternoon, and Dan, Tommy, Shaun, Marty and Eddie had each dropped a tab of acid and gone to the park. They made their way up to their favourite spot: the clearing between the trees in the steep, less populated bit at the top, near where the old packhorse road separated the park from the farmland, where sheep, idly chomping the grass, dotted the hillside.

The drug started to kick in. Dan reckoned he saw a grid under the grass and started trying to scratch it out with his fingertips. The others weren't convinced it was necessarily there and left him to it. Shaun did a cartwheel. Tommy stubbed out a Number 6 on an ant. They watched its death throes as it frazzled away on the end of the cigarette, magnified by the acid and in glorious technicolour.

A familiar figure appeared at the bottom of the hill. It shouted and waved. It was Dave Podmore. Wendy had told him he could find them in the park. Dave wanted to join in; he wanted some acid.

The pills were filed under A in Dan's record box. Drugs in general were filed under D, but acid got its own special spot. He agreed to walk home and get a tab for Dave.

Dan hoped Walter had gone out. Conversations with him were difficult enough, even without acid.

Dan turned the key and opened the door. Walter was diagonally opposite, in the far corner of the living room, talking into the green telephone. Dan snuck past to the bottom of the stairs. He pictured himself like Tom or Jerry doing a bit of exaggerated cartoon-like tip-toeing. Maybe Walter hadn't even seen him; they were, after all, in different universes, which just happened to overlap now and then. He got safely to the foot of the stairs, ran up and into his bedroom and pocketed a tab for Dave. He jogged back down and was halfway across the living room, thinking he'd got away with it, when Walter spoke:

'It's yer mum. Will you have a word.'

Shit.

Dan sauntered over and took the phone from Walter.

'Hello?' said Dan.

A stilted, monosyllabic exchange followed. Dan tried to sound normal, but felt like he was watching someone else have the conversation, and that someone else wasn't doing too well. And Walter was still sat there, right next to him – too close. Dan felt like Walter was marking his performance, and probably agreeing that it wasn't very good. Lily seemed to be somewhere in outer in space, not Brighton. Her voice echoed in from an endless black void, dotted with stars.

Dan tried to be content to let his mum do the talking. He just 'yeah, yeah'd' now and then, in the hope of not having to put together a cogent sentence. Lily had seen this or that down-south relative; they were doing fine. 'Yeah, yeah.' Someone had had a stroke. 'Oh dear.' But then she started to ask questions, and Dan had to try to sound chatty, like anyone else on an ordinary Sunday afternoon – not an easy thing to do when you're in a waking dream in a mischievous passive-aggressive room that keeps sneakily changing shape in the corner of your eye, just to wind you up, and talking to someone who is floating in outer space while pretending they're in Brighton, and all of this on a phone made of lime jelly.

The phone handle started to melt in Dan's hand and wrap itself around his head like a wriggling lizard. He jumped up, terminated the conversation abruptly, handed the perfidious receiver back to Walter, and ran.

Outside, he wondered if that had all been OK. He persuaded himself that it had, more or less. And it was still a sunny Sunday afternoon. He breathed in deeply and relished his escape. He gazed at the cloudless blue sky and soaked up the feeling of freedom. Dashley Dyke was a wonderful place! And he trotted back up to the park.

***

It was important, if you were going to be up all night cranking speed at Tommy and Shaun's or Rick and Sally's, not to run out of fags in the middle of the night, and they always went and stocked up with Number 6 or Benson and Hedges or Sovereign or some combination thereof before the off licence closed at half ten. Even so, they never seemed to *not* run out, and by five or six in the morning they were usually looking for solutions.

Tommy bought a Carlton cigarette maker, to have in reserve. Unlike Rizlas, where you rolled the thing in your fingers and ended up with something shaped loosely like a broken thumb, Carltons were properly preformed hollow cigarettes, complete with filter. The machine that came with them, which was made from red plastic and looked a bit like the top part of an automatic pistol, shoved the tobacco in from the end, and what you ended up with was indistinguishable from any conventional cigarette. They were sold on the basis of economy: a self-assembled Carlton, filled with Carlton's loose tobacco, was marginally cheaper than a readymade cigarette. But there was also the added advantage that you didn't have to use Carlton's tobacco. By choice, or in a crisis, you could use whatever you had to hand.

It was 5am and Shaun had just smoked the last cigarette. In front of them, on the low coffee table with the washed-out picture of somewhere in Italy on it, were two ashtrays, each supporting a small grey mountain of ash and dimps. Using LP sleeves as workstations, Dan and Tommy dismantled the dimps and recovered the last half or quarter of an inch of unused tobacco from each, discarded the paper, filters and ash, and ended up with two not insubstantial piles of unburnt tobacco. This was put into the Carlton machine and a small pile of 'new' cigarettes containing recycled tobacco was created. They'd done the same the night before and the night before that, so, as well as the remnants of the night's new smokes, there was tobacco there that had already had several past lives.

By 6.30, with just the hint of Dashley Dyke life beginning to penetrate from the street, they were again out of fags, but now with two much smaller piles of dimps in the ashtrays. They repeated the dismantling and remaking process and managed to produce a couple more serially recycled cigarettes, which they then shared.

'Here yer go,' said Tommy, proffering the second half of one of the reconstructed fags to Dan. 'Here's a Lone Ranger for yer?'

'A what?'

'You know,' said Tommy, and in the tune from the *Lone Ranger* television programme (or Rossini's *William Tell Overture* if you're posh), sang, 'dimp of a dimp of a dimp, dimp, dimp.'

***

Dan Brody and Tommy and Shaun Coggins sat drinking pints of Boddies' Bitter in The King's Head. They were waiting for Johnny Caswell, who'd got some H.

Johnny arrived at about ten, but as the plan was to go to the Coggins's house to fix up, they had to bide their time until the rest of the household had gone to bed.

Last orders were called at 10.20. They sank one last pint and set off up Sheffield Road. As expected, Wendy, Mrs Coggins and Grandma were in bed, and they had the ground floor to themselves.

It was Shaun's turn for first fix, though it was clear from the pinprick pupils in Johnny's bright blue irises that he'd already made a start on the stuff before he'd reached the pub. Tommy ran upstairs and got the syringe and the dessert spoon that had been specially bent so that the dished part was level and stable. He washed the spoon in the sink and rinsed out the syringe and needle. Johnny handed over the wrap: a piece of neat, folded white paper that looked for all the world like a Beecham's Powder, except that the contents were brown, not white, and considerably more interesting.

Tommy shook a small amount of the powder into the spoon and added 2 mil of water from the syringe. He squeezed in a bit of Jiff lemon juice, then lifted the spoon to eye level and played the flame from a plastic lighter underneath until the contents started to fizz. He put the spoon down on the table and stirred the mixture with the end of the needle. Shaun, meanwhile, had snapped the filter off a Number 6, peeled the paper off and cut it in half. Tommy dropped one of the halves into the spoon, pressed the needle into it and drew up the brown fluid through the filter into the syringe, which he then ran under the cold tap for a few moments, to cool the contents.

Shaun extracted the narrow leather belt from the loops of his lurid blue Dashton Market jeans and tightened it round his bicep. Tommy studied Shaun's pallid white forearm carefully, running fingers up and down, looking for rises that indicated a good strong vein. He found one, inserted the hypodermic, pulled back, got the all-important blood ball, and emptied the mixture into Shaun's arm. Shaun groaned with pleasure and leant back on the settee with his eyes closed. Tommy rinsed out the syringe, put a further 2 mil of fresh water into the spoon, squished the filter a few times to get it to give up the last of its goodness, and gave Shaun a second, less consequential hit.

Tommy rinsed out the syringe once more and prepared Dan's fix.

Shaun's eyes opened and he sat up suddenly. He looked pale and sweaty. He started to retch and ran into the kitchen and threw up in the sink.

Tommy gave Dan his fix. Just as Shaun had done, Dan sagged back into the armchair and gloried in the drug's sensations, as Tommy prepared his own fix and Johnny set about administering it.

Dan felt the beer pushing at his bladder; there was also the hint of that familiar opiate nausea. He didn't know which was coming first as he lurched out through the kitchen door and made his way urgently to the toilet in the backyard. He peed with the shoulder of his ageing sheepskin resting on the old whitewashed wall of the narrow building and felt himself overwhelmed by a gorgeous sense of comfort, wellbeing and relaxation. He grinned to himself as he heard someone else rush out of the backdoor and throw up in the grid. That had to be Tommy: Shaun had got the sink, he'd got the cudgie and Johnny would by now be preparing his own fix. And then the urge to close his eyes and drift overcame him and became irresistible.

Shaun looked up and around the living room. Tommy sat next to him on the settee, Johnny on the armchair, both stoned, eyelids drooping.

'Where's Dan?'

There was a short pause. They looked at each other. The shock of realisation ran across Tommy's face.

'Oh shit!'

They jumped up and ran out into the yard.

The toilet door wouldn't open – Dan's inert body was slumped behind it. Tommy dropped a meaty right shoulder onto the peeling old door and shoved and eased it part way open against Dan's dead weight. 'Dan? Dan?' No reply. 'Shit.' Johnny reached in, grabbed Dan's limp left arm and began to pull him round the door. Shaun grabbed Dan's sleeve and joined in with the effort; Tommy gradually edged the door further back as more of Dan's lifeless body slid out. And then Dan was sprawled motionless on the damp flagstones in the yard, head against the wall, eyes closed, chin on chest.

Shaun staggered backwards and raised his hands to his head. 'Oh my God. He's dead.'

'Is he blue?' yelled Johnny.

'I dunno – it's too dark,' came the panicky reply from Tommy, shaking Dan by his shoulders and slapping his face. 'I think his lips are.'

'Shit. Get him moving. Keep him moving.'

And then Dan was vertical in the yard, but knew nothing about it, and the four of them stumbled out through the back gate in the bit of light that bled from the kitchen window, Dan in the middle, with one arm across Tommy's shoulders, the other across Shaun's, with Johnny propping him up from the back. They blundered in near total darkness across the dogshit wasteland at the back of the house and onto Widnes Street. Dan had the odd flash of consciousness. He was moving. There were streetlights. But then soft, warm oblivion overtook him once more and he was on a warm sandy beach in some tropical paradise with soft balmy winds blowing gently over him.

The three walked briskly down Hacket Lane, with Dan slung between them. His feet joined in now and then, and more assertively as he became more aware. By the time they reached the town centre, vague but continuous consciousness had returned, and they headed back to the house with Dan able to walk unaided. There wasn't much conversation.

Some weeks later, the experience was repeated, but on this occasion Dan viewed it from the other end of the telescope. This time it was Liam Webster who accompanied Dan, Tommy and Shaun back from the pub for a swift wap of H.

They had their fixes and slumped down quietly on the chairs and settee to enjoy the drug. The only noise was the occasional vague flutter from the gas fire.

The near-silence was pierced by Tommy yelling 'Oh fuck.'

Dan and Shaun jerked out of their stupors. Liam was bombed-out at the end of the settee, pale as death. If he was breathing, it was so lightly that it was not discernible.

'Fuck! Fuckin' 'ell. Fuckin' 'ell. Grab 'im.'

Tommy slapped Liam round the face – no response. And again – same result.

'Fuck, shit. Get him moving.'

Dan and Shaun pulled at Liam's arms. They got him vertical and rushed him down the corridor, out of the front door and onto Sheffield Road. Tommy and Shaun had Liam's arms over their shoulders; Dan shoved and cajoled from the back, then went round to look at Liam's face to see if anything positive was happening. It wasn't

They turned into deserted, late-night Hacket Lane. Liam was a lifeless mass – totally unconscious and inert. His feet refused to join in – Tommy and Shaun were just carrying him. The toes of his shoes scraped down the footpath. Shaun began to struggle with the weight, and halfway down Hacket Lane Dan took over, and with Tommy carried Liam the rest of the way. As they got to the town centre, there was some semblance of life. Liam came to and went again, several times over. It was at least clear that he wasn't dead.

Still propping Liam up, they walked in little circles in the town square, around the peculiar glass case the council had installed a few months earlier, which contained some bit of old Industrial-Revolution machinery, as they waited for him to come-to decisively and for a sustained period before returning home. The case was decorated with dried-up dribbles of gravy and curry sauce, but it must have been made of tough stuff, as all visible acts of vandalism had got no further, and as tempting as a pristine minimalist glass box must have been to late-night revellers, no-one had yet been able to smash through it. The machine inside was painted factory-gate green with polished bronze bits and occasional red highlights, and had wheels and shafts on its sides. It looked a bit like an old steam engine, but it was only about the size of a large motor bike and had no chimney, so it couldn't be that. Tommy, Shaun and Dan weighed it up and tried to read the food-spattered plaque in the dim yellow streetlight – something about 'stone-crushing' – while Liam reacquainted himself with consciousness. His shoes, which had been brand new, had worn through at the toe. What had previously been a natty pair of loafers was now an inelegant pair of sandals, with tattered socks visible at the front.

***

It was late Saturday afternoon when the phone rang in the Brody's front room. Walter was out – Saturday was the day for his eleven-while-eleven bender in The White Lion – Dan picked up the receiver. After the usual clicky pay-phone noises and a split-second of silence came Tommy's voice.

'Errr. It's Tommy. I've got Micky Snark with me. D'yer mind if I bring him round?'

'What? What the fuck? Why d'yer want to bring Micky Snark here?'

'He's in a bit of bother – he's hiding from the police.'

'WHAT? And you wanna make me an accessory? What's he done?'

'Erm, well, he's sort of stabbed somebody...'

'Jesus... *sort of?*'

'... in the neck.'

'Oh, fuck me! And you want to bring him *here?*'

'It's just for a few hours. The police are all over Dashton, looking for him. They'll be at his house and his girlfriend's and all his mates'.'

'So what's wrong with your place?'

'I can't take him to ours, what with the stuff we've just had with the Squad. Wendy'd go mad. And they might go looking there anyway. They don't know your place. Come on. I don't ask for much.'

'Oh, bloody hell. All right then. But just for a couple of hours, right? And what happened to the guy he stabbed – is he all right?'

'I dunno. Micky just ran – didn't stick around to find out.'

'Oh, for fuck's sake.'

Twenty minutes later they arrived – Tommy, Shaun and Micky.

'I've parked round the corner on Grover Street – they probably know the car by now,' said Tommy.

Micky was tall and dark-haired, a good-looking lad, with a charming, disarming smile. He was suntanned, due to his outdoor job as a building-site labourer, and wore faded flared jeans and an open-necked olive green shirt.

Dan made tea and handed out Garibaldi biscuits, and they all sat round on Walter's three-piece suite like it was a visit from the vicar. Micky was all smiles and nice as ninepence. His relaxed manner and amiable presence were at odds with his fearsome reputation. He was a junkie, a nutter, a completely out of control guy, prone to acts of extreme violence, and he'd nick anything that wasn't screwed down. You didn't dare leave him alone in your living room – there'd be something gone. Dan scanned the room. There was only one ornament: a copper pot on the windowsill. Lily had left it behind because it was a pain to keep clean. Still, he'd keep an eye on it. Dan also looked for bloodstains on Micky's shirt and couldn't see any, but then it was a very dark shirt.

'So, you stabbed a guy?' said Dan, breaking the ice.

'Yeah,' said Micky, smiling sweetly.

'In the neck?'

'Yeah.'

'So what did you go and do a thing like that for?'

'Well, I was in The Dive, having a few pints, minding my own business, and this guy wanted a fight, and I couldn't be bothered fighting with him,' explained Micky, in a chirpy, cheerful tone, as though he was describing some petty altercation at a kid's birthday party.

'You stabbed the guy in the neck because you couldn't be bothered fighting with him?'

'Yeah,' said Micky, still smiling. 'I was having a good time, enjoying meself. I couldn't be doing with the fuss.'

***

'Suppositories? You've scored suppositories?' said Dan, scarcely believing what he'd just heard. He stood with Tommy and Shaun in their bedroom, sceptically studying the dozen or so small waxy white pellets on the old mahogany sideboard.

'*Morph* suppositories,' corrected Shaun.

'And we've had all the jokes: "you know what you can do with them" and all that,' added Tommy. 'But they're good gear, or so I'm told.'

'Really? OK, so what do you do with them, then – if it's not the obvious?' asked Dan.

'Well, you put them in a spoon, like usual, put water on, then heat it up. The wax melts and floats to the top. The morphine stays in the solution underneath. Then you wait for it to cool. The wax makes a skin on the top. You poke the needle through it into the solution, and draw it up into the works.'

'Well, yeah. Makes sense, I guess,' said Dan, vaguely convinced.

They set about their task. Shaun went and got some fresh water from the kitchen. Tommy put one of the suppositories into the spoon and added the liquid, nearly to the brim. Dan held up the spoon while Tommy played a cigarette lighter underneath. Within a few seconds the water started to bubble. At first it didn't look like the suppository was going to melt, but then, once it started, it went very quickly. Clear wax floated upwards – the spoon looked like a mini lava lamp – and after about a minute and a half the suppository had vanished completely. Tommy removed the lighter. Dan carefully placed the spoon down on the sideboard. They watched as the wax on the surface gradually cooled and turned white, like ice on a winter lake. Shaun rinsed out the works in readiness.

They did this three times and each had a hit. And they all agreed that it was a surprisingly good high, though there was also a consensus that there was a slightly waxy feel with it.

***

Dan, Shaun, Lenny Hughes and Roger Armitage got to Strangeways early: 7.45am. Tommy was due to be released at 8.00. They waited across the road in Carnarvon Street in Roger's hand-painted, pea-green Avenger, with the dark-green

Piccadilly Radio sun strip. They'd all taken the day off work to be there for Tommy. It was a chilly Friday morning and the windows quickly steamed up. Roger took a grubby old T-shirt from the glove box and periodically wiped the windscreen with it to make sure they would see Tommy as soon as he emerged.

Tommy had got six months for possession. They'd busted him three times, and that meant prison. With good behaviour – Tommy was hardly the sort of guy who'd beat up a warden or start a riot – he was getting out after three months.

At a minute past eight, a small door within the gigantic menacing main gate opened and Tommy stepped out, grinning and carrying his little bundle of possessions.

They jumped out to greet him and hugged and backslapped, then they all clambered back into the Avenger and sped off back across town to Dashley Dyke.

First they called into Fat Pat's Caff on Bridge Street Industrial Estate for an enormous, long-awaited Full English with extra bacon and tea and toast, and caught up excitedly with gossip. Not that Tommy had much. He'd just kept his head down and done his time, and one day had been much the same as another – it was all pretty boring, really – though he did set out what he'd learned about prison hierarchy: hard cases and those with gang connections at the top, as you'd expect; 'beasts' – rapists, flashers, child molesters and such – very much at the bottom; and everyone else sort of mixed together in-between. And he was grateful for everyone's letters – they kept him going.

After breakfast, it was time to take him home to Sheffield Road and show him to his mum and gran. After that brief reunion, they withdrew to the front room and got out the booze they'd bought specially the night before – it was clear they'd be making a start before the pubs opened. They figured more gear would have been bad form in the circumstances, so cider, beer, vodka and fags would have to do. They were pissed before the pubs opened at eleven, but they went anyway: to The Nelson, for some fine Boddies' Bitter.

At eleven on a weekday morning, the old Victorian ale house was deserted. They made for the tap room first and played darts for a while. Then, when that became too difficult and arduous, they switched to the best room, where drinking, joke-telling and chit-chat continued, albeit now with the odd slur.

At some point in the hazy afternoon, Kev Barker appeared. The others saw him walk in and looked at each other. Smiles vanished. Conversations stopped. *What's that fuck doing here?* was written on every face. How had he found them? He must have known Tommy was getting out and wanted some of the reflected glory – you'd hardly expect Kev to be there on some altruistic basis. No doubt he wanted to be able to brag that he had a mate who'd done time in Strangeways. He must have figured they'd be in one of the Boddies' houses, then it was just a short process of elimination. There were only four Boddies' pubs in Dashley Dyke, and The Nelson was second-favourite, after The King's Head.

Lenny groaned audibly. Kev was the man for whom the word 'twat' had been invented. When you considered all the qualities you'd want in a friend, things like loyalty, consistency, honesty, integrity, having your back, standing up for you to other people and such, Kev had none of those. In fact, a list of the reverse of those traits would have best characterised him. The irritating, pretentious way he expressed himself, with his DJ-stylee, mid-Atlantic accent, where 't' became 'd' and a 'dirty bass riff' became a 'durdy bass riff', was only the start of it.

He'd drop snide hints in conversations that those naughty tales you'd shared with the lads about things you really wouldn't want to get back to your girlfriend were now knowledge in his possession and he might just let the odd thing slip one day, if he were so inclined.

For his part, though not all that bad looking, give or take the acne and the permanent trace of a sneer, he had very limited success with women – they could see through him quicker than the males could. So he'd schmooze around the lads' girlfriends. Constrained by manners and some vague notion of social obligation, they'd be a captive audience. His gambit was to draw the girls in by making jokes at the lads' expense. He'd done it with Rita, taking the piss out of Dan behind his back. She'd laughed along at first, seeing it as banter, but then it went on too long and started to feel like something else, and she ended up feeling awkward and sullied.

He'd never been to any of the northern soul clubs: he fancied the idea of them in principle, but found the reality a bit frightening, so he lived the scene vicariously, through the stories the others told. As he talked, you got the sense that what he *really* wanted was not to *go*, but to have *been*, so the experience was safely dealt with and the knowledge comfortably owned. He would have been and survived without having been punched, rolled, ripped-off, busted, having experienced the horrors, or an OD, or a comedown, or having found himself stuck a hundred miles from home in the early hours of a Sunday morning with no ticket home and no money in his pocket, and he could talk with casual first-hand authority on the subject, as the others did. And sometimes it seemed that, through all this listening and absorption, he'd actually persuaded himself he had in fact been after all. He'd sometimes be overheard telling a tale one of the others had told some weeks before, but now with himself as the protagonist.

He'd show up at the pub with no money and try to bum drinks from the rest of them. He'd sometimes do it on a whingey basis, expecting them to happily bail him out, because of their affection and understanding, when really few held the esteem that would justify such an expectation. And for those who did enjoy such high regard, it was a self-cancelling thing, as it was a given that, when skint, you did the decent thing and stayed home and didn't leech off your mates. And if they told him to fuck off, he'd get all sanctimonious and call them tight-fisted and say there were no pockets in shrouds. Then, after months of cadging drinks, he'd shown up in the snazzy red Fiat 124 he'd been saving-up for, when most of the others couldn't afford anything but a wreck or the bus.

And then there was the racism. He'd come out with nasty 'jokes' or racist digs and try to get the rest of them to laugh along with him, and he didn't understand when they wouldn't do so. And whereas in the unenlightened 1970s racism was endemic, and many saw the less aggressive end of racist humour as just 'banter', there was something altogether more insidious about Kev's version of it. A subtext of hatred was impossible to miss. Plus, he seemed not to have grasped that the crowd he was preaching to had grown up worshipping at the altar of Otis and Aretha, and from childhood had seen nightly on their TVs footage of Martin Luther King's impassioned speeches, the appalling evil of his assassination, dignified black Americans marching and demanding only that most basic civil right, to be treated as human beings, and that profound, goosebump-inducing moment when Tommie Smith and John Carlos raised their black-fisted gloves in defiance at the 1968 Olympics.

But Kev knew better, and he dragged the conversation round to his racial superiority – one of his favourite topics – and topped it up with evidence. His dad had lived for a while in South Africa and had told Kev the truth of it: he'd worked with black people – well, supervised them – and knew first-hand that they were intrinsically inferior. They had smaller brains and they were all lackeys and dunces.

At this, Lenny Hughes lost it.

'They are NOT inferior,' yelled seething, red-faced Lenny. 'Who the fuck do you think you are? How smart do you think you'd be if your family had lived for generations in a shitty shanty town with no hope, no education and with some fuckin' Boer's jackboot permanently pressing down on your fucking neck? You're not superior – to them or anyone else. You're just privileged and too stupid to see it. You're a wanker and a fucking idiot.'

Lenny and Kev launched themselves at each other. It was like a fight between Godzilla and King Kong – not the giant celluloid Godzilla and Kind Kong, who were hundreds of feet high and could clear Manhattan in a couple of mighty strides; this was like a fight between the twelve-inch rubber Godzillas and King Kongs that kids played with. Neither was much of a fighter. They careered around the room, first Lenny with Kev in a headlock, then Kev with Lenny in a headlock. They fell into tables and chairs, got up and carried on. The others paid little attention, until the two pink-faced entangled bodies crashed into their table and drinks went flying. At that, it was: 'OK, that's enough. Break it up. Break it up. Come on. Sit down. Knock it off,' and Shaun, Tommy, Dan and Roger wrestled the combatants apart and something like peace was restored, and Kev and Lenny sat at opposite ends of the table, each ignoring the other's presence, and the important business of drinking resumed.

The pub closed at 3.40pm and the consumption of spirits and cider resumed in the Coggins's front room, along with a game of Dirty Word *Scrabble*.

Dirty Word *Scrabble* is much like ordinary *Scrabble*, except there are no rules, other than only dirty words are permissible. You can have as many squares as you like, you can look at what letters others have got and try to steal them, you can move any inconvenient pieces, and your words don't have to confine themselves to the board. Tommy thought he'd pulled off something of a coup, with 'quim', but Roger, building out from the letter 'u', won the game with a magnificent 'afuckingbastard', half of which was set out on the green shag-pile carpet.

***

Sunday afternoon, post-Wigan-Casino: comedown time. Shaun lay on his bed in the recovery position, eyes closed, mouth open, face flushed and clammy, kidding himself he might be able to sleep it off. Tommy sat on the edge of his bed, poring over a crossword, which, mind befuddled, he'd made no progress with in half an hour, save for two short words in the top left corner, and he wasn't sure about those. Dan was spinning the tunes on the Sharp music centre: smooth soul ballads, Sunday chill-out tunes, not Saturday night stompers, volume low, as befitted the mood: "I'll be Around", "Just My Imagination", "Ain't No Sunshine"…

A knock at the front door muffled its way up through the floorboards. Wendy shouted up grumpily from the hallway: 'Dan. It's for you.'

Dan plodded disconsolately down the creaky stairs. The front door was open. At the end of the dark narrow corridor, on the concrete flags, stood Rita. She looked good: best frock on, all dolled-up – dressed to impress. Deborah was stood next to her, clearly brought along for moral support.

'I thought you'd be here. You weren't at your dad's,' said Rita. She had her serious, you're-in-trouble voice on, but was struggling to hold back a smile. Dan stood framed in the dark doorway in his black baggies and blue lambswool jumper, dishevelled, doe-eyed, vulnerable. She didn't know whether she wanted to bollock him or fuck him.

'Yeah. Mmm. Right, no. I was here. I *am* here,' mumbled Dan, vaguely. 'This is where I am.'

'I've come to sort things out. You don't answer the phone and you haven't rung me in over a week. What's going on?'

'No, well, y'know...'

Every time they'd seen each other over the last few months, there'd been a row – the meeting of Dan's brittleness and Rita's pushiness, or maybe just Dan's brittleness and Rita's presence – and usually one or the other had stormed off. And there'd been that time when he'd shown up at hers with the big purple love bite on his neck that that mad but very sexy Australian girl who was shagging her way round Europe had given him. That had soured things for a few days. Dan had lost count of how many times they'd broken up.

Anyway, Rita said, it was a nice afternoon and they'd driven all the way over from Salford and they wanted to go out and do something nice. Dan wasn't interested. He had his own internal comedown shit going on and he didn't want to go anywhere. In fact he didn't even want to be where he was, but there was nowhere else to be, so it would do. *Not anywhere* would be his first choice. Rita cranked up the pressure. She'd had enough. This was his last chance. She wanted to go somewhere. She was fed up of him messing her about. She wanted him to get his arse in gear and go and get changed and cleaned up. They'd wait.

No.

She warned him again. She really had had enough. If he didn't sort himself out, it was over – for good this time.

The big sky over The Liberal Club opposite was too bright, and the swishing Sheffield Road traffic was chafing Dan's raw sensibilities. Some *wanker greaser* roared past on a motorbike and drowned out their voices. And with her moaning, it was all just too much. He didn't want this conversation. He didn't want any conversation. He wanted her to fuck off.

She waved her left hand about as she ranted, then twisted it side to side by her face. She'd been doing this for months – years, maybe. At first he thought it was just one of her ways, some random expressive gesture, but then he'd noticed her thumb was on her ring finger. *Hint, hint* – that, on top of regular tales about how this or that friend or girl at work had got engaged. It took ages for him to work it out – never was much good at picking up on hints, Dan. And she was at it again today, when they were on the verge of saying goodbye for ever. Why hint at an engagement ring when you're about to break up? Maybe it had become so ingrained a mannerism that she did it automatically, now. Though maybe that gesture signalled the rest of it: it wasn't just *sort yourself out so we can have a nice Sunday afternoon out,* it was *sort yourself out, step up and be a man and buy me a ring.* Maybe that's what was coming next if they did go off somewhere. Over tea and Victoria sponge, she'd lay down the law.

Deborah said nothing – just stared at him disconcertingly. You could imagine the conversations they'd had before, though: *you've got to put your foot down, Rita, love – get him to man up. Time is passing you by. You're not teenagers anymore. You'll be wanting kids.* Rita's mum and nan had been pissy with him for months as well. They never said anything to him, but you could imagine what they'd said to her: *He's leading you on. He's useless. He's only interested in one thing. He'll never marry you. And he's a druggy.*

Dan studied Rita's face. Was she serious? She looked it. Her eyes were wide open, glaring, but her mouth seemed to be smiling, though it was moving so rapidly it was hard to tell. But then maybe it was a grimace of exasperation and disbelief. Smile or no smile, it looked like it was the end – if he didn't comply. Did he want to rescue it? Did he love her? He couldn't tell. They'd been together on and off for four years, though one of the offs was the year with Eve, and that wasn't without significance. He'd kind of groaned back into his relationship with Rita, after some vacant fallow period after Eve, which he couldn't remember much about. Rita was twenty now, and she'd actually got sexier with time, as she'd grown into her beautiful adult body. The owner of that exasperated face was a very sexy woman. It was a lot to lose. But could he put up with the mither?

'I don't wanna go anywhere. I feel like shit.'

'Well, that's your own fault. You will go to these things, get yourself in this state.'

He was already imagining her as history. He knew that whenever he heard "Every Beat of My Heart" there'd be a twinge. He bought it at the same time as he took her to The Pendulum, way back when they were first going out. She didn't like the place, though – found it a bit rough and intimidating, and wouldn't go again. She liked soul, but not that raucous all-nighter soul. She liked the kind they played on the radio. He could picture her in her red dress playing "Lookin' through the Windows" on the radiogram in her nan's front room and punching the air to that opening fanfare. And they'd listen to baby Michael Jackson's *Got to be There* LP while snogging on the settee and seeing how far they could get before her nan barged in to break things up. And then there'd been that summer and those long, languid Sunday afternoons in the double bed in her friend's flat in Eccles, with Minnie Riperton making the moment perfect with "Lovin' You" and the Moments and the Whatnauts smoothing it out with "Girls". He loved her then. He *definitely* loved her then. She was paradise. Her body was paradise. But over the last few months it was "Never Can Say Goodbye" – that tale of star-crossed lovers who never got it right but never quite got around to breaking up, either – that characterised the pit they'd fallen into. And there'd been that time, after he'd got back together with her after Eve, and he'd bought "One Girl Too Late" by Brenda and the Tabulations and taken it round to her house in his red leatherette record box and put it on the turntable, and she'd fixed him with those piercing green eyes and said 'is that me?' He denied it, of course, but to himself he had to admit that there was something about that record that got to him, that he internalised completely, as though Brenda and the boys were speaking directly to him. Somewhere, down deep inside, he imagined that he was the only person in the world who owned that record and got it so completely.

'I'm serious. If you don't come now, it's over.'
'OK. I understand.'
'You don't care?'
'Care? Erm... I just don't feel right.'

What did he want? Part of him wanted to put his arms around her, feel her lovely warm body next to his, smell her perfume, feel her soft sweet hair on his face. But stubbornness was winning the battle. It usually did. He was nauseous, sweaty and felt like death. His mind was mangled in the way that only an amphetamine comedown could mangle it. Nothing mattered. He couldn't care – about her pain or his own. He wanted oblivion, not a walk by Hollingworth fucking Lake. Rita could hardly have chosen a worse moment for an ultimatum. Whatever the future held, he just wanted this, whatever it was – *this doorstep, soap-opera confrontation* – to be over. It could only go one way.

'You're not coming?'
'No.'
'Then it's over.'
'OK.'
'I mean it. Did you hear me?'
'Yes.'
'Then I'm going.'
'Alright then.'

He watched her vanish down the street. She still had great legs. But then so did Deborah.

Tommy looked up from his crossword: 'who was that, then?' Shaun stirred from his pretend sleep and sat up on the other bed.

'Rita. Seems we've broken up'

'Again?'

'Permanently, I think, this time.'

'Oh. You OK?'

'I dunno... Doesn't matter, really, does it? Nothing matters, when it comes down to it.' Tommy and Shaun looked at him curiously, but said nothing. He continued: 'Could do with the pub, though.'

'Doesn't open for another four hours.'

'Fucking Sundays.'

***

It was Saturday dinner time in The King's Head, and Dan Brody, Tommy and Shaun Coggins, Rick Cooper and Jimmy Bragg quietly discussed their predicament, over fags and Boddies' Bitter. The Drug Squad had been busy again. There'd been busts and was a dearth of gear.

They sipped their beer, glanced around cautiously and leant into each other as they spoke in whispered tones. They kept the jukebox topped-up for further acoustic camouflage: "Silver Star", "Heaven Must be Missing an Angel", "Young Hearts Run Free"... They didn't want a repeat of the 'we won't miss the Airball this time' incident.

'There's this guy,' said Rick, 'a junkie in Dashton: Pete Adamson. You know him?'

Tommy, Shaun and Dan didn't, but Jimmy Bragg did: 'Yeah, I know him from way back. Haven't seen him for ages, though.'

Jimmy had been a nodding acquaintance to Dan and the others – one of scores of local lads who went to Buffy's, Wigan and the rest – but they'd seen more of him lately, now he was into H. He was quite a handsome chap: tall, slim and with long curly black hair, which gave him the look of a dashing seventeenth-century cavalier. And he was good fun to be with: he liked a joke and always seemed to have a smile on his face, though he was by no means a pushover and that smile could vanish rapidly if circumstances changed, and with that long reach he was well known to be a bit of a handful.

'Well, I'm not promising owt,' continued Rick, 'but he always seems to have something – he has to, to keep himself going – so maybe he doesn't score off the same people as us. Maybe he gets it from someone else and maybe his source hasn't been busted. So maybe he's got something. He doesn't usually deal, well not much. He just sorts his own out, but maybe he could be persuaded to part with a bit, in the circumstances. And I bet he gets prescription Methadone. It's worth a crack, and maybe we could find out who he scores from. I know where he lives.'

Pete Adamson lived on busy Glodhill Road in Dashton town centre. Tommy parked the Cortina on a side street opposite. They stood in the rain across the road from Pete's redbrick two-up-and-two-down.

'You stay here,' said Rick to Dan, Shaun and Tommy. 'He knows me and Jimmy. We don't wanna go in mob-handed. Might freak him out.'

Rick and Jimmy waited for a gap in the traffic and crossed the road, while Tommy, Shaun and Dan ducked into their collars and tried to keep the rain out. They watched as Rick and Jimmy knocked on the door and waited. No-one answered. They knocked again, with a bit more urgency this time. Still no answer. They had a conversation, inaudible from the other side of the road, then stepped back to the edge of the footpath, launched themselves at Pete Adamson's door and kicked it in. It seemed to give way very easily. Jimmy and Rick ran in and, a few seconds later, emerged with a small boxy stereo system, wires trailing behind them.

The pair dodged the Glodhill Road traffic in the rain, with Rick shouting 'come on, get the car, let's go.'

Back at Rick and Sally's flat, they studied the stolen contraption.

'It won't work,' said Dan. 'You haven't got the speakers. That's what was on the ends of these wires. It's no good without them.'

'Fuck me,' said Rick, 'I've been had.'

***

It was Mick Henshaw's twenty-first, and there was a good crowd out. Stalwarts, Tommy, Shaun and Dan were there, of course; Eddie Froggatt and Marty Baldock came along too; and Dave Podmore brought a couple of his mates from Verrington: Rob Lilley and Doug Stevens. They met at 7.30pm in The Railway Inn in Woodbridge, a suburb of Verrington, which took the form of a swelling on the main road between Hightown and Verrington town centre. The oldest houses were mostly on or close to the road, then there were layers of 1930s bay-fronted semis, then there were the post-War council estates, and finally there were the 60s and 70s modern townhouses and semis, all pale brick, white wood cladding and big windows, as though they'd been designed for a Mediterranean climate, built on steep slopes and close to railway lines – land which till then had been regarded as unsuitable for housing.

The Railway Inn, being on the main road, was a sturdy Victorian sandstone establishment, with '1875' chiselled into its facade, and it sold some of the finest Robinsons' Best Bitter around. They squeezed in around a couple of old round tables in the best room, next to the etched-glass window, made themselves comfortable on the blue velour benches and stools and set about sampling some of this well-regarded Best Bitter. All except Dave Podmore who, like a complete fanny, drank pilsner lager with a dash of lime.

The atmosphere was loud, raucous and playful. The volume of the conversation had long since drowned out whatever it was that was coming out of the jukebox. They exchanged stories, told jokes old and new, and took the piss out of each other. Eddie told tales about the stupid sods he worked with, with maximum bluster. Someone had dropped a whole fifty-pound bag of cement from a great height and it had hit the ground right next to him and exploded and he'd been 'completely fuckin' covered in fuckin' cement fuckin' dust.' It'd have 'broke his fuckin' neck' if it had hit him full on. Marty did that thing he always did when he felt he couldn't compete in the conversation, he leant back with a smirk on his face, coolly smoking his thin black More cigarettes, imagining he was Clint Eastwood's cigarillo-chewing 'Man With No Name', and doing his best to project the feeling that he was happy to let these simpletons chatter away, but he himself was rather above it all.

They all looked very smart and respectable. Everyone had made an effort because they were going to a club later: Dandy's. They wore proper flared trousers and jackets – not an ounce of denim in sight – and each had a tie in his pocket so as to meet the club's dress code when the time came. Dandy's had been chosen because it was halfway between Verrington and Hightown and so was the best compromise for all concerned. And it was big, so the bouncers were a bit less fussy than in most places about admitting crowds of half-cut lads after pub closing time. All the same, it would probably be best not to mention that this was a twenty-first birthday party. The building was a great, forty-foot high, charmless box of a place, which had originally been built in the late-60s as a speculative factory on the edge of an industrial estate, but no-one wanted it for that, so it became Dandy's. The bar and one of the main seating areas were on the first-floor balcony, overlooking the dancefloor – the place from where a foreman would have kept a watchful eye on workers on the factory floor, had the building been used as intended. The two main downsides were that it was not a soul club – you were bound to spend the evening listening to the worst crap that 1976's pop charts could offer – and there was an act on: The Dooleys, who were a kind of poor man's Brotherhood of Man, who in turn were a kind of poor man's ABBA. But all this had to be tolerated because you had to go somewhere when the pubs shut.

As closing time loomed, they were all thoroughly dazed and happy, though someone had the presence of mind to order a couple of cabs to get them to the club.

In the taxis, they reminded each other of the need to shape-up when they got to the door, to do their best to look reasonably sober and up-together, or the bouncers wouldn't let them in.

They got to the door, then the pay desk. One of the bouncers told them the live act was nearly halfway through, but it was still full price. They told him this wasn't a problem but, not wanting to look like smart-arses, didn't let on that this was a relief and they'd be happier if it had finished altogether. Irony and sarcasm never worked well with bouncers.

They found a couple of high tables with stools by the first-floor bar, got some more ale in, and carried on with the chat and story-telling that had started in the pub. The Dooleys finished and the DJs took over, spinning pop chart and disco records of the moment.

Tommy and Dan gazed over the balcony and mulled over the strange function of music in a place like Dandy's. They figured there must be two kinds of people there: groups like theirs, who just wanted to get drunk, and others who were there in the hope of meeting the love of their life, or at least getting laid. The first lot were totally indifferent to the music; the second lot needed it only because something had to be playing or there wouldn't be a reason to step onto the dancefloor to meet that special person (or that he/she-will-do-for-tonight person). So neither group was actually interested in the music. It was at best a rhythmic noise with a reasonably pleasing melody, designed to give people an excuse to do a bit of wedding-reception-style jigging while getting to know each other. And it sounded like it.

'We have to do the birthday thing,' yelled Dave, piercing the hubbub.

'Yes, the birthday thing!' said someone else. And there were cheers around the two tables.

They all knew what this meant; it was a twenty-first birthday tradition. There'd be a whip-around, and the birthday boy would be bought a pint of his favourite spirit/mixer. Cash crossed the tables. Tommy collected it, went to the bar and came back with a dimpled pint pot, filled to the brim with whisky and dry ginger, which Mick would now have to try and down in one.

They cheered and urged Mick on as he gave it his best. He sank about three-quarters of the drink, took the glass away from his mouth while he recomposed himself, then sank the rest. There were cheers and backslapping.

Mick stood the empty glass on the table and conversation resumed, but Mick didn't join in. He went silent and seemed more concerned about the commotion going on in his innards than what was around him. His face turned red and his cheeks bulged. His right hand jerked up suddenly to cover his mouth. He shuddered, and a narrow jet of liquid shot out from between his fingers. As any student of fluid dynamics will tell you, when a liquid is forced through a small opening, it accelerates. This stuff flew all of two feet, diagonally from Mick's mouth into one of the patch pockets on Tommy's grey and maroon check jacket.

Mick, still holding his mouth, jumped down from his stool and ran towards the toilets. The others noticed but left him to it, knowing exactly what this was about. But then time passed and there was concern.

'I'll go and see how he is,' said Dan.

Mick was sat on the floor in one of the open cubicles. His sleeve was rolled up, his arm was in the toilet and his hand was submerged beneath a thick layer of vomit in the bottom.

'What the fuck are you doing, Mick?' said Dan.

'I've honked up me top set. I can't find it,' gurgled Mick, from a largely toothless mouth.

'Oh, what? Shit. Really?! I didn't know you wore falsies.'

'Yeah, well, just the top plate, and I've lost it.'

'In there?'

'Yeah.'

'Jesus.'

Mick continued to grope around in the stinking pink-and-orange mess. 'I'm worried it might've got round the bend... 'ang on. I think I've got it.'

Mick pulled out the denture, held it triumphantly aloft, then lurched over to the sink, rinsed it and slotted it awkwardly back into his mouth. His face now had in it the usual complete but uneven set of teeth. Mick and Dan re-joined the group at the two tables.

Some fifteen minutes later, Tommy rummaged in his right jacket pocket, looking for his lighter. A startled, confused look spread across his face. 'It's wet!' he yelled, in dismay. 'The inside of me pocket's wet. There's stuff in here. What...? What the fuck?' he continued, as he pulled out small fragments of soggy carrot and other bits of partially digested food and set them out on the table.

***

'Two-one. Two-fucking-one,' said Dan, morosely.

'I know. I... hmm. Yeah,' sighed Tommy in sympathy, shaking his head.

'I mean, I just don't get it. We stood there and watched it, and I still don't get it.'

'I know.'

The pair sat in the desolate, dimly-lit snug of The Cavendish Hotel in Dashley Dyke town centre, early on a Saturday evening. That afternoon they'd watched a first half of Manchester United versus Tottenham Hotspur in which United had played some of the best football they'd ever seen, but, due to bad luck and some exceptional goalkeeping, only led by one goal at half time. In the second half, the roles were bizarrely reversed. It was like two different teams had emerged from the tunnel: Tottenham came out reinvigorated; United gave the impression that someone had slipped a couple of moggies into their half-time tea, and they failed to produce one worthwhile effort on goal in the whole of the second period, and Spurs won the match two-one.

It was a miserable drive back to Dashley Dyke. Mick Henshaw and Shaun had gone home. Tommy and Dan decided to drown their sorrows with Robinsons' Best in the Cavendish.

Suddenly there was a third voice in the room.

'So here you are,' huffed Donna, impatiently.

Tommy and Dan, yanked together by one red-and-white scarf tied round both of their necks – Tommy had lost his at the match – looked up at the doorway to the snug, which now framed Donna and Walter.

Donna was the green-eyed goddess, the girl across the street Dan had followed to Buffy's eighteen months earlier – the one who, much to his chagrin, had been going out with Reevesie. That was long over and neither was particularly heartbroken when it ended. It sort of fizzled out due to a mutual lack of interest, rather than some gigantic blow-up and, after a respectful period, Dan had made his move. Reevesie confided in Dan at the time that he thought Donna was built like a lorry driver. This made no sense at all to Dan, who wondered where Reevesie had encountered lorry drivers with voluptuous lips, 36D tits and an hourglass figure.

Dan half-snapped out of his drunken reverie: 'What? What are *you* doing here? How did yer find us?'

'Boddies' pubs, Robbies' pubs – it wasn't that hard a search. Anyway, you promised me a Saturday night out. Be at yours at half-seven, you said. So what is this shit? It's gone eight,' fizzed Donna, warming to her outrage.

'Did I? I don't remember,' replied Dan, struggling to see his way out of the netherworld he and Tommy had sunk into for the last couple of hours.

'I'll leave you to it,' said Walter, retreating out of the door.

'Thanks, Walter. Thanks for driving me,' said Donna.

'You're OK, love.'

Donna turned her attention back to Dan: 'Yes you did. Now what're you gonna do about it? Your dad's driven me round half the bloody pubs in this town.'

'I'll get you a drink. Take a seat.'

'Rum and coke,' snapped Donna. 'And I don't wanna be in this dump all night.'

'Right.'

Dan went to the bar. Donna parked herself on a red vinyl stool across the table from Tommy, who explained what had happened at Old Trafford and the resulting trauma. Donna remained pouty and unconvinced.

Dan returned and set down a squat glass lined with dark-red rum and a small bottle of coke. 'I've got an idea. Tommy, come 'ere.' And turning his eyes to Donna: 'won't be a minute, love. Just have to make a phone call.'

Tommy got up and the two left a sullen Donna alone in the snug, lighting a Benson and Hedges.

Five minutes later, Tommy and Dan were back in the room.

'Right, we've set up a score: Dex! Lots of 'em! We're off to Wigaaan!' enthused Dan, grinning, arms outspread in a gesture somewhere between celebration and supplication. 'Great stuff, eh? We 'aven't been for weeks.'

'Oh, aye?' replied Donna, darkly, sceptically, 'and how are we gonna get there?'

'Well, I'm the only one with a car,' proffered Tommy.

'And you're pissed out of your mind.'

'No, I'm *not*,' remonstrated Tommy, with great seriousness. 'No way. I'm fine.'

'How many pints have yer had then?'

'Just five, that's all,' Tommy replied, in a tone of hurt indignation. 'Quick wash and that, and I'll be ready to go.'

'And how many did yer have at dinner?'

'Err... that was five as well. Or maybe six...? But that doesn't count. That was ages ago – before the footy. I'm fine, really.'

'Hmmph. OK then. But I'll have to go and get changed. Can't dance in these shoes.'

***

Tommy, Shaun and Dan picked up their foaming pints of Boddies' Bitter from the holey copper contraption on the bar top that allowed excess beer to drain away without mess, and Fred the landlord handed over the change with a business-like half-smile under his bristly white tash. Four of the hard-drinking tap-room regulars leant on the far side of the bar and spoke occasionally, between drags on cigarettes.

The three friends turned into the best room and took their favourite table, by the wall. It was still only 7.20 on a Tuesday evening, and quiet – no-one had put the jukebox on yet. The room was deserted but for old John, who was in his usual place across the room under the big window; the one that used to have an elegant, etched leafy pattern round the edge and the words 'KING'S HEAD' in the middle, but had now been replaced with an ordinary one made from regular obscured glass – bathroom window glass.

They each took a first swig from their pints and replaced their dimpled pint pots on the scrubbed oak table.

'Look.' said Dan, 'there's something I want to say, and I want to get it out now, before we're addled and it descends into one of those pissed-up "I love you man" things. My family moved down south, as you know, and nobody gave a stuff what happened to me. Our Clive's still up here, of course, in Bradfield, but he wasn't interested. I never see him. He's like... I dunno – a stranger. There's blokes at work I know better than him. He's got his own family and that's it. Doesn't wanna know about anything else. Certainly didn't wanna know about me. You have to make an appointment to go round to his house. I mean *really* – literally. Wouldn't even let me kip on his settee. But you – you put me up without a second thought, without a moment's hesitation. You even did the rotation thing with the beds, so I didn't have to kip on the sun lounger permanently. And we've known each other since... well since we've known anything.' He paused for breath. *'You* are my brothers. In all the ways that matter, you *are* my brothers. You always were. That's what I wanted to say.'

Shaun looked at him from across the table; Shaun who couldn't take anything seriously and who took the piss out of everything, without even the trace of a smirk, nodded twice. And Tommy, with equal solemnity, said 'I know. I know.'

And Tommy raised his glass and said 'The Three Musketeers.'

And Shaun and Dan raised their glasses and clinked them with Tommy's and repeated 'The Three Musketeers.'

And they took each another swig of their beer, and, as masculine good form dictates, nothing further could be said. And nothing further was said.

***

Tommy and Shaun parked the silver Cortina on the bit of waste land next to Manchester's famous Ritz all-dayer and swallowed their gear with the aid of a couple of swigs of Fanta. Tommy had never quite mastered the dry swallowing technique. It was just coming up to 2pm and they'd arranged to meet Dan outside the main entrance at 2. They locked the car and strolled the short distance to the front of the building. It was a fine, dry summer day – warm but not hot – and the all-dayer had already started: they could hear the music throb through the building. They itched to get inside and get moving on that fabulous sprung dancefloor.

Dan came into view, tramping happily down sunny Whitworth Street from the Mosley Street end, looking very pleased with himself in his baggy blue Lee Rider jeans, wide tobacco-coloured mock-Oxford shoes and dark blue L for Leather pin-tuck jacket. He'd stayed at Donna's the night before, and it was easier just to catch the 211 all the way into town than to travel first to Dashley Dyke and meet up with Tommy and Shaun there.

He'd necked his gear over an hour ago – those Pirellis, dex and green-and-clears had been too hard to resist – and as he reached the doors of The Ritz, he was clearly flying. His eyes were jammed wide open, his massive pupils exaggerated still further by the narrow pale blue rims that were all that was left of his irises.

'Bloody 'ell,' said Tommy, grimly.

'Fuck's sake,' added Shaun. 'Look at the state of yer. You look like a car with its 'eadlights on full beam.'

It was one of the downsides of all-dayers, as opposed to all-nighters, that much happened in the stark, unforgiving light of day.

'Charming,' grinned Dan. 'Warappened to "nice to see yer, Dan. Did'jer have a good night, Dan? How's Donna?"?'

'Just fuckin' get inside before someone sees yer, yer knob.'

They pulled open the outer doors, slapped quids down onto the pay desk and shuffled past the bouncers, keeping eyes directed downwards till they were in the beautiful silky darkness of The Ritz ballroom. The place was only a quarter full, sizeable gaps separated the shuffling, sliding figures silhouetted against the brightly lit stage. It was still early.

Silvetti's "Spring Rain" faded out and the pungent funk of "Cut Your Motor Off" throbbed into their willing ears. They dropped their jackets and leapt onto that legendary dancefloor.

***

Rick Cooper and Peter Wisneiwski had had a few bevvies in The Highwayman in Hightown town centre and were now back at Peter and Edith's two-up-two-down on Tannery Street, enjoying the effects of a couple of tabs of acid.

It was some time in the deep dark night, not that either was keeping score. Edith had left them to it and gone to bed hours ago – *work in the morning*. With the flame-effect electric fire and a small table lamp on top of the telly for company, Rick and Peter exchanged stories, told jokes, giggled uncontrollably at irregular intervals and watched the strange transformations that the room and everything in it continually underwent.

Suddenly there was the most enormous, explosive crash. The dark brown curtains burst into the room and huge quantities of shattered glass shot out between and around them. Rick and Peter jumped out of their skins in terror and onto the settee, holding onto each other to steady themselves and for reassurance. And with a dull thump, a large brown object dumped itself on the floor beneath them, amid the shattered glass.

Their minds ran through the possibilities: *they were tripping, but this wasn't the trip; this had to be something from the real world. Trips changed things; they didn't invent them from scratch. Well, not normally. But what was it and why here, why them? Had someone chucked a brick? Was someone having a go? What was going on? Why in the middle of the night? Why in the middle of a fucking trip? WHAT THE FUCK?*

They stepped down from the couch and looked at the strange, lifeless brown shape. It defied recognition in the subdued light, but it wasn't a brick. It was bigger and more rounded. Peter, in an unexpected attack of presence-of-mind, reached for the main light switch. And in the sudden, unaccustomed brightness, the two gazed at the brown thing that had shattered both the window and their peace: a dead owl.

'What? WHAT?! What the fuck?' yelled Rick 'An owl. A fucking owl? I mean... why...? And why when we're tripping? It could have chosen a million other windows. Why ours? They fly, for fuck's sake. It could be anywhere. It should be up on Hatton's Moor. That's where it ought to be, innit? Shouldn't it be up there chasing fucking voles or something? What's it doin' down 'ere? Fuckin' bastard.' And he booted the defunct raptor hard with his Dashton Market brogues and it shot across the room, followed by a trail of glass fragments, and thumped against the skirting board next to the telly. 'That'll teach yer, yer bastard. Don't mess with my fuckin' trips.'

'Yeah, and look at the state of my bloody window,' said Peter. 'Edith's gonna be right narked.'

***

Dan and Tommy sat at one of the small round tables in the best room at The Cricketers, drinking Tetley's Bitter and smoking John Player Specials. Accommodation was the chief topic of conversation. Both were having trouble with it. Dan's situation had a long history.

When Dan was little and heard about Hell for the first time, he was naturally very concerned. The news, delivered by the mighty and unimpeachable figure of Headmaster Pop Mayhew at Foundry Street Methodists School, that he and his schoolmates and just about everyone else he knew were likely to be roasted alive for eternity, ruined his day. When he got home, he sought answers urgently. He pestered his mum, Lily. Was this true? Was he really going to burn in Hell for eternity if he didn't do as he was told? It certainly seemed a disproportionate punishment for a kid whose worst crime was throwing dog shit at a neighbour's washing; well, that and saying 'bloody' once; and there'd been that incident when he'd set fire to one of the lockup garages on Beasley Street, but that was an accident, mostly. And where was this Hell place? If it was underground, like they said, why didn't someone go down there and put the bloody fire out? An exhausted Lily, squishing sodden grey clothes through the mangle, explained that he needn't worry about Hell because they were already in it. Dashley Dyke was Hell.

Dan hadn't thought Dashley Dyke was that bad a place, but then he'd never been anywhere else. But Lily had, and this was her view of it. She hated Dashley Dyke and all that came with it: the slum housing, the filthy streets, the oppressive soot-blackened landscape of towering mills and smoke-belching chimney stacks, the perennial choking winter smogs and, most of all, Walter's drunkenness and serial womanising.

It was 13 years later, in the spring of 1975, that Lily had finally made her escape to Brighton. However, by summer 1976 she had had to accept the crushing reality that it wasn't possible for a 50-odd-year-old working-class woman, with no qualifications, few saleable skills, two kids in tow and a bad back to earn enough to live on in coastal Sussex. So, with an awful feeling of dread, defeat and misery, Lily had arrived back in Dashley Dyke. The dream of a life beside the glistening sea was over, and the Brody family was reunited.

It was by no means fair to say that Lily and Walter had settled their differences; they'd just parked them somewhere within easy reach, in order to get on with the basics of having somewhere decent to live and enough to eat.

There was no way that Walter, Lily, Nicky, Janet and Dan would fit into the one-and-a-half-bedroomed Steggs Lane house, so Walter and Lily recombined their money and got a new place a hundred yards away across the cat park on Turner Street. This was a good house – it had three decent-sized bedrooms and a bathroom. Dan shared a bedroom with Nicky, as he had before the break-up. However, the joy of the reunification, such as it was, did not last; at least not for Dan.

Dan had felt hurt and betrayed those fifteen months earlier, when Lily broke up the family and left for Brighton, leaving him to share digs with Walter, the walking dead and hound from Hell. He could have fancied some of that seaside stuff himself, but wasn't invited. And there was his apprenticeship to finish, anyway. On the plus side, these circumstances had given him his freedom, which he'd exploited by turning into a full-on hedonist – not that he knew what one of those was – and ramping up his drug use, which went from prodigious to Olympian. And he could get away with it because he hardly ever saw Walter and when he did they scarcely communicated.

But now Lily was back and full of questions about the state he was in. What was up with his eyes? Where had he been all night last night? Could he really take yet another day off sick? What were those blood stains on his shirt sleeves? Why were his forearms bruised? Who were all these new 'friends' who kept coming round to the house? They looked dodgy. What did they want?

And Dan's resentment at being cross-examined by someone who *vanished and didn't give a fuck* fifteen months earlier turned into rage. And this multiplied when Walter, who had been an absentee for most of Dan's childhood and a ghost throughout his teens, and was himself palpably *unaverse to getting thoroughly shitfaced*, suddenly became a man of great moral conviction and Lily's biggest ally.

Dan really had to get out of that house.

Similarly, Tommy's drug use was something that could no longer be hidden or tolerated at the Coggins house. There'd been the numerous strange behavioural moments, like the day he injected omnopon scopolamine and walked into the living room and, interrupting *Panorama*, told Wendy, Grandma and his mum not to be 'cruel to the rats'. They had no idea what he was on about and, when pressed on the subject later, neither had Tommy. And then there'd been the Drug Squad raids, the three trips to court and one to prison. He'd lost his job-for-life with pension and free van at the GPO and, after a long period of unemployment, was now a delivery driver for a booze company, earning washers. Wendy and his mum were permanently on his case. Tommy might not give a fuck about what anyone thought of him – *what great genius in a dump like Dashley Dyke* could hold him to account? – but Wendy and Mrs Coggins lived in the 'community' and went to church and were all too aware of the chatter and the funny looks.

Tommy also had to move on.

And before last orders was even in sight, Tommy and Dan had resolved to get a place together. They both needed to escape the hassle and to have their independence.

It hadn't clarified in their minds that the chief reason for getting their own place was so they could take more drugs and do so without interference. Nor had they anticipated that, with what bit of parental control there had been now eliminated, their new home would become Grand Central Station for Dashside's druggies, where there'd be a regular turnover of drug-hungry lads wanting to buy, and nervous, sweaty chemist-shop robbers wanting to offload, sharpish.

***

'St Mark's Street, then, eh?' said Rick, in his tangerine first-floor flat, as he jiggled a bit of crystalline white powder from a small sliver of tin foil into a spoon. 'Whereabouts?'

'Number 22 – about halfway up,' replied Dan.

If you approached St Mark's Street from Lowther Street, which you had to if you were in a car because it was a dead end, the first thing you saw was a steep, cobbled incline with flat-fronted, red-brick terraced houses climbing precipitously up both sides. At the halfway point it levelled off, and at the end was a low sandstone wall with a gap in it, where there had once been a gate. Beyond this were St Mark's graveyard and church. The street had twenty two-up-and-two-downs on each side in blocks of ten, with an alleyway in-between for access to the backyards. Tommy and Dan's house was the first one in the second block on the left-hand side. This made theirs an end-terraced, which they liked to think was really, in effect, a semi. When they moved in, the front room anaglypta was painted deep orange and a Bourneville Chocolate shade of dark brown. They overpainted it in yellow and white, to make it a bit brighter and more cheerful. It took many coats, so crappy and thin was the new paint, and so dark and strong were the colours beneath. Dan made a hanging device from a bent-up coat hanger, and with it fixed to the wall a plate he'd won on the air rifles at the fair. It had a country scene on it, with tall trees, a winding lane and a rustic horse and cart, and Dan thought it added a bit of class to the place. The kitchen, which was pink and black, got a pale green paint job. Dan snaffled from work an ancient-but-working cream-coloured gas cooker, which was otherwise destined for the tip, and installed it, soldering the old half-inch lead pipe that dangled down the wall to the union at the back, like he'd been taught at Stretford Tech. While notionally it was Tommy and Dan's house, Shaun slept there most nights too, on a mattress that was shoved under Tommy's bed when not in use. Thus, it became the Three Musketeers' house. Shaun just went back to Sheffield Road for one or two nights a week, to keep Mrs Coggins, Grandma and Wendy happy. Tommy had the smaller, back bedroom. Dan had successfully negotiated the bigger, front bedroom on the basis that he had to have a double bed – a necessity for Donna's visits.

'Handy, that,' said Rick. 'Five minutes from The King's.'

'And two minutes from The Albion,' added Tommy. 'You get a good pint of Marston's Pedigree in there.'

'And a minute from the bus stop for the Number 4,' further added Dan. 'The alleyway at the side goes right through, between the houses on Holmfirth Road. It comes out right next to the bus stop.'

Rick emptied the syringe into his arm, let out a satisfied breath, leant back, then jerked up with a realisation. 'You know who you've got for a neighbour, don't yer?'

'Hmm?'

'Dennis Bradshaw. You know him?'

'By sight, I s'pose' said Tommy.

'I know who he is... seen him about,' mused Dan. 'Never had any dealings with him, though.'

'I could tell you some stories,' grinned Rick, handing the syringe, spoon and silver paper wrapper to Tommy. 'He's really not properly roofed-in, that guy. He's in the last house on the right, right next to the church. And, I gotta tell yer this one: one morning, Dennis is having a lie-in – hangover, or speed come-down, or something – and there's a wedding going on in the church with the church bells giving it some. Y'know, really ringing out loud, like they do. And the noise was driving him crazy. So he got up and stomped into the church, mid-ceremony, with the bride and groom and all the guests there, with just a towel wrapped round his middle, and yelled at the vicar "'ere, marrer, will yer turn that fuckin' racket down. I'm tryin' to get some fuckin' sleep in 'ere. I've got a bad 'ead. Will yer just knock it off," and stomped out again and went back to bed.'

They all rocked with laughter, though Tommy never took his eye off the spoon that was just coming to the simmer before him.

'And there was that time...' continued Rick. 'I was coming out of the post office and something made me look down, and there was a slice of bread – right there on the footpath. And I looked up and there was another, about six feet on. And then there was another, about another six feet on, and I started following them. And I turned right by the war memorial onto the path by the river, and there were more of these slices of bread. And then I saw Dennis, up ahead. He'd got a sliced loaf under his arm, and the packaging had come open, and as he was walking they were just dropping out, one after another. He'd got about half a loaf left by the time I caught up with him.'

***

September was mushroom season, and the Three Musketeers set out in Tommy's silver Cortina to pick the first of this year's crop in the woods at Babel Brook. The lane was too tight and bendy to park on, so they left the car in the pub car park and walked to one of the places known to be most promising. As they climbed up the steep slope into the wooded area, their nostrils were assailed by the sweet damp smell of autumnal woodland, and, heads down, they started to scan the leafy forest floor for the tell-tale light brown caps.

A sudden rustle some way ahead alerted them to the fact that they were not alone, and as they looked they saw a skinny, hippy-looking guy, who had found a batch of the precious little psilocybin goodies and was on all fours, grazing on them like a cow.

***

Johnny Caswell knocked on the door of 22 St Mark's Street, early on a Friday evening. Dan answered the door.

'Got a works?' asked Johnny, expectantly.

'Yep. What have you got?' said Dan.

'Diconal.'

'Ooh, very nice.'

'Let that man in!' yelled Tommy, cheerfully, from the settee on the other side of the room.

'Diconal. Woohoo!' yelled Shaun, excitedly, as he jumped up and extracted the syringe and needle from the sideboard drawer.

'How many have you got?' asked Dan.

'I've got eight here – two apiece – but there's loads more.'

Johnny's dad, Harry, was a painter and decorator, and like many of his profession, he was, after decades of breathing in fumes from paint and white spirit, dying of liver cancer. Diconal had been prescribed for the excruciating pain. Johnny didn't think he'd miss eight.

The great thing about Diconal tablets, from a junkie's perspective, was that unlike other pill-form junk, such as, say, Pethidine and Palfium, they were totally soluble. They didn't need to be crushed-up, semi-dissolved in a spoon and filtered through a fag-end, with the irritating routine risk of fragments clogging the works.

Tommy took the plunger out of the 2 mil syringe, dropped in one of the pink pills and with a finger covering the hole at the needle end, held it under the kitchen tap and allowed in a slow dribble of water, until it was three-quarters full. He replaced the plunger and shook the syringe. Within a minute the pill had gone, leaving a near-opaque cerise solution.

Johnny had the first fix. As the rush hit, he let out a small, involuntary cough. Diconal always made you do this – quite why, no-one knew.

Tommy, Shaun and Dan had their fixes and also each let out a little cough.

Dan put on an LP – *Rattus Norvegicus* by the Stranglers, which Tommy had bought earlier in the week – and they lay back on the yellow nylon cushion-cover chairs to enjoy the drug and absorb the music. They all loved soul, but there was something about this other new music too. They all agreed that "Get a Grip on Yourself" was the best track, though Shaun felt that "Hanging Around" came a close second. "Peaches" was Tommy's second favourite.

Glyn Cousins had started it off some months earlier, when he'd come round with singles by the Sex Pistols and the Buzzcocks. They listened and liked what they heard, and their tastes broadened. Dan bought *Never Mind the Bollocks*, Tommy bought "Gary Gilmore's Eyes" by the Adverts and Iggy Pop's *Lust for Life* LP, and Shaun bought "Mr Blue Sky", "Wuthering Heights" and "Baker Street". But they still loved soul and there were some nights when only it would do. All the same, flopping out on a chair, off your face, listening to the Stranglers or the Sex Pistols or the Damned had much to commend it.

The Diconal wore off pretty quickly, and they each had a second lovely, dreamy pink fix. Then *it* wore off, and they all sat around looking at each other, all nursing the same question: was it OK to steal a dying man's pain medication and could they get away with filching a bit more?

The rationalisation didn't take long: Harry had plenty more; he wouldn't miss them; the nurse would give him more; she wouldn't know how many he'd used in his delirious state, and neither would he...

Johnny vanished for half an hour and returned with the bottle of Diconal. It still had fifty-eight of the puce beauties in it. And they fixed them up and they fixed them up and they fixed them up. And they listened to all manner of music. Even Simon and Garfunkel and a Phil Spector compilation got a spin. The desolate power of "The Boxer" and the soaring strings and soulful vocals of "Unchained Melody" had them in raptures.

By Saturday mid-morning all the Diconal had gone – they'd fixed-up sixty-six of those super-strength painkillers between themselves overnight. And on a cold, dreary Dashley Dyke morning, this was not a good feeling.

'He's got some more,' chanced Johnny, with a half-question in his voice. 'He's got another whole, unopened bottle – a hundred tabs.'

'A hundred?' said Tommy, eyes widening.

'Oh, you can't do that. He needs them. You've got to leave him some,' said Dan, making a half-hearted grab for the moral high ground while hoping to be argued down.

'You could just take a few,' added Shaun.

'It's up to you,' said Tommy.

By early afternoon, Johnny was back with the whole, unopened bottle of one hundred Diconal.

'Didn't you leave him any?' said Tommy.

'No. I've got the lot,' said Johnny, explaining further: 'As I see it, if I take some from a full bottle, they might see there's some missing and suspect something; but if there's no bottle there, they'll assume they were all used up and the bottle's been chucked. Anyway, the nurse'll be round this afternoon – she'll give him some more.'

Tommy, Dan and Shaun silently accepted Johnny's dubious logic and tried to persuade themselves that the decision and the burden of guilt were his, and the four of them spent the rest of the weekend fixing up Diconal. And they forgot about Harry, the ethics of their situation and everything else, and by Sunday evening they had run out of Diconal again.

***

Dan, Tommy and Shaun all got an early finish on Fridays and so, just before five o'clock, were seated together on the settee in the front room of number 22, scoffing fish and chips from greasy paper to get some sustenance down themselves before they got stuck into the big wrap of H that Dan had just picked up on his way back from work. The little black and white telly burbled away in the corner. The kid's TV programme *Crackerjack* started up, and the compere, Leslie Crowther, introduced the show with that catchphrase that everyone up and down the country knew so well: 'it's Friday, it's five o'clock, and it's Crackerjack!' to excited cheering and loud applause from the studio audience.

Tommy sniggered, 'It's Friday, it's five o'clock, and it's crank o' junk.' And they all snorted into their fish and chips, and Shaun spilt his tea.

***

Tommy and Shaun were over at Sheffield Road, on family business. So back at number 22 on Sunday afternoon, Dan and Donna decided to make inroads into the huge batch of mushrooms piled up on the blue Formica kitchen table. They gulped-down a couple of handfuls each of the limp, brown fungi, then made tea and opened a packet of chocolate digestives and settled themselves on the mustard yellow settee in the front room.

After half an hour, the yellow and white anaglypta room took on new characteristics: bendy in some places, slightly crystalline in others. A brief break in the clouds sent a ray of sunlight through the net curtains onto the rust-coloured carpet, and the room became imbued with a magical feeling, which prompted warm, cosy sensations that seemed connected in some imperceptible way to childhood fairy stories and enchanted lands. They got giggly. Each studied the other's face as they battled to speak without laughing and, each knowing this battle was going on – in themselves and the other – laughed all the more. Everything they said, or even started to say, was so funny it was met with fits of laughter, so each sentence had to be delivered in several episodes. And this amused them too.

Suddenly, Donna looked at Dan with intense concentration and great seriousness. 'You look like a… like a… py-<u>thon</u>,' she said. Her voice conveyed amusement as well as a hint of the kind of surprise one might expect someone to express on seeing their boyfriend suddenly take on reptilian characteristics.

'A py-<u>thon</u>?' quizzed Dan, with mock seriousness, his belly now in butterflies with laughter. 'Not a <u>py</u>-th'n – that's how they normally say it – a py-<u>thon</u>?'

'Yeah, yeah. A py-<u>thon</u>.'

And they both howled with laughter and rolled about on the settee.

'I'll have a look,' said Dan, and he stood and weighed himself up in the big brass mirror over the fireplace. And as he looked, the grey of his woollen jumper spread up the back of his neck to his head, and his head changed shape to that of a snake. And when he moved, his head moved in a snake-like way. 'You're right,' he laughed. 'I've turned into a py-<u>thon</u>, a fucking py-<u>thon</u>,' and he poked his tongue out, like a snake sampling the air, and they laughed more than ever.

***

It was Sunday dinner time, and the Three Musketeers sat on the long bench seat in the low, no-nonsense, box-shaped games room of The Labour Club, across the table from Dave Scholes, as blokes nursing their Saturday night hangovers quietly played darts and snooker and sipped the hair of the dog.

Dave was not a soul boy; he didn't belong to any of the tribes. He liked Bob Dylan, Leonard Cohen and Eric Clapton, but mostly just Bob Dylan, and he breezed in and out of the rough pubs, the posh pubs and the regular pubs without discrimination and was mates with everybody. His hair was long, spikey and selectively bleached – the Rod Stewart look – and his eye sockets were permanently red, wet and baggy, so he always appeared to be recovering from a heavy night, even when he wasn't. Though he usually was.

Dave banged on about the deep meaning of Bob Dylan's music and explained at merciless length the profound significance of the lyrics in "Mr Tambourine Man" and "Positively 4th Street". It was all about the lyrics, Dave reckoned – that was all that mattered in music. Tommy and Shaun nodded appreciatively, apparently accepting this wisdom. Dan – not only a soul boy, but a man with the primal throb of The Kinks' "All Day and All of the Night", the soaring glory of the Beach Boys' "God Only Knows", the wistful heartache of Dionne Warwick's "Walk On By", the ethereal magic of Simon Dupree's "Kites", and the manic primordial energy of Keith Moon's drum solos in "Happy Jack" in his formative locker – was unconvinced. Wasn't some of the greatest music ever made wordless – symphonies and that? And why was it that "Exus Trek" sent him soaring into realms of ecstasy when he could take or leave the vocal version on the other side? There had to be more. It wasn't just about the words.

Next, Dave weighed into "Disco Stomp" by Hamilton Bohannon: the lyrics were nothing more than 'a shopping list of American cities.' Dan couldn't deny this, nor could he be bothered to defend a song he didn't much care about. But at the same time, he couldn't escape the thought that its appeal was the meeting of those deep hypnotic rhythms and those fragile, restrained voices: the content of the lyrics didn't matter all that much; what mattered was the way it sounded.

'Yer see,' continued Dave, 'the thing with Dylan is, yer either love him or yer hate him. There's no halfway measure.'

Dan, now bristling at Dave's prescriptive pomposity, retorted 'I just think he's alright.'

'No, yer don't understand,' pressed Dave, patiently, 'the thing with Dylan is, yer either love him or yer hate him.'

'Yeah, I 'eard yer. I just think he's alright.'

Dan and Dave glared at each other. A few uncomfortable silent seconds passed.

'Anyway...,' intervened Tommy, diplomatically, leaning forward and tapping a Number 6 out of its cardboard carton.

'Yeah, anyway...,' reinforced Shaun, shifting in his seat.

The conversation moved on.

Dave bemoaned his luck and the cruelly unfair treatment to which he'd been subjected. His girlfriend had chucked him out, *just because he'd slept with her younger sister* – and it wasn't even as though she was under age or anything. And he was now back at his mum's. 'Still, it's not all bad,' he joked. 'I'm not saying I get molly-coddled, but if I get took short for a pee in the night, by the time I get back, mi bed's been made.'

They all rocked with laughter.

'And I gotta tell yer this, as well,' continued Dave, enthusiastically. 'This was last Saturday night, right. I was in here till about ten, then I went over to The Cavendish. And I was pretty hammered. And then I went back with Black to his place and we had a few spliffs. So when I got home, I was absolutely starving. And I looked in the fridge, and there was an egg yolk in a cup. I figured mi mum had been cooking – used the white for baking or something, and this was left over. So I thought: that'll do nicely. I put some toast on and put it in the frying pan. And I waited and waited, but it wouldn't seem to cook. I flicked the hot fat on it and everything, but it wouldn't go white. I turned the heat right up, and it still didn't seem to make any impression. I was there ten minutes or something. So eventually, I got fed up and stuck a fork into it, and I pulled it out and had a close look. And it wasn't an egg – it was half a tinned peach.'

And again they roared with laughter – and put off the bloke who was lining-up to pot the brown.

***

United were away at Newcastle. Tommy, Shaun, Dan and Eddie made the long journey over the Pennines and up the A1 to see Tommy Docherty's band of red-shirted heroes. It was raining when they parked the Cortina on a side street, a mile or so from the ground: not bitty, inconsequential rain; the heavy, unrelenting stuff that soaks you through – a kind of cold, northern appropriation of the tropical monsoon. It was still raining when they reached the ground, where United's fans were directed by stewards and mounted police to the unroofed, unpromising-sounding Gallowgate End.

The rain clattered down just as hard as they waited for kick off. It carried on at the same merciless lick throughout the first half, and through half time. And on it went, unchanged, through the second half, through injury time, and during the twenty minutes the police kept them locked inside the ground, while they cleared the waiting Newcastle fans from outside to prevent post-match punch-ups. And it continued to hammer down relentlessly during the sodden fifteen minute walk back to the car.

They were all soaked to the skin – literally. Dan had on his long black double-breasted raincoat. The rain had overcome what limited resistance it was able to offer before the first foul. It had made similarly light work of Tommy's denim jacket, Shaun's cotton bomber jacket and Eddie's Harrington. It had then penetrated their shirts, their baggies and even their underpants. Their shoes, filled with water, squished as they walked. As they got to the car, Dan extracted the three stuck-together pound notes from his jeans pocket and squeezed the water out of them onto the footpath.

They shivered and their teeth rattled, and cold water ran down their legs and turned into puddles in the foot wells, as Tommy piloted the steamy Ford the 150 miles back to Dashley Dyke. And they concluded that they couldn't have got any wetter even if they'd jumped into the Tyne.

The match was a two-all draw: Cannell and Burns; Greenhoff (B) and Pearson.

***

It was late Saturday morning. Tommy put down the receiver. Dan and Shaun sat opposite on the settee, mugs of tea in hands. 'That was Steve Mahoney. He wants to see us – well, me – right now, in The Dive. Sounded narked.'

'What was up with 'im,' asked Shaun.

'Didn't say. Sounded pretty pissed-off though.'

Tommy, Dan and Shaun hopped into Tommy's silver Cortina and rumbled down St Mark's Street for Dashton and The Dive.

They'd scarcely reached the bottom of the stairs of the subterranean boozer when Steve spun round from the bar, grabbed Tommy and rammed him up against the wall with a beefy, tattooed forearm pressed hard under Tommy's chin.

They could all scrap a bit, if pressed, but Steve Mahoney was in a different league. Already in his mid-twenties, he was the real deal, a proper hard man. He'd been in and out of borstal as a kid, prison as an adult, and his approach to problem-solving almost always involved extreme violence. Steve had more in common with Glasgow gangsters and the Kray twins than scrawny-arsed Dashley Dyke pillheads. He looked hard at the best of times – shaved head, flattened boxer's nose and a torso that looked like it was made from reinforced concrete, today wrapped skin-tight in a red check Jaytex shirt – but angry, he was a terrifying sight, and Tommy looked suitably terrified. He said nothing, though it wasn't clear if this was because he was shocked, or because Steve's forearm was shoved so hard under his chin that he couldn't work his mouth. So Dan did the talking instead: 'What the fuck, Steve? What's goin' on?'

'Keep out of it, Dan. This has nothin' to do with you,' came the yelled, ferocious reply.

'But what is it? Can't we just talk about it, civilised, like?'

'I told you, Dan. Keep the fuck out of it.'

'But what the hell can be this bad, Steve?'

'Right that's it, Dan, that's your last warning – SHUT IT,' seethed Steve, with the forefinger of his free hand in Dan's face.

Dan complied, knowing what was coming next if he didn't, and Steve turned his attention back to Tommy's reddening face. 'Right. Did yer grass me up, you cunt?'

Tommy looked bewildered. 'What? I-I. No. Fuck's sake. No. What are you on about? No, course not. Whaddya mean? What's happened?'

'The Squad came round and busted us, just after yer scored at our place.'

'Shit. I don't know anything about it, Steve. I just came, bought the gear and went. That's it. Why would I grass you up, for fuck's sake? We score off yer. What's in it for me if you get busted?'

'You didn't say anything to the Squad?'

'I never even saw them. I don't know anything about it.'

Steve relaxed his arm. Tommy's weight transferred back to his feet and the floor.

'You don't know anything about it? And that's gospel truth?'

'Yeah. Absolutely. Gospel truth. I'll swear on anything yer want. Why would I speak to the Squad? Why would I dig meself a hole like this?'

'Yeah, well. It wasn't you then?'

'No. Definitely not.'

Steve's tone went from rage to sad resignation. 'Well, anyway, we got busted big time. I mean, fuckin'... ahh... they got a load of stuff. I'm gonna get sent down again. I know it. I just... I dunno. Look, sorry. I just didn't know what had happened, and you can see how it looked. Sorry I kicked off at you, Dan. I'll get some beers in. Let's all just calm down, eh. What'll you have?'

And they sat down and they had some beers, and Steve lamented his fate, and Tommy, Shaun and Dan sympathised and tried to think of ways in which things might not be as bad as they looked.

And in the event, Steve didn't get sent down again.

A couple of weeks later, he was driving back to Verrington from his score in Whalley Range in his metallic green Hillman Hunter, when he realised he was being followed by members of the Drug Squad. He sped up to shake them off. And then he wasn't being followed, he was being chased. And he went faster and faster and jumped red lights and flew down the wrong side of the road to overtake, weaving side to side to avoid oncoming cars. And now the chase was manic. The Hillman roared and skidded and screeched, and still the Squad were behind him. And then Steve's car hit a bollard and veered instantly across the road and hit the kerb and a lamppost, and then it somersaulted. Steve, of course, was not the kind of guy who'd wear a poncey thing like a seat-belt, and as the car spun and the roof struts gave way and the windows shattered, he was thrown clear. As he exited through the now narrowed jagged gap where the windscreen had been, an arm was momentarily trapped. It went one way, he went another, and the car cart-wheeled on down the road. Steve ended up upside-down in a shop doorway and bled to death from the open wound at his shoulder before the ambulance could arrive. It was the sort of death Steve would have respected. He wouldn't have wanted a namby-pamby death, though it still took him by surprise when it happened.

***

Adey Martin and Dan Brody sat swigging pints of Bass Charrington's iffy bitter in The Norseman; a newish place put up when the estate Adey lived on was built. From the outside, it looked like a council health centre. Inside, it was a Scandinavian cave, complete with faux Nordic memorabilia and a bar constructed from wooden planks that curved up at the ends so it looked like the side of a Viking longboat, sort of.

'How's the new job then?' asked Dan.

'Great. Love it,' replied Adey in a buoyant tone, clearly very pleased with his new circumstances.

'Yer've done well. First job you applied for.'

'Yeah. Woodwork teacher. That's what I always wanted to do.'

'Right. Yeah. But I can't imagine anyone ever wanting to go back to Hightown High School. Just going past it on the bus still creeps me out.'

'Nah, it's fine. It's a different kettle of fish when you're the teacher.'

'I guess,' said Dan, wistfully, not entirely convinced.

Adey looked grown up now, like a teacher should. He'd grown a beard, though whereas his sensibly short hair was still the brown it had always been, the beard had a tinge of red about it. And he still wore a petrol-blue Trevira jacket; not tonic, though. Shimmering, chat-show-host two-tone was a bit too flashy for a woodwork teacher.

'Anyway,' said Adey, switching the subject, 'I'm off to see Bobo in Bristol this weekend. D'you and Donna want to come – share the petrol and that? She'd love to see yer both. S'been ages.'

Adey and Bobo had been together, on and off, since school days. She was now at Bristol University, studying Chemistry – another decision that made little sense to Dan, though being at university at all was a pretty amazing thing. He'd known her as long as Adey had. She'd been one of the girls they'd first met at Mars. A very pretty one, mind: a Diana Rigg/Emma Peel lookalike. And now she was at university. She was 15 back then – they all were. Who'd have thought it? Who knew she was that smart, little Bobo? And soon she'd have a degree and BSc after her name. Dan didn't know anyone else who'd done that.

'Yeah. Yeah,' said Dan, enthusiastically. 'That'd be great. I'm sure Donna'll be up for it. I've never been to Bristol.'

'You've never been anywhere, yer daft cunt!' laughed Adey.

'Fuck off! I've been to Blackpool, Stoke, Wigan and Cleethorpes, and everywhere United have played away.'

Late on Friday evening, Adey parked his pale blue Triumph 1300 on a Clifton side street, near the house Bobo shared with five other students. Dan had never seen anywhere like it. The house was gorgeous: a big, beautiful Georgian semi, made from soft yellow stone, with a wrought-iron archway and tangled old garden out front, separating it from the road. There was a cathedral four doors away. The garden seemed to spread into the house: a big-leaved, gangly plant filled a corner, while another dangled from a ceiling-mounted basket; the hall and living room were painted deep green and red; the floor was a mixture of uncovered varnished wood and oriental rugs; the lighting was warm and comforting. Walls were decorated with colourful textile hangings, reproductions of old paintings, and posters recalling Impressionist art exhibitions and psychedelic rock concerts. Delicious, fragrant smoke drifted up from a joss stick in an exotic-looking carved brass bowl.

Bobo welcomed them warmly and showed Dan and Donna to a room they could use because one of her housemates had gone home for the weekend. They dumped their bags and followed Bobo back to the kitchen, where she was preparing lamb casserole. On the chopping board were these things she called peppers. Dan thought at first this was a wind-up. Pepper, as far as he was concerned, was a grey powder you sprinkled on cheese on toast. These things looked like oversized, shop-display apples, made from shiny plastic. But they were real enough and they tasted alright. She also had these flat fawn things called pitta breads. Dan was dubious about these too – thought they bore too much of a resemblance to Odor Eaters. And there was no beer in the house. Bobo drank red wine. Dan tried that out, and it tasted alright too.

If all this was a culture shock, then so were Bobo's friends – all subtle, thoughtful people who talked quietly in measured terms and listened when you spoke, as though what you had to say was important, and weren't off their heads and screaming at each other all the time.

It was another world.

***

Back at St Mark's Street, Tommy scanned his forearms, wondering where he could fix today. They were a mess. Each vein was a raised ridge, dotted at quarter-inch intervals with a small scab, or an angry red blotch. Not infrequently there were purple-yellow bruises, where a blunt needle had done battle with resistant skin, or where the vein had been clumsily torn and blood had spread under the surface. It was Tommy's turn for first fix.

Dan crushed four Palfium in a spoon, added 2 mil of water, applied heat with a lighter, then threw in half a cigarette filter. He fitted the fine, orange needle to the hypodermic, pressed its tip into the white fibres of the filter and pulled back the plunger. But instead of drawing up fluid, the plunger became hard to move and nothing but a few bubbles appeared in the bottom of the syringe, while air passed downward past the plunger to compensate.

'Fuck. Shit. It's blocked again.'

Dan removed the works from the spoon and pressed the plunger back in, in the hope of squirting the blockage back out. But instead, the needle flew off the end and impaled the carpet like an airgun dart. The four of them, Tommy, Shaun, Dan and Philbo, trooped into the kitchen with the syringe and needle. They all had an investment in this. They'd got the Palf, but there was only one works and it was knackered. They were only meant to be used once. They'd kept this one going for weeks. Syringes were hard to come by. You had to know a nurse, or someone had to lift a handful on a trip to the doctors or A&E and sell them on. They'd had to use butter on this one to lubricate the plunger, it had got so stiff; and the needle was so blunt that you could shove so hard to penetrate the skin that when you did finally break through you shot straight through the vein and out the other side. And needle blockages were getting more frequent.

Dan ran the needle under the gushing cold tap, then the hot. Tommy put it to his lips and tried to blow through it. They reattached it to the syringe and tried to squirt the blockage out with fresh water. They held it in the steam from a boiling kettle to see if expansion might dislodge it. They blew again and ran it under the tap again. Eventually the blockage gave way, and the syringe sent a satisfying arc of fresh water across the kitchen.

Back in the living room, Dan drew up the Palfium mixture, located a rare unspoiled bit of vein in Tommy's arm, forced in the blunt needle, pulled back the plunger slightly, got the confirming blood ball and completed the injection.

Tommy gasped with pleasure as sweet euphoria followed instantly the famously awesome rush of the Palfium. Dan rinsed the works, crushed up more of the tablets and prepared another fix. It was Philbo's turn next. Dan dropped the filter into the spoon, pulled back the plunger, and it blocked again.

'Fuck fuck fuck fuck fuck,' said Dan, followed by a sigh of resignation. He'd had first crank of the Pethedine they'd had the night before, so it was his turn to go last today. It could be a long wait; it might never happen, the way things were going, and he longed to get himself outside of some of that lovely Palfium.

'You know what we *have* still got,' mused Shaun: 'that massive 10 mil works with the green needle.'

They'd disregarded that. It had been shut way in the sideboard drawer for ages and forgotten about. The works was so big that the slightest push of the plunger pushed in too much too quickly, and the big green needle – nearly an eighth of an inch across; the kind nurses used to take blood – made such a big hole in your vein that it bled for hours.

But as time wore on and efforts to clear the small orange needle failed again and again, and as the plunger jammed again and again – even with the liberal application of Lurpak – that other, super-sized works, with the big green needle, started to look ever more viable. And they finished off the Palfium using a 10 millilitre syringe and a giant, green phlebotomists' needle, and they all went to work on Monday morning with sticking plasters on their forearms. And they resolved that they really had to find some way to get a new syringe and needle that week.

***

The North Western Gas Board had become North West Gas, and everything had been rebranded in royal blue and white, with a little blue-to-purple rainbow motif here and there, representing the colours of a gas flame: the company's spanking-new brand identity. In the Verrington office, the Distribution Planning team sat around chatting, enjoying the last ten minutes of their dinner hour.

There was old Aileen, the tracer, who was homing in on retirement. She'd been there since the 1950s; since long before the giant, factory-sized open-plan office they now worked in was built. When she was little, she'd lived in a slum house in Dashton West End. The front room was separated from the cellar by a floor made from sandstone flags, supported on wrought iron girders. One day – mercifully, when she and her sister were at school and her mum and dad were at work – the rusty old beams had given way and the great, heavy flagstone floor had dropped through into the cellar. Luckily, no-one was hurt, though it was still a shock to come home at teatime and open the door and find your front room and everything in it ten feet below where it ought to be. But Aileen had married well and now lived in a well-appointed semi in the plastic-gnome belt between Woodbridge and Verrington.

Angela was also a tracer. She was 25 and relatively new to the department. She had got married just a year earlier. She was feisty, loud and blonde, and regarded as attractive by those attracted to such things. She was also far too intelligent to only be a tracer, and the job seemed to be just a stop-gap, while she worked out what she really wanted to do.

At the front desk was Roy, the good-hearted but lecherous, 26-year-old scouse distribution planning technician, with the receding hairline and ever-expanding forehead. He'd obsessed, usually for a two-week period, over every viable young woman in the office, until by now he'd obsessed over all of them and had had to go back to the beginning and start again. However, in spite of all this passionate intensity, he'd only ever managed to get one of them to go out with him. That was the lithe, long-limbed Elaine from Accounts. They'd only gone out on a few dates, and while Roy was clearly smitten, Elaine had only gone out of curiosity and for something to do. And fate dealt Dan the uncomfortable task of telling Roy he'd seen Elaine draped over a Tom Selleck lookalike in The Flemish Weaver in Woodbridge. So Roy dealt with his inflamed passions privately: at dinner times, he'd pick up a wodge of canteen serviettes – or 'wanky wipes', as he called them – and exhaust his urges later, often with the help of Pan's People.

At the back desk was Geoffrey. He was 40 years old, thin, neurotic and constantly agitated by some or other minor vexation: the gristle-packed dinners in the canteen, the stewed tepid tea served up by Hilda from her mobile urn at 11am and 3pm, or his crappy pre-War desk, which moved and wobbled every time he leant on it to write. Geoffrey was kind of a 'half' distribution planning technician, in that he did most of what the others did, but had no qualifications and had been slotted in as an emergency measure when things had been busy. He had then learned the job from the others, and with his having now become a fixture in the department, he had not been sent back to his previous job as a clerk. However, the precariousness of his situation added to his neuroses and prompted not-infrequent diatribes about how he was as good as anyone else and qualifications meant nothing next to experience. He smoked almost continuously and his marriage was coming apart, and he spent at least a third of each day staring at Angela's arse.

Then there was Dan, the newly qualified distribution planning technician, who always showed up late and in various states of dishevelment. He'd be nauseous, distracted, glazed and sometimes scarcely coherent, and in the afternoons would often be seen battling with the urge to fall asleep on his drawing board. At the age of 21, he was corroding away before their eyes.

Dan told the tale of his recent trip to Bristol and his encounter with exotic foods and how at first he'd refused to believe peppers weren't plastic shop display apples. Angela related the tale of how, when she first married Paul, she'd cooked-up some chips and served them with cheesecake, thinking it was a savoury.

Just then, the main door opened and in walked Rosemary Neild, a well-dressed, sturdy, barrel-shaped woman in her fifties. She and Aileen exchanged nods and perfunctory smiles as she passed Distribution Planning, on her way to Marketing. Once she was a suitable distance down the office and out of earshot, Aileen leant forward and in a low voice shared with the others, 'bloody Rosemary Neild – she's a nightmare. She takes working medicine to keep her thin, and…'

'Working medicine?' interrupted Dan, always keen to hear about anything pharmaceutical. 'What's that?'

'You know: working medicine – laxatives, senna pods and that. She thinks it'll keep her slim: if she eats what she likes and then takes working medicine the food'll shoot straight through and she won't put weight on.'

'And does it work?'

'Well, it doesn't look like it, does it,' grinned Aileen. 'But the worst thing is in the ladies' in the morning. If you're in there when she is – my God! The noise and the stink! It's just… it's appalling.'

Dan's attention flipped to Geoffrey: smoke was rising from his head.

'Geoff! Smoke! Smoke! You're on fire,' yelled Dan

And as Geoffrey jumped around in his chair, it became clear that the smoke wasn't coming from his head, but from just behind him. His bin was on fire. He'd thrown a dog end onto piles of screwed-up A4, and flames had taken hold. Geoffrey wasn't unused to this – it was the third time it had happened in the last few months. He leapt up from the chair and spun round. A decent blaze was under way – flames rose fifteen inches above the standard-issue green steel bin, and grey smoke billowed up towards the ceiling. Geoffrey rammed his foot into the bin and stamped repeatedly, and black embers, glowing red at the edges, flew up round his leg and floated down the office.

***

Dan called round to his mum and dad's on Turner Street, on his way home from work. They'd had a row and sat seething at each other on opposite sides of the front room.

Lily had always longed for a garden but had never had one, and she'd tried to brighten up the back yard a bit with tubs and pots, which she'd planted with flowers and shrubs.

She'd been out and poured salt on the slugs that threatened to devour her precious bit of greenery, and Walter had gone out after her, rescued them, washed off the salt in a bucket of water and transferred them to the alley outside the back gate, in the hope they might move on and live long and fulfilling lives elsewhere.

'He even apologised to them. Bloody idiot,' steamed Lily.

***

Just after 7pm, Dave Podmore swung by 22 St Mark's Street and picked up Dan, Tommy and Shaun in his Citroen GS Pallas, ready for a night out dancing to Ian Levine and Colin Curtis's latest fabulous soul discoveries at The Blue Room in Sale. The four then swished up Sheffield Road in Dave's space-age motor to collect Donna from Shipman's Fields Estate. From there, they dropped down the hill to The Railway Inn, in Woodbridge, to collect Rob Lilley and Doug Stevens. After a couple of snifters in The Railway, the seven happy soul enthusiasts crammed into the Citroen and sped off to Verrington, to join the newly opened stretch of the M63, which made short work of the trip round south Manchester to Washway Road and The Blue Room.

Dave saw a little too late the police check point just short of the roundabout where the motorway started. Due to that, the fact that he was doing forty when he should have been doing thirty, and because of the great weight of bodies in his car, he struggled to stop in time and avoid hitting the police officer who was trying to wave him down. He almost made it, but the policeman had to leap out of the way, as the Citroen skidded to a halt a yard or so past where he had just been stood. The copper was already alongside the driver's door as the car came to a halt, and visibly angry. Dave wound the window down and the narky constable looked in.

'Look at the state of it. LOOK AT IT!' yelled the fuming law-enforcer. 'You're way overloaded. There's SIX of you in here.'

And Donna's sweet, charming voice chimed in helpfully from the back: 'no-o: seven'.

***

Reevesie showed up at number 22 late on a Saturday morning. He'd got a score lined up: Physeptone ampoules. Did they want in?

There was only ever one answer. Shaun, Dan and Tommy rummaged urgently in pockets and drawers to cobble the money together.

The front room was filled with the previous night's debris: fag packets, mugs, glasses, cider bottles, beer cans, cigarette papers, the pewter tankard with the naked lady handle that the lads had bought Dan for his twenty-first... Reevesie gazed around the room. His eyes settled on the fireplace. In pride of place, top centre, was a small piece of turf lifted from Old Trafford during a pitch invasion, surrounded and set-off by an imitation gold bracelet left behind by one of Dan's one-night stands. Beside and below were keys, coins, a book of crossword puzzles, yesterday's Guardian, punk and soul singles, some book about modern art that Tommy had bought – still in its brightly coloured dust jacket – and a pile of LP sleeves: one, The Stranglers' *No More Heroes,* with a mutilated orange Rizla packet, blue Bic lighter, and fragments of tobacco and cannabis resin scattered about on it.

"Kin 'ell,' laughed Reevesie. 'The thinking man's tip!'

***

Next door to number 22 on the attached side lived a long-suffering middle-aged couple, who somehow got through Tommy, Shaun and Dan's nightly parties with only one complaint. In truth, they would have complained more often, but they generally found that knocks at the door after midnight tended to go unanswered, though the music might go down just a notch soon afterwards.

Next door on the other side, across the alleyway, was occupied by an indeterminate number of grown-up greasers. Like the Three Musketeers' place, it was a bit of a party house, albeit with different music. Not infrequently there'd be motorbikes with chrome chopper handlebars parked outside, but it wasn't clear who actually lived there and who was just visiting. Dan wondered at first if there'd be trouble, what with his crowd being made up of soul boys and grown-up skinheads, but there was never any hassle. Number 20's occupants and guests were all in their late teens or early twenties, like those at number 22, but back in their formative years had gravitated to Dashley Dyke's other youth cult. A few years earlier, they and Dan's skinhead mates might have been on opposite sides in a street brawl outside Mars, but now everyone had mellowed and all of that other stuff was in the past and a bit embarrassing. They nodded on the street and only once came to Tommy and Dan's door – to borrow a cup of sugar. They had their share of bad luck, though.

Azzer Cunliffe was twenty-one years old – a stocky guy, with long black hair and a slightly confused expression. All who came and went from number 20 had long hair – it was an essential greaser thing. Azzer had a tough, heavy job at the abattoir on Burton Street and liked nothing better than a good piss-up, especially if it was topped-up with a few spliffs. So when Dashley Dyke Motor Cycle Club set up a Saturday coach trip to see a blockbuster exhibition of motorbikes at Earls Court, which would inevitably involve a pub crawl afterwards, he jumped at it.

After an hour or so at the exhibition, Azzer, Lol Bradshaw – Dennis's big brother – and the two Franklin brothers, Harry and Pete, separated themselves off and caught the tube over to Soho, to get on with some serious drinking.

By 2.30pm they were in The Lyric. They then found a club – a deep red underground dive bar – so they could drink all afternoon. At tea time, they moved on to The King's Head. By 10.30, after eight hours of power drinking, interspersed with puffs on Lebanese Woodbines, they stepped out from the rammed Intrepid Fox into the cool night air, thoroughly arseholed.

They staggered and reeled, and in the dim light of late-night Wardour Street, and before the others had a chance to grab him and arrest his fall, Azzer lurched and fell through the window of a trendy boutique. His beer-filled belly came to rest on the upward-pointing shards of glass at the bottom of the window, while the top two-thirds dropped like a guillotine onto his back. With his nose at the feet of two nattily turned-out, insouciant manikins, Azzer was more or less cut in half.

Lol and the others didn't think he'd survive, but the doctors at St Thomas's did an amazing job. They slotted Azzer's organs back into their proper places and stitched him up, and by Tuesday he was back in Dashley Dyke. The doctors hadn't wanted him to leave – he was nothing like ready – but if he insisted, they couldn't stop him. But, whatever the case, he must definitely not drink.

But he did drink. As soon as he got back to Dashley Dyke, he was in the greasers' pub, The Golden Calf, joking about what happened in London and making light of his injuries, which got ever more painless as the soothing lager filled his belly. At closing time Azzer staggered home and climbed into bed, and as he slept his stiches came undone and his patched-up stomach and bowel gave way, and his spirit left his body in a sticky pool of blood and booze.

Lol Bradshaw and Harry Franklin died within three months of Azzer and within days of each other, though in much less dramatic circumstances.

Lol was twenty-three and Harry twenty-two. Harry had long dark hair and a bit of a tough-guy reputation. His job as a Water Board labourer made him heavy and muscular, with overtones of a Saturday afternoon wrestler. He wasn't the sort of bloke you'd want to mess with, and it didn't take much for him to want to mess with you, or so it was said. Lol, on the other hand, had long fair hair and was tall and slim, with more than a passing resemblance to Iggy Pop. He looked nothing like his brother – stubby, dark-haired Dennis – and his charming, friendly demeanour made him very different from his mate, Harry. Dan, Tommy and Shaun knew Lol well, because they scored off the same people and periodically met in The King's and The Albion to set up deals.

Lol and Harry were both killed by the same batch of heroin. They both made the same serial mistakes: they underestimated its strength, injected after drinking and did so alone, with no-one to stop them slipping away.

***

Bev Atkins was always good for a score, especially if her boyfriend Des Barlow wasn't in the nick, which he frequently was. Des was Dashley Dyke's most prolific chemist screwer. But then, the Drug Squad knew that, and every time a place was turned over within thirty miles of Dashley Dyke, it was Bev and

Des's door they'd knock on first. The last time Des was in court, charged with relieving Furber's Chemists on Glodhill High Street of the contents of its controlled drugs cabinet, he'd asked for 200 other similar offences to be taken into account. In fairness, they weren't all his, and the Squad had simply taken the opportunity, while they had him available, to get things off their books. But a lot were his.

Even when Des was away, Bev knew enough people to make sure she got what she needed. And what she needed was quite a lot, because she had a long-standing opioid habit. What Bev could shift in a session might kill another person. And because of the amount she bought, she was able to buy at better prices, and then cut and sell some on, to make her money go a bit further. And if she hadn't got the money, there was always her body as payment in kind, though the value of that had slipped markedly as time passed.

At 23 and 24 respectively, both Bev and Des were a couple of years older and considerably more experienced than Dan and his mates. They'd had their first gear way back in the days of The Twisted Wheel and had never stopped. And they knew everybody – if there was one thing to envy about them, it was their connections. They lived in a second-floor flat in Belgravia House – a 1960s development of deck-access flats in Dashley Dyke town centre.

Bev was junkie thin, with bleached blonde hair and hard angular features, her face a skull with sickly yellow wax drawn taut across it. Years of herculean drug abuse had dissolved most of her teeth, though there was a joke going round that owing to this she gave an amazing blow job. Not that there were many takers.

Des was tall, muscular and reasonably good looking, with short dark hair and a hint of the young Richard Burton about him. And for someone who had shifted in his time at least as much gear as Bev, he looked in surprisingly good shape. The not-infrequent enforced fasting stints in Strangeways no doubt played a part.

The news was that they'd got some good H. Not chemist stuff – the brown variety that started life in Afghanistan and travelled across Europe shoved up someone's arse in a condom.

Tommy, Shaun, Dan and Eddie called round after tea on a Wednesday evening, money in pockets, ready to roll. Des was out – both of the nick and on business. Sure, she'd got some, Bev said, and she'd sort them out in a bit, but she was having her fix first. This wasn't good news. They knew they'd be there for an age, watching Bev off her face and listening to her turgid stories.

Tommy, Shaun and Eddie sat on the smelly brown corduroy settee and pretended not to see the various unidentifiable stains. Dan took the armchair. Bev sat in the middle on the half-circle hearth rug, holding court.

She tipped a sizeable amount of brown powder from a small, folded piece of foil into a spoon, squirted water onto it with a 2 mil works, added a little vinegar, heated it with a lighter and drew the fluid up into the syringe. She examined her arms while giving the mixture a little time to cool. She then wrapped a narrow leather trouser belt round her left arm, held it tight with her few remaining teeth and located the most promising stretch of vein. Then she did what she usually did: because she used such a large amount of H nowadays, she injected it in stages.

With only one third of the mixture in her body and her eyes drifting and her head lolling with the power of the drug, she sat on the floor, legs crossed, with the blood-filled hypodermic dangling from her forearm.

She then got on with her stories, the usual ones: what a cunt her dad had been – *and* her husband. Good riddance to that slimy, two-faced twat.

With her free hand, she deftly shook a Number 6 from its packet, inserted it between her narrow lips and lit it with the red plastic lighter. She stopped speaking only for as long as it took to take in and exhale her first drag, then resumed with the tale of how she once fancied that she'd seen her mother's ghost. She wasn't saying it was real, she wasn't saying it wasn't, but she knew what she'd seen, and she hadn't had much that night.

Her attention went back to the syringe hanging from her arm. She looked at it carefully and squeezed in another third of the blood-heroin mix, then lolled again.

Dan and his mates stifled their boredom and impatience. Bev's kids didn't. Troy, aged three, and Mary aged four, charged happily round the room screeching and yelling with great gusto: around the dining table, behind the settee, in front of Dan, between Bev and the gas fire, back up to the dining area, then round again, and again.

'Don't mind them. They're just having fun,' slurred Bev, eyes three-quarters shut, before going on to explain that both of them were the outcome of pragmatic pregnancies: she'd twice got herself knocked-up while awaiting trial, because judges were reluctant to send expectant women to prison. And it worked. And she'd do it again without hesitation. She wouldn't let them bastards catch her. It was a shame Des couldn't get pregnant.

And she told again the story of the enormous bully at school she'd levelled when she was seven with just one well aimed punch – the bully was even bigger, and Bev even smaller, than on their last visit. And then she told the one about her awful, snobby boss at the shoe shop, and how she'd put her right in her fuckin' place. Who did she think she was? Mrs fuckin' high and fuckin' mighty. It was only a fuckin' shoe shop for fuck's sake. And then she slipped into wistful mode and related, once more, the tale of how she'd been doing really well at school but had to leave when she was 15 and get a job because her mum needed the money. She loved Geography. And the teacher, Mr Derbyshire… he was so lovely. He was her first ever crush. He was so kind, and he had these gorgeous eyes. Big and brown they were, with such long black eyelashes – almost like a girl's. She could still picture his face now.

There was a noise at the front door, and Des walked in carrying a lump hammer. He and the lads exchanged brief greetings. The kids joyfully threw themselves at him, then resumed their game in the dining area.

'Hiya, love,' said Bev, with her eyes still half shut and the one-third filled works still swinging from her vein like a red plastic parasite. 'How did yer get on?'

Des grinned and explained for the benefit of his customer-guests that he'd had to go up to Brushwood Estate to collect money from Simon the hippy. Simon had persuaded Des to lay gear on him three times in three weeks, hadn't paid for it, and had now turned into the Invisible Man. Des had gone round to his house to collect his money or otherwise resolve the matter. He wasn't hopeful, hence the lump hammer. The curtains were drawn, but he knew Simon was in because his car was outside. And after several attempts to get him to come to the door and threats yelled though the letter box, Des took decisive action and reshaped every panel on that bastard hippy's Vauxhall Viva.

***

Dan had passed his driving test and got himself a car: an eight-year-old, white Morris 1300, with, like Tommy's Cortina, an imitation vinyl roof, done in black paint. Even so, he was always last home because he had to get back from Verrington, with all the nightmare traffic that entailed, while Tommy and Shaun's work places were close to St Mark's Street. And he never knew what to expect when he walked through the door. They usually scored on Thursday night or sometime Friday, ready for the weekend, though sometimes the gear would last into the week. And sometimes they'd score again during the week, if they had the funds. And sometimes folk would just bring stuff round because they had some to spare and needed the money, or because they needed urgently not to be in possession of it, on account of the company they were expecting, or just because number 22 was a place where they could fix when they couldn't at home. And when there was little or nothing midweek, they drank cider – mostly Dry Blackthorn, which got renamed Bly Drackthorn, because it ceased to be worth fighting the mispronunciations that routinely occurred late at night. And sometimes they weren't able to get anything for the weekend, and that was regarded as a bit of a disaster.

It was 6.15 on a Monday evening. Dan turned the key in the lock of number 22. Tommy and Shaun were on the settee opposite. They looked glum and close to sobriety, but Dan still got the sense they'd had *something*, even if it wasn't much, or wasn't anything especially exciting.

'What have yer had?' asked Dan

'Vodka.' replied Shaun.

'How much?'

'2 mil,' said Tommy, with a note of irony.

'We thought we'd give it a bash,' explained Shaun. 'Might've been instant pissed or something, or some kind of rush.'

'But it wasn't?'

'Nah. You might as well drink the stuff.'

***

Dan, Shaun and Tommy never knew what state they'd wake up in, other than it wouldn't be good. Dan got up first, on account of the fact that he worked furthest away. To put off the dreaded waking hour as long as possible, he set the alarm for 7.30, which allowed 10 minutes to get ready and 50 minutes for the tedious, traffic-clogged drive to Verrington. Neither was quite enough, and no-one could remember when he last got to work on time, though five or ten minutes late was justified in Dan's mind, by the fact that it wasn't his fault that the traffic was that bad, and 50 minutes for 7 ½ miles ought to be enough. There was never time for breakfast or even a cup of tea – that would have necessitated getting up earlier. The basic stuff of making himself presentable – wash, clean teeth, put on clothes – was enough.

Dan's neat little Timex alarm clock, which had done no more than tick politely away for the last 23 hours and 59 minutes, clicked into hateful banshee mode. Screeching at a zillion painful decibels, it battered him into painful, resentful consciousness. An incomprehensible but vivid dream, involving brightly coloured skulls with red, yellow and blue lines emanating from them, fizzled away to nothing, leaving just strange ephemeral echoes, like friends who'd been trying to tell him something vitally important giving up and drifting sadly away, disappointed that they never quite made him understand. Dan looked with loathing at the implacable malevolent truth on the dial, slapped the top of the black plastic beast to make it shut up, and dragged himself grudgingly out of bed.

It was *freezing*. And Dan was in his underpants.

A blizzard of big fluffy snowflakes, painted lemon by the streetlights, billowed past the bedroom window. Ice crept across the glass from the bottom and edges, inside and out. Down on the street, snow had settled on the cobbles. The view might have made a good Christmas card, were it not for the fact that this was uncomfortable real life, not some imagined bucolic wonder. The only heating in the house was the gas fire in the front room, which was never put on in the morning because no-one went in there, other than to pass through on the way to the front door.

Dan dragged his befuddled brain and leaden muscles into the bathroom and yanked the light puller. There was water in the pink wash basin, with a bar of green Palmolive soap and a multi-coloured flannel submerged beneath, evidently there from the night before. This had to be Tommy's or Shaun's – Dan didn't use a flannel. On second glance, this wasn't water. The soggy ensemble had turned into a solid block of ice over night. With no time to chisel it free, Dan turned on the taps, intending to throw water into his face directly from the spout, but nothing happened – they were frozen solid too. He tried the bath taps: same result. And for the first time ever, Dan went to work unwashed. Chewing gum in the car stood in for teeth cleaning.

***

It was Saturday dinner time, and the Three Musketeers were seated in the agreeably anonymous darkness of Rowntrees Spring Gardens in the city centre, quaffing ale, puffing on Number 6's and dealing with the effects of Ephedrine.

The music was fantastic: northern soul interspersed with that new modern stuff they played at Blackpool Mecca, The Ritz and The Blue Room. The throbbing, mesmeric sound of Donna

Summer's "I Feel Love" and Chic's cool-as-fuck "Everybody Dance" filled the air.

The Ephedrine was less fun, though. They'd bought it because it was all that was on offer, but the effects were less than thrilling. It made your heart race and it made you sweat, but it brought none of the joy of speed; none of that gorgeous, uplifting high that made you feel you could conquer the world and dance till Tuesday. Ephedrine was like speed with all the good bits removed.

They sank a few more beers and enjoyed the music, in spite of the Ephedrine, then decided to look for a change of scenery – The Shakespeare, maybe, or The Swan with Two Necks.

Immediately outside the door, they were accosted by four lads who looked to be about 15 or 16 years of age.

''D'yer wanna buy any gear?' asked the boldest one.

'Might do. What have yer got?' replied Dan, interest reservedly piqued.

'Clean-and-greers.'

'Clean-and-greers?!' said Tommy, and the three of them howled with laughter.

'Yeah, so? What's wrong with that?' said the kid, now fidgeting with a mixture of confusion and embarrassment.

'Let's have a look then,' said Shaun.

'Err, they're not here. We'd have to go and get them.'

'But they're definitely clean-and-greers, are they?' said Dan, trying not to laugh.

'Yeah. Straight up: clean-and-greers. Good stuff.'

'So,' said Tommy, 'you want us to give you some money, and then you'll vanish with it – somewhere – and we'll just sit here and wait, and you'll come back at some point with some clean-and-greers?'

'Yeah. Tenner's worth?'

More laughter.

'See ya, lads. Good luck,' said Tommy, and the three turned and strolled off up Market Street towards The Shakespeare.

***

It was a Wednesday evening, and Glyn Cousins had popped round to number 22 with a handful of new punk records, all in picture sleeves, but Tommy, Shaun and Dan had nothing to share with their guest but tea. They'd run out of gear, booze and money.

'There's the empties,' ventured Shaun, hopefully. 'You get money back on them: two pee each. We must have quite a few by now.'

There were two of the brown glass, 1.5 litre Dry Blackthorn bottles on the top of the mantelpiece and three on the tiled base, either side of the gas fire. A further six were lodged between the stereo and the side of the settee. Five more were parked on the sideboard and seven or eight loitered under the settee, gathering dust. In the kitchen, a dozen or so competed for space with the evening's dirty plates on the Formica table, and on the floor underneath were several neat rows of them, like little brown soldiers on parade. Dan opened the pantry door. The whole floor was lined with empty cider bottles, right to the back, where the mop bucket lived. Tommy and Shaun checked out the backyard, where dozens more had been exiled due to lack of space.

They ferried the big brown bottles in shifts out of the front door and into Glyn's grey Renault 10, most in the front-mounted boot, but a fair few on the back seat and in the foot wells.

Tommy and Dan hopped in – there wasn't room for Shaun – and Glyn drove them the 200 yards to the off licence on Lowther Street. Barry, the shopkeeper, looked on in silence as they brought the empties in, in armfuls, and lined them up on the floor at the side of the counter.

'Right,' said Tommy, 'I make than 78 – count them if you like – and at two pee apiece, I make that one pound fifty-six.'

Barry opened the till with noticeable air of irritation, and counted out the money.

They bought another five bottles of Dry Blackthorn, some Magic Wands and a bag of chocolate caramels.

***

It was a busy Saturday afternoon at 22 St Mark's Street. Donna had stayed the night, and Greg Platt and Philbo had showed up with a load of Pethedine, plus a few Palfium and

Physeptone. Then Nick Norton had called round, wanting to score. Philbo and Greg had brought a works with them, and Tommy, Shaun and Dan had theirs, so there were two to share between six – Donna didn't touch injectables – and the little twelve-foot-square front room was packed with people preparing fixes and firing them up. Those who were neither preparing nor fixing enhanced their pleasure with cigarettes, and the air was thick with grey smoke. Even floor space was at a premium, with mugs and ashtrays dotted around, plus the kitchen bowl and two buckets, placed within easy reach for the inevitable opioid-induced vomiting.

Dan prepared himself a fix of Peth, but when he weighed-up his forearms, nowhere seem usable. Every findable vein was peppered with needle marks and bruises. The best ones, those in the crooks of his arms, both seemed to have collapsed completely. He decided to go for the big blue tube on the front of his biceps and got Nick Norton to fix him up. That was a visibly unmissable vein, but in practical terms it was not so easy, because it was on the high point of the muscle and it wriggled and moved when you tried to spike it. Still, he was short of options, so it was worth a try.

Nick was a decent sort, the kind of guy who always tried to do the right thing. He was of medium build and muscular, with a broad, serious-looking face and short fair hair. He'd just left the army and was getting himself back in touch with old friends and their developing pastimes.

Dan tourniqued his left arm close to the armpit, and the vein swelled. Nick, with a look of intense concentration, closed in with the hypodermic on the raised blue pleasure conduit. The needle deflected then penetrated the skin, and a tiny amount of blood appeared in the thick white liquid in the syringe – evidence Nick had hit the vein. He pressed the plunger and emptied the works into Dan's arm. But there was no rush and, instead, a bulge, which looked slightly paler than the rest of Dan's arm, appeared next to the vein.

'Shit. I've popped it,' said Nick.

Dan looked at the lump. It was clear what had happened: the needle had nicked the side of the vein, hence the blood, but the drug had been deposited next to it, under Dan's skin.

'Oh, shit,' said Dan. 'We're gonna have to cut that out, or it might go septic.'

Dan ran upstairs and got a razor blade from the bathroom cabinet. In the kitchen, using his Gas Board pliers, he held it in the gas cooker flame to sterilise it, then ran it under the tap to cool it and handed it to Nick. The others came to have a look at what was going on, then went back into the front room. Tommy, Shaun and Donna stayed.

Dan held his arm up to the window to get the best possible light. Tommy gripped it at the wrist and under the elbow to help hold it steady. Nick paused, breathed deeply and set himself, then carefully sliced into the skin of Dan's bicep, through the bulge and as close to the vein as he could safely get, and squeezed out a bubbly pale-pink mixture of blood and stray drug.

There was palpable relief in the room.

'Nice bit of field surgery, Nick,' said Tommy.

'Yeah. Nice one, Nick. Thanks. That's sorted it,' added Dan

'Phew. Yeah,' replied Nick. 'You had me going for a minute there. I was really worried about cutting that vein.'

'Well, that would have been a mess wouldn't it,' joked Dan.

Nick laughed. 'Yeah.'

Tommy, Shaun and Donna returned to the front room to resume the business of having a good time, while Dan washed and put a sticking plaster over the neat, inch-long cut. Nick stayed to see the process concluded. Someone switched on the stereo; Iggy Pop's "Lust for Life" blasted through the doorway.

Alongside a triumphant looking Nick, Dan walked back into the crowded, smoky front room, with its buckets and slouched bodies.

'Right,' announced Dan, 'I'm gonna need some painkillers now,' and the one or two who weren't comatose laughed.

***

United were away at Norwich. It was one of the worst journeys of the season, and the Three Musketeers were all close to broke. So they decided to give it a miss and instead, for entertainment and a bit of a change of scenery, took themselves off for a few dinner-time bevvies at The County Arms. It was an old, white-stuccoed Boddies' pub in that odd bit of no-man's-land between Hatterston and Hightown: a wide vale with a sparse scattering of houses and an almost rural feeling, plonked incongruously into the midst of that cramped industrial melee; quite pleasant, as long as the wind wasn't blowing from the direction of Turley's bone yard.

Thursday's, Friday's and even Saturday morning's phone calls had produced no gear and there was no-one else they could think to call. So it looked like Saturday night was going to be a drugless affair. No football, no drugs – it didn't seem right. Still, there was the Boddies', which flowed very well.

'There's always Potter's Asthma Fags,' proffered Tommy, tentatively.

'Potter's Asthma Fags? I thought that was all bullshit, like smoking dried banana skins and other such nonsense,' replied Dan, sceptically.

'I've heard they work – to an extent, in their own way. You don't smoke 'em. You mix 'em up in boiling water – make a kind of tea. They're a bit trippy.'

'Well, I'd give it a crack – for what it's worth,' said Shaun 'It's not as though we've got owt else, is it.'

And at 3.45, when The County Arms turned out, they drove over to that strange orange and green wholefoods and alternative medicines shop on Stanniforth Street in Dashton, which none of them had ever been in before, and purchased a packet of Potter's Asthma Cigarettes.

They drove back to Dashley Dyke listening to the football scores on the car radio. United had lost 2-1, and their team's solitary goal had been a Norwich own-goal. They felt comforted and vindicated that they hadn't travelled all that way for that.

Back at number 22, they broke open the cigarettes and dropped their strange cowpat-coloured contents into the tea pot, poured on boiling water, stirred and waited.

After giving the mixture time to cool, they filled three mugs and started to drink the strange black fluid.

'Gor streuth! It tastes like shit,' said Dan.

'Just get it down yer,' said Tommy. 'Hold your nose or something.'

With the dubious liquid consumed, they sat around the gas fire in the front room and put on a few albums: *No More Heroes, Lust for Life, Rattus Novegicus*....

And then the feeling was strange: a bit like a trip, but not quite. It had gone dark outside but, gazing at the fire and listening to the music and feeling the peculiar effects of the asthma fags, they hadn't noticed, so there were no lights on in the house and they sat in darkness, but for the glow of the gas fire.

Dan felt he was in a dream. The gloom added to this sense. It was like waking in the near-total darkness of an early-hours bedroom, with your mind still coming to terms with the fact that you were something like conscious, while the dream narrative and its hallucinations were yet to get the message and depart. But this was continuous, and because you were there, awake, it was like a dream in which you actually took part, rather than imagining you do, like in a real dream.

A knock at the door shattered the spell. It was Glyn Cousins with his girlfriend, Jess. Glyn was another skinny speed-freak soul boy; a bit like another Reevesie, with long fair hair and a friendly face and demeanour. He was a tremendous dancer at the soul clubs and did the most startling, prolonged spins, which had other folk dizzy just watching. Jess was good fun too – mucked in with the lads and didn't seem to mind what Glyn got up to. The most striking visual feature of Jess was her hair. It was dark brown, nearly black, and she wore it in the hot fashion of the day: wrapped tightly round her head, until it reached the front, where it flared out abruptly, giving her face the look of a pink sunflower, or of someone wearing a parka with the hood tied too tightly. It was evident, however, that the hair didn't want to cooperate with this design and that it took industrial quantities of hairspray to hold it rigidly in position. Dan couldn't help but wonder if you might cut yourself on it if you got too close and if Glyn was in mortal danger when he snogged her.

Glyn and Jess stepped into the room. Dan switched on the small table lamp on the sideboard – he couldn't fancy a room full of proper light just yet. Glyn wore his long, maroon leather trench coat. Jess also wore leather: a long black coat with grey fur trim at the edges, echoing somehow the look of her hair.

Were they ready? Glyn wanted to know.

'Ready for what?'

'The party. Don't tell me you've forgot.'

And then it came back. They were all supposed to be off to a knees-up at Bradfield Reform Club: some girl Jess worked with was having her twenty-first there. They'd said they'd go. They didn't know her, but any excuse for a piss-up... But in their deranged, other-worldly state, the affairs of this one had been eclipsed.

Tommy and Shaun, in their indescribable but demented condition, no longer fancied it. They weren't going. Dan, irritated at the darkness that surrounded him, said he would. He scurried upstairs, threw cold water in his face and got changed. Minutes later, he was zooming up St Luke's Brew in the back of Glyn's grey Renault on the way to Bradfield Reform Club. But, looking out of the window as the town streaked by, Dan still wasn't sure about the revised dreamscape environment; it was still dubiously dark and its reality remained questionable.

The party was loud, packed and bright. People pushed and swished past Dan, like they had in London that day, and they laughed too loudly and got too close to him, too. Glyn and Jess fought through the crowd to find the birthday girl and hand over a card and present. Dan bought a pint of bitter and stood around. He wasn't sure if he wanted a conversation – the comfort of human company – or if that would be too much to deal with and he'd prefer solitude, not that that was really possible in these circumstances. Either prospect looked tricky. A couple of girls did try to speak to him, but he didn't reply because he wasn't sure if they were real or, if they were real, whether it was him they were actually talking to, such was the strange, echoey spirit-world quality of their voices. It was all just too complicated. He found a corner with a squishy, satsuma-coloured bench seat under a window and sat down for a bit, but didn't like that much – he felt awkward and alone and could only see people's backs. So he stood up and mingled, and found he didn't much care for that that either. The world had gone from too dark to too bright – garish, clattering, flashgun bright. And why was everyone talking so loud? And it dawned on him that he didn't like parties in the first place, even when he wasn't having to deal with a dream and reality going on at the same time.

He stepped outside into the cold night air. He wasn't sure where to go or what to do. He couldn't fancy a pub – it would have the same issues as this place. He started to walk towards home. If he hadn't thought of anything better by the time he got there, that's where he'd go.

He clacked down the hill in his leather-soled brogues, past Eagle Mill, which was just a dark disused skeleton now. As he turned left onto St Luke's Brew, he became aware that Tommy and Shaun were following him. He had in fact suspected they were there a quarter of a mile back, near the mill. But now they were closer and it was obvious. They were chatting about something. He ignored them for a while, but they kept at it and had now started giving him a bit of stick.

'Look,' said Dan, without breaking his stride or turning round, 'I know you're not there, you're not real.'

They laughed and took the piss some more.

'You're not gonna make me turn round. I know you're not really there.'

And they gave him still more playful abuse and dared him to turn round.

'All right. If it helps, I'll turn round and then we'll know for certain you're not there and that'll be the end of it. That OK?'

Tommy and Shaun agreed to Dan's terms, and he stopped and turned around, and they weren't there. No-one was there. The street was dark and deserted in both directions.

'Right, I'm glad we've put that to bed. Now can I get on with my walk home in peace? And no bloody sulking.'

Tommy and Shaun muttered some sullen riposte, but now suitably chastened said nothing more, and Dan's walk home continued without incident or further conversation.

Back at the house, the little table lamp on the sideboard was still on, but there was no-one in the front room. The kitchen was in total darkness.

'Hello?' yelled Dan.

'We're up here,' came Shaun's voice down the staircase.

Dan entered the bedroom. Tommy was leant over his neatly made bed in deep concentration, his left hand on the bedspread, his right arched out behind his back, moving slightly, back and forth. Shaun looked on thoughtfully from the side.

'What are you doing?' asked Dan.

'Shsssh! You'll mess up his shot,' said Shaun

'What? What are you on about?'

'You blind or something?' said Shaun, with a tone of exasperation. 'What's it look like were doing?'

'I dunno. What?'

Shaun looked at Dan and shook his head in disbelief: 'We're playing pool, you fucking idiot.'

***

It was late Saturday morning. They'd phoned every number they could think of and couldn't find anyone with any gear to sell – the Squad had clearly been very busy – though one guy, Andy Parkin from Dashton, said he'd got some stuff called Largactil. It wasn't junk – it was some kind of heavy-duty tranquiliser – and he wasn't recommending it especially, but it was there if they wanted it. Having no alternatives whatsoever, and with Potter's Asthma Fags now definitely off the list, they said they did. The three friends hopped into Dan's Morris for the short drive down to Dashton.

Andy lived in a ground-floor flat in one of the big old houses on Lancaster Square. He let them in without enthusiasm. A couple of Andy's friends were there already, splayed out on the armchairs. They looked spaced and shared Andy's lack of enthusiasm – for Dan, Tommy and Shaun, and probably everything else, by the look of them.

Andy produced the drug. Conveniently, it came in ampoules, and Andy had a works with a decent needle on it. Fixing up was therefore quite an efficient process.

There was a rush of sorts. Thereafter, they became almost entirely immobile. It was scarcely possible to move or speak.

After half an hour, it was clear that they'd outstayed what little welcome they'd ever had. They slowly gathered themselves up and fumbled like geriatrics out into the communal hall, then out onto the street. The door clunked closed heavily behind them.

They staggered slowly down the side streets to the car. Dan dropped into the driver's seat and raised his arms to the steering wheel. 'I can't drive. Me arms are like lead. I've got no control over them. They're somebody else's arms. And me legs are the same. I don't know what I'm doing. Everything's down a fucking tunnel.'

'I'll have a go, if you want,' said Tommy.

'Are you sure? Yer can't. You've had the same.'

'I'm not great, but I think I can do it.'

'We could go somewhere – take a walk or something – and let it wear off a bit and come back and get the car later.'

'No. I'll be OK…. I think.'

And somehow, slowly and painstakingly, Tommy did get the Morris back to St Mark's Street. And they got back into the house and collapsed onto the settee.

***

It was just shy of nine-thirty pm. Shaun, Dan and Eddie were seated around a small square table in the loud, smoky main bar of The Cavendish Hotel. Eric Clapton's "Layla" filled the room. A couple of long-haired, flared-kecks greasers near the bar played the riff on imaginary guitars. Tommy was under the staircase, on the phone – receiver to one ear, finger in the other, trying to keep out the racket. He hung up and swung back around the table onto his stool. 'Right. Got her at last. She's got some H and she'll flog us a bit. We need to go now.'

An icy wind whipped around them as they crossed the darkened town-centre by-pass to Belgravia House and climbed the cold concrete steps up to the second-floor deck and Bev's flat. Bev opened the door. The warm orange light and familiar dull pong of fags and stale chip fat were welcoming after the biting, wintry wind outside.

Mercifully, Bev was already off her head – this meant they'd get their gear and the use of the works pretty quickly. There'd be less of Bev's tedious stories to sit through; or rather, they'd be off their heads too by the time she was telling them, so it wouldn't matter too much.

Each had a fix, and they sagged like lumpen sacks on the settee. Dan rummaged in his sheepskin pocket for his fags and realised he'd smoked the last in the pub. He fancied some chocolate too. It wasn't half ten – the offie would still be open. 'I'm goin' for some fags and chocolate. Anyone want anything?'

Tommy said he was low on fags too – would he get him a packet.

Dan, half dazed, head tucked down into the collar of his sheepskin, crossed back over the by-pass and through the alley into Cavendish Square. Light blazed from the aluminium-framed off licence – the only shop on the square not now in darkness. He shoved the door and stepped into an experiment in sensory overload. Colour-saturated adverts, sweet wrappers, chocolate bars, beer cans and fag packets, pulsated under blistering fluorescent light – super-bright, to put off shop-lifters. The chief research scientist tilled Dan's money and handed over the goodies: a packet of Number 6 for Tommy, and John Player Specials and an Aero for Dan.

He felt himself losing the battle to keep his eyes open, but forced them apart just long enough for a glance each way at the by-pass. He dragged himself back up the breezy staircase and had the feeling he was somewhere near Bev's flat. And even though the icy wind blasted around his ears, an irresistible feeling of warmth and serenity swept over him, and he slumped down in the darkness.

And then there wasn't anything – the universe and everything in it had vanished.

Dan went from not being anywhere to being somewhere intangible, with his arms being pulled. He felt his weight shift. He seemed to be in some great echoey void, beyond which invisible people were shouting, arguing... something about an ambulance. Dan moved upwards and forwards, but he wasn't doing this – he was weightless, being carried. There was warm air and an orange glow, and more shouting, closer this time – male voices, then a female one: 'No! No way. No fuckin' ambulance. You'll 'ave the Squad 'ere.'

Someone was shaking him. There were slaps around his face. Someone had him by the forearms and pushed and pulled so that his body rocked back and forward, while his head lolled, helplessly. He could feel consciousness returning, while most of him wanted nothing more than warm oblivion.

His eyes half opened. Bev's toothless jaundiced face filled his field of vision. 'He's alright now. See. He's coming round.'

And there was Tommy's face and, behind it, Shaun's and Eddie's, all inspecting his, thoughtfully.

'I'll get 'im some coffee,' said Bev.

***

It was another drugless Saturday night, and Tommy, Shaun and Dan sat in the best room of The County Arms, downing pints of Boddies' Bitter with Rick Cooper and Jimmy Bragg, alternately mulling over this wicked turn of fate and trying to distract themselves from it. And the more the beer flowed, the more daring and inventive they got about rectifying this appalling situation.

Rick knew this chemists' in Glodhill that was dead easy, and Jimmy knew one less than half a mile from there that he reckoned was even easier. But they should leave it till late, till after closing, so there'd be fewer folk about. And they did – they stayed till the landlord turfed them out at twenty to midnight. And while others staggered out into the darkness looking for a takeaway, sex or a fight, the five friends sped off in the Cortina towards Glodhill on business.

'That's it,' said Rick, pointing out a darkened corner shop on a nondescript terraced street on the Manchester side of Glodhill. Tommy brought the silver Ford to a stop twenty yards further on and kept the engine running, while the other four got out and surveyed the scene. The shop had facades on two streets, with a front door that linked them diagonally across the corner. The door was glass in an aluminium frame, and both the top and bottom panels had tell-tale strips of silver tape around their peripheries, linked to the alarm system.

'Well, we've no chance here, have we?' said Jimmy.

'Don't be so quick to judge,' said Rick. And he crossed the road to some cleared demolition ground and returned with half a house brick. 'What often happens,' he explained, 'is that as the glass breaks, the alarm fuses and doesn't go off.'

Dan, Shaun and Jimmy looked at each other sceptically, and Rick spun on his heels and launched the half-brick at the bottom panel of the door.

The alarm seemed to start ringing almost before the brick hit the glass. They sprinted back to the Cortina and Tommy put his foot down, and the 1300 engine, with its heavy load, did its best imitation of a getaway.

'That was *good*,' said Shaun, in a tone of deep irony.

'Well, look, see: you have to try things don't yer. Yer'd get nowhere in life if yer didn't try things,' replied Rick, cheerfully.

'What about the other one – the one Jimmy knows?' proffered Dan.

'Well that's down here, right and right again,' said Jimmy. 'But we can't go there now. It's only a few hundred yards from this one. The police'll be all over here in a minute.'

'I know one on the other side of Glodhill,' said Tommy, 'right in the hills. Quiet. And you can get round the back.'

They drove sensibly through Glodhill shopping centre, at the speed limit in order not to attract attention, and out into the suburbs on the Pennine side of town.

'There it is,' said Tommy, pointing at one of a line of shops in a grey gritstone terrace.

Tommy pulled the car into a dark side-street at the end of the row. The shops all had small, conventional northern backyards. Beyond this was nothing for a hundred yards. Houses had been demolished, nothing had been put in their place, and it was usefully dark.

Tommy got the jack and a crowbar out of the boot, handed them to Jimmy and got back into the car. 'I'll wait here,' said Tommy, revving the engine.

'You go out front, Shaun – keep an eye out,' said Rick. Shaun complied. Rick's couple of years' seniority over even the oldest of them, and his predisposition to unpredictable acts of demented violence earned him deference from the others.

The back gate was open. There was little light, but it was clear that the yard was disregarded space, littered with bins, flattened old cardboard boxes and other unidentifiable crap. Beyond was a single storey lean-to with a barred window. Rick smashed the glass with the jemmy and waited. No alarm. He raked out the broken glass, inserted the jack between the bars and cranked open a gap. Dan gave Rick and Jimmy a leg up and waited in the yard for the goodies to be passed out, and to keep watch.

Metallic noises, conversation and swearing bled out from the opening. Then, after ten minutes, Jimmy's face appeared between the bars. 'We can't get the DDA open. It's like a bloody safe. We'll just get whatever we can.'

Rick and Jimmy came to the window in turns and passed out large quantities of sunglasses, bottles of Brut 33 aftershave and larger, brown bottles, which turned out, once they got them into the light, to be Sanatogen. And for the next few weeks they all went around in Aviators and stinking of Brut 33. No-one drank the Sanatogen, though.

***

There was a knock at the door of number 22 St Mark's Street at 11.30pm on Saturday night. Tommy, Shaun and Dan were home. Donna was in the bath. It could be trouble, or it could be someone with a big bag of goodies from a freshly turned-over chemists', so Dan answered the door with mixed feelings.

As Dan's eyes adjusted to the darkness, he recognised the short, dark-haired figure of Dennis Bradshaw: not a bloke he'd ever met in person; someone he knew only by sight and reputation – a reputation for not being properly roofed-in. Dennis, being on the footpath beyond the doorstep, looked even stubbier than usual. In the darkness, he seemed to be wearing all black or dark blue – dark jeans and a donkey jacket, probably – and his face looked dirty.

''Ave yer gorany wanmough?' gruffed Dennis.

'Yer what, pal?'

'Wanboh, ave yer gorany wanboh?'

'I'm still not getting it. Wakboffs?'

'Wanboofs, wanboofs,' pressed the increasingly exasperated visitor.

Dan turned back into the room. 'Tommy, 'ave yer heard this? Can yer make any sense of this fucker?'

Tommy came over to the door. 'What is it, pal? What'jer want?'

'Wanboofs. Fuckin' wanboofs.'

'It's wank books! He wants wank books: pornography,' said Tommy, with a hint of triumph in his voice. 'Have you got any?'

'Me? No,' replied Dan, slightly surprised to be asked. 'I've got Donna. Kinda covered for that department. Have you got any?'

'No,' replied Tommy, and turned back into the room, where Shaun sat, half stoned, gazing at the telly: 'have you got any wank books, Shaun? Y'know, porn.'

'Me? No. Well, not here.'

Dan turned back to Dennis. 'Sorry, mate. No wank books.' And Dennis grunted, turned and stomped off up the street.

***

In 1970s Britain there was a marked tendency for things to explode. Some of this was due to terrorism – the Irish trying to bomb the British into giving them back the top third of their country – but far more was due to gas leaks, which seeped silently into people's cellars and old coal chutes, then drifted up through floorboards and blew up at the next flick of a light switch. There was major loss of life due to a huge gas explosion in Sheffield. Houses were blown apart in Blackburn and Bristol. A whole street was demolished in Bolton. So commonplace had this become that it was starting to look like an epidemic.

The government set up an enquiry under a gentleman by the name of Lord King, to work out why this was happening. After sifting through the evidence, Lord King and his team discovered that multiple issues combined to cause the catastrophes.

Natural gas, which the country was in the process of being switched over to, had to run at a higher pressure than the old, manufactured town's gas, on account of its burning characteristics; this meant that it was less forgiving of leaky old gas mains. And natural gas was dry, unlike town's gas, which was infused with steam during manufacture; this meant that the new gas dried out the old jute-and-lead jointing systems used on the thousands of miles of Victorian cast-iron gas mains that lay under Britain's streets. If this wasn't enough, the old, small-diameter cast-iron pipes, laid in the nineteenth century perilously close to the UK's vast number of densely packed terraced houses, were worn out and corroded and prone to breaking catastrophically and without warning. And then there was the fact that when the optimum concentration of natural gas was ignited in air, it expanded massively and devastatingly in a few millionths of a second. In short, natural gas was to town's gas what nuclear fission was to cosy old TNT. It produced a very big bang.

The upshot of the King Report was an urgent, countrywide programme to replace all the suspect old gas mains before they could cause any more devastation. And gas distribution engineers all over the land frantically set about identifying at-risk areas and organising new pipe-laying projects. It was for this reason that Dan Brody was at work, doing overtime, on the Saturday morning when the Drug Squad raided 22 St Mark's Street.

Tommy and Shaun were there, and so was Mick Henshaw, who'd called round ready for the fortnightly pilgrimage to Old Trafford in the afternoon.

Detective Inspector Coleman was chirpy – almost friendly. 'Morning, Tommy, Shaun, Mick,' he said and, glancing round the room, 'Dan not here?'

Tommy explained about Dan's overtime. Detective Inspector Coleman expressed his disappointment at not seeing him.

Detective Inspector Coleman's colleagues searched the house for offending substances. They found nothing other than the syringe in the sideboard, which they confiscated. Tommy said it was his and that no-one else used it.

Three weeks later, Dan took half a day off work to go to Dashley Dyke Magistrates' Court, to give Tommy moral support, and because he felt guilty that Tommy was carrying the can for all of them. In the old, brown-panelled courtroom at the back of the town hall, Tommy's neat lady brief explained to the magistrate that the amount of heroin the police had been able to extract from the confiscated syringe was so minute that it was worth only 0.43 of a penny at street prices, and that the syringe had been lying around for ages – a vestige of the old life Tommy had long left behind – and that Tommy was now an upstanding and much-loved member of the community, as evidenced by the fact that he was now gainfully employed and by Dan's taking time off work to come along and support him, and it would be a shame to send him down again now, just when he was sorting his life out.

The grey, grim-faced Dickensian magistrate said he took a dim view of drug-taking, and Tommy's record did not make inspiring reading, but he had taken account of the brief's arguments, and he handed down a two-year sentence, *suspended for two years*, with the sternest and most final of stern final warnings. If Tommy fucked up again in the next two years, he'd get whatever was coming for that, plus the two years just allotted.

Dan and Tommy left the courtroom chastened, and didn't score again till the weekend.

***

Dan parked the white Morris outside the block of flats in Glodhill where Mark, the new score, lived. The sky was the colour of lead. Cold, hostile rain hammered down. The three friends gazed up at the tall building. Already in a bleak, windswept part of town, it was a grim spectacle: a huge, labyrinthine development of system-built, grey, deck-access concrete flats. The parapet walls were streaked alternately with seeping water and black grime. A few of the flats were boarded up. Some had broken windows, one with a pathetic bit of red curtain hanging out from it, which flapped back and forth in the pitiless wind – a sad vestige of someone's vain attempt to make the place homely. Only a dozen or so years old, the block already looked wrecked and desolate, like some vast, bombed-out World War Two gun emplacement.

Inside was no more promising. Dan had been in dozens of junkie dives and they didn't bother him – he scarcely paid any mind to such things – but this one creeped him out. There was something strange and sick about the place. It was chaotic mess, with clothes, blankets, dirty plates, bottles, fag packets and drug-related stuff scattered around, and it didn't smell too good. Not that any of that was unusual when a bunch of drug-using young men lived together, as Dan knew from personal experience, but there was something different here. Three of Mark's friends were sprawled out on the settee and armchairs. All were strangely subdued and silent. They didn't just look smashed, they looked ill. Dan's gut instinct was that there was something deeply wrong about this place. He looked at Tommy and Shaun and got the sense that Shaun shared his disquiet; not that it was feasible to say 'this is bit of a shithole, innit?' while stood so close to Mark. And as for Tommy, he was all tunnel vision: none of this had registered; he just wanted that gear.

They made a deal and took the opportunity, while they were there, to use Mark's works. It was a decent hit, and they left with the remainder of the wrap to use over the weekend.

By the following evening, they were all feeling very unwell, and the whites of their eyes had turned yellow.

***

It was a Sunday afternoon at 22 St Mark's Street. Tommy, Shaun, Dan, Philbo and Greg had each consumed thirty-odd psilocybin mushrooms and were enjoying the ensuing madness. The planes in an air display on the telly left the screen and flew past the chimney breast like a set of grey porcelain ducks. Donna was there too, but had not imbibed. She had an exam the next day and wanted a clear head.

Some familiar looking silhouettes passed the net curtains and there was a knock on the door. Before Dan could stop him, Tommy had opened it. Dan's entire family had popped round. Lily, Walter, Nicky, Janet, and Clive and his wife and two kids trooped in.

The room fell silent. No-one knew what to do. Dan stood there trying to work out how to deal with the situation – this was his family, his problem – but he was so deeply in trip land that he couldn't even look at them, let alone to speak to them; nor could anyone else. Some lost voice, some deeply buried part of him wanted to erupt onto the surface, make everything normal and OK, and say, chirpily, 'I'll put the kettle on – tea everybody?' And they could sit around and have a nice, cordial Sunday-afternoon chat. But he couldn't get there; he couldn't break out of the strange parallel universe he'd slipped into. And as his mind wrestled with what was possible and what was not possible and came to no conclusion, he remained frozen to the spot and speechless. And after a further few minutes of excruciating silence, someone – Clive, probably – said, 'Er, right, we'll be off then,' and the extended Brody family, sans Dan, trooped back out.

Dan was shellshocked. He fought to think of ways in which the debacle might not have been quite as ghastly as it looked. Tommy leant into his ear. Dan hoped to hear some comforting words: 'that wasn't as bad as it seemed', would have been a good start. But Tommy just said 'that was *baaad*.'

At that, a sudden sick feeling, somewhere between guilt, shame and embarrassment, hit Dan. In an instant, the feeling, magnified by the drug, expanded and exploded and bored deep into his psyche, and sensations of horror and dread overwhelmed him. The room erupted and chairs and walls shattered into scraps and splinters. The floor fell away and revealed a burning black hole that connected the house to Hell. And Hell roared up through it, and everything collapsed, and shards and fragments of room swirled in incomprehensible grey space, and there were beasts and demons, and deafening noise and hysterical terror. Everything was horror, violence and loathing. Dan's friends became grotesque, warped and evil, full of malevolent intent. They'd joined forces with the demons and turned against him. Reassuring smiles became mocking, hateful sneers. Bodies distended and snapped in the unreal space. Faces twisted into sickening pink spheres that smeared across the room. Eyes expanded into great pits of boiling pitch and exploded out of blood-dripping heads. He fought to get out of the trip and into his own rational mind, but there was no way back. The world was chaos, madness and thundering, terrifying violence, which swept over him in giant dreadful waves and pulled him under. He closed his eyes to shut it all out, but that was worse. With its view of the world cancelled, his mind, now no longer compelled to work within the limits of (distorted) reality, expanded to create its own unimaginable terrors. The shuddering horror went from massive to absolute. He was no longer his own man. He had no control. This thing had taken over and he was helpless inside it.

    Donna rushed him up to the bedroom, but Hell came with him – there was no escape from the insanity. He wasn't hallucinating; this was real and he was in it. Donna held him on the bed and tried to reassure him. But there was nothing she could do. When she was close, he was horrified by her evil, shape-shifting presence and told her to get away; when she got up to leave, he begged her to stay. He couldn't be alone with this. Whatever was going on in the chaotic maelstrom of Dan's mind was all consuming and was as real to him as the pink anaglypta bedroom was to Donna. His terror, the waking nightmare Dan could not escape from, was invisible to her. She just had to hold on. Hell had ridden up from its subterranean pit and absorbed everything. The house and the town and maybe the whole world were all now caught up in the swirling demonic horror and everything was lost.

Some hours later, the drug's effects started to diminish, and Dan gradually came to be able to see the real room and Donna and everything else. And he turned to her and said: 'That's it. That's the end. I'm done with drugs. I'm never taking anything ever again. What I've just experienced I can't even begin to explain. Imagine the most terrifying thing you can think of and multiply it by a million. I didn't know that that was even possible. I've been to a place I didn't even know existed. It's just... I can't tell yer. It's the worst. No, it's worse than the worst. It's the end.'

Outside the light was fading. It was evening.

And then it was properly dark, and Dan, still on the bed, with Donna's warm body next to his, felt the warm glow of peace – the silence of a reassuringly ordinary Dashley Dyke Sunday evening which, after all that had happened, could just be absorbed and enjoyed for its quiet, peaceful nothingness.

They heard the front door open and close, followed by muffled conversation. Some minutes later footsteps rocked up the stairs and there was a knock at the bedroom door. Tommy walked in with a big grin on his face: 'Phil Murphy's just been round. Look at this.' And he tipped his palm and poured onto the pink polyester carpet next to the bed a kaleidoscope of different amphetamine pills and capsules: Bustaids, Pirellis, dex, green-and-clears, Filon and a couple of black bombers.

Dan propped himself up in bed and looked down at the collection, which still sparkled in the residual effects of the psilocybin. And his eyes widened and he looked at Tommy and he looked down at the drugs again and touched them with his fingertips to reassure himself they were real, and a smile crept across his face, and he turned to Donna and said 'I may have to rethink my renunciation of drugs.'

***

Adey had given up his job at Hightown School and taken himself and his rusty beard to Bristol to be with Bobo. He and Dan exchanged frequent letters: Dan told Adey of his latest, mostly drug-related, exploits; Adey told Dan about his new job at Hartcliffe School and about what it was like to live in Bristol and how Bobo was going on at university. She was in her final year, exams were coming up, her degree would soon be over. And he remonstrated with Dan to give up the drugs. 'Quit while you're ahead,' Adey said, amongst other things. And he invited Dan and Donna to come to Bristol again, and Dan leapt at the chance. He'd been wowed by Bristol – Clifton in particular – and needed no persuasion to visit again. And Dan had a car now, so that made it easy.

Bobo and Adey's flat was within a few hundred yards of her old student digs, still in beautiful Clifton. It only had one bedroom, but in the lounge it had a settee that folded out into a double bed, for guests, for Dan and Donna. It was a first floor apartment in another big old house. It was a recent conversion, much plainer and less elegant than the old place, but neat and pleasant, and it had a view of the cathedral.

With the culture shock of the first trip behind him, Dan was more able to look and absorb the place as Adey and Bobo showed them round. They took photos of each other on Brunel's famous suspension bridge; they crossed the busy road in front of the art gallery, which looked like something from Rome or ancient Greece; they nipped into the university – the magnificent Wills Building – where Bobo chatted briefly to a couple of her intelligent, studenty friends. They window-shopped on steep, elegant Park Street; they strolled around the city centre and the docks; and then they visited a couple of warm, cosy pubs.

Bobo was working on her thesis, and she asked Dan if he'd mind doing the illustrations for her. Dan was honoured and delighted – any excuse to draw, and it was a thrill to be doing something associated with such an elevated level of learning. Her subject was Chemistry, and within that, the thesis had something to do with the way crystals bond. It was way beyond Dan, but Bobo was able to explain by describing and by showing him photos in a book, taken through a microscope. And Dan was able to complete the drawings, with full black lines for what would have been visible and dotted red ones for what was hidden behind, and Bobo was thrilled with the results.

And Dan started to wonder – even though his contribution had been so minor – what else he might be able to do.

***

It was Saturday dinner time. Thursday's and Friday's phone calls had produced no gear. There had been numerous busts in the East Manchester towns once more, and there was a dearth not only of H, but of any worthwhile synthetic substitute. The one spark of hope lay in a phone number obtained from a contact of a contact of a contact of someone Tommy knew, for a guy called Rocky in Blackpool.

Dan and Shaun looked on hopefully as Tommy picked up the receiver and dialled Rocky's number. And as the conversation unfolded and a grin spread across Tommy's face, it was clear that at last this was a successful call. Tommy hung up. Rocky had some H and was happy to sell them a wrap. The Fylde Coast was a 150-mile round trip, not like a quick dash out to Brinnington or Levenshulme, but what the hell – they weren't exactly fighting off offers and they used to go up there regularly for nights out at Blackpool Mecca – it wasn't that arduous a drive.

Tommy had arranged to meet Rocky at 7pm in South Beach car park. Rocky would be in a white Escort; they would be in Tommy's silver Cortina.

They arrived at 6.45, climbed out of the car, stretched their legs and looked around. It was October. The tourists had mostly gone, the place was quiet and peaceful, and they had the car park mostly to themselves. The sun was low in the sky, waves sloshed onto the beach, there was a bracing, salty breeze, and they were about to get some H. They felt good. They were a little early, so there was no need to expect to see Rocky just yet. But he wasn't there at 7, or at 7.15, or at 7.30. By 7.45, anxiety had set in. Had they gone to the wrong place? Was there a mix-up over times, or even days?

They found a call box and rang Rocky again. His flatmate answered – he didn't know where Rocky was. They waited a bit longer, and at 8.30 rang again. No answer this time.

They strolled into town to get food to eat back in the car. They also bought some booze, but not much – just a four pack of crappy Skol lager – because they'd only brought enough money for the gear and there was little left over to spend on anything else. They should have been home and wrecked by now.

There was still no sign of Rocky. At 10.30 they rang again and got the flatmate again: Rocky was in hospital; he'd OD'd. He wasn't too bad, though, and ought to be out in the morning.

It was late and they had nowhere to go, and without even the benefit of enough booze to make them drowsy, they decided to sleep in the car: Tommy in the driver's seat, Dan alongside, and Shaun in the back with the luxury of a bench seat to sprawl out on. But Dan couldn't sleep sitting up, and neither could Tommy. And it was cold. And after an hour or so of fidgeting, Tommy got out and tried to sleep on the tarmac. He slid as far as he could under the car, in the hope of escaping the icy wind, and so he wouldn't be run over if some driver swung in without seeing him. But that didn't work either, and soon he was back in his seat, still failing to get off to sleep. Even in the back, with the bonus of 4 ½ feet of horizontal cracked black vinyl, Shaun fared no better – he couldn't stretch out and, in just a T-shirt, he was freezing.

As the sun came up, none of them had had any sleep whatsoever, but it was a relief that they could now stop trying. Tired and fed-up, they ambled over to the old Victorian toilet block, which was conveniently placed next to the car park, and did their best to freshen themselves up a bit.

At just 7.30 in the morning, they concluded it was too early to give Rocky another try, and they had no money for breakfast, so they took a walk along the prom, then returned to the car and listened disconsolately to the crap on Radio One.

At 10, they rang Rocky again. He was back home and he was alright, if a bit shaken up. He'd come down and join them straight away.

Twenty minutes later, the white Escort, turned into the car park and pulled up next to Tommy's Cortina.

Rocky was in the passenger seat, still too wobbly to drive. His flatmate, who didn't get out of the car, had chauffeured him. Rocky swung open the door and eased himself out and into the cold sea breeze. He was a big, heavy guy, in his early twenties – it was clear how he'd got his nickname – and he wore cool, punky fashions: black winkle-pickers, skin-tight sky-blue denims and a big furry black jumper, *à la* Johnny Rotten. They felt a bit passé in their baggies and Donald Duck shoes.

They shook hands and exchanged niceties. They asked him how he was after the previous night's OD. He reckoned he was OK, but they could see it had rattled him. He looked like a man who'd learned a harsh lesson. They handed him a wodge of notes and he slipped them a sliver of folded white paper. He then smiled and nodded and climbed back into the white Escort, which spun back round to the car park entrance and vanished from sight.

They returned to the Cortina and weighed up the wrap. It looked like good stuff and it was a decent-sized deal. They drove home, a little tired and jaded, but very happy with the transaction and looking forward to a sweet, consoling fix. And they racked their brains and tried to remember if they'd ever had to work so hard for a score.

Back at number 22, with the heavenly wrap open and ready on the windowsill, Tommy rinsed out the syringe and squirted fresh water through the needle into the air to check it was clear. A fine line of silvery liquid glinted reassuringly in the afternoon light and fell silently onto the carpet. Dan snapped off a couple of cigarette filters, stripped away the brown paper and cut them in half.

Shaun, who had nipped out for a loaf, opened the front door. As he did so, a draught picked up the open wrap and blew it off the windowsill and onto Dan's record collection, below, and a million molecules of precious heroin vanished into the sleeves of a thousand soul singles.

***

Sheffield Road climbed a thousand feet in the two-and-a-half miles between Dashley Dyke town centre and where it peaked at the top of Ebbert's Moor. From there, it fell a hundred feet in half a mile, to meet the Pennine sandstone village of Butterworth.

Butterworth had four pubs, and Dan and Donna were seated at a secluded corner table in the best of them, The Woodcutter. From the outside it was quite an unprepossessing place – a small gritstone bookend on the right of a row of terraced houses; the butcher's shop, a hundred yards away, was the equivalent on the left. But inside it was warm and cosy, with rough, cream-coloured walls and lots of nostalgic villagey stuff: horse brasses, pairs of dinky little wall lamps with imitation candlewax drips and frilly shades, and framed pictures of empty streets from the lost but yearned-for days before the motor car and Manchester sprawl came to town. It was only a Wilson's house, but the beer was excellent because the landlord knew his craft, and every foaming jug was served up just as the brewer intended. Each of the bar-top beer pumps was a horizontal glass cylinder containing a piston, which shunted from one side to the other and dispensed a half pint with each throw of the lever; and what emerged from the spout was a match for all but the very best-kept Boddingtons.

Two weeks ago, they'd been in the second best pub in Butterworth – The Stagecoach – because it served food, like a restaurant. They'd been out with two of Donna's respectable friends: Amanda, Donna's fellow trainee lab technician at Manchester University, and Amanda's boyfriend, Anthony, who was middle class and whose dad drove a Jag and played golf. Dan had shown up after a substantial fix of heroin and struggled to be mentally present with the other three and, while doing battle with a recalcitrant bit of steak and kidney pie, which he wasn't especially interested in anyway, he'd banged down too hard with his fork and flipped his plate and its contents into his lap. Amanda and Anthony were very nice about it, but Dan, with a lapful of pie, chips, garden peas and gravy, was mortified.

Dan sipped his Wilson's Bitter, and Donna her rum and coke, and they talked about the debacle of that night and Dan's situation in general.

'What's it like, then, addiction?' asked Donna, almost casually.

'What's it like?' repeated Dan, slightly taken aback at a question which, in spite of its overwhelming pertinence, he'd never thought to address.

'Well, yeah, I know there's the longing and that…' pressed Donna.

'Well that, I guess, is the headline thing, the thing people always talk about: "addiction equals longing". But, it's more than that… it's… it's visceral.'

'Vissa-wot?'

'Visceral. You know: to do with yer guts, yer innards. Tommy's always saying it. It's not just about your mind; your whole body's involved. I mean, for starters, opiates are emetic. They make you throw up. You don't mind it so much because you're anaesthetised, but it still happens, and it's disgusting really, but you get used to it. And that's the thing – degradation becomes normal. And then, when it wears off you feel like shit, because it makes you constipated, and you get all bunged up and just sort of lose your sparkle and become befuddled. And there's that bit in between, when you're not high but it hasn't completely worn off either, and you're like a zombie. And it does for your skin as well. It makes you itch like crazy, especially round your nose, and you scratch and you rub and it gets red and raw. You can probably see it now, can't yer – look.' Dan pointed at his nose; Donna examined it. There were tinges of red and small areas of peeling skin, on and next to the nostrils. 'So you wander round feeling dopey and awful with your face coming to bits. And it rots your teeth, though amphet sulphate's worst for that. Your teeth just sort of corrode away. I can remember, when I was doing a lot of speed, this white powder appearing from nowhere in my mouth, and I wondered what it was. Then I realised: it was tooth enamel; it was mi teeth just crumbling away. And then there's all the other stuff. You live in a constant state of tension. Where's yer next wrap coming from? Are yer gonna get busted? A car door slams late and night and you're wondering if it's them, if the door's gonna knock. And then there's all the knock-on stuff from there. Say you get busted: then you're in court, then you're in the papers and everybody knows, and then you lose your job, and you've got a record, and it comes up when you try and apply for another job, and you're fucked, ruined. And there's the people you have to deal with: other junkies, people you buy off... And there's the rip offs and the bad gear, and sometimes you get ripped off and the guy's a hard case and you know you can't take him, so you walk away, humiliated. In fact, humiliation is a big part of it, because you spend time with other, sober people, at work and that, and you're out of it, incoherent, and you make a fool of yourself in so many ways, like me the other week with that fucking plate of chips in The Stagecoach, and when someone talks to you and you can't string a sentence together. And people who you know who aren't exactly bright sparks are suddenly smarter than you. And then you wake up one day and find you've moved into another, darker world, because ultimately it's a criminal activity, and whereas you started out just buying a few pills from a mate, you're now involved with serious, heavy-duty criminals – dangerous people. I've seen guns, Donna. Fucking guns! And you might think you're just having fun, but they're not fuckin' about – it's business. And then there's the guilt, because you're letting your family down, and other people you care about, and you lie to them and deceive them. Everything revolves around keeping your two worlds apart: your gear world and the other one, where people think you're just this ordinary chirpy guy. Oh yeah, junk makes you an expert liar... and actor. And so you're no longer an honourable person. You think of the people you admire and respect, and you're not on the list. You've turned yourself into the sort of person you don't like. You're on the other list: the liars, the two-bit thieves, the bullshitters, the blokes who'd sell their granny for their next fix. That's the club you've joined. The guy in the mirror's a cunt. And speaking of people – you start to lose control of your life to other people. It just sort of happens. Things drift and suddenly you're in a situation you never asked for. You know I love Tommy and Shaun – we'd do owt for each other – but there's never a private moment, no peace. Mi house is always full of people –

junkies – zonked out on the settee or fixing up or nicking mi food, sometimes people I don't even know. I never know what, or who, I'm gonna come home to when I get in from work. And I can't complain because I want the gear, and they come with it. So much of it comes through them and their contacts. If I tell them to fuck off, the gear dries up too. But sometimes I just want to sit down in the front room, quiet, with a clear head, and paint, *just paint* – like I used to do. Why can't I do now, at twenty-two, what I could when I was twelve? How did it manage to get worse? What happened to that freedom? How did I lose control of my own fucking life? And I don't wanna sound snobby or anything, but some of them aren't too bright. Tommy, Shaun and Reevesie are sharp, as you know, and Johnny Caswell, but some of them... my God... I mean – Philbo... Y'know – nice enough lad and all that, but I've had more enlightening conversations with me mum's cat. Did I tell you about the other week...? Tommy and Philbo were having a row about some missing gear, and it got pretty heated. And Tommy called Philbo "peevish", and Philbo rounded on him and tried to rule him out of order for "using long words". And Tommy, sort of gobsmacked, said "but it's only got two syllables". And then Philbo got even more narked because he didn't know what a syllable was. And I dunno, maybe I *am* a snob, but I think I've got more about me than that, and I don't think I should be ashamed of it. But what happens? We all get fixed up and we all sit around stupefied – or maybe stupidised – together. And we sit there with our fags and our plastic buckets like human vegetables. Though I guess it's a great leveller, because we're all then as dumb as each other.'

'But I thought it was creative. We did Taylor Coleridge and De Quincy at school. They were opium addicts.'

'Well, yeah. Your mind goes to all sorts of places when you're on it. And it gives you vivid dreams and that carries on for a bit when you wake up. But what would any of us lot do with that? What do I know about literature? The only books I've ever read are *Skinhead, Suedehead* and *Clockwork Orange*. And I can't imagine Shaun or Tommy being moved to verse. We just sit there dumfounded. Maybe our minds *do* do something in those moments – people take it for a reason, it does make you feel good – but we don't do anything with it. We just sit there. Then we get up after a few hours and we're so mind-fucked that we can't even remember where we left the gear. I don't call that mind-expanding.'

'But you're good at art.'

'Art? No, I'm not good at "art". I don't know anything about "art". What I'm good at is drawing. I can look at a thing and create a reasonable likeness of it with a pencil on a piece of paper. That's it. But "art"? No, I don't know anything about that. I've flicked through Tommy's modern art book, and there are some amazing things in there. But I don't know what they mean, how you get to that, what goes on in an artist's mind to produce those things. That's why I wanted to study art. I always wanted to study art. Fuck.' Dan let out a great heavy sigh and took a swig from his pint. Donna looked at him keenly. 'Anyway,' Dan continued, 'people... and places. Where was I? Yeah, there's the Dashley Dyke factor in this, too. Dave Scholes – I know he's not a junkie, but he knocks back the ale like billy-o and uses a lot of dope, and he's not averse to a bit of Charlie when there's some about – but when he's sober he's got a lively, perceptive mind. He really has – you've met him. You know what he's like. And what does he do with it? He's just the funniest man in the pub. That's it. If he'd been born somewhere else, I don't know what he'd have done, but he could have done a lot more than tell jokes and bang on about Bob Dylan. And all he does is drink and smoke to quieten his bouncy mind and fit in with all the clodhoppers. And then there's the big one: people keep dying. I've lost count. There's been, what: Molly, Al Waterhouse, Terry Wardle, Pete Clayton, Steve Mahoney, Azzer Cunliffe, Lol Bradshaw, Harry Franklin...? And there were a couple of lads in Dashton the other week – I didn't know them, don't know their names. Reevesie knew them. That's not all junk, but it's all connected to drugs one way or another. And then there's all the near-misses. I've OD'd twice, and that could have turned out differently, and... you know what...? I've had enough... I'm tired. I'm tired of it all, Donna. The light's gone on. I've got to get away. I've got to go. If I stay here, sooner or later I'm going the way of Lol and Terry. And I can't stop while I'm here. I'm surrounded by the stuff.'

Donna gazed studiously into Dan's face, looking for clues: '*Sounds* like you want to stop... but you've said that before... quite a few times... a lot of times.'

'I know, I know, but it's the temptation. I *do* want to stop, but when it's there in front of you, and if someone else is having some, you can't not. It's like someone eating in front of a starving man.'

'Hmm...'

'Seriously. I've got to leave. I've got to go. I've got to be somewhere else, or this'll never stop. I'll die if I stop here. I *am* dying. This stuff is death; it's just coming in instalments... For a long time, I didn't care if I lived or died. The world didn't give a fuck about me and I didn't give a fuck back. I expected to die. I just didn't want to know anything about it when it happened. And I wouldn't – you know why. I'd have just gone out in one final blaze of glory and got my name in the paper. That's it. Over and out. But things have changed. I want to live now.'

'That's cos of me, isn't it,' said Donna, waggling her head side to side and grinning coquettishly.

'Yes, well, hmm... Let's not get carried away, should we, eh?' came the abrupt reply. Donna's face dropped and she shrank visibly in her seat, still not entirely used to Dan's bluntness.

Oblivious, Dan continued: 'Would you come with me?'

'What? Wow! Come where? Go where? I dunno... Where would we go?'

'Well... Bristol. We could go to Bristol, where Adey and Bobo live. It's lovely there, isn't it? You liked it. There's another life there. It doesn't have to be like this, y'know. Just because we were born here, that doesn't mean we have to stay here. It doesn't mean that's all there is. What'jer think? Would you go with me if I went?'

'I dunno. That's sudden. It's a lot... Let me think about it. There's me mum and dad to think of. And there's me exams to finish.'

***

Dan knocked on the grey office door marked 'H. Carrington, Area Distribution Planning Engineer'. Senior staff got their own rooms, protected by two inches of matt-finish Sapele from the migrainous melee of the open-plan office. Harold was 50 and very short, with an oversized head, greased-back black hair and an ego the size of Canada. Dan neither liked nor disliked his boss – he was just *there*, an inevitable part of the workplace – someone to be dealt with as required during the day, then forgotten about at five. Dan was, however, never quite comfortable with the stick Harold got – always behind his back, of course – about his strange appearance: his great, sumo wrestler's torso and tiny, toddler's legs. Roy the scouser would ring Harold's extension while Harold was out talking to someone in the main office, just to watch him slalom at full tilt with his little legs around the desks and drawing boards, to get back breathlessly to his desk, because any phone call to the Area Distribution Planning Engineer had to be an important one. The instant Harold reached his phone, Roy would hang up, leaving Harold 'hallo, hallo-ing' at the dialling tone. But then, it was Harold's own pomposity *combined* with his odd looks that completed the aura of absurdity that followed him around and goaded people into action.

'Come in.'

Harold, in his shiny brown suit with neck-throttling shirt and tie, was seated behind his big, executive-sized desk. Arranged neatly before him were three piles of official-looking papers, a messy ashtray, a two-tone brown telephone, and a wire in-tray, full of folded-up technical drawings. The putty-coloured walls were bare but for a calendar with a picture of a lake and a hill and the days of the current month, December 1977, and a neatly framed black-and-white photo of a young Harold standing between two older and much bigger gas engineers, all towered-over by two gigantic grey gas holders. Dan thought he recognised the place: Bradford Road Gas Works – its gas holders were reputed to be the biggest in the world.

The air was dense with cigarette smoke. Harold looked up from his blotter. 'What can I do for you, Dan?'

'Well, it's an awkward one, Harold,' said Dan, tentatively, 'but, erm, is it possible to get a transfer?'

'A transfer? How do you mean?'

'Well, you know, to another region.'

'You mean outside the North West?!' said Harold, with eyebrows raised and a tone of disbelief. People didn't leave the North West; the home, in Harold's view, of all the country's greatest gas engineers – like himself, for example. 'The North West has a reputation for producing high-calibre men,' Harold had once said, snootily, over cod Mornay in the canteen, to a table full of faces fighting desperately not to cough up their food.

'Yeah, I think I wanna go down south.'

'Down south, eh? Well, no – not just like that you can't. It doesn't work that way. You can't just transfer – or everyone would be working in Devon!' Harold chortled at his own joke. 'No, you have to find a job and apply for it – *and get it.*'

'Oh, right. How do I apply? How do I know what there is to apply for?'

'There's the list – the fortnightly jobs list. Have you never seen it?'

'No.'

Harold rummaged through a pile of papers with his short, podgy fingers, extracted three sheets of A4, stapled together in the top-left corner, and flicked them across the desk to Dan.

Dan glanced quickly at the pages. There were scores of jobs of all kinds, all over the country: clerks, engineers, accountants, managers – required everywhere, from Truro to Inverness. Why had he *never seen this before?* 'Right. Thanks, Harold. I'll have a look through. But where does it come to? I mean, where do I see the new one when it comes out?'

'In here. It's always on my desk – every other Friday.'

***

Dan said goodbye to his family on Saturday afternoon and to Donna Saturday night. On Sunday morning, Tommy and Shaun helped him load his stuff into the white Morris. He'd sold his thousand-plus collection of northern soul singles to a dealer, because they wouldn't fit in the car. Or rather, they would fit in, but only at the expense of everything else, and clothes were vital, while records, however treasured, were not. So, in went his stereo, a handful of LPs, the portable telly, a suitcase, and boxes and polythene bags containing clothes, bedding, towels, kettle, kitchen utensils and his demonic alarm clock.

With everything loaded and the Morris visibly low on its suspension, Dan, Shaun and Tommy, stood on the footpath between house and car and looked each other in the eye. Shaun looked close to tears. He threw his arms around Dan. 'You're breaking up the Three Musketeers.'

This almost triggered Dan, but he tried to hold onto it. He was the oldest one, after all. 'It'll be alright. I'm not going to Australia. I'm just down the road in Bristol – a couple of hours away, well three, maybe. And I'll come and visit every few weeks, and you can come down there.'

Shaun stood back and Tommy stepped forward with his chin jutting out, the way it always did when he was trying to control his emotions. He and Dan embraced and backslapped. Tommy stood back. 'Anyway, go on, fuck off, you fucker,' he said, grinning. 'Hmmm... now, what shall we do tonight – have a few pints of Boddies, maybe? Maybe some H? Maybe both...? And United are playing Chelsea midweek.'

'Yeah, well, you're not gonna make me jealous,' grinned Dan, wryly. 'Well, you *are* making me jealous, but that's the thing, innit. That *is* what I'm trying to get away from.'

Dan climbed into the car, wound down the window. 'See you soon, right?'

Tommy slapped the imitation vinyl roof and Dan and all his possessions rumbled down St Mark's street, turned right onto Lowther Street and vanished from view.

***

It was 1979, a January evening, dark and very cold. Dan and Donna watched *Coronation Street* on the portable black-and-white telly, which was perched precariously on an upturned packing crate in the mostly empty living room. Grainy grey characters fought out their domestic dramas on the 12" screen, while Dan and Donna took turns at using the only armchair. The chair-less one sat on the floor and leant against the other's legs. They'd got the keys to the 1960s Bristol semi just before Christmas, and the place still had that Spartan, 'just moved into' look.

Dan had lived in the city for a year, and Donna had joined him in July, when she finished her training in Manchester. They'd rented a tiny, mildewed bedsit in Redland for the first few months, and they'd fancied getting a place in Clifton, near Bobo and Adey, but it was too expensive. So, for now, an estate on the south side of the city would do.

Dan had landed a job as a technical training instructor with South West Gas in Bristol soon after that brief conversation with Harold Carrington. He'd have been the first to admit that he wasn't best suited to it, and he seemed to have a permanent cold along with strange mental distortions for the first few months, which didn't help. But it got him away. And he made a point of avoiding temptation – something Bristol wasn't short of. Apart from beer – rather a lot of beer – and the odd spliff, he was clean. He could roll up his sleeves at work without being inhibited by what folk might see. And Donna was very happy: she'd just secured a job as a lab technician, supporting an amiable old academic in the Pharmacology Department of Bristol University.

From the moment of Dan's arrival, he and Tommy had exchanged letters at least weekly. There was regular, developing news of what was happening: Dan told Tommy about life in his new town; Tommy told Dan about events in his old one.

Shaun was doing well. He was properly settled in at Crosby's grocers now, and they thought well of him and gave him more responsibility; he more or less ran the place. And he had a girlfriend, kind of, on and off: Gina. She was 18 and lived on Crowley estate. She worked on the perfume counter at Boots in Dashton. It was all pretty casual. He'd see her once or twice a week, and they'd vanish somewhere and do their thing. But he was still doing the usual stuff with Tommy: pub, footy, Buffy's, gear...

And there'd been a bit of a fight. They were coming back from The King's, late on, pretty hammered, and found themselves catching up with this old bloke who was walking funny. So Tommy got behind him and mimicked him, taking the piss. And the geezer heard them laughing and turned round and said 'are you taking the piss?' And Tommy thought for a moment and said 'yeah, I guess I am.' And the old fella said 'then I'm gonna punch you out.' And he swung a surprisingly effective right hook at the side of Tommy's head. As Tommy reeled backwards Shaun flew past him at shoulder height and drop-kicked the fucker. And then they were all on the ground, swearing at each other. 'Wanker.' 'Tosser.' 'Arsehole.' And that was the end of the matter: they all got up, dusted themselves off and went home.

Every letter contained a self-devised crossword, in which the clues and answers related to something they'd got up to years ago, or an in-joke. The solution, in case anything remained unworked-out, would be in the next letter. But, most importantly, as Adey had done with him, Dan took the opportunity to remonstrate with Tommy to stop taking the gear. Following that old adage, 'there's no zealot like a reformed sinner', Dan was 100% on Tommy's case in every letter, arguing, cajoling, persuading, lecturing... doing everything he could think of to try and get him to stop, as it seemed clear that it was only a matter of time before Tommy, always the most reckless of the Three Musketeers and most fervently committed to drugs, OD'd. He knew Shaun would be OK: there was something about Shaun that gave the feeling that, even though he was the youngest, he was an old soul and it wouldn't be long before he jacked all this in and settled down and started a family.

The phone rang. 'Who could that be?' mused Donna. 'No-one rings on a Wednesday night.'

'I'll get it,' said Dan, and jumped up and stepped into the darkened hallway. He picked up the ivory-coloured receiver. It was Dan's mum, Lily. He felt a bolt of anxiety shoot through him. Lily rang on Sundays, and only on Sundays – there had to be something wrong.

'I've got some bad news,' said Lily.

Oh shit, oh shit. This is it. He's done it. He's fucking done it, screamed Dan's internal voice, while his public one yelled 'What is it? What's happened?'

'I don't know how to tell you this... but Shaun's dead. Overdosed, last night.'

'Oh for fuck's sake, fuck's sake, fuck's sake...' Dan dropped the phone, slid down the wall and collapsed onto the floor and yelled into the living room 'Take the phone, Donna, take the phone.'

Donna darted into the hall. 'What is it?'

'JUST TAKE THE FUCKING PHONE,' screamed Dan, distraught, in a dishevelled heap on the floor.

***

The world had changed. All the usual stuff was there, but it looked wrong, alien: the familiar now unfamiliar, like a room viewed over the shoulder through a corroding old mirror, or a magical childhood place revisited in adulthood and found to be grubby, small and churlish. At first it seemed unreal. Then it dawned that it wasn't less real, it was more real. This was the world as it really was, stripped of optimism, enchantment and colour. Dumb streets, dumb houses, dumb cars, dumb job, dumb life. Dumb, all of it. Dumb.

***

They met up again in The Nelson at noon the day before the funeral, and took a corner on the red leatherette chairs and benches in the empty best room: Tommy, Dan, Lenny Hughes, Johnny Caswell, Roger Armitage, Rick Cooper. Tommy had aged ten years: face grey, eyes red, black shadows beneath. There was only one subject, but no-one knew how to broach it. So Tommy started: he and Shaun had had a few in The King's, left at closing time, gone back to Number 64, had a fix of morph, then one of H. That was it. Next thing Tommy knew it was daylight. Shaun was flopped forward with his head between his knees, face in a bucket. Cold. Blue. 'I knew he was dead straight away,' said Tommy, gazing at nothing in the middle distance, 'but I tried all the stuff – pumped his chest, mouth-to-mouth and all that. I even tried dragging him in front of the fire to warm him up. It's *ridiculous, I know,*' he added, beginning to sob into his words, 'but I didn't know what else to do.' The others jumped up. Arms closed around his back. Lenny's eyes were streaming. Dan felt his tear ducts filling.

Tommy related what the coroner had said: that Shaun, while unconscious, had vomited as far as his throat. Heroin cancels your gag reflex, and he'd suffocated without ever regaining consciousness.

Rick said he wished it was him instead of Shaun. There was silence: at first, irritation at Rick drawing attention to himself, then the realisation that he probably half-meant it. He did seem to live with a kind of death wish, or as though he had accepted the inevitability that something, the shape of which as yet unknown, was coming his way in short order. Later, back home in the evening, he lay down on the bed, smashed the window, picked up a dagger-shaped splinter and slashed at his wrists. It was messy but inconsequential; more a combination of cry for help and self-harm as antidote to real pain than genuine pursuit of death. And Sally intervened before it became more than just another of Rick's overreactions and persuaded him that this wouldn't be taking Shaun's place, it would be going as well.

As booze temporarily eased the pain, Tommy told stories – funny two weeks ago; bittersweet now – of Shaun's antics as a kid. There was laughter of a sort, smearing over both the pain and the guilt – because Shaun was the youngest, and all or any of them should have saved him. If they'd stopped, Shaun would have stopped.

It was fair to say that Lenny had stopped some time ago, and Roger was only an occasional dabbler, and Dan had stopped too. Though Dan had cheated – he'd gone away to make his recovery and taken what influence he might have had with him. But they'd all been there at the start. They were all part of this, and it would have taken a collective commitment to rid the group of drugs – something that was never going to happen. Plus, everyone else they knew who partook was still at it.

They stumbled out of the pub mid-afternoon and wandered around the town centre with no particular destination in mind, mainly because Tommy couldn't face going home yet.

As Dan glanced around the familiar streets, a feeling, a fragment of disquieting energy, flickered into life in some dark recess at the back of his mind, then grew and accelerated and roared to the front. Where was Shaun? Yes, he knew he was dead. He understood the word, but where was he? The word and the reality didn't correspond. They were out having a drink. It didn't make sense that Shaun wasn't there. He was always there.

The town became unreal – a pulsating dreamscape. Clumps of painted metal flashed down the street, conversations wowed in and out of earshot, an exhausted exasperated mother yanked her skriking kid by the arm. All that was normal was bent out of shape and slyly malevolent.

The sky was blue, cloudless, and the sun was shining. What was it doing, doing that in February? Didn't it know what had just happened? Were it not for the cool air and long shadows, this could have been August. And Dan had the thought: *that's Shaun in Heaven telling us he's alright.* And then he heard himself say it out loud. There were affirmative noises all round, but Dan couldn't work out why he'd said it. Was he trying to make the others feel better, or just trying to persuade himself? And he *didn't* believe it. And his mind rolled. It was absurd: stupid... *stupid, stupid, stupid – he isn't fucking anywhere. He's gone. That's it. That's all there is. And we can't ask for a rerun. There's no appeal. We can't go to the church tomorrow and say, 'look, we made a mistake, we won't do it again, lesson learned, can we have him back now?' He isn't coming back.* Little Shaun. Cheeky, funny, mischievous, loyal Shaun. Shaun, he'd known since he was a toddler. Shaun, the Third Musketeer. Shaun, his brother. *Gone. Just gone.*

And a feeling of grief like he'd never known swept over him. He couldn't hold anything back. There were voices, and arms fell around his shoulders, trying to console him. And he felt he had no right to this. This was Tommy's grief – and Wendy's and Mrs Coggins's and Grandma's. And they'd been having theirs every second of every day since that unspeakable night. And what was it like for them to climb into their beds at night and turn out the light and be alone with the dark and their thoughts, knowing all this? The pain felt like it could have no end.

But there, still, was the town, *their* town and all their places: the streets they'd walked down a million times, the market hall where their flustered mothers had scratched anxiously into the bottoms of shabby purses hoping there were enough pennies for this week's food, Foundry Street Methodist School where they'd started to awaken to life together, the pubs where sometimes they'd gone crazy and other times just talked reflectively. Every brick, flagstone and cobble glowed and echoed with meaning. The town was at once loving and indifferent. It had borne them and held them like a mother – the soft heather moors that wrapped around the place had always felt like a comforting, protective embrace. But then it was a psychopath – just so many cold, heartless stones sneering back at them.

They bundled Dan off the High Street into the memorial gardens and dropped onto the benches. Dan looked up at the blurred, smeary edifice. He'd always found it moving, ever since he'd first seen it as a kid. It was the only well-kept place in town; always neatly trimmed, with rows of brightly coloured flowers, when in season, and wreaths and little wooden crosses with paper poppies every November, all blown down and washed away by New Year. The structure spanned the High Street. Two huge plinths stood guard at the bridgehead. On top of each, a sorrowful sculpted angel comforted a dying soldier. Below, two dignified arcs of marble famously carried 778 names, many of them teenagers, few past their twenties. Age had long since ceased to weary them. Below, an inscription read: 'THE YOUNG RESIDE IN THE HOUSE OF GOD – HEAVEN RESOUNDS TO THEIR LAUGHTER.' Dan retched.

***

The funeral service took place in Foundry Street Methodist Church. Dan sat near the back, between Lenny and Roger. Donna couldn't face it and stayed at her parents', watching the clock. Dan scanned the room. The place was packed. Had Shaun known all these people? But it wasn't just friends and family – people Dan knew. It was Shaun's old school friends and teachers, lads from the brass band he'd played with until he was sixteen, others from the fishing club, Gina and her friend, the extended Coggins family – aunties, uncles and cousins – Mr Crosby and his wife from the shop, Shaun's old workmates from the mill, and members of the church congregation, whom Wendy and Mrs Coggins knew well. It felt like half the town was there. Everyone who knew the Coggins's, and many who didn't, felt for them. And they looked at their own children and tried to grasp the agony of losing a son or daughter just a few days out of their teens.

There was a collective gasp as the pale pine coffin was carried in, and audible sobbing around the room.

The vicar did his best. He talked about Shaun's boisterous personality and the things he liked, like United and soul, and how he'd been a talented cornet-player with the school band. He went on to say something about how young people experiment and push boundaries – it's an aspect of growing up – and how some fall by the wayside, like lads who go too fast on motorbikes. Dan felt this was meagre stuff, from possibly the best-educated man in town and someone with a direct line to God. And the vicar himself, seeing the inconsolable faces before him, seemed almost apologetic as he said it, but what else could he say, *poor sod?* What sense was there to be made of this? What comfort to be had?

Eight days later, Grandma, having seen all she cared to of this world, left it to join her ancestors and Shaun.

Millennium Tale

It was early evening on 23rd December 1999. Dan Brody and Johnny Caswell met at Dashley Dyke station. It wasn't that either was arriving by train, it was just that the station bar was the best pub in town and the one that sprang to mind when Dan rang Johnny to say he would be travelling home from Bristol for Christmas and to bring in the new millennium with his mum and dad, and it would be good to see him.

They shook hands in the doorway and joined the noisy, good-humoured throng inside. The station bar was long and narrow, following the shape of the platform it stood on, and as smoky as one of the long-obsolete steam trains it once served. The walls were covered in railway memorabilia: station name plaques, bits of old-fashioned signalling gear, and sepia photos of long-dead locomotives, along with cheerful old enamelled adverts for cigarettes, ales and dubious medications. The bits of wall that were visible were painted in the deep claret-colour of the old-style train carriages, and there was an abundance of exposed, timeworn timber: bar, tables, stools, doors and floor. A fire blazed in the corner. It was a warm, comforting, homely place, in stark contrast to the cold, dark December night outside.

Dan glanced up and down the room. The station bar had become something of a local legend – everyone knew its story. Somehow it had survived the ravages of twentieth-century modernisation. For the large part this had been a consequence of accident or neglect rather than design. Dashley Dyke had been an important town for a brief moment at the height of the Industrial Revolution. It had then declined and become invisible to those who didn't live there, and as all the other station bars got their red-and-grey Traveller's Fare makeovers in the 1970s, Dashley Dyke's was overlooked. By the time the authorities finally noticed the oversight and presented plans for a lemon and white, minimalist coffee-bar makeover, it was too late. Locals knew what they'd got – a genuine unspoilt Victorian bar, worth using even when you didn't have a train to catch – and they were not prepared to have it changed. There were petitions, and a publicity campaign was launched. Even the BBC took notice: a sulky journalist drew the short straw and was sent out from the air-conditioned city-centre bubble to find the place and discover how a station bar could be the object of such commotion. Her report was characterised by a mixture of almost-convincing concern and condescending amusement at her interviewees' accents and old-fashioned phrases, betrayed by conspiratorial glances back at the camera, which she evidently believed were too subtle for the locals to decode. Yet it was this report, and the nationwide coverage that followed, that clinched the victory, and apart from improved sanitation and the welcome addition of a few European brews, the bar remained largely as it was in the 1890s.

This wasn't just about nostalgia. Some things simply happen to be right as they are and cannot be improved upon. Just as they knew how to do cemeteries, the Victorians knew how to do bars. The whole town was Victorian, but it had all been remodelled several times over in the style of the moment. The pubs had been modernised in the 1950s and '60s with beige anagylpta, vinyl floor tiles and Formica tables. The Red Barrel and Double Diamond served up from behind the bar meant that the beer, like the furniture, had very much a functional quality about it. In the 1970s it happened again, but this time with red-flock wallpaper and velour-topped, barrel-shaped stools and, in some less-reputable places, with Whitbread's Gauntlet Ale, which in spite of having been an ad-men's wet dream, only ever managed to dribble in a distinctly un-virile way from its vainglorious faux-medieval pump. There was an unmistakable, if vague, glance backwards in this. And as the millennium drew to a close in what had been defined by some as the 'post-modern' era – when all things had to be revisited by some semblance of the past – the pubs had all been made-over to be Victorian once more. But of course, they were no longer really 'Victorian'. A typical pub was now a mixture of tithe barn, western saloon and burger-bar, the last remaining fragments of actual Victoriana having been driven off to the tip in a melancholy fug of damp mortar and replaced by something more 'authentic'. Hogarth and Lowry street scenes completed the fantasy. Nobody evidently noticed or minded that their centuries were either side of the one in question – it was near enough. A vague simulacrum of The Past had been contrived, cobbled together from a collection of disparate but recognisable tokens. The appeal of the station bar was ever more apparent.

Dan had known Johnny Caswell since they were teenagers in the 1970s. Back then Johnny was the gorgeous, curly-haired production-line worker at Seedley's Toy Factory. He spent his days fastening red plastic wheels onto blue plastic tractors, his nights and weekends boozing, speeding, chasing girls and dancing at the north's soon-to-be legendary soul clubs. He was so full of confidence and energy in those days; you wouldn't recognise him as the same man now. In his mid-forties, he looked a good decade older. His teeth had gone and his receding hair was dyed an implausible shade of blue-black. He wore one of those 1980s jackets: the shiny, box-shaped ones that you were supposed to wear with the sleeves rolled up, *Miami-Vice*-style. At the turn of the new millennium, this was not a good look; not that Dan didn't bear traces of his own time warp. He'd been a skinhead of his own volition thirty years ago; he was one again now, this time at Nature's insistence. And his dark green Harrington-esque bomber jacket, faded 501s and black AirWair shoes carried visible overtones of those earlier fashions, though these items had since taken on a certain universality and timelessness, or so Dan liked to think.

Once, things had looked so promising for Johnny. He'd been the first of Dan's mates to go to university. Something switched on: he did A-Levels at night school and, by the time he was 22, he'd gone from a dead-end job to studying for a degree in English at Reading University. It would be another decade and more before the handful of others in the group who would do this would find the self-belief that would make it possible. Lads from Dashley Dyke did not go to university. So it was astonishing when Johnny went, and even more so when, on his visits back, he told them that it wasn't all that hard: listen, read the books, do the essays and you get there, he said.

After three years of entertaining himself in pretty much the same ways as when he was a production-line worker, and putting enough effort into his studies to get by, Johnny left university with a 'two-one', which, whatever it was, was an indication that he'd done pretty well. There was speculation in The King's Head at the time that if he'd done *really* well he might have got a 'three-nil' or something. With his new qualification, and another new thing the others hadn't heard of before called a 'cee-vee', he was able to get a white-collar job and work wherever he wanted. He took himself off to London, where he got a job selling 'office systems'. Precisely what 'office systems' were was not clear. The selling of them, however, seemed to be very lucrative, and Johnny was good at it. He moved into a trendy apartment, bought a new car, wore pricey suits and pubbed and clubbed the night away with a succession of elegant girlfriends. His grinning, pan-shined face was regularly to be seen in the trade press, as he hit a remarkable new sales landmark or received some special industry award or other. He was the epitome of 1980s new-money success. But something wasn't quite right.

On trips home, it was evident that Johnny had something to prove. He might have been away, got educated, lived the high life, but he did his best to make it clear that underneath it all he was still the same rough, tough, who-gives-a-shit Dashley Dyke lad he'd always been. He had to drink the most beer, take the most drugs, tell the crudest jokes, and cause the most trouble. Dan, Tommy and the rest of the crowd had all shared Johnny's upbringing and developed the same self-destructive tastes, but by their mid-twenties, those who'd survived had started to grow out of it. Not Johnny.

After a series of mysterious job changes, which had accelerated in frequency, Johnny returned to Dashley Dyke. And by the second half of the 1980s he had settled in an old stone terraced house on the edge of town with his girlfriend, the blonde, smart and graceful Toni.

Johnny and Toni had known each other since university, been part of the same group of friends, but it wasn't until after they had both graduated and gone to London that they began to see each other regularly. Toni had landed a job with a PR consultancy and, like Johnny, started rapidly to make a name for herself. As the stopovers at Johnny's place gradually became seamless, keeping her own flat on became pointless, and she moved in. But, even though Toni was originally from London and had been keen to get back there after university, the subsequent move north to Dashley Dyke was something that she and Johnny had been in full agreement about. It was after this move that what had transpired in London gradually came to light.

Johnny's fantastic sales figures had not been achieved cleanly. He would say anything to get a sale. Unfeasible deals were clinched; clients were sold massively expensive systems which, once installed, would not do what he'd said they would. But for a brief, glittering moment, he was a valuable commodity – rival sales managers were only too keen to have him on their books – and he could move on to another job just before the shit hit the fan. Then there were the expenses fiddles. And then there comes that moment when fiddles spill over into clear-cut criminality. It's great to have the company pay your mileage, even better if you've exaggerated the mileage, and better still if you haven't paid for the petrol. But if you're going to do that, it's important to be invisible, and lots of London petrol stations had had closed circuit TV installed by then.

The casual pill-popping of Johnny's teenage years had turned into opiate use even before he left Dashley Dyke. But once in London, with lots of pretty green in his pocket, he'd quickly acquired a full-on heroin habit, and his wages alone did not cover the costs. As addiction took hold, his sales figures collapsed. Important clients were neglected, meetings were missed and when he did put in an appearance, his behaviour would be noticeably odd. It soon became apparent that in spite of his impressive CV and amazing sales figures, Johnny had made himself unemployable. The move back to Dashley Dyke in the mid-80s was therefore to be a fresh start: an attempt to get the London experience, and the heroin, out of his system. With the support of his friends and family, and Toni, and in the comfort of familiar surroundings, he would rebuild his life.

The good intentions lasted a matter of days. Within any industry, people move around, and stories and reputations travel with them. Such was Johnny's notoriety and so tightly-woven was the office systems industry that even back up in the North, hundreds of miles from his misdemeanours, everyone knew about him. He could have gone to Aberdeen and they would still have known. And it was necessary to find solace, though he promised himself he wouldn't let it take over this time. The odd fix would be harmless enough, and no-one needed to know. Old connections were re-established and channels of supply re-opened. It all had to be paid for, however, and Johnny was out of work. Friends, family and Toni were unknowingly co-opted into supporting Johnny's secret new habit. They would experience those strange moments of disbelief, as they gazed into purses where they could have sworn there were two tenners, not one; or as they picked up that tub of pound coins that was supposed to take the edge off next summer's holiday and felt somehow that it was slightly lighter than before.

Toni had a demanding job and long commute, and would go to bed early. Johnny, with nothing to get up for, would stay up late. Sometimes Toni would be awakened by a knock at the front door very late at night. Johnny would still be up. He would deal with it, which meant getting into a car with some strange men and vanishing for a few hours in order to do what he would describe dismissively as a 'business deal'. After these visits, Johnny would be very happy, if somewhat detached, for a few days. But there would then be other visits. These didn't involve Johnny going out. Instead, Johnny and the visitor – usually a sick-looking adolescent who Toni didn't know and who would dip his head into his collar and avoid eye-contact – would nip briefly into the kitchen. There would be muffled conversation, the shuffling of paper, the careful opening and closing of drawers. The visitor would then leave. The explanation would be that the visitor owed Johnny money, and he'd popped by to give it back. What Toni couldn't know was that there was usually another event that coincided with these periods of happiness: a chemists' shop, somewhere within a thirty-mile radius of Dashley Dyke, would have been broken into late at night and relieved of the contents of its controlled drugs cabinet.

Johnny's periods of detached happiness never lasted. Euphoria would gradually give way to depression, then to bouts of rage. He was never physically violent towards Toni – a Caswell would never hit a woman; that was reserved for whichever poor sod came too close to him in the pub on the wrong day – but nevertheless, Johnny's increasing unpredictability, the paranoid accusations and the ferocious, pointless, middle-of-the-night rows got ever harder to bear. As if this were not enough, on his good days he would sometimes go out until the early hours, in Toni's Fiesta, and come home with a whiff of unfamiliar perfume on his clothes. The explanation for the late night would be some kind of booze-up with his mates. For the perfume there would be no plausible explanation. He would have no idea where it came from: Toni must be imagining it. Maybe someone had spilt something on his jacket – it was all a bit of a blur. Maybe it was a prank – one of the lads winding him up. It could have been anything, but it was all perfectly innocent, he could assure her. If she pressed the point, he would counter-attack: she knew he was going through a difficult patch – was she deliberately trying to provoke him? Was she trying to divert attention from something she was doing? After all, she went out every day and met lots of other people while he was stuck at home...

The final and decisive row occurred when Toni found a knuckle duster and a flick-knife at the back of the sideboard drawer. She was horrified. What kind of double-life was he leading if this was a necessary part of the paraphernalia? Had he ever used these things? She had to admit to herself that Johnny had another, parallel existence, beyond the one she was part of and from which she was studiously excluded. She really didn't know this guy. And still he lied: when confronted, he made out he was just keeping these things for a friend.

Johnny had become a consummate liar. He would sometimes lie just for practice, even when the issue was hardly worth the effort. He lied because this was what he did. He lied to keep people in the lied-to condition he wanted them in.

Toni put up with Johnny's malignant behaviour for a remarkably long period – nearly 5 years in total – but for the sake of her own sanity, and in spite of the massive, heart-bursting love she had always had for him, she had to go.

There was something kind of perfect and well-rounded in Johnny's misery. It had a sort of completeness. His career and bright future had vanished, he had alienated most of his family and lost most of his friends, and now he had lost Toni. He tried to get her back, of course, but deep within himself he knew that there was something half-hearted even in this. He came on with all the ever-so-predictable stuff: charm, followed by pleading, followed by threats.... but it didn't work. He didn't expect it to, really. She'd seen it all before. And Johnny knew that this time things had gone too far. He could read her feelings: she felt pity, she still loved him, but she wasn't stupid, and she had watched and waited long enough to know that things would never improve. And when she finally found the resolve to leave, the feeling of relief was overwhelming – an epiphany – and she would never go back to that life.

That 'each man kills the thing he loves,' as Wilde put it, was never truer of anyone than it was of Johnny. The reasons for these destructive impulses were manifold. Although he would never admit to it directly, self-doubt crept out again and again when he spoke. 'Imposter Syndrome' loomed large and was amplified by the self-loathing induced by his prodigious drug use. The university education, the well-paid white-collar job, the fantastic London flat and the gorgeous, sophisticated fiancée – he could never quite bring himself to believe they were really his and that this could be permanent. He never quite believed in his London life – it was all about money and, in the end, meaningless and empty. His druggy, night-time netherworld was the real life; everything else was just inconsequential froth. Then there was the warm, salt-of-the-earth embrace of his home town. But that had its own price, in its backwardness, lack of opportunity and the sense that returning was an admission of failure. Ultimately, he didn't know where he belonged or who he really was – he was a poor fit in either setting. He couldn't take the yuppie lifestyle seriously, and the boors and bumpkins in The King's and The Cavendish bored him shitless. Both had to be blotted out.

Without Toni's wages, Johnny couldn't keep up the payments on the house, and before long it was repossessed. As a single young man, he was a low priority for council housing. However, the council's policy of shifting families and single mothers into semis on the outlying estates had the effect of releasing space in the considerably less desirable high-rise and deck-access flats dotted around Dashley Dyke town centre. So it was that Johnny moved into what was known locally as 'Junkie Towers'.

The council made an effort with the flats – there had been periodic makeovers and refurbishments – but ultimately, there was no way they could keep up with the determined efforts of so many disaffected people. If someone really wants to graffiti a wall, set fire to a neighbour's door, or piss in the lift, they surely will.

For Johnny, his circumstances now matched what had become his self-image. He was thoroughly degraded. He had always resisted 'registering' before. There was too much of a stigma attached. But now he had to. He needed the methadone, and in any case being 'registered' had a certain kudos, in the circles in which he now moved: if you were 'registered', you'd made it.

The drugs took their inevitable toll. His health suffered, his good looks faded and his teeth first crumbled and then fell out. He became a well-known face in Dashley Dyke's most beaten-up pubs, where he entertained himself by cavorting with the town's most desperate drunken women. But as the last vestiges of his self-worth evaporated, so did his confidence with the opposite sex, and as he descended still further, he began to regard himself as too worthless and too ugly to present to any woman. And whereas, before, he had always been a fervent womaniser, he now had a different reputation. Going down on men in back alleys in a drugged and drunken stupor gave him the affirmation he needed. It seemed that masochism could destabilize sexual orientation and create a paradox: the thrill came from being degraded, and it was even more degrading to be used by the gender you didn't even fancy.

All of this was well known to Dashley Dyke's bar flies and blabbermouths, but as Dan looked at Johnny while they vied for the barmaid's attention, he reflected that maybe there was something more to this, that there was another, more mysterious layer, which had always been there from way back.

In spite of his rampant heterosexual libertinism, there was always an element of misogyny in Johnny's attitude towards women. He called women 'split arses,' and his jokes and wisecracks always seemed to include some direct or indirect reference to female bodily odours or secretions and, in doing so, betrayed a hint of repressed revulsion. On one of his trips to see Dan in Bristol, Johnny related some of his gut-churning jokes to Dan's friends in the pub, who later made it clear that they'd be grateful if Dan didn't bring that sick fuck along again. These, however, were ambiguous allusions: indirect – maybe meaningful, maybe not. But as Dan thought about it, another incident from the early-80s came back and suddenly seemed to have more pertinence than it did at the time. It was the era of the New Romantics, when androgyny and the wearing of makeup by men had not only come out of the shadows; it was being loudly celebrated by the young and fashionable. Johnny said he'd given it a go, himself, when he was at Reading. And from there, the conversation moved on to bisexuality, and Johnny quizzed Dan over whether he'd ever had bisexual urges. He hadn't; he'd liked girls ever since he found out they existed. He was engaged to Wendy Coggins when he was five – till she lost the Lucky Bag ring he gave her down the back of the sideboard. And at that, the subject seemed to have run its course and they drifted on to another topic. In that moment, Dan had seen this only as an abstract conversation – not an attempt on Johnny's part to unburden himself of something. Given Johnny's reputation as a relentless womaniser, why would he? Though maybe this was another one of those moments when Dan had seen only the surface. Had he failed again to read what was beneath? It was certainly beginning to look that way. Nevertheless, in the following years, the subject never came up again, and Johnny continued to present himself as the most vehemently hetero guy in town. And maybe this should be no surprise. For those who grew up in Dashley Dyke in the 1960s and '70s, homosexuals did not exist. This was a town of 25,000 people, in which no-one was gay. 'Puffs' and 'queers' were talked and joked about in bars and playgrounds, but they were the stuff of myth and legend; no-one knew a real one. So Dashley Dyke only had straight men: straight men who liked women; straight men who preferred the bachelor life and funnelled their energies into hobbies and pets, and felt it was important to stay home and look after their mothers; and a small number of straight men who committed suicide and no-one knew why. There were also other straight men who looked like the first of that trio and were ostensibly happily married, and had kids, but in reality lived out mutually-unfulfilling shadow plays with their miserable, tight-lipped wives. As for lesbians and bisexuals – they hadn't been invented. So maybe it was no surprise that the real nature of Johnny's sexual wiring was never entirely made clear, possibly even to himself, and this was another contradiction and source of shame that tore him apart and led to his self-destructive horrors.

Dan toyed with the idea of bringing the subject up, to satisfy his own curiosity, but concluded that he and Johnny, estranged for all those years, were no longer close enough for such an intimate conversation. It was Johnny's business – he'd talk about it if he wanted to. Plus, the odds of getting a straight answer were pretty remote anyway.

Dan bought a couple of pints of Stella and, for his trouble, got sniffy looks from the real-ale buffs at the bar – a bedraggled Henry VIII look-alike competition that made humble bar stools and catalogue jeans look like the most extraordinary feats of engineering – and he and Johnny took a table in a cosy corner. Dan hadn't seen Johnny for the biggest part of ten years, though they'd kept track of each other through acquaintances and the occasional letter. So Johnny knew that Dan was doing OK, and Dan knew that Johnny wasn't. But since they'd known each other from way back – back when style mattered and Johnny was a successful man-about-town – it was important for Johnny to muster some form of dignity, to make Dan believe that things weren't so bad. It was OK to be degraded amongst the degraded, but for Dan he had to put on a show. Hence the hair dye and his best Crockett and Tubbs jacket.

Johnny talked vaguely about sorting his life out. Things had got better, he reckoned, and he'd had a girlfriend for a while. Pauline, she was called, from Longsight, though that was over now. And he'd been doing a bit of work – labouring for a bloke called Frank, who was going out with his sister and had a demolition company. And he'd cut down on the gear – mostly just dope nowadays, though he still had his methadone. And he'd long since stopped injecting. Apart from anything else, he'd run out of veins. 'When you're cranking into your toes and contemplating the big blue vein on top of your dick, you know you've got problems,' he explained. But he also thought chasing the dragon was a better thing, because you didn't share needles and because if there was something dodgy in the gear you'd got a chance, whereas, if you'd pumped it straight into your tubes, you'd no chance. But anyway, like he said, he didn't do much gear nowadays – just when he was feeling a bit flushed, and as a treat.

When Johnny wasn't working for Frank or signing-on, he would read. He was a regular at the library. He'd go in for the company, for a warm when he couldn't afford to have the heating on in his flat, and to be near the books. He read everything: adventures, biographies, big fat romantic novels. He was a particular fan of Thomas Hardy; felt he could relate to the tragic inevitability of disaster in Hardy's characters' lives. What had become a focal point, however, was Dashley Dyke itself. He didn't know much about his own family history, but that didn't matter. They had always lived in Dashley Dyke and, in Johnny's view, it was the town, as much as his family, that had shaped him. He felt he had learned a great deal about what had made him what he was and where his destructive internal battles came from. His career had taken off in that moment when mass unemployment in one half of the country met selfish indifference in the other, but, still tied to his roots, he had never quite been able to muster the appropriate level of cynicism to live successfully in the privileged part of that world. And now – as a walking compendium of sexually-transmitted and drug-induced diseases – he didn't have the strength to muster much of anything. If he'd known how things were going to turn out, maybe he would have made a firm step into one life or the other, but it was too late now.

Dan bought a couple more beers – Johnny had no money for trips to the bar – and they talked about the old days and who was still around and who wasn't.

In addition to those who'd died in the '70s, Rick Cooper, Jez Reeves, Ian Caldwell, Adey Martin, Glyn Cousins and Jimmy Bragg had now gone; the first three taken by drugs, the others by tobacco.

Dan and Donna had got married a few years after the move to Bristol, but Dan's continued excesses, even though they had long since ceased to involve narcotics, had put an end to that. They'd divorced, and Donna had gone off and married a soldier. But Dan had then taken that strange moment of freefall, of misery mingled with nothing-to-lose liberty, to finally leave his job and study art. And he was now doing what he'd always wanted to do: teaching art and, when he had time, painting in a shed rigged-up as a studio at the back of the house. He had no idea of what had become of Eve and Rita, though he'd heard that Brenda still lived in Dashley Dyke and was married to some fella who worked at the airport. Lucy was happily married to a guy she met at university and now lived in Buckinghamshire.

Bobo's relationship with Adey only lasted another year after her graduation. Adey no longer fitted in with her lifestyle, she reckoned, now that she was a successful chemical engineer. Lifestyles were a new thing then – Bobo was one of the first to have one. Later, she was headhunted by an American company and was last heard of living in New York. Si was also working abroad somewhere, in civil engineering.

Liam, like Johnny and Dan, had gone off and got himself an education, and now lived in London, where he was a director of a telecommunications firm. Neither Dan nor Johnny had seen the Halliwell twins in ages, but when last heard of they were both living in South Manchester and doing fine. Dan had had no contact with Charlie Broadhead since that disastrous night in Salford, though word was that he married mousy Monica. Dave Podmore had married an accountant from Wakefield, but that had lasted all of eighteen months, and he now ran a record stall in Hightown Super-Market, specialising in old soul vinyl.

Mick was happily married and living on one of the sprawling hillside estates in Bradfield, as was Eddie – Mick on the one where all the avenues and closes were named after poets; Eddie on the one where they were named after species of tree. Marty, however, had become town drunk, and nasty with it, and so was barred from every pub on Sheffield Road, and a few others. Philbo had managed to go from angelic boy to craggy middle-aged man without having ever been an adolescent or young man in between. This was his most remarkable achievement. And Dave Scholes was still the funniest man in Dashley Dyke and still didn't let up about Bob Dylan.

Lenny and Roger were both doing well, and Dan planned to have a pint with them in Dashton before he went back to Bristol.

Kev had emigrated to Australia. The informal but marked segregation between the white Europeans and black Aborigines suited his values. Sydney, in particular, with its indigenous community largely isolated in the inner-city district of Redfern, while the whites enjoyed the neat suburbs and, especially, the paradisiac harbour-view promontories, was especially well-geared to his outlook. While the drugged and drunken behaviour of many Aborigines, sent crazy by the destruction of their ways of life and alienated by what now surrounded them, validated his prejudices.

The bit of Tommy that had still been on the rails before Shaun's death left them completely after it, and he abandoned himself to his fate. He'd stopped working, become a full-on junkie and moved in with Bev. This had been made possible by Des getting sent down again – a long stretch this time. Bev always needed some gullible bloke as her thief and gofer, and as Tommy was always round at her place, buying gear or getting wasted with her, he eventually stopped going home and slotted into the job. But when Des got out of the nick, Bev had to make out that Tommy had only ever been a guest, and Tommy was edged out to the spare bedroom, which he had notionally lived in throughout, even though it didn't have a bed or any furniture. On hearing of Tommy's desperate circumstances, Dan and Donna invited him to come and stay with them in Bristol while he sorted himself out. Over six drugless months, Tommy gradually returned from orbit, stopped talking bollocks, and partially rediscovered his love for life. He then retrained, got a decent job as a computer repair guy, moved back up north, and was now married with four kids. And they were all still together and living in a bow-fronted semi in Blackpool. However, shortly after Tommy's move to Bristol, Des had showed up at 64 Sheffield Road demanding money and to know where Tommy was. Des reckoned Tommy owed him £500 for back rent, unpaid-for gear and the use of Bev's orifices. Wendy said she hadn't got that sort of money and she wouldn't tell him where Tommy was. Des showed up again the next day – same demands but this time with threats, big ones – said he'd burn down the house, with them in it, if Wendy didn't say where Tommy was or come up with the money. Wendy was resolute and told Des to fuck off. And the next day, someone shoved a burning, petrol-soaked rag through the open window facing Sheffield Road. It fell onto the windowsill and, from there, set fire to the net curtains and then the main curtains. A taxi driver, momentarily idling outside the house, waiting for the traffic lights, saw the blaze, leapt of out of his car and hammered on the door. He and Wendy managed to put out the fire with kitchen-bowl-fulls of water and the hearth rug. The police were called, but the fact that Des had threatened to burn down 64 Sheffield Road one day and someone had tried to burn down 64 Sheffield Road the next day wasn't evidence enough. It proved nothing – this could be a coincidence. It could just have been the case that some random arsonist had randomly chosen their house and just happened to have done so the day after Des said he'd do the same. So, whatever offences Des got sent down for in the following years, the attempted murder of Mrs Coggins and Wendy wasn't one of them.

It was nearly twelve and the landlord was showing signs of impatience. Dan and Johnny drained their glasses, stepped out onto the platform, and descended the long concrete ramp to the street. The sky was moonless, the air crisp, cold and black. Odd bits of the massive sandstone pillars that supported the bridge by the station were made visible here and there by the golden glow of the street lamps. The distant voices of a couple of bellowing drunks gradually faded to nothing. Dan told Johnny he was heading back down south in a few days, and wished him luck. They shook hands, embraced and patted each other on the back, then took a step backwards and looked at each other, and smiled – grinned, maybe – as they each reflected for a moment on the teenagers they used to be, on the things they had got up to together, and on how life had turned out. They agreed that they must do this again some time, though they both knew that it would almost certainly never happen. And Johnny turned round and disappeared into the darkness under the railway bridge.

Afterword

When my previous book, *The Truth About Northern Soul*, was published, it attracted a lot of feedback, most of it positive, I am pleased to say. Of all the comments I received, the one that struck me most resolutely came from an old friend, who knows me very well and was around when much of what is described in *The Truth About Northern Soul* took place. She asked why I hadn't included certain other stories – events she knew I'd been involved in – that would have enriched the book in many ways. The answer is that *The Truth About Northern Soul* set out to do a very particular thing: to counter, with accounts of real lived experiences, the skewed, sanitised and ahistorical views of the northern soul scene that now exist in some quarters. For that reason, it only needed so many anecdotes and pieces of evidence to sustain its arguments; any more would just belabour points and add little to the debate. However, it was my friend's question that got me thinking and made *Soul Stories* an inevitability.

The question then arises: how real are the events in *Soul Stories* and how close are these fictional characters and towns to real people and places? Two of the books I read while writing this may be helpful: *Goodbye to Berlin* by Christopher Isherwood (for the third time – it is a wonderful book) and *Rule of Night* by Trevor Hoyle.

While *Goodbye to Berlin* is widely understood to be semiautobiographical, Isherwood nevertheless includes this rider in his introduction: 'Because I have given my own name to the "I" of this narrative, readers are certainly not entitled to assume that its pages are purely autobiographical, or that its characters are libellously exact portraits of living persons. "Christopher Isherwood" is a convenient ventriloquist's dummy, nothing more.'

In *Rule of Night*, a fictional work about youth culture in Rochdale in the 1970s, which includes references to the northern soul scene, in particular Manchester's Pendulum club,

Hoyle explains that the roots of his story are deliberate encounters with real people with whom he spent time in order to understand their attitudes and learn about how they lived. Hoyle explains: 'From this material I started making notes, trying to work out a structure or a shape for the book. This was intentional. The kind of novel I had in mind wouldn't work if it was too tightly structured, following too rigid a plot-line. It needed room to breathe.' He goes on to say that, after the book was published, two or three actual Rochdale probation officers reckoned they knew who Hoyle's fictional lead character, Kenny Seddon, was in real life: 'Each one gave me the lad's name they were confident was the real Kenny – and each one was different. This demonstrated, I like to think, that the fictional character had sufficient depth and authenticity to convince them that they had encountered and had to deal with Kenny's real-life counterpart. They couldn't have done anyway. Kenny Seddon wasn't a particular person, he was a pick 'n' mix of several different individuals.'

I would like to think that *Soul Stories* has a relationship with both of these positions and reality is liberated by being set to the music of fiction.

I should add, also, that whereas *Soul Stories* is the follow-up to *The Truth About Northern Soul*, and in fact includes a handful of stories from it, refined and elaborated by fiction, it is by no means only about the northern soul scene. *The Truth About Northern Soul* was aimed at audiences who wanted to read about the subject because they were part of the scene back in the day, or because they weren't but would like to have been, or because they had an academic or a casual interest of some sort in the northern soul scene. While *Soul Stories* should appeal to those same audiences, I would like to think that, as a work of fiction, it will also have meaning for a broader audience with little or no attachment to the northern soul scene, just as it is possible to enjoy Nick Hornby's *Fever Pitch* without being an Arsenal fan, or Irvine Welsh's *Trainspotting* without being a junkie.

Soul Stories is a book about people, rites of passage, youth culture and northern life in the 1970s. Whilst it refers to the soul scene, it is also a series of stories 'from the soul' and about the souls who populate the book. I would like to think that, ultimately, *Soul Stories* is a universal tale of coming of age.

Discography

Songs and tunes mentioned or alluded to in this book.
Just to be clear: these are not all soul records, nor are they by any means all recommended listening. They are, however, all tunes that in some way played a part, for better or worse, in the lives of the souls in *Soul Stories*.

10cc – I'm Not in Love
5th Dimension, The – Train Keep on Movin'
Adverts, The – Gary Gilmore's Eyes
Al 'TNT' Braggs – Earthquake
Al De Lory and Mandango – Right On
Al Martino – Spanish Eyes
Al Wilson – Help me
Alessi – Oh Lori
Alvin Cash and The Registers – Philly Freeze
America – A Horse With No Name
Archie Bell and the Drells – Here I Go Again
Archies, The – Sugar Sugar
Arthur Conley – Funky Street
B. T. Express – Do It ('Til You're Satisfied)
Barbara Acklin – Love Makes a Woman
Barnaby Bye – Can't Live This Way
Barry White – You're the First, the Last, My Everything
Beach Boys, The – God Only Knows
Beatles, The – Lucy in the Sky with Diamonds
Bee Gees – You Should be Dancing
Bill Harris – Uptown Saturday Night
Bill Withers – Ain't No Sunshine
Billy Preston – Billy's Bag
Black Nasty featuring Herbie Thompson – Cut Your Motor Off
Blue Mink – The Banner Man
Bob and Earl – Harlem Shuffle
Bob Dylan – Mr. Tambourine Man
Bob Dylan – Positively 4th Street
Bobby Bloom – Montego Bay

Bobby Hebb – Love, Love, Love
Brenda and the Tabulations – One Girl Too Late
Candi Staton – Young Hearts Run Free
Chic – Everybody Dance
Chicory Tip – Son of My Father
Christie – Yellow River
Chubby Checker – (At the) Discotheque
Cindy Scott – I Love You Baby
Cliff Richard – Goodbye Sam, Hello Samantha
Cozy Powell – Dance with the Devil
Crow, The – Your Autumn of Tomorrow
Curtis Mayfield – Move on Up
Daniel Boone – Beautiful Sunday
Danny Monday – Baby, Without You
Dawn – Knock Three Times
Dee Dee Sharp – What Kind of Lady
Detroit Executives, The – Cool Off
Detroit Land Apples – I Need Help
Detroit Spinners, The – Could it be I'm Falling in Love
Detroit Spinners, The – I'll Always Love You
Detroit Spinners, The – I'll be Around
Dionne Warwick – Walk On By
Dixie Cups, The – Chapel of Love
Dobie Gray – Out on the Floor
Don Thomas – Come on Train
Donna Summer – I Feel Love
Doris Troy – I'll Do Anything
Du-Ettes, The – Every Beat of My Heart
Duke Browner – Crying Over You (Instrumental)
Earl Jackson – Soul Self Satisfaction
Earl Wright and his Orchestra – Thumb a Ride
Ed Crook – That's Alright
Eddie Parker – Love You Baby
Edison Lighthouse – Love Grows (Where My Rosemary Goes)
Edwin Starr – Agent Double-O Soul
Electric Light Orchestra – Mr. Blue Sky
Eric Clapton/Derek and the Dominoes – Layla
Esther Phillips – Catch Me I'm Falling

Esther Phillips – What a Difference a Day Makes
Ethics, The – Standing in the Darkness
Exciters, The – Blowing Up My Mind
Father's Angels – Bok to Bach
Four Larks, The – Groovin' at the Go-Go
Four Seasons, The – (December 1963) Oh What a Night
Four Seasons, The – I'm Gonna Change
Four Seasons, The – Silver Star
Four Tops, The – Ask the Lonely
Four Tops, The – Baby I need Your Loving
Four Tops, The – Without the One You Love
Frankie Valli – You're Ready Now
Frankie Valli and The Four Seasons – The Night
Fred Hughes – Baby Boy
Fuller Bothers, The – Time's a Wasting
Garland Green – Sending My Best Wishes
Garnet Mimms – Looking for You
George 'Bad' Benson – Supership
Gerry and Paul – The Cat Walk
Gerry Rafferty – Baker Street
Gioachino Rossini – William Tell Overture
Gladys Knight and the Pips – The Look of Love
Gloria Gaynor – Never Can Say Goodbye
Golden Earring – Radar Love
H. B. Barnum – Heartbreaker
Hamilton Bohannon – Disco Stomp
Hoagy Lands – The Next in Line
Iggy Pop – Lust for Life
Inspirations, The – Touch Me, Hold Me, Kiss Me
Invitations, The – What's Wrong With Me Baby
Isley Brothers, The – Behind a Painted Smile
Jackie Wilson – The Who Who Song
Jackson 5, The – I Want You Back
Jackson 5, The – Lookin' Through the Windows
James Bounty – Prove Yourself a Lady
James Bynum – Time Passes By
James Wells – Baby I'm Still the Same Man
Jerry Cook – I Hurt on the Other Side

Jimmy Radcliffe – Long After Tonight Is All Over
Johnnie Taylor – Who's Making Love
Johnny Copeland – Sufferin' City
Johnny Jones and The King Casuals – Purple Haze
Johnny Moore – Walk Like a Man
Judy Clay and William Bell – Private Number
Juggy – Thock It To Me Honi
Karen Young – Too Much of a Good Thing
Kate Bush – Wuthering Heights
KC and the Sunshine Band – That's the Way (I Like It)
Kinks, The – All Day and All of the Night
L. J. Reynolds and Chocolate Syrup – The Penguin Breakdown
Larry Williams and Johnny Watson – Too Late
Lenis Guess – Just Ask Me
Leroy Hutson – Ella Weez
Liars, The – Tell the Truth: the song does not exist and no such band existed at the time, though in the years since Dan invented The Liars a real band of that name has existed.
Linda Jones – My Heart Needs a Break
Lou Pride – I'm Com'un Home in the Morn'un
Lou Ragland – I Travel Alone
Luther Ingram Orchestra – Exus Trek
Lynn Anderson – (I Never Promised You A) Rose Garden
Magic Disco Machine – Control Tower
Major Lance – You Don't Want Me No More
Martha Reeves and The Vandellas – Jimmy Mack
Marvin Homes and Justice – You Better Keep Her
Mel and Tim – Backfield in Motion
Mel Britt – She'll Come Running Back
Middle of the Road – Chirpy Chirpy Cheep Cheep
Millie Jackson – My Man a Sweet Man
Minnie Riperton – Lovin' You
Miracles, The – Love Machine (Part 1)
Moments and Whatnauts – Girls
Moses and Joshua – Get Out of My Heart
Moses Smith – The Girl Across the Street
Mr Flood's Party – Compared To What
Mungo Jerry – In the Summertime

Neil Diamond – Cracklin' Rosie
Nite-Liters, The – K-Jee
Olympics, The – Baby Do the Philly Dog
Otis Redding – Respect
P. P. Arnold – The First Cut is the Deepest
Paul Anka – You're Having My Baby
Paul Kelly – Chills and Fever
Peaches and Herb – I Need Your Love So Desperately
Philip Mitchell – Free for All
Promised Land, The – Cheyenne
R.P.M. Generation – Rona's Theme
Rex Garvin and The Mighty Cravers – Sock It to 'Em JB
Righteous Brothers, The – Unchained Melody
Robert Knight – Branded
Ronnie Walker – You've Got to Try Harder (Times are Bad)
Roy Docker – Mellow Moonlight
Roy Hamilton – Crackin' Up Over You
Ruby Andrews – Casanova (Your Playing Days Are Over)
Rufus Lumley – I'm Standing
Sam and Kitty – I've Got Something Good
Sandy Posey – Single Girl
Shangri-Las, The – Leader of the Pack
Shine On, Harvest Moon: a song written in 1908 by Nora Bayes and Jack Norworth, sung by the cast in *Soul Stories*; numerous versions are out there in real life.
Shirelles, The – Last Minute Miracle
Shona Stringfield – I Need a Rest
Silvetti – Spring Rain
Simon and Garfunkel – The Boxer
Simon Dupree and The Big Sound – Kites
Sister Sledge – Love Don't You Go Through No Changes on Me
Solomon King/Levi Jackson – This Beautiful Day
Soul Twins, The – Quick Change Artist
Stealers Wheel – Stuck in the Middle with You
Steely Dan – Haitian Divorce
Stranglers, The – (Get a) Grip (On Yourself)
Stranglers, The – Hanging Around

Stranglers, The – Peaches
Supremes, The – Stoned Love
Supremes, The – Up the Ladder to the Roof
Sweet Things, The – I'm in a World of Trouble
Sylvia – Y Viva Espana
Symarip – Skinhead Moonstomp
T. Rex – Telegram Sam
Tavares – Heaven Must be Missing an Angel
Temptations, The – Just My Imagination
Thin Lizzy – Whiskey in the Jar
Three Degrees, The – Reflections of Yesterday
Toys, The – I Got My Heart Set On You
Triumphs, The – I'm Coming to Your Rescue
Twinkle – Terry
Tymes, The – Here She Comes
Upsetters, The – Return of Django
Van McCoy and the Soul City Symphony – The Hustle
Velvet – Bet You If You Ask Around
Vibrations, The – Gonna Get Along Without You Now
We All Hate Leeds and Leeds: a song popular with all UK football fans, except Leeds United fans, sung to the tune of The Dam Busters March, which was written by Eric Coates as theme music for the film The Dam Busters, released in 1955.
White Plains – Julie, Julie, Julie do Ya Love Me
Who, The – Happy Jack
Willie Kendrick – Change Your Ways
Wilson Pickett – Mr. Magic Man
Wonder Who, The – Lonesome Road
World Column, The – So is the Sun
Yvonne Fair – It Should Have Been Me

Bibliography

Books mentioned in the foregoing:

Anthony Burgess – A Clockwork Orange. 1962
Christopher Isherwood – Goodbye to Berlin. 1939
Irving Welsh – Trainspotting. 1993
J. D. Salinger – The Catcher in the Rye. 1951
Nick Hornby – Fever Pitch. 1992
Richard Allen – Skinhead. 1970
Richard Allen – Suedehead. 1971
Trevor Hoyle – Rule of Night. 1975
William Golding – Lord of the Flies. 1954

Glossary

Some terms that may have been specific to the location, culture or time and might need further explanation:

crank (also 'wap') – verb and noun: fix, drug injection

Crockett and Tubbs – two handsome and stylish characters from the popular 1980s TV series *Miami Vice*.

cudgie – outside toilet

DDA – the secure cabinet in a chemist shop where drugs controlled under The Dangerous Drugs Act were kept.

dimp – cigarette butt

Discassette – a portable device that played cassettes and 7-inch 45 rpm records. Also around at the time was the Discotron, which played 45s and had a radio.

div, divvy – a person lacking in sophistication

Emitex – a velvety cleaning cloth for vinyl records

green-and-clears – a type of amphetamine (Drinamyl) capsule, much prized amongst the 1970s soul fraternity.

johnnies – condoms

Jubbly – a large, fruit-flavoured, frozen confection

kecks – trousers

Lucky Bag – a cheap, shoddy confectionery item sold to kids, comprising hard sugary pellets, gone-off caramels and some Christmas-cracker-level knickknack.

Magic Wand – sherbet-filled liquorice stick

marrer – marrow: friend, mate, pal, workmate

micey – edgy, awkward, nervous, lairy, of a demeanour likely to spread unease to others.

mither – verb and noun: to pester, to irritate, to hassle. Hassle, nuisance, aggravation; the vexation, anxiety and irritation caused by being mithered.

moggies – Mogadon: a kind of sleeping tablet

narrer – narrow

neck – verb: to swallow

Paki bashing – a nauseating pastime indulged in by racist skinhead gangs in the late 1960s/early 70s, involving beating up non-white people, all deemed to be 'Pakis' (Pakistanis) wherever they came from.

rolled – mugged

Royals – a style of brogue shoe

SK&F and Riker – pharmaceuticals companies

skriking – crying

tonic – a kind of cloth, traditionally made from mohair, in which two different colours are cross-woven so that the material shifts from one colour to the other depending on viewing angle.

tonked – hit

works – syringe, or syringe and needle combination